JESSICA, NOT HER REAL NAME

S.K. MUSKAT

PROLOGUE

ADDISON HURRIED DOWN EMERALD STREET, her breath hitching with each step. Damp scrubs clung to her back, the fabric sticking to her skin. Every step sent a dull, crawling pain through her bones, but she couldn't stop.

Not now.

Ahead, the sidewalk lay deserted. Most businesses along this stretch of road were shuttered, their roller doors heavily tagged. Missing persons posters were tacked to the windows. A ribbon of yellow crime scene tape fluttered from a nearby utility pole like a grisly party streamer. To the north loomed the elevated tracks of the Market-Frankfort line.

Addison stumbled on, growing ever more desperate. Finally, she spied the light at the end of her tunnel. The Emerald Street underpass.

The empty sidewalk became dense with people. They were huddled under sleeping bags and slumped down in plastic lawn chairs along the damp wall of the underpass. Some lay curled up in sagging tents.

She slowed her pace, frantically searching their faces. Most looked through her, pupils blown and empty. But then, a pair of lucid eyes met hers. A man hunched forward in a wheelchair, a black beanie pulled low over his ears. Ricky Somes. Her breath left her in a shaky exhale, her knees nearly buckling with relief.

When he spotted her approaching, he nodded like he'd been expecting her. He rummaged in the pocket of his hoodie and produced a glassine baggie. It contained a single glorious gram.

Just the sight of it made the knot of anxiety in her stomach loosen.

He held it out to her, gesturing with his other hand for the cash.

Addison swallowed and tried to adopt a casual tone. "Yeah, uh, I'm a little strapped for cash right now, Ricky."

The corner of Ricky's mouth twisted up like she'd said something funny. "You know the deal, sweetheart. No freebies. No samples. No credit." The baggie disappeared from between his fingers like magic. "I feel like I should get that tattooed on my fucking forehead."

"Please," she said. "You know I'm good for it."

Ricky wheeled his chair back and angled it away from her. "Look, lady, I don't know shit about you. So pay up or fuck off."

Addison let the desperation show in her voice. "I'll pay you back Ricky, I swear. It's just been a terrible week, you know? My landlord's about to kick me out over the rent. And it's my kid's birthday tomorrow—"

He interrupted her in a tone that made it clear he didn't want her life story. "Yeah, we all got problems, sweetheart. The difference is, I'm not making mine yours."

His face showed no signs of softening, and she knew it wouldn't. Ricky didn't do feelings. He was numb from the waist down and, apparently, the neck up. And she could understand why. Kindness wasn't a currency. And in this world, anything you couldn't spend wasn't worth shit.

She hesitated for a moment longer, then pulled the wad of cash out of her pocket. It was money she was supposed to be spending on Noah's birthday present. She'd promised him a Harry Potter Lego set and had been putting a few dollars aside for months now. She pictured the look of disappointment on his face when he woke up tomorrow to nothing. It felt like a needle stab to her heart.

But the pain was insignificant compared to the agony awaiting her if she didn't get the contents of that baggie into her bloodstream right now. She'd rather saw off her own arm with a dull knife than go through the torment of withdrawal again.

So, with trembling fingers and a pit of guilt in her stomach, she handed over the money.

Ricky made a big show of counting it, passing the singles from hand to hand like he was shuffling cards. Satisfied she wasn't short-changing him, he finally parted with the packet. She buried it deep in the pocket of her scrubs and hurried away from the underpass.

A light rain was falling. It cooled nothing down, just made the sidewalks steam and heightened the stink of diesel fumes and uncollected garbage.

As she moved east down Emerald, the back of her neck prickled.

She glanced behind; a man, nearby, wearing an Eagles jacket, pushed a shopping cart. It was loaded with electrical junk: old microwaves, a cracked computer monitor, and a stack of dirty keyboards. His gaze was fixed on her. She quickened her pace.

A few yards on, she crossed the street and headed east down a narrow lane. On either side were crumbling brick row houses. Most looked abandoned, with rusted metal bars over their ground floor doors and windows. Their upper windows were boarded over like they caged in violent animals. The only fresh paint was graffiti. She was no expert on gang tags, but she recognized the spray-painted symbols of LMN-13: an all-seeing eye topped with a crown. That gang ran all the streets east of the railway tracks and south of Kensington Avenue, right down to the expressway.

It had stopped raining. She looked behind her again, but the Eagles fan was no longer following her. He'd probably never been following her; it was just her paranoia kicking in.

She stopped, unslung her backpack, and sat on the steps of a vacant building. Her whole body ached, like someone had injected acid into her bones. She clenched her teeth against a rising tide of nausea. She reckoned she had about ten minutes, tops, before she got so dope sick she'd wish she'd never been born.

A dirty white sedan cruised down the adjacent street, rap music blaring out its windows. It set off a dog barking somewhere in the building behind her.

She glanced around to check she was still alone. Then she slipped the glassine baggie out of her pocket. It bore a black ink stamp of a hand print with the number thirteen on its palm. Even drug dealers prized good product branding.

She opened her backpack and pulled out a plastic Paw Patrol lunch box. It was an old one of Noah's that she'd repurposed for her kit. She opened it and took out its contents: rubber tourniquet, syringe, foil, cigarette filters, lighter. First, she prepared the dose and drew it up into the syringe. Then she tightened the rubber strap around her upper arm and let her hand hang down against the concrete step for a minute to let the blood pressure build up. Then she took the needle and rolled the skin of her forearm, searching amongst the scabs for a usable vein.

She would feel a brief stab of pain when the needle pierced her skin, but then she wouldn't feel anything. There would be no more anxiety. No more fear. No more guilt about the myriad ways she'd failed Noah, or regret about all the terrible things she'd done that had led her to this point.

The door behind her opened. She sensed the gap at her back, heard footsteps fill it. She twisted around, saw an enormous man towering over her. He had a tattoo of a spider web covering his scalp and running down both sides of his neck.

He looked down at her and grinned. Dangling from one hand was an aluminum baseball bat. He raised it, double-handed, like a slugger about to hit one home.

Addison felt a sharp stab of pain.

And then she felt nothing at all.

ONE

PRESENT

JESSICA MEEKS HAD ten minutes to pack everything she would need to start a new life into a suitcase, watched silently by the armed man in the doorway.

She yanked clothing from hangers, grabbed armfuls of makeup and toiletries from the bathroom and upended drawers onto her crumpled bed.

"Shit." She scraped her hair back from her face. "I can't find my phone. I must have left it at work."

The man in the doorway stepped forward. "Leave the phone, ma'am. And all your other devices. We'll get you new ones."

She rolled up a pair of jeans and stuffed them in her suitcase. Then she stopped to survey the room. The place looked like a hurricane had ripped through it, and not just because of her hurried packing. Clothes spewed out of her wardrobe. Someone had rifled through her underwear drawer; its contents were draped obscenely over her dresser. The mirror on her chest of drawers was shattered.

The rest of her house was in a similar state. Nearly every possession she owned had been pulled from drawers and knocked off shelves. Someone had torn the pictures from the walls. Her TV had been kicked over, and the contents of her

7

refrigerator spread across the kitchen floor. In the bathroom, her vanity had been raided, the mirror smashed.

Her bedroom had suffered the greatest devastation. In the fractured image reflected by her dresser mirror, she could see the wall above her bed. Red spray paint scrawled across the wallpaper. It depicted a crudely drawn all-seeing eye topped with a crown. The still-wet paint dripped down the wall from the corners of the eye like tears.

The man in the doorway cleared his throat. "Five minutes, ma'am."

She tore her gaze from the awful artwork and swung the lid of her suitcase shut. "Just one more thing."

Before he could object, she dashed down the hall to the kitchen. She pushed open a screen door and stepped out into the backyard.

The sun was setting, casting long shadows across the lawn. Her washing hung stiffly from the clothesline strung between two pine trees.

She glanced over her shoulder to check she wasn't being followed, then jogged down the crushed shell path that led to the laundry room by the side of the house. She pulled the door shut behind her, flicked on the light, then reached up into the cupboard above the dryer and took down an old box of laundry powder. Lifting the lid, she found what she'd stashed in there years ago. A little pink and silver revolver and a box of cartridges. She wrapped them in an old dish towel, then ran back to the kitchen.

She stuffed them in her shoulder bag, then returned to the bedroom. Pausing in the doorway, she took a moment to survey the debris of her life scattered about. Her fragmented reflection stared back at her from the shattered mirror.

"Ready to go, ma'am?"

She hoisted her bag onto her shoulder and faced the man. "You don't have to call me, ma'am, you know. My name's Jessica."

The man said nothing, just left his post by the door to lift her suitcase from the bed and carry it out into the hall.

As she watched him go, it occurred to her that her name wouldn't be Jessica for much longer. Soon, she'd be someone else entirely. Someone no one had ever met before.

Not even her.

———

Forty minutes earlier, she'd been onstage at the Femme Fatale Strip Club, wearing nothing but a pink thong and a couple of strategically placed silver stars. She was upside down, hanging onto a pole with just her knees when she spotted the man standing near the lighted exit.

He was leaning against the wall, both hands clasped in front of him. Broad shouldered, his shirtsleeves rolled up to the elbows, the veins jumping out of the tanned skin of his forearms. Handsome, in a square-jawed, clean-cut kind of way.

He'd stuck out like a sore thumb among the sweaty frat boys and assorted lowlifes that frequented the club. Partly because he looked deeply uncomfortable being there. But mostly because he had a silver star of his own. His was made of chromium and attached to his belt, beside a slim black handgun. When he shifted his hips, it glinted in the light.

U.S. Marshals.

He wasn't a customer. He wasn't a creep. He was something far worse.

And he was there for her.

She climbed down off the pole as gracefully as she could in six-inch Lucite heels. Then she gave up on grace and fled the stage.

She pushed her way past the other girls backstage, yanking off her shoes as she went. But the man with the badge had been fast on his feet because he was already waiting for her beside her locker. He flashed his ID wallet in her face and said, "Ma'am, I suggest you put some clothes on. You need to come with me."

Jessica bristled at the order but caught the way his gaze stayed on her face, not dropping below her neck. Like he was trying very hard not to look anywhere else. She considered doing the exact opposite of what he said and hightailing it out the side exit. But then she thought better. You didn't run from a U.S. marshal. Because if you did, you didn't get very far. Hunting people down was what they did for a living.

Jessica knew that better than most.

"What's going on?" She tried to keep her voice calm, but there'd been an audible tremor in it.

The marshal's voice was steady. "Get dressed. There's been a break-in at your house."

———

Her house was only a short drive from the strip club, yet it had felt like an eternity. The world outside the marshal's car appeared blurry and distorted as anxiety clouded her vision through the backseat window. *It's just junkies,* she'd told herself, repeatedly. *Looking for cash or valuables.*

When he pulled to a stop on her street, she saw multiple police cruisers parked in her drive. Their red and blue strobe lights were bouncing off the white walls of her house.

She clambered out of the marshal's car and ran across the yard. Several officers had been milling about on her porch, but her attention went straight to her front door. Or to what was left of it. The old wood had splintered around the handle and lock, leaving a semi-circular hole. Someone had clearly kicked it in with considerable force.

She climbed the porch steps in a daze. "What the…?"

Waiting inside for her was another deputy marshal. This one was a petite redhead with a pale, freckled complexion. A heavily pregnant belly protruded over her gun belt.

Jessica had recognized her immediately. Her name was Inez Sharrow, and she'd been Jessica's sole liaison with the U.S. Marshals Service for the ten years she'd lived in southwest Florida.

"A local PD unit reported the break-in," Sharrow said, leading the way down the hall. Progress proved difficult; broken ceramic shards and soil from a shattered pot plant littered their path. "They spotted your door hanging off its hinges from the road. They entered the premises to investigate, but the intruder was already gone."

Jessica didn't respond; she'd been too preoccupied with the sight of her belongings reduced to rubble underfoot.

Nothing she owned was especially valuable. She lived a flat-pack existence, accumulating nothing that couldn't be broken down or abandoned at short notice. Still, seeing what she did own abused in such a way hit her like a physical blow.

Ahead of her, Sharrow paused in the door to her bedroom. "It's a bit of a mess in there too, I'm afraid."

Jessica stopped beside her. The red painted eye had stared down at her from above her bed.

Her stomach dropped, along with her hopes. Not just junkies then.

Sharrow had been speaking, and Jessica tried to tune her back in.

"—you need to pack a bag, just the essentials, and be ready to leave in ten minutes—"

Jessica returned her attention to the new mural decorating her wall. The graffiti eye seemed to watch her.

A cube of cold fear slid down her throat.

The Marshals Service had promised she was safe here. That she was invisible. That no one would ever find her.

They were wrong.

TWO

JESSICA WAITED BY THE CURB, arms crossed tightly over her chest, as the male marshal loaded her suitcase into the trunk of his car. The night air was thick and still, carrying the scent of asphalt and distant rain. Sharrow appeared beside her, phone pressed to her ear, her brow furrowed in concentration.

Sharrow ended the call and nodded toward the other marshal. "This is Deputy U.S. Marshal Ryan Inglis," she said. "From the Two Rivers Violent Fugitive Task Force."

Jessica turned toward him, intending a more dignified introduction than their one at the strip club, but he was too busy with her suitcase to even glance her way. His movements were efficient, practiced, as if she were just another package to transport.

Sharrow continued, "He's taking you to a neutral site in Baton Rouge. You'll be safe there while we make new arrangements."

Over Inglis's shoulder, Jessica caught a glimpse of black metal drawers bolted to the bottom of the trunk. Rifle cases. She knew what they were. What they meant.

Her stomach twisted.

She turned back to Sharrow. "You're not coming with me?"

Sharrow shook her head. "I'm afraid you're on your own now."

Jessica had known that before she'd even asked the question. Still, hearing it out loud sent a cold ripple through her chest. Sharrow's role in her life was over. There'd be another Witness Inspector waiting for her in Baton Rouge, another name she'd have to memorize. Another person guarding the identity of a woman who didn't exist yet.

Her gaze flicked to the swell of Sharrow's belly. She was close. Nine months, at least. Their infrequent meetings meant Jessica hadn't seen her since before the pregnancy. Other than a once yearly check-in, Sharrow had existed in Jessica's life solely as a contact on her phone, under the name "Aunty Sam".

There was no round-the-clock monitoring like Jessica had imagined when she'd first entered the federal Witness Security Program. No marshals sitting in darkened cars at the end of her drive. No surveillance of her phone or checking of her mail. The USMS left her to her own devices, provided she followed their extensive list of rules. And she had followed all those rules. To the letter. Changed her habits, erased her past, learned how to live without leaving a footprint. She had built a new life, one small, cautious step at a time.

And yet still, somehow, they had found her.

"Ma'am." Inglis's voice was low, firm. He held the car door open.

Sharrow gave a single nod. "Good luck, Jessica." Not goodbye, but good *luck*. It sounded fittingly ominous.

Jessica climbed into the car, and Inglis shut the door behind her. He slid into the driver's seat, buckled in, and met her gaze briefly in the rearview mirror before pulling away from the curb.

Through the rear window, she watched her house shrink into the distance. It had never been much, just an old clapboard bungalow with an iron roof that turned into a furnace in the summer. The paint on the fascia was peeling. The porch sagged. The lawn was more dirt than grass.

But it had been *hers*. The place where she had learned to breathe again. The place where she'd finally felt safe.

Except now she understood—safety had only ever been an illusion.

Jessica let her head rest against the seat, staring out the window as they passed darkened houses and the swaying silhouettes of date palms.

She had the strange, overwhelming sensation that she'd forgotten something. Left something behind.

The thought almost made her laugh.

She was leaving everything behind.

THREE

A NEUTRAL SITE in Baton Rouge. That was government-speak for a safe house, a secure location where she'd stay while the USMS created all the documents she'd need to start again. Birth certificate, social security number, driver's license, bank accounts. They'd fabricate education records and medical certificates. They'd invent a whole new life for her and hand it over in a brown manila folder.

She knew all this because she'd spent three months in just such a place, eleven years ago. Right after the trial. Right after...everything. The brief stay had permanently etched itself into her memory.

The Witness Security Safe Site and Orientation Center in Washington, D.C. had been a fortress. A compound within a compound. Armed marshals had patrolled the outer perimeter; the internal building had been a prison-like warren of segregated rooms, separated by doors that opened and closed by themselves. The only entrance had been via a bomb-proof underground car park. Everywhere, there were cameras.

Her room had been self-contained, with a closet-sized bathroom and a tiny kitchenette. There'd been no internet. No phone line. No cell signal. The only form of entertainment had been a stack of mostly kids' DVDs and a shelf of decaying paperbacks.

Twice a day, they'd let her into the communal yard for fresh air and sunlight. The high concrete perimeter walls had meant it was hard to enjoy much of the latter. Guards carefully timed each of her outdoor excursions so she wouldn't meet other residents. She'd heard them though, through the walls. Banging. Shouting. And at night, crying.

Her own crying had been done silently, curled up in bed, where she'd spent most of her time.

Other than the marshals, her only human contact had been the doctor who'd administered regular medical examinations. The Bureau of Prisons had dispatched a psychologist to decide if she posed a risk to herself or others. He'd sat opposite her and asked inane questions from a clipboard about her state of mind. The joke was, being holed up in that place was enough to scramble anyone's mind, regardless of the trauma she'd already gone through.

It had felt like a prison, but it wasn't. She could have left anytime she wanted. Somehow, knowing that only made it worse. On the days she could get out of bed and muster enthusiasm for life, escape had consumed her thoughts. What had stopped her was the knowledge that the moment she walked out of that place, she'd have been completely on her own. WITSEC was a onetime offer. If you elected to leave the program, you were effectively dead to the USMS.

And, pretty soon after that, you'd be dead to everyone else, too.

When she'd discovered that Florida was to be her new home, she hadn't exactly been thrilled. Her perception of the place had been of killer storms, dog-eating pythons, and gators on golf courses. That impression hadn't improved after a few months of living there, during what had been one of the hottest and wettest summers on record. God, she'd missed snow. And sleet. And freezing westerlies.

Slowly, though, the place had grown on her. First, she'd stopped hating it so much. Then she'd begun to like it.

Now, it was in her rearview mirror, just as Illinois had been. And soon, Jessica Meeks would be erased, just like Julia Mikkelsen had been.

Jessica rested her head against the cool glass of the car window and wondered how many times a person could do that before they erased themselves entirely.

———

Florida became Alabama, night fell, and the heat rose.

With her head lying back against the seat and the cool draft of air conditioning against her face, Jessica slipped into a light doze. Images that weren't quite dreams, weren't quite memories shimmered before her eyes. A big white stone house that overlooked a lake. The faces of her parents and sister, frozen as if trapped in a photo. Pointe shoes on her feet. The sensation she used to get when she danced. Like she was liberated from the laws of gravity, like she might never land from the next leap.

A man's voice, soft in her ear. *"Nunca tienes que tener miedo de mí."*

You never have to be afraid of me.

With a jerk, she awoke, her heart beating fast and her back damp with sweat. She hadn't heard Daniel's voice in her head in years.

She blinked the images away. It took a few seconds to remember where she was. In a car, with a deputy U.S. marshal, heading for Baton Rouge. It took another second for her to realize that the car had stopped.

She looked up and saw the marshal twisted around in his seat, staring at her. He must have said something to wake her.

Glancing out the window, she saw they'd pulled in a truck stop off the interstate and were now parked at the pumps of a

Shell station. Across a wide concrete lot was the illuminated sign of an all-night diner.

"Where are we?"

Inglis unfastened his seat belt. "Mississippi, ma'am. Just outta Biloxi."

He had a nice voice. Low, a little husky. Permanently slurred with that thick Southern drawl.

She glanced down at her watch. It was nearly two in the morning. It felt like she'd only closed her eyes for a moment, but it had been hours.

Having gotten out of the car, the marshal leaned back in. "You hungry?"

She shook her head. But she needed to use the bathroom, so she unfastened her seatbelt and got out too.

A fat yellow moon was beating down like a sun. She looked around the forecourt, illuminated by the harsh overhead lights. There were public restrooms in a small concrete building to the left, but from the look of the overflowing rubbish bins out front, they received little in the way of servicing. She hitched her bag strap over her shoulder and headed for the diner instead.

It was almost empty, with just a guy in a trucker cap seated alone at a table and a couple of teenagers at a booth by the door. Cold air blasted down from a HVAC unit in the ceiling, strong enough to lift strands of hair from her face. There was a TV fixed to the far wall, tuned to a local news channel.

She paused for a moment to watch it. A reporter was standing on a pier, her back to the darkened sea. She was wearing a thick PVC parka, even though it wasn't raining. The audio was inaudible, but the report was clearly focused on the approaching storm.

Hurricane Petra had been occupying all the media channels for a week. Meteorologists had been tracking its progress since it began life hundreds of miles away, off the Ivory Coast. It was now a Category Three storm and had already left a trail of destruction across the Yucatán Peninsula. A screen graphic depicted its swirling eyewall around the deep low-pressure system at its center. It was a deadly spinning Catherine wheel of reds, oranges, and greens. Arrows illustrated its path toward Louisiana and Mississippi in the coming hours.

Hugging her bag to her side, she headed for the restrooms at the rear of the diner. Either the place lacked a no walk-in bathroom policy, or the waitress chose not to enforce it. She just leaned against the counter and eyeballed Jessica from afar.

As she walked past the trucker, she could feel his eyes following her every step of the way.

She used the toilet, then washed her hands. Her reflection in the mirror gave her a jolt. She was still wearing her work makeup: heavy winged eyeliner, fake eyelashes and far too much bronzer. Her pink hair was pulled up into a high ponytail. She looked like Fuck Me Barbie. No wonder people were staring.

She found a pack of makeup remover wipes in her bag and took off what she could. Then, for a long moment, she studied her reflection, examining the face that remained behind. It was the face of the girl she could never outrun.

Every time she looked in the mirror, she was reminded of that fact. Reminded that no matter how many times she changed her name or her address, she could never change what she'd done. Could never fix what she'd destroyed.

The marshals had told her long ago not to dwell on the past. That everything and everyone in it was gone. And that the sooner she made peace with that, the better.

But it was impossible not to dwell. The memories felt magnetized. They tugged her mind back of their own accord.

The past wasn't something she enjoyed revisiting. In fact, it was a place she tried to avoid at all costs.

For there be monsters.

FOUR

ELEVEN YEARS EARLIER

JULIA GRIPPED the edge of the vanity and stared at her reflection, wondering why there were two of her staring back. Focusing hard, she had to squint to make her mirror twins become one.

Her gaze swept the bathroom. A grimy sink. Mold blooming across the walls. She had no idea where she was. She'd lost that rather vital piece of information somewhere between her fourth and fifth vodka shots.

The door behind her burst open, and a girl stumbled in. She looked panicked. Julia was about to ask what was wrong when it became obvious. The girl groped for the toilet with outstretched arms, but she couldn't get the lid up in time. A torrent of vomit spattered over the cistern and dripped onto the floor.

Julia pressed herself against the vanity to avoid it. "Are you okay?" she asked, but the words didn't seem to come out in the right order.

The girl ignored her. She just kneeled over the bowl, panting.

Julia had to get out of there before the smell made her puke, too. She stepped over the girl's legs and went back out to the hallway. There was thudding music coming from downstairs. It was so loud she could feel it vibrating the floorboards under her feet.

Behind her, a man's voice said, "There you are."

She spun around, stumbling in her stilettos.

The man was very tall with black hair slicked back in an old-school quiff and a silver hoop glinting in one ear. He held a red Solo cup that reeked of bourbon.

That voice. That earring.

The memory came back in pieces. The club downtown. Sweaty and loud, the bass pounding like a second heartbeat. He'd been behind the DJ booth, headphones slung around his neck, eyes locked on her from the second she walked in. Her pink minidress and sparkly Louboutins had clearly caught his attention.

She remembered the heat of the crowd, his hand on her lower back. The sting of the first shot. Then more. After that...

She blinked.

A taxi ride. His hand on her thigh. The rest was fog.

What was his name? Finn? No—Floyd.

She was swaying a little, and he took her arm to steady her. "Woah. You okay?"

She said nothing, just continued to stare stupidly up at him.

He handed her the cup. "You didn't finish your drink."

She didn't want to drink anymore but took a sip out of politeness. The tip of her tongue felt numb.

He said, "You wanna go someplace quieter?"

"What?" she shouted back.

He grinned, then nodded towards the staircase. "Come on."

She followed him, hitching up the strap of her handbag. "Oh, wait," she called after him. "There's a girl in the bathroom. She's sick."

Again, she got the feeling her words weren't coming out in the right order because Floyd didn't respond. He just kept walking down the stairs, weaving between the loved-up couples pressed against the wall and the passed-out loners splayed across the steps.

Not wanting to be left there on her own, she teetered after him.

Downstairs, in the crowded living room, the air stunk of weed and spilled beer. The bass from the speakers was so loud it made her eardrums ache. Following Floyd, she forced her way through the jam of bodies. He led her through the kitchen to a backdoor, then down a short flight of concrete steps.

The chilly night breeze raised goosebumps on Julia's bare skin. She shivered and crossed her arms.

Light spilled out from the windows of the house, pooling on a small, cobbled courtyard. People had nodded off in patio chairs. A circle of guys stood off to the left, their faces illuminated grotesquely by the flicker of a lighter as it was passed around.

She felt like her head was floating about two feet above her body. She stumbled on an empty beer bottle, sending it skittering across the courtyard. The drink in her cup splashed over her hand, so she dropped it.

"You good?" Floyd said.

"I want to go back inside," she said. At least, that was what she wanted to say. But the words that came out of her mouth sounded like they were in a foreign language. Floyd seemed to understand what she meant though, because he nodded and took her hand and led her back towards the house. Relieved, she gripped his fingers and stumbled after him.

The sounds of the party grew distant. She realized they weren't going back to the house at all. They were moving around the side of it. She looked behind her, but the shadowy figures in the yard were no longer in sight.

To her left, a dog gave two sharp barks, then a low, menacing growl.

Her feet hit metal. He was leading her up steps.

She forced herself to wake up and assess where she was—standing in the doorway of an old RV. It was dark inside; she had to strain her eyes to make out the room. The air felt thick.

She stood still for a moment, confused. Had she wanted to come in here? She focused hard, but trying to think seemed to require an enormous effort.

The door closed behind her. She whirled around and found

Floyd right there, his hands on her shoulders, walking her backwards.

Her back hit something solid. A wall, or a cupboard. He was crowding in against her, his hands gripping her upper arms, his breath on her face, hot and alcoholic.

She tried to push him off her, but he was pinning her arms, pressing all his weight against her. He leaned in close, his face near hers, clearly intending to kiss her. She turned her face away and his teeth grazed her jaw. Both hands were tugging at her dress; she heard a rip as the fabric tore.

She shoved him again, harder this time, but all it did was make his smirk grow.

I should be stopping this, she thought. *I shouldn't just be letting this happen.* Angling her face away, she hissed, "Get *off* me."

Outside, the dog was whining by the door. Its claws made a grating sound as they scratched against the metal. She inhaled, intending on screaming as loud as she could to set the dog off barking again.

Floyd raised his hand to her neck and squeezed it between his fingers and thumb. He shoved her head back until it hit the wall behind her with a thud. Screaming became impossible.

She sobbed against his hand, hot tears leaking out of the corners of her eyes. Again, she tried to mobilize her arms, but they felt numb and useless.

She couldn't breathe. She tossed her head from side to side, trying to shake his grip off, trying to make a space so she could suck in some air. But he was too strong. Bright white spots danced in front of her vision.

This is it, she realized. *This is how I'm going to die.*

Bright yellow light filled the room. Instinctively, she clamped her eyes shut.

Behind Floyd, she heard a faint metallic *snick*.

Floyd's body tensed against hers. His grip on her neck eased.

Julia gulped a lungful of air. The bright spots receded. She opened her eyes, squinting against the harsh light.

Floyd was still pressing his hips against hers. But he'd let go of her. She watched as he lifted both hands toward the ceiling like he was being compelled by a higher power. His sour breath washed over her face. "What the actual fuck?"

She raised her chin to see over his shoulder. There was a man standing behind him. He was taller than Floyd and was calmly holding a pistol to the back of his head. Tattoos crawled up his neck. When he spoke, his voice was soft but laced with menace. "This is private property, *pendejo*."

Floyd, hands still in the air, gave a nervous laugh. "Bruh, chill out, alright? We didn't think anyone was in here."

The other man said nothing, just continued to press the pistol to Floyd's head like he was trying to bore a hole in his skull.

Floyd's colorless face went even paler. He flicked his tongue over his lips, then said, "We're sorry, man. We just wanted a little privacy. My girl couldn't keep her hands off me."

The man with the gun shifted his gaze from the back of Floyd's head to Julia's face. She dropped her head, so she didn't have to make eye contact, but still felt his stare travel over her. She realized how she must look, pressed against the wall, her face streaked with mascara-laced tears.

There was a dull crack, the sound of metal hitting bone, then a loud thud. The trailer quaked beneath her feet.

Her eyes flew open to find Floyd out cold on the vinyl floor. The other guy stood over him, the pistol he'd just used as a club still outstretched in his right hand.

Julia took a shaky step to one side. The guy jerked the gun in her direction.

Instinctively, she raised her hands. "Please," she whispered.

Then everything went black.

———

Her limbs felt wrong. Heavy. Disconnected.

Sheets rasped against her skin—cheap, scratchy fabric—but

she couldn't remember lying down. There was a bitter taste in her mouth, like stale liquor and something metallic.

Her head throbbed. Somewhere nearby, a bass line pounded. No, maybe that was her pulse.

She kept her eyes shut. The dark behind her eyelids felt safer than what might be waiting when she opened them.

A whiff of something chemical drifted past—cleaning product? Cologne?

Her stomach turned.

This wasn't her bed.

This wasn't her room.

She forced herself to open her eyes. The blur slowly hardened into shapes. A bed. A narrow room. Daylight leaking through the slats of a grimy window

None of it felt familiar.

She pushed herself up onto her elbows. Her head felt as light as a balloon. Then it exploded in pain, like someone had driven a metal spike into her skull. She squeezed her temples between her finger and thumb, feeling a vein pulsing thickly under the skin. Her mouth was tacky, and she had a desperate thirst.

Peering around, she saw she was in a cramped trailer, on a double bed that occupied the entire width of one end. Small windows ran down the right wall, curtained with faded yellow fabric strung on a plastic cord. There was a kitchenette down the far end—a sink, a tiny bar fridge, and a trestle table. Cupboards lined the other wall. Hanging above the door was the Mexican tricolor.

She tried to remember what had happened last night. In her mind, images flickered like a faulty fluorescent tube. The club downtown. The party in the house. The DJ, Finn. No, Floyd.

Then, with a jolt that felt like being zapped with a cattle prod, she remembered how he'd pushed her up against that cupboard over there. How he'd put his hand up her dress. How he'd almost…

Then, with an even bigger jolt, she remembered what had happened next.

There'd been another man. With a soft, sinister voice. And a gun.

After that, the memories flickered and died out.

She covered her eyes with one hand. God, she felt so stupid. How many times had she heard about girls getting wasted and waking up with no memory and no underwear? How many times had she told herself that would never be her?

Pushing back the covers, she was relieved to find her underwear was still accounted for. In fact, she was wearing more clothing than she'd had on last night. Over her dress was a black hoodie. It had white writing running down the sleeves, which were so long they hung off her hands. She lifted one and sniffed the fabric at her wrist. It smelled of gasoline and smoke. Underlying those scents was another. The faint whiff of cheap cologne.

She looked around the trailer again. It was empty. Whoever the man with the gun was, he was gone now.

Near the bed, a beer crate served as an improvised nightstand. On it was a glass of clear liquid. She picked it up and gave it a cautious sniff. Discovering it was just water, she gulped it down.

The moment it hit her stomach, it tried to come back up again. She gripped the edge of the mattress, willing herself not to be sick. Slowly, the nausea passed, and she felt strong enough to stand up, bracing one hand against a cupboard to ward off a wave of vertigo.

The exertion made her head pound. It also drew her attention to another source of pain: her neck. She pressed a damp hand to it. It felt tender to the touch. She had a vivid memory of Floyd's tight grip around her windpipe, and of the white spots dancing across her vision.

Lowering her hand, she discovered her necklace was missing. It must have broken off during the attack.

She cast her eyes across the cracked linoleum floor. Nothing gold glinted up at her. Her spirits sank even lower. The necklace had been a gift from her dad; she hadn't taken it off since she was a kid.

But she couldn't stay here any longer to search for it. She had to get out of this trailer before its owner returned.

Her handbag and heels were lying on the floor near the end of the bed. She scooped them up, then tiptoed to the door and cracked it open. Its old hinges squealed.

She paused in the doorway, shielding her eyes against the bright sunlight, and looked around.

The trailer sat in the far corner of a weedy lot. A chain-link fence separated it from the next property. Objects poked above the shin-high grass. An overturned wheelie bin. An old car covered by a blue tarp. A rusted motorcycle that looked like it was returning to the earth.

Still barefoot, she stepped down onto a dirt path. Taking her phone out of her purse, she checked her messages.

None. Nothing from her mom or sister. Not one of her so-called friends had phoned or texted her, wondering where she'd disappeared off to last night. No one had noticed that she hadn't gone home, or checked that she wasn't dead in an alley somewhere.

A volley of barking came from her right. She got such a fright that she felt her body cleave from her skeleton.

Whirling around, she saw a white Rottweiler emerge from under the trailer. It was tethered to a piece of metal rebar stuck in the ground. Suddenly, it tested the limits of its chain by launching itself at her legs. It was short by about a yard, but she stumbled backwards anyway.

From behind her, a man called out, "¡Tequila! *¡Cierra la puta boca!*"

Heart pounding, she spun back around.

But there was no one there. Just the old wreck of a car, covered with the tarp and propped up on concrete blocks.

Then she spotted a pair of denim-clad legs sticking out from under it. The man attached to them scooted out on a trolley. He sat up, shielding his eyes against the sun.

It was the man with the gun. She took a few stumbling steps backwards.

He pushed himself to his feet. He was tall. Latino. Dark hair in a high fade. No shirt, just low-slung jeans revealing the top of his white boxer briefs. Tattoos covered his torso and arms.

He had a tool in his hand, some kind of wrench. Both his hands were black with engine oil.

"Don't worry about her," he called, gesturing to the dog. "She's just being friendly."

Julia looked at the dog's bared incisors and raised hackles.

Friendly. Right.

She looked back at the guy. He didn't look friendly either. But he was keeping his distance, so she resisted the urge to bolt.

"You okay?" he called in a soft Spanish accent.

She nodded, not looking at him. "I'm fine."

He dropped the wrench on the ground, wiped his hands on a rag. She realized they weren't black with oil, but black with more tattoos.

He slid one hand into his back pocket and pulled out a baggie of white pills. "You sure? You took a shitload of benzos last night."

She stared at the baggie, feeling sick at just the sight of them. "Those aren't mine."

"I know," he said, shoving them back into his jeans. "They were in that asshole's pocket. I'm guessing a bunch of them wound up in your drink."

She swallowed hard and looked away. Part of her brain registered the sinister notion that this guy had gone through her attacker's pockets. A far larger part realized she didn't care.

A cool breeze rattled the trees along the fence line and raised goosebumps on the bare skin of her legs. She crossed her arms over her chest in their overlong sleeves.

It occurred to her he must have dressed her in his hoodie after she'd passed out. Then put her in his bed and slept…where? In that old car?

"I'm Daniel, by the way," he said. He had a small cross tattooed under one eye, and the word ALONE running along his jaw up to his ear.

She hesitated for a long moment, then said, "Julia."

He didn't seem fazed by the cold, just stood there, shirtless, with both hands stuck into his back pockets. "Where do you live, Julia?"

"Lake Forest."

"I can give you a ride home."

She glanced at the old wreck behind him. It was the only thing resembling a car that she had seen in the yard or on the street. "In that thing?"

His eyebrows shot up in mock offense. "Uh, that 'thing', actually, is a 1970 Plymouth Hemi 'Cuda."

He paused, as if expecting her to be bowled over by that fact. When she wasn't, he grinned and added, "Only one of the greatest American muscle cars ever built. Four hundred and twenty-six horsepower. Four-ninety pound feet of torque. Original Tor Red. Incredibly rare." He was looking at it with what could only be described as a loving expression. "She's my ride or die."

Julia looked more closely at the car. Beneath a raised corner of the tarp, she saw a shiny red fender. Okay, so maybe it wasn't a wreck after all. In fact, it looked brand new.

But it was still missing several vital components, even to her untrained eyes.

"You realize it doesn't have any wheels, right?" she said.

He grinned again, revealing white teeth and a dimple in one cheek. "Minor detail." He pointed at the motorcycle that looked like it was dying a slow, rusty death. "I actually meant, I'll take you home on that."

She raised her eyebrows, thinking he must have been joking. His face appeared serious. "Thanks," she said. "But I'll pass."

He shrugged, like it was her funeral. Which she was pretty sure it would be if she'd said yes.

"Alright then," he said, bending to pick up his wrench from the ground. "*Adiós*, Julia."

He lowered himself onto the trolley and disappeared back under the car.

She turned to go, then spun back, waving her stupidly long sleeves. "Oh, your sweatshirt."

"Keep it," came the voice from under the car. "I got others."

She walked down the dirt track that led to the street. Scrolling through her contacts, she pulled up the number of a car service.

While she waited on the sidewalk for her ride, she turned to look back at the house. It had plywood boards on its windows, rotten siding, and weeds sprouting from its gutters. From the outside, it appeared uninhabited.

There was no sign of last night's partygoers. It looked so creepily deserted she could almost believe she'd hallucinated the whole thing.

The only thing that reminded her she hadn't was the dull ache of the hand-shaped bruise around her neck.

FIVE

DANIEL CASTAÑO SAT on the steps of his trailer, watching as his old white Camry lurched over the rutted driveway, its shocks groaning under the abuse. The early morning air carried the scent of damp earth and gasoline.

Beside him, Tequila lifted her head, ears pricked. She got to her feet and whined, pacing anxiously.

The car came to a stop, and the door swung open. An enormous man unfolded himself from the driver's seat, using the doorframe for leverage. Terry "La Araña" Bidois was built like a bulldozer—barrel-chested, thick-necked, with arms like slabs of meat. He was nearly as wide as he was tall, and unlike most older white guys who carried that kind of bulk, his wasn't just fat. The guy could bench-press a truck.

He tossed Daniel the keys.

Daniel caught them one-handed. "Where?"

Terry pushed his sunglasses onto his forehead, revealing the intricate spiderweb tattoo covering one side of his bald scalp. His gold teeth flashed in a grin. "Dumpsters," he said. "Back of the Yards."

"Dumpsters," Daniel repeated, noting the plural.

Terry's grin widened. "Let's see if those crime scene guys know their assholes from their elbows." He chuckled. "Literally."

Daniel said nothing. Just stretched his legs out in front of him, exhaustion sinking deep into his bones. He hadn't slept last night, and not just because his bed had been occupied. It had been a night from hell in every possible way.

Tequila had been the first to sense the intruder. By the time Daniel got inside, the bastard had his hands all over that girl, trying to pull up her dress while she sobbed. The look on her face —terror-stricken, eyes wide and glassy—was burned into his brain.

The guy was lucky Daniel hadn't put a bullet in him right then and there. Instead, he'd knocked him out, dragged him outside, and beaten him until his fists were raw and bloody.

When his anger had finally subsided, he'd stood up and stared down at the guy. He'd still been alive. If Daniel had called an ambulance right then, the guy'd probably be alive now. Breathing through a tube, sure. But alive.

But Daniel hadn't called an ambulance.

He'd called Terry.

La Araña had showed up ten minutes later and walked right up to the guy lying there face down in the grass. He'd pulled out his Ruger with the silencer and put two nine-millimeter holes in the back of his head.

"Any more?" Terry had asked, scanning the yard like he expected an entire battalion lying in wait.

Daniel had looked down at the body. "No."

They'd wrapped him in an old groundsheet and shoved him into the backseat of Daniel's Camry. And then Terry had gone off to do what Terry did best—make people disappear.

Daniel had stood there a long time afterwards, staring at the dark, wet smear the body had left behind. He didn't regret that the man was dead. But he did regret needing to get Terry involved. Help from *The Spider* always came with long, tangled strings attached.

When he finally headed back to his RV, Tequila nosed at his palm as he passed.

The girl was still where he'd left her, curled on the floor in the recovery position, her blonde hair tangled across her face. He'd washed the blood from his hands, then kneeled beside her and brushed the strands away. She'd shivered, mumbling something incoherent.

He'd pulled her dress back down, then fetched the cleanest hoodie he owned, easing it over her head and sliding her arms into the sleeves. It swallowed her frame, falling longer than her dress had.

Then he'd lifted her onto his bed, pulled a blanket over her, and sat against the wardrobe, watching her sleep as the sun crept over the horizon.

Now, Terry nudged his chin toward the trailer. "She still out?"

Daniel shook his head. "She's gone."

Terry blinked. "You let her go?"

Daniel just shrugged.

Terry swiped a hand down his sweaty face, even though the sun had barely risen. "Big mistake, man."

Daniel chewed the inside of his cheek. "She didn't see anything, Terry. Like you said—she was out for the count."

Terry made a face. "Doesn't mean she won't go to the cops. Even if she doesn't remember much, they'll still investigate." He replaced his sunglasses. "And you realize what happens if a bunch of cops come sniffing around here, right?" He gestured to the yard. "You got that guy's blood all over your grass. His DNA's in your trailer. And hers."

Daniel clenched his jaw. Said nothing.

"They'll have you in cuffs on sight, Danny." Terry's voice was sharp now. "You know how the cops in this city are. One look at you, and you're the fucking rapist."

Daniel forced himself to stay still, but his stomach churned. He looked at the spot where Terry had ended that guy's life. He'd thrown a bucket of water over it this morning, but the blood had dried into the grass. Even if he dug up the whole lawn—which wouldn't be suspicious at all—forensics could probably still pull DNA from the soil.

Terry let the silence stretch before playing his trump card.

"If you go down for this, think about Sebastián." His voice was lower now, more calculated. "Think about what happens to your little brother. He'll be on a bus back to the border before you can blink."

Daniel exhaled through his nose. His fists flexed against his thighs.

Terry was right.

Letting the girl go had been a mistake.

A big one.

Terry studied him, then nodded to himself. "You'd better find her, Daniel. And deal with it." He paused. "If you don't, I will."

Daniel had a vivid, stomach-turning image of what 'dealing with it' would look like in Terry's hands. La Araña had been an Army Ranger for fifteen years, deployed everywhere from Beirut to Somalia, and had acquired skills even a surgeon couldn't match. And he really enjoyed using them.

The thought of Terry applying those skills to Julia made Daniel's gut twist. He didn't want her hurt. But if it came down to it, he'd rather take that sin on himself than let Terry near her. He shook his head. "No. I'll handle it."

Terry smirked, reading his hesitation. "I didn't say you gotta hurt her. Just scare her a little. Remind her that actions have consequences."

Daniel nodded, relief washing over him. Just scare her. A little.

He could do that.

Terry jerked his thumb toward the Camry. "Oh, and by the way, you got a big clean-up job in there. Fucker bled all over the backseat. Hope you got a bucket. And a shitload of bleach." He slid his sunglasses back into place. "And don't use hot water," he added over his shoulder. "Cooks the blood into the upholstery."

Then he turned and walked back to his truck, a late-model Chevy Suburban. Conveniently evidence-free.

Daniel watched him go, then looked down at the keys in his hand, exhaling sharply.

Apparently, he had a lot of cleaning up to do.

————

Daniel held up the dainty gold chain so that it caught the fading light coming through the windshield. He'd found it under his bed a few days ago. The clasp was broken, yanked apart as if someone had ripped it from her neck. He'd fixed it with a pair of tweezers.

A ballet slipper dangled from the end. And engraved on it, in tiny words, was a name.

Julia Mikkelsen.

He looked up through the windshield at the Mikkelsen mansion. The gaps in the huge wrought-iron gates gave him a good view of the place. It was one of the fanciest in the neighborhood. And it was a pretty fucking fancy neighborhood.

The house was massive. A monolith of gleaming white stone, set back from the road down a sweeping circular drive. In front was a giant marble fountain he could probably swim laps in. The garage was at least a six-car job.

For a very long time, he just sat there, across the road from her house, his Beretta clutched in his palm.

It was a little after ten at night when a black BMW coupe came down the lane and turned into the drive. As it passed, he caught a flash of blond hair and knew from that brief glance it was her.

The gates closed behind her. She eased the car up beside the garage but left it idling, neither parking inside nor getting out. From where he watched, he had a clear view through the window. Night had fallen, but the lights of the house cut a sharp silhouette of her. Her head was bowed, like she was praying to the steering wheel.

Long minutes passed, and still she made no move to get out.

It hit him like a slap—maybe she'd seen him parked there. Maybe she was already on the phone with the cops, tucked safely in her car, waiting for backup to roll in, sirens wailing.

His grip tightened on the gun, slick with sweat. *Should I go?* The thought stabbed through the haze of adrenaline.

But the minutes dragged on, heavy and silent. No flashing lights. No sirens.

Still, unease prickled along his spine. This was the kind of neighborhood where a call about someone like him—brown skin, sitting alone, not belonging—wouldn't be ignored. Not for long. If she'd called, they'd be here already.

So, no, she hadn't spotted him. And he knew what he had to do. He had to stride up to her car door, shove his gun in her face and tell her that if she didn't keep her fucking mouth shut about what had happened in his trailer, she'd wind up in a dumpster along with the other guy. Or bits of her would, anyway.

And yet he couldn't coax his body to carry out that plan.

Time stretched on for so long without her moving that he reached for the door handle to get out and check if she was still breathing.

The irony struck him hard. Here he was, one hand gripping a gun that could easily end her life, the other poised to perhaps save it.

Thankfully, before he cleaved himself in half with indecision, she abruptly sat up in her seat and opened the car door. She climbed out, head still downcast, and swiped at her eyes with the back of her hand. Even from this distance, it was obvious she'd been crying.

His gun was sweaty in his grip. Terry's voice was in his head. *Remind her that actions have consequences.*

Right now, though, the only thing he could remember was how she'd felt in his arms as he'd lifted her onto his bed. How her hair had fanned over his shoulder. How the skin on the back of her thighs had felt impossibly soft against his forearm.

"Fuck," he muttered, tossing the gun onto the passenger floorboard. He started the car, reversed in a wide arc, then slipped away into the night.

———

Julia dried her cheeks with the back of her hand, took a big sniff, then glanced around to make sure no one had witnessed her crying alone in her car. But, as usual, she was the only one at home. Her mom and stepdad's cars were both parked in the garage, but she knew neither of them were here. Her mom was in Rome with her sister for a dress fitting, and her stepfather was in Japan for a charity golf event.

It wasn't unusual for her to find herself rattling around in this big house on her own. Her family spent more time apart than together. It was rare for them all to find themselves in the same city, let alone the same house.

She slung her dance bag over her shoulder, still dabbing at her eyes. She tried to blame her sudden bout of tears on exhaustion from eight hours of rehearsal and two more of performing. But, deep down, she knew that wasn't it.

It had been four days since the night of the party. The bruises on her neck were buried under a thick layer of stage makeup. And she thought she'd done a pretty good job of burying the memories of it, too. She'd shoved the whole incident into a box in the back of her mind and nailed the lid shut. If there was one thing that she was good at, it was compartmentalizing. It was her superpower. She ran her life with the rigidity of a barre routine. Trauma was put in boxes. Smiles were painted on. And the show went on.

She shut the car door and headed toward the house. When she reached the front door, she paused on the threshold and cast another glance behind her. While she'd been sitting in the car, she'd had the strangest feeling she was being watched.

But there was no one out there. Her drive was empty. Nothing disturbed the still night air, save for the distant sound of a retreating car.

SIX

TODAY'S THE DAY.

Daniel gripped the steering wheel with both hands and tried not to think about how he'd made the same pact with himself yesterday.

And the day before.

In the backseat, Tequila let out a restless whine. She'd been cooped up too long, just like him.

He looked through the car window at the Mikkelsen mansion, as if he hadn't memorized its facade many hours ago. Despite Terry's order, he couldn't bring himself to get out of the car and carry it out.

He drummed his fingers against the steering wheel, trying to justify his reasons for stalling. One came easily: he had to wait for her to leave the house. The plan was to follow her in his car, then make her pull over on a secluded stretch of road and do it. He'd missed her yesterday and had seen no sign of her BMW today.

There'd been plenty of other vehicles coming and going. Contractors' trucks, several vans emblazoned with a florist's logo. One belonged to a caterer who specialized in weddings.

He leaned back in his seat, shoved his hand into his jeans pocket and pulled out her gold chain. He had taken to carrying it everywhere with him. For reasons that baffled him as much as the ones that had him sitting in front of her house for hours on end.

Maybe it was because she'd begun to occupy parts of his mind that didn't listen to reason. Parts that liked to replay how good she'd looked in his sweatshirt. In his bed.

He closed his eyes and exhaled. Then he reached over and opened the glove box. Took out his Beretta. Bent forward in his seat and stuffed it down the back of his waistband.

He wanted to be ready.

An uncomfortable fullness in his bladder made him think he should take a piss before doing anything else. He opened the car door, went round to the back, and unzipped his jeans. He was mid-leak when he realized he was being watched.

A huge black cat was sitting on the stone wall that bordered the Mikkelsen property. It had yellow eyes, and a mushed face, and was staring at him with a look of pure disgust. With a flick of its eyes, it switched the target of its loathing to the dog in his backseat.

Tequila had her head all the way out the window. She grinned at the cat, then gave a high-pitched squeal.

Daniel saw it all unfold a millisecond before it happened.

"Tequila, no—"

Too late. The dog leaped from the car in a single bound. She dashed across the road and galloped through the open gate after the cat.

Fuck's sake.

He zipped up and jogged across the road. "¡Tequila! ¡*Vuelve aquí!*"

The dog paid him no attention, focused as she was on the flash of black ahead of her.

Daniel paused halfway up the drive and wiped sweat off his forehead. He glanced around, conscious of being in full view of the house and grounds. There were several vehicles in the driveway, but no one was about.

He gave a shrill whistle, then watched with dismay as Tequila loped cheerfully after the cat, past the fountain and all the way around the side of the house.

He reached under his t-shirt to check if his pistol was still in his waistband. Then he took a deep breath and followed.

———

Julia grabbed the shank of her pointe shoe and hurled it at the wall. It hit with a satisfying crack, leaving a dent in the plaster. She picked up the other one and flung it after it.

Then she marched across the studio, retrieved both, and beat them against the wall some more. Breaking in new pointe shoes was brutal. A workout in itself.

It was also the only thing keeping her from having a meltdown. She poured every ounce of frustration into those dainty pink slippers, taking it out on them instead of the thing she really wanted to destroy.

The memory of Floyd's hands on her.

Sadly, the relief was fleeting.

Satisfied she'd softened them enough, she collapsed onto the floor, applied her toe pads, taped them down, and wrapped her toes in paper towels. Then she laced up her shoes, stood, and rose en pointe, testing the support through her arches.

Today marked the first day of her summer layoff from the Joffrey Ballet Company. Not that it meant rest. She hadn't taken a real break since she was eleven. During the season, she rehearsed for nine hours and performed for three. Off-season, she wasn't in the studio quite as much, but she still treated it like a full-time job.

She moved to the barre, pushing through demi and grand pliés, before shifting into échappés, sautés, and passés, her toes hammering out a steady drumbeat against the Marley floor. She'd done these moves thousands of times. They came to her as naturally as breathing.

Until a sudden barrage of construction hammering and the earsplitting whine of a power tool shattered her focus.

She stopped, sighing, and turned toward the full-length glass doors that separated her studio from the pool area. It was normally a serene view. Lately, though, it resembled a construction zone. Workers had been swarming the backyard for a week, racing to finish the gazebo renovations in time for her sister's wedding.

Her mother had been planning the event for five months. Julia had been dreading it for the same amount of time.

It was being heralded as the society wedding of the year. Five hundred guests, most of them rich and powerful. And, as her mother loved telling anyone who would listen, two minor royals.

Her sister was a soloist with the American Ballet Theater, and a rising star in the ballet world. She was destined to become a principle, and a great one, like their mom had been. At least, that's what everyone said.

Julia, a lowly corps dancer at the less-revered Joffrey, got no such fanfare.

Which was fine. She didn't need it. One day, if she worked hard enough, it would be her turn.

Scowling in the direction of the builders, she grabbed the sound system remote and cranked up the volume.

Back to work.

She returned to the center of the floor, composed herself, and prepared to restart—only to hesitate. One of the workers was sitting at a table near the pool. His head was turned toward her, watching.

A flicker of unease passed through her, but she pushed it away.

She launched into trickier jumps—piqué manèges, grand jetés —bounding from one end of the studio to the other. But despite her best efforts, her mind kept circling back to her observer.

There was something…familiar about him. And the dog panting at his feet.

She took a breath and forced herself into fouettés, the hardest move in ballet. Whipping around and around on one pointed foot, a human spinning top. It took perfect balance. Perfect concentration. Eyes locked on a fixed point, or she'd get dizzy.

Twenty-three, twenty-four, twenty-five—

Her gaze flicked to the man by the pool. And in an instant, she knew who he was.

Her focus shattered.

She stumbled, the momentum of her spin tipping her into a downward spiral, her elbows and knees slamming hard against the floor.

For a moment, she just sat there, winded. Then she turned toward her unexpected audience.

He was still watching.

And then, unbelievably, he started to clap.

Heat flared in her cheeks. She leaped to her feet, stormed to the glass doors, shoved them open, and strode toward him. But as she reached his table and looked down at him, she realized she had no idea what to say.

So, the only word that came out was, "You."

Daniel looked up at her, shielding his eyes from the sun. "Don't you get dizzy doing that?"

She blinked. Then glanced over her shoulder at the studio, realizing he meant her fouetté fail.

"Yes," she said, then quickly shook her head. "No."

He smiled, a dimple appearing in his left cheek.

"What are you doing here?"

The dimple deepened. *"Disfrutando del espectáculo."*

She frowned. "I don't speak Spanish."

"Enjoying the show."

She stared at him. He was very good-looking. Smooth, tanned skin. Bright hazel eyes under dark brows. A dangerous smile. A thin scar cut through his left eyebrow, disappearing into his hairline. That, and the tattoos on his face, kept him from being too pretty.

He wore a backward blue ball cap, a white tank, and battered jeans. Silver glinted in his ears and around his neck.

His dog stood, sensing her attention.

"Tequila," Daniel warned. *"Compórtate."*

Julia tensed, but the dog just grinned up at her, tail wagging. "She's friendly?" she asked.

He nodded.

Tentatively, she held out her hand. Tequila butted her head into it, drooling in gratitude.

She looked back at Daniel. "You're a builder?"

He chewed a thumbnail and stared out at the pool, seeming to give the question a lot of thought. Then he sat back and shrugged.

Before she could probe, he reached into his pocket and pulled something out. Something small. Something that glinted in the sun. He placed it on the table.

"My necklace."

"I found it in my trailer," he said. "Thought you might want it back."

He lifted it and held it out. She opened her palm, and he dropped it in.

"Thanks," she murmured, closing her fingers around it. "I thought I'd lost it forever."

Daniel scratched his jaw. His knuckles were raw, like they'd recently been scraped. Across his fingers, she noticed the letters inked into his skin.

L-M-N-1-3.

"How are you?" he asked quietly.

She swallowed hard. Looked away. "I'm okay."

A lie.

As much as she'd tried to seal shut the lid on the box of horrors in her head, she couldn't stop the flashbacks. They came, relentless: dark rooms. Sweaty fingers. Hot breath against her skin.

She forced herself to meet his gaze. "I didn't tell anyone, you know."

His expression sharpened, though his voice remained relaxed. "Why not?"

She shrugged. "Didn't think you'd appreciate cops showing up at your door."

A long silence.

Her voice was quieter when she finally said, "I'm not thrilled he got away with it."

Daniel's jaw tightened. "He didn't."

She glanced at his knuckles again. At the letters on his hand. A chill passed through her.

Then decided she didn't want to think about either. Ever again.

Daniel cast his eyes up at the house. Julia followed his gaze, taking in the Beaux-Arts mansion that loomed over the manicured grounds. Four stories of limestone and glass, a palatial display of excess. Seven bedrooms. Nine bathrooms. A private gym, a cedar sauna, a theater. And that was just the house. Beyond the tree line were the tennis courts, the staff quarters, and the garage stocked with luxury European cars. It was the kind of house that looked like it belonged in a magazine, not in real life.

Daniel let out a low whistle. "This place is insane. Your dad own a bank or something?"

She shook her head. Her father had been a musician, brilliant but broke. After his death, when Julia was six, her mother had apparently made a vow never to marry for love again. Because every marriage after that had been for money.

"Glen's my stepdad," she said. "And it's a finance company."

Daniel nodded, his gaze drifting to the half-finished gazebo where his coworkers hammered and sawed away. "It's not your wedding, is it?"

Julia blinked, then let out a short laugh. "Oh, God, no. It's my sister's."

Something in his expression shifted. A barely-there flicker of relief. It was subtle, but she caught it. Which was ridiculous. He didn't even know her.

A quiet settled between them, the hum of drills and distant chatter filling the space. His eyes flicked over her, not in the way men usually looked at her. It was more like he was trying to figure her out, slot her into some frame of reference that made sense to him.

"So," he said finally, "you're a ballerina. For real."

She nodded. "I'm a corps dancer with the Joffrey."

Daniel considered that, chewing on his thumbnail. "Does it hurt?"

She frowned. "Does what hurt?"

"When you fall down like that."

A flicker of embarrassment crept in, but she brushed it off with a shrug. "I've been dancing since I was four. I don't think I have nerve endings in my knees anymore."

His gaze lingered, not on her knees. Any other time, she might have felt a warning bell go off, a sense of unease creeping in. But she didn't. Instead, a strange awareness curled through her, a tingling beneath her skin, like a million nerve endings coming back to life.

She scrambled for something to say. "So...how's your, um, Cuba?"

"'Cuda," he corrected with a smirk. "And she's finished. Got wheels and everything. You wanna see her?"

She glanced toward the driveway, assuming that was where it was parked.

"Tomorrow night," he clarified.

She narrowed her eyes at him, trying to work out if she was understanding him correctly. "Are you asking me out on a date?"

Daniel shrugged. "Maybe. Guess you'll have to come and find out."

Her rational mind jumped in first, fast and firm, running through a checklist of reasons to say no. She had practice in the morning. She shouldn't be out late. And after what had happened with Floyd she definitely shouldn't be getting into cars with strange men, no matter how charming their smile or soft their voice.

Her fingers curled around the necklace in her palm, knuckles tight. She could feel her heartbeat in her throat.

But then there was the other part of her. The restless part. The part that hated the silence in that big, echoing house. The part that couldn't stand another evening with her mother's polite concern and veiled disappointment. The part that had always ached for something else, something bigger than routines and early mornings and chasing a dream that felt more like someone else's idea of success

And it was that part of her—the one that still hadn't learned, maybe—that opened her mouth and said, "Okay."

————

Daniel turned the key in the ignition, yanked the gearshift into drive and peeled away from the curb, tires spitting dust as he hit the gas harder than he needed to.

His pulse hammered. His knuckles were white on the steering wheel.

One fucking job.

All he had to do was put the fear of God into her. Make sure she kept her mouth shut. Make sure she understood that talking— *even thinking* about talking—wasn't an option.

Instead, what had he done?

Asked her out.

Like some lovesick idiot.

He exhaled sharply, bracing his forearms on the wheel, shaking his head at himself. He should've walked away the second he'd seen her, left her standing there with her wide, unblinking eyes and that trembling little breath she'd taken when she realized who he was.

But no. Instead of fear, he'd seen something else in those baby blues.

Curiosity.

And worse, something dangerous. Something warm.

He should have shut it down. Instead, the words had slipped out before he even thought about what they meant. Before he considered the consequences.

And there would be consequences.

A rustling sound came from the backseat. Then warm, damp breath panted against his neck.

Daniel cut his eyes to the rearview mirror. Tequila was sitting up, her big tongue hanging sideways, her tail thumping once against the seat.

He sighed. "This is all your fault."

She blinked at him. Then drooled on his shoulder in silent agreement.

———

DEA Special Agent Belinda Weck folded her arms and leaned back against the long trestle table, exhaling through her nose. The overhead fluorescents buzzed softly, casting a sterile glow over the war room.

The whiteboard in front of her was a collage of horror—crime scene photos arranged without any regard to anatomical order. Some of the remains were still half-wrapped in black plastic bin liners, others were unrecognizable as human at all. Whoever had taped them up hadn't bothered trying to piece them together. No point.

Belinda's expression tightened, but not from squeamishness. She'd spent years in the DEA's satellite field office in Ciudad Juárez during the late '90s, when the gang bloodshed was at its worst. She knew what the drug trade did to people. She'd seen its consequences stacked in morgues, buried in mass graves, hung from bridges.

But there was something about seeing a person reduced to so many chunks that still got to her.

The speakerphone on the table crackled to life, cutting through her thoughts. "What are we looking at?" came the voice of AUSA

Malcolm Oates, calling in from his ivory tower at the Dirksen Federal Building.

Belinda exhaled. "Well, right now, I'm looking at about three-quarters of a man formerly known as Floyd Monaghan."

A pause. Then, dryly: "Where's the last quarter?"

She glanced at the photos again. "Still digging him out. Thankfully, the dumpsters on the South Side don't get emptied too often." She reached for a manila folder and flipped it open. "Doubt they'll ever find the hands or the teeth, though."

Oates sighed. "Of course not."

"Luckily," she continued, "the guy had titanium screws in his left tibia from a skiing accident a few years back. The coroner traced the serial numbers and got an ID that way."

"So who was he?"

"Floyd Monaghan. Twenty-eight. DJ from Salt Lake City. Popular, apparently."

"I've never heard of him."

Belinda resisted rolling her eyes. Oates was a forty-three-year-old Black man who wore tailored suits and listened to Coltrane. He was hardly the target audience for whatever Monaghan had been spinning.

"He had a hit last summer. Remix of that Bee Gees song," she offered.

"'More Than A Woman'?"

"'Stayin' Alive'."

A short, amused exhale from the speaker. "You want to say it, or should I?"

"It's been said," she muttered. "Several times today."

She flipped another page. "Monaghan was touring, doing clubs and festivals across the country. Three shows in Chicago. Last one was at a club in the Loop called Code. His manager reported him missing two days later. That was a week and a half ago." She turned her gaze back to the photos on the board. "Fast forward to two days ago, and he's in a bunch of trash bags in Canaryville."

Oates sniffed. "Tragic. But what's it got to do with us?"

"It hit our radar because the last place Monaghan was seen was a well-known LMN shooting gallery in South Lawndale. Place has a reputation for wild parties."

A pause. Then she added, "And it's also known to us as the long-time abode of one Daniel Castaño."

Silence.

Belinda could feel Oates sitting up straighter in his chair.

"You have witnesses placing Monaghan there?"

"Not good ones," she admitted. "Most of the people at that house that night were in no state to remember their own names, let alone who came and went. And those who do remember?" She shook her head. "Not exactly lining up to talk. Even the ones who don't owe LMN a damn thing aren't willing to get involved."

Oates let out a slow breath. "And yet, you're telling me we do have something."

Belinda tapped the folder against the table. "Not yet. But we will. Someone saw something. Someone always does."

SEVEN

Julia stood stiffly, arms locked around herself, her gaze fixed on the narrow gap in her bedroom curtains. Through the sheer fabric, she could see the front gate and the stretch of concrete bathed in the glow of the security lights.

Every time headlights flickered through the trees, her breath hitched, her stomach coiling tight. But none had turned down her drive.

It was after nine. He wasn't coming.

"Julia."

A light tug on her arm. She barely registered it, her eyes locked on another pair of approaching headlights. They slowed as they neared the gate. Her pulse tripped. Panic warred with excitement. Now that he was here, she didn't want him to be. What had she been thinking—

"Julia."

Her mother's voice, sharp and insistent. The tone she used when correcting Julia's posture mid-routine. Julia wrenched her eyes away from the window.

"Stand up straight. Colette is trying to get the fit right in the shoulders."

Julia blinked at the seamstress, who had been gently trying to pry her arms apart.

"Oh. Sorry," she murmured, relaxing her posture.

Colette gave a small nod and resumed her work, pinning the delicate fabric into place. Julia's attention darted back to the window just in time to see the headlights continue past the gate.

She exhaled, the tension draining from her limbs. Then, with effort, she kept herself from slumping again.

From the bed, Natalie scrolled idly through her phone, propped on one elbow in that casually perfect way she always managed. Every inch of her looked like it belonged on a stage or in a perfume ad—long, lean legs, willowy arms, a swanlike neck. Even her feet had those high, elegant arches ballet teachers swooned over.

Natalie had been born for ballet. She looked like she'd been sculpted for the stage.

Julia had not.

She was taller, but it was the wrong kind of tall. Her height lived in her torso, not her legs, throwing off her lines in every arabesque. Flat feet, a head a shade too big for her frame, and the most unforgivable offense in ballet: hips. Real ones.

She'd been on a diet since she was twelve. Not because anyone had told her outright, but because they didn't need to. Her mother's carefully worded suggestions—*Maybe skip the bread this week, love. Let's try some lemon water in the mornings*—were enough. And Natalie, with her delicate appetite and natural thinness, had been the gold standard. Always the example. Always the blueprint.

The seamstress finished her work and stepped back.

Julia turned to the full-length mirror, catching herself in the custom Valentino bridesmaid dress for the first time. Blush pink, sweetheart neckline, mermaid hem. It was objectively stunning. She looked...fine. Pretty, even. But she still felt like a draft version of someone else's design.

From the bed, Natalie looked up and grinned. "You're gonna pull a Pippa Middleton on me in that."

Julia managed a tight smile. Lately, everything Natalie said felt dipped in something sticky-sweet.

Or maybe she was just becoming bitter.

Their mother appeared behind her, fussing with the fabric around Julia's thighs.

"Hmm," she said, eyes narrowing slightly. That one sound, that slight purse of her lips, said more than words ever could.

Julia went still, spine straightening instinctively.

Her mother nodded toward Colette. "Thank you for coming so late. There's still so much to do, and the wedding is only two weeks away…"

Julia tuned her out, eyes flicking back to the window. Nothing. No headlights.

The comment about the dress barely registered—she'd heard worse from her mother—but the thought of Daniel standing her up stung far more.

Then she heard it.

A low rumble. Distant but growing. Headlights swept around the bend.

They slowed. Stopped. Right across from her gate.

Holy crap. He's here.

Julia flailed behind her, reaching for the zipper.

After a few seconds of struggling, a hand behind came to her rescue. Her sister helped peel it off her, then scooped up the gown. "Try not to let her get to you," she said quietly. "She's just impossible to please sometimes."

Julia paused in pulling her top over her head. For a moment she thought she'd misheard, because Natalie never spoke of their mother. Neither of them did. Not of endless early morning starts or untold number of hours they'd committed to ballet since they could walk. Or the sacrifices, the pain, the diets, the injuries. They'd never commiserated together because neither wanted the other to think was weaker. Their mother had raised them as rivals and not sisters.

She hesitated, half-tempted to say something. Instead, she

forced a smile. "The dress is perfect. Everyone's going to be looking at you, anyway."

Their mother clapped her hands once, briskly. "Colette, we'll finish the hem tomorrow. Natalie, come with me, we'll check your fittings in my room."

Natalie rolled her eyes but obeyed, gathering her phone as she slid off the bed. A moment later the door clicked shut behind them, leaving Julia alone. The muffled rise and fall of their voices drifted down the hall, then faded.

Julia seized her chance. She grabbed her bag and bolted.

By the time she reached the front door, her heart was hammering. She half-expected Daniel to be waiting on the doorstep, but he hadn't ventured up the drive. The engine was still idling, its low growl vibrating through the night. Like he wasn't sure he should be here. Like he, too, had wondered if he'd be stood up.

She quickened her pace, and the car came into view.

It was sleek and aggressive. Six angry-looking grilles glared from between the headlights. Angled shark gills cut into the fenders. A massive hood scoop sat like an open mouth, ready to swallow the road whole. The thing had the subtlety of a sucker punch.

Daniel got out and rounded the car to open the passenger door for her.

Julia wiped her sweaty palms on her skirt and climbed in.

The interior was all gleaming black vinyl and polished wood grain. A crucifix dangled from the rearview mirror, swaying with the engine's vibrations.

Daniel slid back behind the wheel, shutting the door behind him.

"So," he said, watching her reaction. "What do you think?"

She stared at the car. Then at him.

"It's hideous," she said at last.

Daniel grinned. "I knew you'd like her."

———

They left behind the pristine estates and tree-lined streets of Lake Forest, heading south. The transition was stark—one moment, the world was manicured golf courses and gated driveways, the next, it was the steady hum of the Edens Expressway, stretching like a vein into the heart of Chicago.

Julia sat back in the seat, watching as the landscape shifted from suburban affluence to urban sprawl. The rhythmic clatter of 'L' trains overhead blended with the distant bass of car speakers from the traffic around them.

She glanced at Daniel, his hands steady on the wheel, his profile illuminated by the passing streetlights.

He took an exit just past Chinatown, weaving through the narrow streets of Back of the Yards. Aged brick buildings, some with boarded-up windows, stood side by side with vibrant murals and lively taquerias. Streetlights flickered, barely illuminating the figures lingering near shuttered businesses. This was a city within a city, a place where the undocumented, the unseen, and the forgotten carved out a life.

Julia shifted in her seat. "So, what exactly are we doing tonight?"

Daniel glanced at her, the corner of his mouth quirking up. "Ever been to a mercado?"

She frowned slightly. "Like a market?"

"Sort of," he said, cryptic. "But maybe not the kind you're thinking of."

After turning onto 47th Street, he navigated a series of alleys until they pulled up beside an unmarked warehouse, its entrance illuminated by a single bulb. Somewhere in the distance, the wail of a siren echoed.

He killed the engine and turned to Julia, his expression unreadable. "Ready?"

———

Daniel knocked twice, then three more times. A metal slot in the door slid open, revealing shadowed eyes. A hushed exchange in rapid Spanish followed, too quick for her to catch more than a word or two.

A latch clicked. The door swung inward, releasing a rush of heavy, humid air thick with the scent of grilled meat, gasoline, and something acrid—burnt sugar? Plastic? Her stomach tightened. This was not the kind of place you found on a travel itinerary.

Daniel stepped inside after her without hesitation, placing a light touch on her lower back. The heat of his palm burned through her shirt. She exhaled and moved forward.

Inside, a makeshift maze of tarps and rusted steel beams formed a tunnel, crammed with knockoff sneakers, bootleg liquor, and counterfeit designer bags. Music throbbed from crackling speakers. Conversations hummed around her, fast and low, punctuated by bursts of laughter and the occasional sharp curse.

To her left, a man twirled a knife between his tattooed fingers, his stall lined with an array of gleaming blades. A woman in a cropped hoodie braided a little girl's hair while another customer handed over cash for a trim.

Julia turned, taking it all in, pulse thrumming beneath her skin.

"How do you even find a place like this?" she asked, keeping her voice casual.

Daniel's response was just as smooth. "You don't. That's the whole point."

He moved through the market like he belonged there, nodding at a few familiar faces, ignoring others. A vendor flashed a gold chain in his direction; Daniel dismissed him with a flick of his fingers. Further down, a group of men huddled around an old sedan, cash exchanging hands in a quick, quiet rhythm.

Then—

"*¡Hermano!* About time."

Julia turned and saw a young man perched behind a cluttered

table of cracked iPhones and suspicious-looking USB drives. He grinned at Daniel, finishing a rapid-fire sales pitch to an unimpressed customer. He looked about seventeen, his shoulder-length hair tucked neatly behind his ears. His eyes—hazel, like Daniel's—gleamed with curiosity as they locked onto her. The resemblance between them was obvious. Same sharp cheekbones, same quick dimple when he smiled.

He went up to Daniel and pulled him into a quick hug. Daniel clasped a hand on his shoulder and turned to Julia.

"Julia, this is my little brother, Sebastián."

Sebastián gave her a once-over, then nodded. "Hey."

She returned the greeting, still taking in how much they looked alike.

Then Sebastián turned back to Daniel, his expression playful. "Is she your girlfriend?"

Daniel smirked. "She's my none of your damn business, *hermanito*." He folded his arms and jerked his chin at the table. "Tell me you're not selling bricks again."

Sebastián scoffed, shoving a phone into the customer's hands. "First of all, it works. Second, I offer a money-back guarantee." Then his gaze flicked to Julia again, interest sparking behind his smile.

Julia surveyed the table of electronic flotsam and jetsam behind him. "Do you work here?"

Daniel cut in before Sebastián could embellish. "He hustles here. One week it's tech, next it's sneakers. Supply and demand."

"Smart," Julia murmured. She wasn't sure she meant it as a compliment, but Sebastián took it as one anyway.

"And you?" Sebastián's eyes gleamed with mischief. "What's the deal, *hermano*? You bringing her here to impress her, or—"

"We're just passing through," Daniel interrupted, voice clipped.

Sebastián sighed theatrically. "That's a shame, 'cause I might've made a small bet with the wrong guy, and I could use some backup."

Daniel groaned. "Sebastián."

"I know, I know," Sebastián said, lifting his hands. "But it's fine! Probably. I just—"

His words cut off as his shoulders stiffened, his gaze flicking past them, over Daniel's shoulder.

Daniel turned.

A broad-shouldered man pushed through the crowd, his face set like a thundercloud.

Sebastián muttered a curse. "Time to go."

He moved fast, vaulting over the table in one fluid motion. Julia barely had time to register what was happening before Daniel's hand found her wrist. His grip was firm, but not rough.

"Hope you're fast, ballerina."

She didn't need to be told twice.

They ran.

The mercado blurred around her—faces, stalls, neon lights flashing past in a haze. The air pulsed with bass-heavy music, the rhythm matching the pounding of her heart.

Behind them, a shout. Then another.

Sebastián veered left, disappearing into a curtain of hanging tarps. Daniel tugged her right, shoving past a stack of crates into a narrow alley. The glow of a beer sign flickered weakly above them, casting shadows against damp pavement.

Daniel didn't slow until they made it all the way back to where the 'Cuda parked. He pulled out his keys, glancing at her.

Julia wasn't winded. If anything, she felt alive. She let out a breathless laugh, brushing her hair back. "That was intense."

Daniel smiled, unlocking the door. "Yeah? You kept up."

She met his gaze. The adrenaline still crackled between them, hot and electric.

A different kind of danger.

And for a moment, she wasn't sure which one thrilled her more.

———

Daniel leaned against the 'Cuda, fishing in his pocket as the lake stretched out before them, silver under the moonlight.

The night air carried the scent of damp earth and gasoline, mixing with the distant hush of waves against the shore. The chase, the market, the city—it all felt distant now. Here, the night was quiet, the world smaller.

Julia got out of the car and joined him. "You're not what I expected."

Daniel finally looked at her. "What did you expect?"

Julia thought for a moment, then just shook her head, smiling. "I'm still figuring that out."

He flicked open the lighter attached to his keyring, the flame briefly illuminating the palms of his hands. He touched it to the tip of the joint between his lips, inhaled, then exhaled a slow stream of smoke that curled into the cool night air. "Let me know when you do."

She looked back at the water. "Where'd you learn so much about cars?"

He tapped his joint, watching the ember glow in the dark. "My dad taught me," he said, watching the lake. "He had this big old Chevy Impala. I'd set up obstacle courses in the gravel lot at the end of our street—cones, bits of wood, whatever junk I could find. I was eleven, could barely reach the pedals. But I was shit-scared of knocking over a single cone 'cause I knew he'd make me rework the whole body of the car." He took another drag, then held the joint out to her. "And that was one big motherfucking Chevy."

She eyed it. "I don't smoke cigarettes."

His grin was lazy. "It's not a cigarette."

Her lips parted slightly. "Oh."

He waited.

She hesitated another beat, then reached for it, her fingers grazing his as she brought it to her lips. She inhaled.

And immediately choked.

Coughing, she shoved it back at him.

Daniel chuckled. "You good?"

She pressed the back of her hand to her mouth and nodded, though her eyes were watering.

Shaking his head, he took another drag and turned his gaze back to the lake. Beside him, she shifted, pressing closer against the car. Out of the corner of his eye, he stole a glance at her.

In the moonlight, she looked unreal. Ethereal. Perfect, full lips. Eyes like some glacial lake.

As if she could feel his gaze, she turned her head, looking up at him. He dropped his chin, scuffing the toe of his boot against the gravel.

"Where in Mexico are you from?"

For a moment, he didn't answer. Just kept watching the water. Then, with an exhale of smoke, he said, "Torreón. We left when I was thirteen."

"With your parents?"

He nodded.

"Do they all live in Chicago with you?"

His voice was quieter this time. "No. They're not here."

She kept looking at him. He flicked the joint onto the damp sand, where it sizzled out. Leaning back against the car, he closed his eyes.

She sighed. Then sighed again.

He cracked one eye open. "Are you freaking out?"

"No," she whispered. A beat. "Yes."

He smiled. "Just relax. It'll wear off in a couple of hours."

"Really? Because I feel like I might die right now."

He chuckled, turning toward her. "You're not gonna die."

She nodded quickly, though she didn't look convinced. Her breathing had quickened, her chest rising and falling in a way that was—

Distracting.

"I just keep thinking," she panted, "that if I stop thinking about breathing, I'll actually stop breathing."

His smile deepened. Without thinking, he reached for her hand.

She didn't pull away. Instead, she slid along the car until their shoulders touched. Lifting his hand, she turned it over, tracing the ink along his fingers. Her thumb ran over the ridges of his knuckles, following the letters tattooed there.

Her touch was light, almost reverent. She traced a line along the back of his hand, over the rosary beads at his wrist, then up his forearm, pausing at the eagle with a snake in its mouth. Then the skull crowned with marigolds. The deeper she explored, the more she seemed to find—tarantula, scorpion, rose. She went to push his sleeve higher.

"You having fun there?"

She froze, looking up, startled.

Her face was inches from his. Her lips slightly parted, soft and tempting. He had the sudden, urgent need to run his tongue over her Cupid's bow.

A breeze rolled off the lake, making her shiver slightly. Whatever trance she'd been under seemed to break. She looked embarrassed, dropping his arm.

He stepped forward, closing the space between them.

She pressed back against the car. His hands braced the roof, caging her in.

She looked like she'd forgotten how to breathe again. In the quiet space between them, he could almost hear the rapid beat of her heart.

Bending down, he placed his lips just shy of hers. *"Nunca tienes que tener miedo de mí."*

A tiny furrow appeared between her brows.

He repeated himself in English. "You never have to be afraid of me."

Her eyes searched his, frantic back and forth. Whatever she was looking for, she must've found it.

Because she surged forward and kissed him.

It took him by surprise. But only for a second.

Her lips were soft, tentative. Unlike in his fantasies, they were chaste. But he tilted his jaw, deepening it, and she melted. Her mouth parted for him. His tongue slid in, tasting her. Warm, sweet, a little salty.

He slipped a hand behind her neck, thumb pressing lightly over her pulse. She whimpered.

A slow burn ignited in his stomach. He fought the urge to drop his hands to her waist, knowing exactly how much faster things would escalate.

But things were already going there.

She was fully open for him, pressing into him, responding like she wanted—

And then, suddenly, she tore away.

They were both breathing hard. She ducked her head, avoiding his gaze.

He exhaled sharply, dragging a hand over his face. He swung away from her, staring out at the lake. Trying to get himself under control. Trying not to think about the way her mouth had felt against his.

"I'll take you home."

She didn't answer. When he turned back, she had her hands pressed to her cheeks.

And to his horror, she was crying.

His stomach dropped. "Jesus, Julia..."

She wiped her eyes quickly. "It's fine. I'm fine." She nodded, like she was convincing herself more than him. Then she turned and fumbled for the door handle.

He exhaled, raking a hand through his hair.

He'd known he was going to fuck this up.

But just once, it would've been nice to have been wrong.

———

"I'd take you right up to your door, but I don't wanna freak your parents out."

Julia had been staring out the passenger window, seeing nothing. She took a moment to register where they were. Idling in the lane opposite her drive.

She looked across at Daniel. His profile was cut out of the lights of her house beyond. It was a perfectly fluid line. Smooth forehead. Straight nose. Crisp jaw.

"They're not home," she said. Then she realized what she should have said. "And you wouldn't freak them out."

In her head though, she was thinking, *he has face tattoos. They would definitely freak out.*

He raised an eyebrow and gave her a smile that implied he'd heard her thoughts and not her words.

"I'm sorry," she said. But she wasn't sure if she was apologizing for intolerant parents, or for her own freak out on the beach. She wanted to blame it on the weed, and maybe that had something to do with. But it wasn't the main reason.

The kiss had been incredible. Lips and tongues and burning heat. He'd known what he was doing, whereas she'd felt like a total amateur. And right in the middle of it, Floyd had appeared, like a jump scare in a horror movie.

She shuddered. Even the mere memory of that night in the trailer could kick-start a panic attack.

Daniel sighed. It was almost imperceptible, just a slight rise and fall of his chest. He reached over and took her hand in his. "Julia. None of this is your fault."

She looked down, studying his hand on top of hers. He wore a silver ring with a cross on it on his pinkie, and a chunky platinum watch on his wrist. Veins snaked under his skin from the back of his hand all the way up his forearm.

She wrapped her fingers around his wrist, tightly enough to feel his bones and muscles and the tic of his pulse under his skin. It made her wonder what the rest of him felt like.

She swallowed, her throat suddenly dry. "I should go get your hoodie."

"I don't want it back."

"Why not?"

He looked up and met her eyes, steady and unblinking. "Because I like knowing you still have it."

The air caught in her chest. Something flipped in her stomach, like a trapdoor opening. She let go of his wrist as if it burned and turned abruptly toward the door, fingers fumbling for the handle.

She had to get out. Now. Everything was moving too fast, her thoughts tangling with the heat in her skin.

She ducked out of the car and slammed the door behind her. Head down, arms clutched across her chest, she crossed the lawn in quick, uneven strides.

Behind her, the 'Cuda rumbled to life. She heard it pull away from the curb, the engine's low growl cutting through the still night air before it finally faded into silence.

Or maybe that echo wasn't the car at all. Maybe it was just the roar in her head.

EIGHT

DANIEL WATCHED the claw of the grappler pick up his old Camry and crush it between its huge steel talons. Then it swung the car's carcass onto a pile of other scrap with a metallic crunch that vibrated the dirt beneath his work boots.

He stared at the twisted body, with its concave roof and popped windshield. Two years ago, that car had taken him and Sebastián from L.A. to Chicago. To what should have been a new life, but what had soon felt a fuck of a lot like his old one. Doing the same thing. Hoping for a different result.

Now, looking at the car, he only remembered that night a week ago in his trailer. He'd never got the stink of that guy's blood out of the upholstery. So, it had to go. Soon it would be buried under a shimmering mountain of scrap metal, being warped and bent and broken down by the elements. Rust to rust.

He wouldn't miss it.

Tequila was sitting at his feet. He bent down to scratch her ears. She grinned up at him, tongue lolling out.

A familiar voice came from behind him. "Daniel! Been looking everywhere for you, man."

He suppressed a sign, then turned to see Terry making his way up the dirt track towards him. His gait was slow and rolling, like his hips ached.

Everything Terry did was slow. Right until it wasn't. The waddling gait, the huffing and puffing, the constant fumbling and fidgeting—it was all an act. Daniel had seen Terry switch from ambling buffoon to prize fighter at the drop of a hat. Seen him pound a man with his ham hock fists until the man didn't have a face no more.

Terry stopped a yard away, put his hands on his hips and sucked in air like he'd just sprinted here. "Where you been at? Paq said you didn't show up at work today."

Daniel looked up at the crumpled wreck that had been his Camry.

Terry followed his gaze. He grunted, then plucked a cigarette out from behind his ear. "Car trouble?"

Daniel said nothing.

Terry grunted again, then lit his smoke and took a long pull. He squinted at Daniel with one eye. "You been distracted lately, Danny. And I've been wondering if maybe it might be girl trouble instead."

Daniel felt a chill from his tone. Terry had only one rule for the guys that worked for him. Relationships were off the cards. In his mind, girlfriends and wives made you weak and unfocused. They fucked up your priorities and skewed your sense of loyalty, which was to him and the gang, and *only* him and the gang.

Apparently, it was something he'd seen in the military. Men getting married and having kids and losing their edge on the battlefield. "It happened all the time," he'd once told Daniel. "These guys would go from ruthless killers to total pussies overnight. One minute they're attaching battery probes to some poor Iraqi's nutsack, the next all they can talk about is strollers and school zones and fucking minivans. It was a goddamn tragedy, man."

But Daniel knew Terry's problem with females didn't just stem from his time in the army. The big man had some grade A trust issues with people in general. His paranoia was legendary. And he insisted an internal threat posed the greatest danger to their operation. He believed it would come from someone they trusted, someone they let into their inner circle.

Someone like a girlfriend.

Terry was still observing Daniel, waiting for a response.

Daniel swallowed something sharp in his throat. Then he said, with as much nonchalance as he could muster, "Nah. Nothing like that."

Terry chuckled, like he'd said something funny. "I'm glad to hear it." He took another drag from his cigarette. "'Cause you know it don't pay to let anyone get too close, right? Life we lead, they just end up getting hurt." He blew out a stream of smoke. "Sometimes real bad."

Under his soft tone, the threat was loud and clear.

He took another deep pull, the ember flaring close to his knuckles. "If you got needs, there's plenty of girls at SINoritas. And you know the best thing about hookers, right?"

You get to fuck them. They don't get to fuck you. Daniel intoned the words in his head in perfect sync with the ones that came out of Terry's mouth.

Terry dropped his cigarette butt, grinding it into the dirt with his heel. "Take your little brother along. Introduce him to Gabriela. She'll put some hairs on his chest."

Daniel managed a smile but mentally deleted everything he'd just heard.

Terry clapped an enormous hand on Daniel's shoulder. "Oh, nearly forgot to tell ya. Whole point of this little meet and greet. You're doing a run to Philly tonight."

Daniel stared at him blankly. "Philly."

"Big shipment coming in tonight. I'm gonna go round up Milo. You head back to base and start unloading. Make sure it's ready to go by eleven."

Shit. The Philly run was a two-day round trip. Stuck in a van. With fucking *Milo.*

Terry turned and ambled away. Then he halted and looked back. "By the way," he called. "I gotta ask. Did you deal with that little loose end we had?"

Daniel's gut clenched. He was talking about Julia.

He opened his mouth to ask, but no words came out. Lying to Terry was a bad idea. Telling him the truth was worse.

No, Terry, I didn't "deal" with her. I watched her dance, which was easily the most beautiful thing I've ever seen. I kissed her by my car, and now I can't get her out of my mind for longer than two seconds.

And no, I'm not dealing with any of it.

Since remaining silent would be worse than lying, he cleared his throat and mumbled, "Yeah, she ain't a problem no more."

Terry nodded. Then he gave Daniel a wide grin. The man had surprisingly white teeth for someone who smoked as much as he did. His eyes, however, held a coldness. It made Daniel think the man didn't quite believe him.

He turned and kept walking, with that rolling gait of his, like he was wading through deep water.

Daniel watched him go. A spider of fear crawled up his neck. He didn't like that Terry was still thinking about the girl in his trailer. And he really didn't like him referring to her as a *loose end*.

What he hated, though, was knowing that for the next two days, he was going to be eight hundred miles away from her.

And Terry, less than forty.

———

El Paisano Restaurante Mexicano was wedged between a laundromat and a *tienda de licores* on the West Side. The *taquería* had no piped-in mariachi music, no waiters pushing oversized margaritas or novelty sombreros. Just good food, the kind that didn't need gimmicks. The kind that made the place packed wall-to-wall despite the scuffed floor and plastic chairs.

Daniel stepped inside, setting off a small bell above the door.

Conversations faltered as heads turned. He felt their gazes slide over his arms, down the inked skin of his hands. A few of the regulars—men who'd seen his kind before—went back to their food. Others took a little longer, eyes lingering in wary recognition.

Martín Tostá didn't bother with pleasantries when Daniel approached the counter. He just stood there, wiping his hands on his canvas apron, his sharp black eyes taking him in with something between indifference and contempt.

Daniel leaned his elbows on the counter. "*¿Dónde está mi hermanito?*"

Martín jerked his head toward the kitchen. "*Arriba.*"

His brother was upstairs.

Daniel straightened, feeling the older man's gaze on him as he moved past the counter and into the back. The kitchen was a humid mess of sizzling oil and rapid-fire Spanish. Nobody looked up. They'd all learned that much.

Upstairs, he tapped on the door before pushing it open.

Sebastián was sitting cross-legged on his bed, a textbook propped against his knees. His dark curls hung over his face as he read, but Daniel caught the title: *Applied Anatomy for Students in a Clinical Setting, Fifth Edition.* He tilted his head, smirking. "Sounds riveting."

Sebastián didn't look up. "Caleb left it behind this morning."

Daniel sat with that for a beat. His eyes flicked around the room. The same sparse furniture as always, just a bed, a chest of drawers, and a whole lot of empty space.

"So," he said, clearing his throat, "this guy is spending nights here now?"

Sebastián's gaze lifted, blank as a closed door. His little brother had always been like that, good at keeping his emotions locked down.

"I thought you said it didn't bother you."

Daniel exhaled through his nose, gave a quick shake of his head. Seb was seventeen. It's not like Daniel had been celibate at that age. Far fucking from it. "It doesn't, *hermanito*," he said softly. "You know that."

Sebastián studied him for a moment, then looked away. "We broke up this morning. So, I guess it doesn't matter anyway."

Daniel frowned. He wasn't sure what he was supposed to say to that, so he sat down on the edge of the bed. "You wanna give me his address?" he offered. "I'll go round and return his book. Maybe shove it somewhere… anatomical."

That earned him a tiny smile. "Thanks, Dani but I'm good."

"You sure? I can send Terry round. Dude's a fucking ninja with a bone saw."

Sebastián's smile faded. Daniel knew he hated it when he talked like that, when he let the darkness of his life slip into their conversations like it was normal. Bone saws. Bloodstains and bleach. The things he didn't want his little brother to think about.

But the truth was, that was his life. And most of the time, it wasn't the blood or the violence that got to him. It was the loneliness.

Sebastián sighed. "You know that guy creeps me out."

Daniel smiled. "Terry creeps everybody out. That's the whole point of him."

Sebastián made a face but let it drop.

After a beat, Daniel swiveled toward him. "*Escucha, hermanito.* I gotta leave town for a couple of days."

Sebastián looked up, closing his book. "Where?"

"Philly."

He didn't ask why. Sebastián never asked why.

Daniel rubbed a hand over his jaw. "You know that girl that was with me at the mercado?"

Sebastián frowned. "*¿La chica rubia?*"

"*Sí.* The blonde."

"Julia, *¿claro?*"

Daniel nodded.

Sebastián's eyes narrowed slightly. "What do you need?"

Daniel exhaled. "A favor."

NINE

THE DOLLHOUSE WAS in South Philly, in an austere black building across the road from a Popeyes and an AutoZone and shrouded in a haze of traffic fumes from the freeway. It was not the most glamorous locale, but the owners clearly understood one basic fact: it was a strip club in South Philly. No one went there to look out fucking windows.

Daniel parked the van behind the club and quit the engine. Mercifully, the music quit too. Whenever he rode with Milo, the little shit made him listen to drill rap at full bore. The kid seemed to believe he had a future in the music industry, and that if he listened to enough Chief Keef, he'd somehow absorb the rapper's talent. It wasn't working. Daniel had suffered through Milo's version of "I Don't Like" for two hours now, and it had taken every ounce of his self-control to not reach across, open the passenger door and shove him out.

The only thing stopping him was the fact that Milo was Terry's half-brother. The family resemblance was faint, but Daniel knew better than to antagonize the younger Bidois, as the elder Bidois was a stone-cold psychopath.

He looked down at the phone in his lap. The screen showed nothing. All the way from Chicago, he'd been checking it every few miles, dreading a text from Seb. A text telling him that Julia was in danger—that Terry had found her or sent some of his goons to show up at her house. Daniel had instructed his brother to tell him immediately if something like that happened, all the while knowing there'd be nothing he could do about it if it did.

He got out of the van and stretched his stiff back. Pocketing his phone, he walked around to the back of the van, climbed in, and tossed out the duffle.

It landed on the gravel, close enough to Milo's feet to make him skip backwards. The idiot was always too busy scrolling his screen to pay attention to his surroundings.

Daniel stared down at the guy and shook his head. Milo Bidois was easily the ugliest man he'd ever seen. But not because he'd been born that way. No, he'd gone to a lot of effort and expense to look as bad as he did.

His face was a mess of tattoos. Weird doodles and scrawls of cursive that no one could read. It was as if he'd passed out drunk one night and someone had gone to town on his face with a Sharpie. Then he'd woken up and decided to make that shit permanent. His hair was braided into tight cornrows, each one dyed a different color of the rainbow. He wore several thick dookie chains around his neck and gold grills in his mouth that made him spit when he talked. All up, he looked like something you'd scrape off the road after Mardi Gras.

Daniel jumped down, then closed the van and locked it. He shoved the keys in his pocket, then headed for the rear entrance. Milo tried to jog after him, grappling with the duffle that was heavier than he was.

As he approached the door, he nodded at Sonny Fai, the club's head of security. Daniel handed him his phone, then submitted to the obligatory pat down. Sonny let him pass. Behind him, Milo tried to saunter past, only to have Sonny clamp a massive hand onto his shoulder and drag him backwards.

"Come on, man," Milo whined.

The Samoan was twice Milo's size, in both height and girth,

making the idiot's protestations pointless. By the time he was done with his search, Sonny had extracted from his person a drop-point knife, a bong, a baggie of Oxy, a phone, and two Glocks.

"No outside drugs," Sonny said, pocketing the pills. The rule seemed ironic, given the contents of the duffle. But the Samoan only gave the interior of the bag a cursory glance.

Daniel led the way down a dark hallway into the club itself. It was like descending underground, even though the place was still on street level. Plush black upholstery padded the walls, and pink fluorescence seemed to ooze from the air.

Runways connected three circular stages, all tiled in shiny mirrors. A glass mezzanine floor wrapped around three sides of the room, accessed by an illuminated staircase. The nearest wall housed a long, neon-lit bar.

From the overhead speakers, a trigger-pull bass line was thudding, but there wasn't a patron to be seen. The girls were all out in force, though, wrapped around poles and writhing on the mirrored stage floor. They appeared to be on show solely to entertain the four men seated at the table in the center of the room.

Daniel led the way across the club towards them. Milo's eyes were on stalks, taking in as much skin as he could.

"Bad *bitches*," he said, making a full turn while hanging onto the crotch of his jeans.

Sasha Sokolov sat at the head of the table. Daniel recognized him instantly—mirrored aviators, gym-honed arms, that cocky lounge-lizard energy. He was the younger Sokolov, flashy and volatile. His brother Borya, the real power behind the name, never came to these deals in person. But Daniel had clocked him already, staring down from his usual perch on the mezzanine above, arms folded, eyes cool. Always watching.

A more mismatched pair of brothers you'd be hard-pressed to find. While Sasha was all about the silk shirts and sealskin loafers, Borya dressed like a high school math teacher: cheap polyester suits and butt-ugly floral ties.

But despite his bland appearance, Daniel knew—from the odd

jobs he'd run for him in the past—that you didn't fuck with the older Russian. Borya had a ruthless streak that ran deep. Rumor had it he'd had to leave Vladivostok after he'd had his wife and two kids murdered, their bodies discovered in a burnt-out car. Apparently, family life hadn't suited the guy.

The Sokolovs now owned strip clubs across the East Coast and were expanding along the Gulf. But their yacht money came from porn. They owned a major distribution company stateside, although they'd recently moved all production to Eastern Europe. Allegedly, the laws there were more accommodating to your average sex industry capitalist. The brothers' foray into narco-trafficking was a new venture, but one that was paying off if the diamond-encrusted Rolex on Sasha's wrist was anything to go by.

The other men at the table were well-dressed lackeys that Daniel had seen around before. It was only ten in the morning, but the party had started early: three magnums of champagne stood open, and a crystal tray of freshly lined coke sat in the center of the table.

Daniel took a seat, yanking Milo down beside him.

The Russian exchanged pleasantries, then offered their choice of refreshments. Daniel bypassed the booze and did one line of coke for appearance's sake. It burst on the back of his synapses like fireworks.

A beautiful redhead appeared at the table and promptly parked herself down on Daniel's lap.

"Hi," she purred.

He considered the logistics of moving her off his lap, but the fact that she was completely naked made that…tricky.

Sasha smirked and said in his thick accent, "Looks like Svetlana's taking a liking to you."

Milo came up from snorting a line, pinching the end of his nose. "Serious question. Why is every Svetlana either a stripper or a hooker?" He looked around the table, expression earnest. "Is that name Russian for "slut" or something?"

Sasha turned his mirrored lenses on Milo, his tone flat. "Careful. My sister's name is Svetlana."

Milo blinked. "Oh shit, not this Svetlana, right?" He jabbed a thumb toward the girl in Daniel's lap, grinning like it was a joke worth making. "That'd be wild."

The mood at the table became frostier than a Siberian winter.

Daniel reached out a hand and smacked the back of Milo's head, just as he was lowering it back to the lines of coke. His head hit the table with a meaty thud, shattering the glass tray. "Ow, fuck, man!" he said, trying to dust off the blow and shards of crystal embedded in his forehead.

"Sorry," Daniel said to the table at large. "That's his off button."

Sasha's face remained inscrutable, thanks to those ugly-ass glasses. But apparently, the whole deal wasn't about to go south because of Milo's mouth, because he said, 'You have our product?'

Daniel reached down with one arm, lifted the duffle off the floor, and placed it on the table. "Five keys. *Certificada.*"

Sasha opened the duffle and pulled out one brick of heroin. It was wrapped in white plastic and stamped with a black hand print and the number thirteen.

Svetlana was doing her utmost to get his attention. She ran a hand down his chest and across his stomach, close enough to the waistband of his jeans to make a tremor start in his knees. When that still didn't work, she placed the same hand on his cheek, tilted his face towards her and kissed him.

He kissed her back, using that brief interval of time to work out how he was going to handle this situation. Specifically, how he was going to handle it if she didn't stop in her relentless pursuit to get into his pants.

Something hard pressed flat against the small of his back. Daniel didn't need to look to know it was a pistol, with a short barrel and a thick grip.

Svetlana.

He didn't know where she'd hidden the weapon, given her

lack of...pockets. But the answer was, of course, obvious. When she'd sauntered up to their table a moment ago, not a single man at it had been looking at her hands.

She pulled away from the kiss, eyes flicking upward.

Daniel followed her gaze—to Borya, who was still on the mezzanine. Watching. His face unreadable. Borya's eyes went to his brother below him, then back to Daniel. He gave a single, almost imperceptible nod.

Daniel closed his eyes. He experienced a sinking sensation, like his soul was dropping out of his body.

Borya had just sent him a message. And Daniel was powerless to do anything but follow it.

Sasha had been busy conferring with his comrade in muttered Russian. He reached down and placed a large leather satchel on the table. "Two hundred and forty k," he said to Daniel. "As agreed."

Daniel wrapped his fingers around the gun behind him. "Apparently, the price has gone up," he said calmly, leveling his gaze at Sasha.

Sasha raised his eyebrows in confusion. That expression—half confusion, half arrogance—was the last thing his face ever did.

Daniel fired once. The shot cracked like lightning. Sasha's skull disintegrated, splattering the room with brain and bone.

A millisecond before that happened, Svetlana threw herself under the table. That action alone made her the smartest one at that table, because everyone else at it got sprayed in Sasha's brain matter.

Daniel didn't realize he was on his feet until he felt the ground shift and he had to grip the table to stay upright. There was a roaring in his ears; it was his own blood blasting through his head. The sour tang of copper and spilled champagne filled the air.

In the immediate aftermath, there was total silence. Then it abruptly gave way to screaming, feminine and high-pitched. Daniel thought it was coming from one of the girls—maybe Svetlana under the table—but then he realized it was coming from Milo. He was crouched on the floor, covered in Sasha's blood and brain matter. "What the fuck, man?" he squealed.

Daniel didn't answer, just strode to the stairs, wiping the grip of the pistol on his shirt before tossing it aside. Ears still ringing, he took the steps three at a time, not slowing his stride till he got to Borya's glass walled office on the upper floor.

The older Russian was standing behind his desk, waiting for him. His face was a mask of calm, like he regularly watched the execution of his family members. Which, apparently, he did.

"*Gracias,*" he said, in an even thicker accent than his brother's.

Daniel was still panting. "What the fuck was that all about?"

Borya shuffled some papers on his desk, like the answer lay in one of the spreadsheets on his desk. Which, as it turned out, it did.

"My brother was lying to me," Borya explained. "And stealing." He slid some papers across the desk, as if providing proof of Sasha's treachery. "Hundreds of thousands of dollars."

Daniel kept his eyes on the Russian.

"He was doing side deals all over the place," Borya said. "Taking payments in cryptocurrency, hiding them from my accountants. I cannot tolerate that kind of treachery in my organization." He looked up at Daniel. "And you understand why I couldn't do it myself, of course."

Daniel just shook his head. He understood none of it. Not the part about killing your own blood. And definitely not the part about not having the balls to do it yourself.

Borya inclined his head toward the window overlooking the main floor of the strip club. "We'll clean this up. Make sure none of it comes back on you. Or the gang."

Daniel followed Borya's gaze to the strip club floor—to the forty-odd dancers, slowly emerging from their hiding places and running, panicked, for the exits. Witnesses. Every last one of them.

"Next time," Daniel said coldly, "you let me in on the plan before you hand me the murder weapon."

Borya smiled thinly. "Terry said you got the message."

Daniel didn't answer. He just stared. Wondering, confused, if the message had been meant for him all along.

A message about what happens to those who lie.

To those who *steal*.

Daniel said, "I meant what I said about the price going up."

Borya nodded, and Sonny appeared over Daniel's left shoulder. He was holding a thick brown envelope.

"Ten thousand," the Russian said. "For you, my friend."

Daniel looked from the envelope to Borya, then back to the envelope. He snatched it. "Fuck this shit," he said, and left.

Downstairs, he saw the leather satchel of cash lying on the table. It was wet with blood and gore and split champagne. He grabbed it and headed out the way he'd come.

Outside, the sunlight hit the back of his eyeballs like a trip flare. Cocaine was still fizzing in his veins, making everything feel a thousand times more intense. He bent double and vomited onto the gravel.

Milo appeared in the corner of his vision. He was doing a comical little jig, trying to re-pocket all his paraphernalia and run toward the van at the same time. "We gotta get the fuck outta here, bro."

Finally, something intelligent out of that idiot's mouth.

Daniel straightened and wiped his mouth. He tucked the brown envelope down the waistband of his jeans. Then he tossed the leather satchel to Milo and strode toward the van.

He cranked the engine while Milo scrambled into the passenger seat. He didn't even wait for him to shut the door before reversing in a wide arc and peeling out of the lot.

Out of the corner of his eye, he watched Milo get out his phone, queue up Chief Keef and reach for the aux cable to plug it into the car stereo.

Daniel smacked his hand away. "Don't even fucking think about it."

TEN

BELINDA WECK SPLIT her gaze between the three whiteboards set up at the front of the ops room, as if she hadn't already memorized their contents days ago.

Oates' voice came from the speakerphone on the table behind her. "Where are we at?"

She folded her arms and drummed her fingers against her biceps. "Well, we finally have our witness. A young man who was at the party and who saw Monaghan there."

Oates waited for her to continue, but she could hear the skepticism in his pause.

She exhaled through her nose. "Admittedly, he was fairly intoxicated at the time. But he told detectives he'd been standing in the backyard, smoking weed with some of his friends. He saw Monaghan leave the house and head for Castaño's trailer."

She paused, sensing Oates sitting up a little straighter in his chair.

"And he wasn't alone," she went on. "He was with a young blond woman. Heavily intoxicated."

"So…his girlfriend?"

Belinda made a skeptical sound. "From what I've gathered, Monaghan wasn't exactly the girlfriend type. But whoever she was, they arrived at the party together, then, at some point, made their way out to Castaño's trailer. The witness said they heard several gunshots sometime later."

"So that was the cause of death?"

Belinda nodded, even though the AUSA couldn't see her. "Two bullets to the head. Close range."

"Execution style."

Belinda made a sound in the affirmative.

"Hmm," Rigg said. "So, I'm guessing Castaño didn't take kindly to trespassers."

Belinda didn't respond. It was the same conclusion she'd drawn.

Rigg said, "Have we found Blondie yet?"

She caught the missing but implied part of that sentence: *have we found Blondie's* body *yet?* "No. We do have the security footage from earlier in the night of her leaving the club with Monaghan. But it's black and white and grainy as hell."

"Can they clean it up and run facial rec?"

"They're trying."

Another long pause down the line.

"And do we know why Monaghan was at the house party in the first place? Was it to buy drugs?"

"Probably," she said, "he might have gone there to pick up some weed, a little coke. Maybe some pills. He had a couple of priors for possession, but it doesn't look like he was dealing in a big way. What he did have was a lengthy list of sexual assault charges leveled against him, going back a decade. Two attempted rapes, one rape, and an indecent assault. None of them made it to trial, but there's a pattern there."

"Hmm," Oates said again. "Maybe not such a great loss to humanity, then. Catchy Bee Gees covers notwithstanding."

Neither of them spoke for a minute, having exhausted their evidence and theories. Finally, Oates said, "So, now what?"

Belinda uncrossed her arms and blew out a breath. "What now is that I'm desperately fending off CPD. They have their body, their ID, their ballistics and their witness. All the probable cause they need. They're champing at the bit to get a warrant and raid Castaño's trailer. And if they find their murder weapon, that will be that."

Daniel Castaño would be in police custody, staring down the barrel of a life sentence for murder. And the case that they had been working for the past eighteen months would be in tatters. A case that they hoped would net a much bigger fish than Daniel Castaño.

She looked across at the two other whiteboards facing the table in their operations room. Both were also covered with taped photos, but these had been placed in a much more deliberate order. The one nearest her had the words LA MANO NEGRA—CHICAGO scrawled in her own untidy handwriting at the top. Below it, they'd laid out the gang's hierarchy, as far as they knew it. Daniel Castaño's mugshot was there, as well as ones of Paquito Vasquez, Che Cardenas and Milo Bidois. About ten others joined their names at various levels of their criminal family tree. And at the very top, beside the scrawled acronym "CPOT", was the frankly terrifying visage of Terry "La Araña" Bidois.

The other whiteboard showed the wider criminal enterprise, extending from *La Mano Negra* in Chicago to the Sinaloa Cartel in Mexico. It represented the pipeline of heroin that ran from the poppy fields of the Sierra Madre Occidental, under the border at El Paso, then spread like veins on the back of a hand across the East Coast and Midwest.

There were a lot of holes in that hierarchy, a lot of black silhouettes standing in for photos and initials substituting proper names. Some were just big hand-drawn question marks. They'd tentatively placed the names of the Russian Sokolov brothers in Philadelphia in the far-left corner. But the biggest question mark had been reserved for the identity of the one they called "El Merc". He was the one who got the product over the border and into the hands of the likes of Castaño.

And all this work, all this combined intel from their multi-agency task force, would be for nothing if the Chicago Police Department went wading in with their dirty boots and took down Castaño. He was the only piece on this board that Belinda believed she could get through to. The only one who had lost enough to know he didn't want to lose any more. Castaño's life story was a cautionary tale if ever she'd heard one. A story in which he was both the villain and the victim. The problem, and—potentially—the solution.

"You want me to make a call?" Oates said. "Tell CPD to back off?"

She pictured him sitting in his brand new, plushly furnished office, in his thousand-dollar suit. The Justice Department considered Oates a rising star, and he could probably accomplish much with one phone call.

But Belinda was the one in the trenches with this case. If anyone was going to be making any calls, it would be her.

"They're backing off," she said. "For now."

"So, what's our next move?"

She put her hands on her hips. "Daniel Castaño has a brother. Sebastián. Sixteen. Undocumented. Works at a Mexican restaurant in Little Village."

"Yeah. And?"

She turned back to the whiteboard in front of her and its gruesome scrapbook of the man once known as Floyd Monaghan. "And strangely enough, I've got a sudden hankering for Mexican food."

Martín Tostá looked down at the business card the woman was holding out. He didn't take it. "I have got nothing to say to you."

The woman, who was Black with cropped graying hair and a crumpled shirt, pointed at the logo on the top of the card. "You see what it says there? D-E-A. Not I-C-E."

Martín gave her a chilly look. "I can read."

The woman titled her head at him. "What I mean, Mr. Tostá, is that I am not here to poke around into anyone's immigration status. It's not my job."

He folded his arms over his apron. "I am a legal resident of this country."

The woman gave him a tight smile. "But one of your employees isn't."

Martín involuntarily cast his eyes toward the ceiling where Sebastián's room was. He chewed the inside of his cheek but said nothing.

The woman followed his gaze upward. "Mr. Tostá, I am aware of Sebastián Castaño's legal status. Or lack thereof. I also know you gave him a job when few others would have. And that you let him live up there for almost nothing."

Martín said nothing for a long moment. Everything the woman had said so far was true. A year ago, Daniel Castaño had sidled into his restaurant, his teenage brother in tow. Martín had eyed the gang ink on the elder's hands and had edged closer to the baseball bat he kept on a ledge under the till. *La Mano Negra* gang members were a common sight on the streets of La Villita, and their bad blood with rival gangs often spilled over as actual blood on those same streets. Martín had no affiliations with any gang, but that didn't mean he wasn't ready for trouble when it presented itself.

But Daniel had not been there to cause trouble. Not that day, anyway. He'd asked Martín to take his brother on, to give him a job and a place to stay. Martín had agreed, if only to make sure that none of that gang ink, or blood, made its way onto the younger boy's hands.

He raised his chin at the woman. "Sebastián is a good kid. He works hard. He stays out of trouble."

The woman nodded. "And I'm guessing you want to make sure he continues to stay out of trouble, correct?"

Martín sniffed and looked out at the busy restaurant floor. "I thought you just said you weren't interested in making problems for him?"

"Oh, I'm not here for him. I'm here for big brother."

Martín felt his lip curl. Obviously, Daniel was the reason for her visit. That guy was bad news from head to toe. "You want to deport Daniel, you go right ahead. Don't let me stop you."

The woman smiled. It didn't reach her eyes. "Like I said, I'm not here to deport anyone. I just want information."

"What kind of information?"

"I want to know everything you can tell me about Daniel Castaño. His movements. His girlfriends. I want to know if he so much as grows a goatee or buys new sneakers."

She was still holding out the card. He fidgeted with his apron but still didn't take it.

She said, "If you help me out with that, I can help Sebastián out."

"How?"

"I can get him his Form I-551."

He narrowed his eyes at her. "I thought you said you weren't immigration."

The woman didn't blink. "I work for the government, Mr. Tostá. There are certain strings I can pull when the situation requires it."

Martín stared at the card. He thought about all the things Sebastián could do if he could become an American citizen. He'd be able to travel freely. Get his driver's license. Qualify for financial aid so he could attend college. Go to the doctor. Report a crime to the police. Just walk down the street without fear of someone asking to see ID.

She seemed to grow tired of holding out the card and placed it on the counter beside the register. "Think about it." She picked up the plastic bag of carnitas she'd ordered. "Then call me. Anytime. Day or night."

Martín watched as the woman left his restaurant. He glanced

behind him toward the kitchen door. Then slipped the card into the pocket of his apron.

89

ELEVEN

WITH EVERY MILE WEST, Daniel felt the pull of home tightening around him.

One hundred and seventy miles to go. Maybe two and a half hours. Three at the most, and then he'd see Julia again. The thought gnawed at him, urging him forward, keeping him sharp despite the exhaustion that blurred his vision and made his head pound.

He'd told Sebastián to keep an eye on her while he was gone, but there was only so much a sixteen-year-old could handle.

Beside him, Milo sat hunched over his phone, thumbs tapping, lost in whatever bullshit he was scheming. Neither of them had spoken in miles, and Daniel relished the silence.

But, of course, Milo ruined it.

"You thinking about her, huh?"

Daniel kept his eyes on the road. "Who?"

"That blond chick you're banging."

The words hit him like a sucker punch. Without thinking, Daniel slammed on the brakes, sending Milo lurching forward. He barely caught himself against the dashboard before whipping around, eyes wide. "Jesus, man, what the fuck?"

Daniel grabbed him by the back of his T-shirt and yanked him upright. His voice was low, dangerous. "What did you just say?"

Milo huffed, rubbing his neck. "Relax. I saw you, alright? At the mercado, with your brother. And that blond girl."

Daniel's grip tightened on the steering wheel.

Milo grinned, flashing those gaudy gold teeth. "At first, I thought she was with your brother. But we both know she ain't his type, right?"

Daniel resisted the urge to put his fist straight through Milo's face.

Milo chuckled. "Damn, bro. You got expensive taste. That bitch is like the Patek Philippe of pussy."

Daniel's knuckles went white on the wheel. His vision tunneled. And suddenly, everything made sense.

How Terry had found out about Julia.

Milo.

This stupid little *pendejo* had gone running his mouth. And Terry had taken that one scrap of information and spun it into a full-blown conspiracy.

Daniel turned, his voice ice cold. "So you snitched to Terry."

Milo's face twisted in offense. "I ain't a snitch." He held up his phone. "I just took a couple pics of you two. Just in case, you know..."

Just in case he ever needed leverage. Just in case he wanted to hold something over Daniel's head.

Daniel held out a hand. "Give me the phone."

"In a sec, man—"

"Now."

Milo hesitated, then sighed like he was being so inconvenienced and passed it over.

Daniel unlocked it and started scrolling. Jesus Christ, the guy took a fuckload of selfies. Hundreds of them. Shirtless, flexing, flashing gang signs, holding twin Glocks across his chest like he was some kind of action hero.

No photos of Julia so far. But knowing Milo, they could be buried deep.

Problem was, if he kept scrolling, he would stumble across a dick pic. No doubt about it. Probably one where the little weirdo had dyed his pubes blue or some shit. Daniel had seen a lot of bad things in his life, but he knew he wouldn't be able to come back from *that*.

He selected all the photos and hit *delete*, then dug into the "recently deleted" folder and wiped those too. That was as good as it got.

He tossed the phone back.

Milo caught it and groaned. "Aw, come on, man! One of those was gonna be my album cover."

Daniel ignored him. "So Terry doesn't know about her?"

Milo was still sulking over his lost masterpieces. "No. And I wasn't gonna tell him. Bros before hoes, right?"

Daniel nearly decked him right then and there. Not just for calling Julia a hoe, but for ever thinking they were bros.

Instead, he smacked the back of Milo's head, hard enough to make a point. "You ever talk about her again—you even *think* about her again—and I'll shove that phone so far down your throat your followers will see what you had for breakfast."

Daniel yanked the van back onto the road, gravel spraying behind him.

As the engine rumbled beneath him, he exhaled slowly, trying to let the rage drain out.

Relief crept in, replacing it.

Milo was a snake, but he was a stupid one. If he said Terry didn't know about Julia, then Terry didn't know.

That didn't mean she was safe forever.

But it meant she was safe…for now.

———

Julia leaned down and knocked on the window of the 'Cuda.

The young man in the driver's seat looked up and blinked at her. His expression flitted from alarm, to relief, then to something like embarrassment. He took out his earbuds and wound down the window.

She said, "It's Sebastián, right?"

"Yeah." He sighed, looking down at the phone in his lap. "Shit. I think I'm meant to be doing this covertly or something."

"By 'this', do you mean stalking me?"

Sebastián's eyes widened. "No! I mean, not me." He gave a quick shake of his head. "I mean…not Daniel either."

Julia raised her eyebrows but said nothing.

"Daniel had to leave town for a couple of days, and he was worried about you, so he asked me to come by and check on you." He sighed and dropped his head. "Yeah, that kinda sounds like stalking, right?"

She didn't reply, letting her silence answer the question.

When she'd come home and found the 'Cuda parked in the lane opposite her house, her immediate response had been excitement at the thought of seeing Daniel again. She'd quickly shelved that feeling and replaced it with one of wariness. When she'd plucked up enough courage, she'd walked down her drive and crossed the road to find out what he was doing there, only to discover it was the younger Castaño sitting in the driver's seat.

She looked back down at Sebastián. "Is there any reason why your brother is suddenly so worried about me?"

Sebastián's expression became cagey. "Yeah, you're going to have to ask him that."

The sun was setting, and a chilly breeze was raising goosebumps on her arms. She pointed at the passenger side. "Can I?"

"Oh, sure."

She got in the car. They were both quiet for a spell. Then Sebastián said, "You're not bothered? By the whole stalking thing?"

"I thought you said it wasn't stalking."

He regarded her in silence for a long moment, then said, "How much do you actually know about my brother?"

She kept her gaze straight ahead, out the windshield. Not much, admittedly. But what she did know felt pretty significant. She knew he'd taken care of her when she'd been at her most vulnerable. She knew the way he'd looked at her right after he'd kissed her, as if she were the most beautiful thing he'd ever seen. And she knew she hadn't been able to stop thinking about that kiss for days.

She turned her head to look at Sebastián. "I'm sensing you're trying to tell me I should be scared of your brother," she said. "Well, I'm not."

Sebastián met her gaze and held it for a long moment. "I'm not saying you should be scared of him. I'm saying…" He shook his head, like he was trying to work out what he really was trying to say. "Daniel has friends."

She frowned. "Friends?"

"Yeah. The kind of friends that if they ever become enemies…" He gave a smile that was more like a grimace. "Well, your life expectancy goes down a lot. Put it that way."

It was her turn to shake her head. "I haven't met any of his friends."

"Yeah," he said again, and there was something almost sad in his tone. "You should probably keep it that way."

———

As soon as he got back to his trailer, Daniel went straight to his wardrobe and pulled out a black sports bag. He unzipped it and gave it a shake, gauging the amount of cash inside. The denominations ranged from singles to hundreds. He hadn't counted it recently, but he knew how much was in there.

Not enough.

He emptied the cash from the brown envelope into the bag. The ten thousand would boost the tally a lot. He should thank Terry, really. But the cash came with a warning. A warning that if anyone found out about this bag of cash and where the rest of it had come from, he'd be praying his end was as quick and painless as Sasha's had been. Even while he knew it wouldn't be.

He zipped up the bag and tossed it back into the bottom of his wardrobe. Shut the door and locked it. Then he peeled off his blood-stained t-shirt and jeans, and bundled them up into a black trash bag.

His phone buzzed on the table. It was a text from Seb. His brother was at Martín's, and he wasn't alone. Julia was with him. He assured him she was safe, and that Daniel should meet them at the restaurant when he got back to Chicago.

He tossed the phone on the table. Then he went to his tiny bathroom and turned on the shower. He got in and stood with his head under the stream of hot water, with both hands pressed against the shower wall. He closed his eyes. Pictured Julia. Her face. Her body. Her eyes. Her smile.

Her image faded, and Sasha Sokolov's head abruptly took its place. The perfectly round bullet hole in the center of his forehead. The horrific mess at the other end of that hole. It was chased up by an image of the guy he'd dragged out of his trailer last week, his blood like black paint on the grass. And other images, too. A nightmarish parade of them.

He stood there under that stream of water for a long time, trying to imagine it was a baptism, washing away his sins. But the hot water ran out long before he felt even close to feeling clean.

———

Julia looked up at the menú chalked onto a huge blackboard on the far wall of the restaurant. She turned back to Sebastián and said, "Iguana?"

Sebastián chuckled. After their chat in the car, he'd offered to take her to this little Mexican place on the West Side for a bite to eat. Since she didn't have any other dinner plans, she'd agreed.

"*Sí*," he said. "*Y cabrito, y caimán*. Baby goat and alligator." He laughed at her expression of horror. "So, I guess that's a no for the *criadillas* then."

"The what?"

He grinned. "Bull's testicles."

There was a small balding man watching them intently from behind the counter. He had black eyes that reminded her of a bird's: sharp and fierce.

"Who's that?" she said.

"The boss man, Martín."

She raised her eyebrows in surprise. "You work here?"

Sebastián pointed at the ceiling. "Live here, too." He tugged her over to introduce her. "Martín, *es* Julia."

Martín's eyes traveled from Sebastián to Julia and back again, a look of comical confusion on his face. "*¿Ella es tu novia?*"

Sebastián rolled his eyes. "*No. Es la novia de Daniel.*"

Julia's tiny amount of Spanish was enough to deduce that Sebastián had just called her Daniel's girlfriend. It wasn't true, but the mere idea of her being that sent a stupid little thrill through her.

Martín's reaction to that news was very different. He looked at Julia with a mixture of pity and horror, like he'd just been told she had some incurable, life-shortening disease.

Sebastián laughed at his response. Then he tugged Julia away, through a doorway curtained by long plastic strips. It led to the kitchen, which was cramped and hot and loud, with servers and cooks bustling between the counters and speaking loudly in Spanish. She pressed herself against a refrigerator door and made herself small. Sebastián went over to one grill and spoke to the cook manning it. A minute later, he came back with a plate containing two overstuffed fried sandwiches.

"Tortas," he explained, handing her the plate.

She trailed him out of the kitchen and through the dining area to a small table near the door.

While they ate, she kept snatching glances of him across the table. She tried to spot differences between him and Daniel. Sebastián's face was thinner, more sculpted. None of Daniel's scars or tattoos. More handsome, but less animated. Daniel's eyes contained all his thoughts, swimming right on the surface. She sensed Sebastián kept his much deeper down.

He said, "So how'd you and my brother meet, anyway?"

She bit the inside of her cheek and said nothing.

"Sorry," he said. "I didn't mean to pry."

"It's not that."

She looked down at her plate. Every time she thought about telling anyone what had happened in Daniel's trailer that night, she felt a stab of panic.

Her eyes flicked back to Sebastián. "It's just a long and kind of awful story."

He didn't seem surprised that they hadn't met in some adorable, romantic way like you see in a rom-com. Or maybe his guarded expression was just Sebastián's standard reaction to everything.

She said, "How long have you worked here?"

"About a year and a half. Since we got here from LA."

"Just you and Daniel?"

He nodded.

"Why'd you leave LA?"

He didn't answer, just pushed his plate away. He sat forward, crossing his arms on the table. "Listen, Julia. I'm not trying to scare you away here. But there's a lot of stuff you don't know—"

Behind her, the restaurant door banged open. Sebastián fell silent.

She swiveled in her seat and saw Daniel standing in the doorway, wearing baggy jeans and a green checkered shirt over a white singlet. The color of his shirt seemed to make the hazel in his eyes even more striking.

His gaze went straight to Julia. And she instantly felt like there was no longer enough oxygen in the room.

She couldn't seem to make her tongue work, so she just stared at him. Daniel's eyes went to his brother, and something passed between them, deep and unspoken. Something like gratitude, only a hundred times stronger.

Sebastián stood and tossed him the car keys.

Daniel snatched them out of the air. He nodded at Julia, then turned and left the restaurant without a word.

She got up and pushed her chair in. Her hands were shaking, so she pressed them to her sides. "Thanks for dinner," she said to Sebastián.

At the door, she paused and looked back. Martín was standing over by the counter, serving a customer. She gave him a little wave. He just shook his head and went back to punching buttons on the cash register.

———

Julia's heart was thumping as she crossed the street to where Daniel was waiting for her in the 'Cuda. Outwardly though, she tried to appear calm as slid into the passenger seat.

He turned his head to look at her but said nothing. The orange cast of the streetlights illuminated his face. He didn't smile or attempt any pleasantries. He just looked her right in the eye.

It didn't feel awkward or weird. It just felt like they'd skipped a bunch of the usual steps in the getting-to-know-you part of a relationship. The self-conscious small talk, the forced niceties, the bad jokes. The parts where you figure out if you actually like this person or not. Where you decide if you have chemistry.

For her and Daniel, they'd figured that out a long time ago. All that other stuff felt redundant. It was like they'd skipped straight ahead to the staring into each other's souls' bit.

"Hi," she whispered.

He gave a tiny smile. "Hey."

He started the engine and pulled into the street. She stared straight ahead, hands clasped in her lap. The air between them seemed to shimmer, like it was suffused with gasoline fumes.

She had a million questions backing up in her throat. Questions about where he'd been and what he'd been doing there. Questions about his job and his family and why'd he'd moved to Chicago two years ago. Questions about these friends of his and why he felt the need to protect her from them.

She realized that all the questions boiled down to one.

Who are you?

But by the time he brought the car to a stop in the lane outside her house, she hadn't worked up the courage to ask a single one.

Maybe they'd skipped too many steps. Because they didn't really know a thing about each other.

The interior light of the car lit them both in a soft yellow glow. The silence stretched. Then, out of nowhere, they both spoke at once.

"Listen—"

"Daniel—"

A second silence followed, this time imbued with humor.

He looked down at the steering wheel and made a soft sound. Like Sebastián's almost-laugh.

She swallowed and forced the words out of her mouth. "Why did you tell your brother to watch out for me while you were away?"

He lifted his gaze to meet hers and winced slightly, like he had something sharp stuck in his eye. And she saw it in his face. The fear.

He was scared. Of whom? Of her?

Or of someone else?

He exhaled and chewed his tongue for a moment. "There's a lot of complicated shit in my life, Julia," he said, not looking at her. His gaze was fixed on the windshield, his thumbs hooked around the steering wheel above his knees. "Shit I don't want you getting involved with." He glanced at her now, and that same haunted look was in his eyes. "Shit that could get you really hurt."

His words settled with a heavy weight on her skin. She swallowed a lump in her throat. She knew that when he said 'hurt', he didn't just mean her feelings.

He looked down at his hands on the steering wheel. "I keep Sebastián away from it. And I'm gonna keep you away from it, too."

She said nothing, just bit her bottom lip, thinking. Then she looked at him and asked, "What are you saying?"

He swallowed, the column of his throat working. Then he looked at her, right in the eyes, and said in a low voice, "We shouldn't do this."

When she spoke, her voice was just as husky. "Do what?"

His eyes settled on her lips. And with that one look, every single one of her questions was incinerated in a blaze of need.

Their kiss was like a collision. His lips pressed against hers. His hands were everywhere. Gripping the back of her neck. Cupping her breast. Sliding around her waist to press against her lower back. Squeezing her butt. It was like he'd grown ten more hands in a very short space of time.

She didn't even realize he'd pulled her over the console until she was sitting in his lap. He ran his hands up under her skirt, over the bare skin of her thighs, stopping to cup her ass. There was a burning sensation in her stomach, like she'd swallowed something hot.

His mouth had become the center of her universe. His tongue glided over hers, pressing deeper into her mouth.

Unseeing but feeling, she pushed his shirt down off his shoulders and traced the muscles of his chest with her hands. She could feel the thick ridge of his hard-on through his jeans.

She gave an experimental rock of her hips. He broke off the kiss with a sharp intake of breath. His fingers dug into the skin of her thighs, hard enough that she could feel the blunt edges of his fingernails. When he kissed her again, he nipped her bottom lip with his teeth.

She pressed down on him again, gentler this time, enjoying the way it made him gasp and the way it made his heart beat faster under her palm.

"Fuck," he breathed. "Julia, I want you so bad."

She froze. It dawned on her where this was leading. To him unbuttoning his jeans, pushing aside the fabric of her underwear and…

Her face must have shown her fear, because he reached up a hand to cup her cheek with his palm. "Hey," he said, dragging a thumb across her cheekbone. "It's okay. I'm not going to do anything you don't want."

She swallowed, then nodded. Then shook her head. Then, because her indecision was bordering on comical, she smiled. He smiled too and placed a hand on the back of her head, pressing her forehead to his.

"I'm sorry," she whispered.

He retreated, gazing into her eyes. He brushed a strand of her hair behind her ear. "Baby, the first time I have you, it's not gonna be in my car." A smile tugged at his lips, not quite enough to bring forth the dimple. "She gets very jealous."

Smiling too, she pushed at his chest with both hands. She was trying to appear aloof and cool, but inside she was burning up.

The first time I have you. The way he said it, like it was a foregone conclusion, this having. A matter of when, not if. It was like he'd set a timer for a bomb to explode between them, and she had no idea when it might go off. And she knew that for every second until it went off, she'd be thinking of nothing else.

He was watching her, that little smile on his face, like he knew exactly the effect he had on her. At least now she knew she had the same effect on him. Physically, anyway.

She slid off his lap and climbed back over the center console. The gear stick jabbed her in the ass on the way, making her think that maybe the car really did have jealousy issues.

She settled back in her seat and stared straight ahead. They were both quiet. The only sounds were their breathing and the little thuds of bugs dive-bombing the glass.

She sat there, waiting for the alarm bells to ring. Warning her to get out of this car right now and walk away while she still could. End this before it went any further.

But the only fear she felt in that moment was the fear that he would drive away from her. Put her in his rearview and not look back.

We shouldn't do this.

She looked across at him, his expression soft in the dim light.

Too late.

———

Martín Tostá shut the restaurant door and locked it, flipping the sign in the window to Closed.

His gaze went to the table where Sebastián and Julia had been sitting earlier, before Daniel had swaggered in and she'd followed him out. He'd seen how she'd stared up at him with cartoon hearts for eyes.

He shook his head. Stupid girl.

Martín had come to Chicago from Guadalajara two decades ago to escape gang warfare in his hometown. He'd seen violence —real violence—up close. His sister had been killed right in front of him. His business burned to the ground. It had cost him everything to come to America and start again. To make something of himself. To build a good life, in a city he was proud to call home.

So, to see young men like Daniel Castaño strut around these streets with a pistol shoved down the back of his pants, with tattoos all over his face, made him sick to his stomach. Guys like him played at violence. It was all a game to them, something they did for the attention and the cred and the power. They flooded the streets with their drugs so they could buy more gold chains to hang around their necks and more fancy cars to roar up and down the streets of La Villita in. They were corrosive, and they were eating away at this city from within.

But this time, Martín would not watch it happen and do nothing. He didn't want to flee again and abandon another place to the gangs.

He buried his hand into the pocket of his apron and took out the crumpled card the DEA woman had given him. Then he picked up his cellphone, punched in her number, and hit CALL.

TWELVE

"FIRST POSITION." Julia stood straight and tall, arms curved in front of her, legs in a perfect ninety-degree turnout. She outstretched her arms, shifted her legs further apart. "Second position."

Daniel was sitting on the sofa in the corner of her home studio, facing the wall-mounted barre. He'd adopted a classic alpha male pose, legs spread, one arm draped over the back of the sofa, taking up as much room as possible. Tequila sat at his feet, wearing her silly grin.

She lifted one arm above her head, holding the other out, crossing her feet. "Fourth position."

Daniel nodded at the barre. "Can you put your leg up on that thing?"

She did.

His eyes scrolled down her body. "Yeah," he murmured. "I think that's my favorite position."

She took her leg down and crossed her arms. She tried to adopt a prim expression, but her cheeks were on fire. "Daniel, I'm trying to teach you ballet fundamentals here."

He grinned and held up his hands. "I am one hundred percent focused."

Oh, he was focused, alright. On certain parts of her anatomy in this leotard.

She fanned herself and went to take a sip of water. It was hot in the studio. The cantilever doors were closed because the builders were still making a racket outside. But that wasn't the only reason she was sweating before she'd even begun any routines. Having Daniel lounging over there, with his spread legs and damp singlet and slow smile, was like having the thermostat turned up to the max.

She kept her eyes off him and swept her gaze over the pool area and the path that led around the house. Checking the coast was clear. Her mom had wedding-related appointments in the city and wasn't due back for another hour. But occasionally one of the other girls from the Joffrey would show up at her studio to rehearse with her in the afternoons.

She looked back at Daniel, feeling a stab of guilt that she was so worried about anyone finding out about him. She reminded herself that they'd both agreed to keep this thing a secret. And while she didn't know the reasons why he wanted to shield her from everyone in his life except for his brother, she knew why she was reluctant to introduce him to her family and friends. And it wasn't because she was ashamed of him. Far from it.

It was because she was afraid of discovering that she was ashamed of them.

She sat down on the floor and took off her leg warmers and ballet slippers and started prepping her feet for pointe shoes. She applied Second Skin, then tape and gauze. Laced them up tightly, then got back to her feet and tested the flexibility in her insteps. She bent her knees, bearing down on her ankles. Feeling for pain, feeling for tenderness.

Then she did a bourrée, a little wandering movement on the tips of her toes, like she was shimmering over the floor.

Daniel had been watching her silently the whole time. "What's this *Giselle* thing about, then?"

She'd told him she was going to perform the *Peasant Pas de*

Deux from the famous ballet. She went over to the iPod that was connected to the sound system and queued up Adolphe Adam. "It's about a beautiful peasant girl who falls in love with this rich nobleman called Count Albrecht. But he's already engaged to this other woman and doesn't tell her. When she finds out about his betrayal, she's so devastated she dances until her heart gives out." She took a sip of water. "In some versions, she stabs herself. Then her body is buried in the woods."

Daniel snorted. "Wouldn't it be better if she stabbed Count Asshole and buried *his* body in the woods?"

She looked over her shoulder at him. "That wouldn't be very romantic, would it?"

"Be a hell of a lot smarter."

She walked back to the center of the floor. "Well, maybe one day you can choreograph your version and see how popular it is. You can get Quentin Tarantino to direct it."

He just shrugged, his look saying he might just do that.

"Anyway, that's not the end," she said. "After she dies, Giselle comes back as a ghost. And there are a bunch of other spirits living in the forest with her called the Wilis. They're the ghosts of all the women who have been betrayed by men. And they want to kill Albrecht by making him dance to his death. But Giselle intervenes and saves him. She forgives him, and lets him go, and then goes peacefully back to her grave."

Daniel, far from being enthralled by the story, appeared unimpressed. "That's it?"

She nodded.

"Tell me she at least gets to kick him in the balls at some point."

She laughed. "Yeah, I have a feeling ballet's not for you."

He smiled, spreading both arms across the backrest of the sofa. "Hey. I'm enjoying it so far."

She had to admit he had a point about the storyline. *Giselle* wasn't a feminist masterpiece. She knew it was meant to be about the redemptive power of forgiveness, but she'd always hated how the Wilis were portrayed. Instead of showing them as a sisterhood of tragic women fed up with being treated poorly by men, the ballet presented them as creepy, man-hating harpies with axes to grind.

Maybe one day she would choreograph her own version, too. One where the Wilis were the heroines of the story. But she suspected it wouldn't be any more popular than Daniel's version. Classical ballet isn't exactly known as a progressive art form.

She picked up the remote and hit play, feeling strangely calm. She usually felt riddled with nerves before any performance. Stage fright had crippled her for most of her life; it had gotten so bad in her teens that her mom had sent her to a psychiatrist who specialized in performance anxiety. Her diagnosis: Julia was far too fixated on perfection, to the point it was interfering with her mental health.

Julia's response had been, *no shit, Sherlock.*

She took a second to relish this feeling of waiting to start and not quaking in terror. She looked over at Daniel, lounging on the sofa. Maybe it was because she was performing in front of someone who probably couldn't tell a pas de deux from the Chicken Dance. Or maybe it was because she got the feeling that if she broke out the Chicken Dance and called it a pas de deux, he'd love it all the same.

The music started. She threw herself into every movement, with as much energy as if it were an audition. It wasn't a long variation, but there were some complicated beated steps en l'air which required all her concentration. She ended the piece delicately perched on one knee; her arm gracefully extended. But inside, she didn't feel delicate or graceful. Pheromones were dancing their own little jigs in her bloodstream, and her heart had taken up gymnastics.

He didn't applaud. He just sat there, his face flickering through a dozen tiny expressions. Awe and amusement and even something that looked a bit like pride. Then he reached out a hand to her. She got up and took it and he gave a little tug. Unbalanced, she toppled onto his lap. Both her knees collided with his thighs, but if it hurt, he gave no sign. Just wrapped both his hands around the small of her back and looked up at her, his expression settling on wonder. *"Eres increible,"* he murmured. "You're so fucking incredible, baby."

She placed both her hands on his chest. She could feel the heat radiating off him through the fabric of his singlet. Sweat glistened on his clavicle.

He placed his mouth a fraction away from hers but didn't kiss her. When she moved to kiss him, he pulled back and smiled teasingly. So, she placed both hands on the sides of his face and held him still and kissed him.

He liked that because he gave a soft moan in the back of his throat. His mouth was hot, and his tongue was not shy, and he was gripping her hips with both hands. And she was enjoying it, right up to the moment when she wasn't anymore, and she broke off the kiss.

She was still holding his face, and they were so close they were still breathing into each other's mouths. He looked up at her, something unreadable in his eyes.

He leaned forward and planted a quick kiss on her mouth. Then he smiled and tilted his head in the barre's direction. "Come on. I paid to see the whole show."

She smiled, too, and climbed off his lap.

He settled back on the couch, both arms draped across the top. "Can you do that spinning around on one foot thing again? Only this time, don't fall down."

"It's called a fouetté," she said over her shoulder. "And they're very difficult. I only fell because you distracted me."

He smirked. "Alright. Just picture me naked. Then you won't be distracted."

She threw her water bottle at him. Unfortunately, it was empty.

He swatted it away, still smirking.

She folded her arms and said, "When I was little I used to get nervous before every performance. So, my ballet mistress told me to picture people in the audience as cabbages. Rows and rows of cabbages."

He laughed. "Okay. Picture me as a cabbage, then."

She smiled. Pictured him as a cabbage. Then executed thirty-two perfect fouettés. And didn't fall down once.

———

The breeze coming off the lake was balmy, and the sky was clear but starless. Julia lay on her back on the sand, her damp clothes sticking to her skin.

She hadn't intended to go swimming, but Daniel had gone in first, wetting his jeans to the knees. Tequila had thrown herself in after him. Julia had waded in up to her ankles. Then Daniel had turned and run back and scooped her up, throwing her over his shoulder. He'd become unbalanced, and then they'd both ended up in water up to their necks.

Together, they'd sloshed out and then lain flat on their backs on the warm sand. Tequila was a few yards away, trying to dig something out from under a log.

She turned to Daniel, just a dark silhouette on the sand next to her. "You've never told me about your parents."

There was a dry rasp and then a burst of brightness. Daniel's face was illuminated as he lit the joint pressed between his lips. He inhaled, then blew out the stream of smoke and held it across his body to her. "You've never told me about yours either."

She took the joint and put it to her own lips. Sucked in, and this time, didn't cough it all out again. She handed it back to him. "What do you want to know about them?"

He blew a stream of smoke into the air, then turned his head to look at her. "What happened to your dad?"

Her fingers brushed the tiny ballet shoe pendant at her throat—the gift from her dad on her sixth birthday. He'd died just weeks later, and somehow, the necklace had come to represent him far more than ballet. She exhaled softly. "He died when I was a kid. Aortic aneurysm."

She felt Daniel's eyes on her. "Do you miss him?"

She looked up at the night sky and said, "I was so young, it's like there was no one to really miss. But I can still feel the absence at the same time. Does that make sense?"

He rolled over to face her. They were just inches apart. He reached out a hand to capture a strand of her hair. He considered it carefully, then tucked it behind her ear. "Yeah, it makes sense."

His eyes flicked to the pendant she was still absently turning between her fingers. "You must really love it."

She glanced down, confused. "What?"

"Ballet."

The word hung between them, heavier than she expected. No one had ever asked her if she loved ballet. It was always assumed.

She let the question settle, turning it over in her mind. Then she tried to answer it honestly.

"I love to dance," she said slowly. "That part, I love." She hesitated, her grip tightening on the pendant. "I just don't know if I'll ever have an actual career in it." A beat passed before she added, almost reluctantly, "Not like my sister does."

The admission left a strange weight in the air, yet at the same time, she felt lighter. The words echoed back at her, and she realized it was the first time she'd ever said them—out loud, or even to herself.

She had spent years pushing down doubts, swallowing them whole. To admit them had always felt like failure, like giving up.

But now, for the first time, it felt like something else.

It felt like freedom.

"So, this is our thing now?" she whispered. "Getting high on the beach?"

He ran his hand over her bare shoulder and down to the dip of her waist. He ran his eyes down the same path his hand had made. When they met hers again, they were drowsy with desire.

"We could make our thing getting high and having sex on the beach."

He leaned forward and kissed her. She kissed him back, and it quickly grew hotter and more intense. He gently rolled her over, so he was on top of her. He was heavy; his body pushed hers down into the sand. But the weight of him felt good, and the way he was pressing himself against her made her whole lower body throb.

He dipped his head and kissed her again, his tongue gliding against hers. She couldn't help but wonder what else he might be good at.

He braced both his forearms on the ground above her and was pushing his hips against hers in a way that made her think she was about to find out.

Panic and desire were fighting an epic battle inside her. Panic won.

He must have felt her body stiffen because he abruptly broke off the kiss and looked down at her.

She whispered, "Daniel, I'm sor—"

He pressed his lips to hers, cutting her off mid-word. "Don't," he said, right against her mouth.

He rolled off her, lying on his back on the sand beside her. He exhaled, then ran his hands through his hair, leaving them resting on the back of his head.

She curled around to face him and said in a small voice, "Don't what?"

He swiveled his head to look at her. In the darkness, his expression was impossible to read, but his voice was gentle. "Don't keep apologizing to me. You know you don't need to."

There was something hot rising in the back of her throat and she tried to swallow it down, but there was too much of it and it overflowed. And then she was crying, and he was wrapping his big arms around her and holding her. And they lay together in the sand like that for a long time, until her tears subsided, and she grew quiet.

He kept his arms around her, his chin resting on the top of her head. The only sounds were the cicadas and the soft lap of water and Tequila's little whines as she tried to extract whatever she wanted from under the log.

Then she sighed into his neck and said, "Maybe I shouldn't smoke weed anymore. It just makes me cry. And want pancakes."

He laughed, and she could feel it in his whole body. He kissed the top of her head and said, "You want me to drive us back into the city so we can go find pancakes?"

She nodded, and he chuckled again. Then he got up and helped her to her feet. They walked across the sand, his arm around her waist, her head leaning against his shoulder.

When they got to his car, she turned so her butt was against the hood. He placed both his hands on the metal on either side of her hips and leaned forward. But before he could kiss her, his phone went off.

He dropped his head and pushed back from the car. Retrieved his phone from his back pocket. The screen lit his face up as he read the text, and she watched as his face hardened right in front of her eyes. Became a different Daniel's face.

He sighed and shoved the phone back in his pocket. "Julia, I'm sorry. I gotta go."

"What? Where?"

"It's a work thing."

She shook her head, confused. "A work thing? But it's one o'clock in the morning."

"I service freight haulers, baby. They come in at all hours."

She stared at his face. It was a lie. She wasn't sure how she knew it, but she did with absolute certainty.

She had a fleeting fear he might go to see another woman. But his expression hadn't been the one of a man reading a booty call text. It was the expression of a man who had, as he'd put it, *complicated shit in his life.*

Shit that could get you really hurt.

He lifted her chin between his thumb and forefingers. Kissed her once on the mouth. "Julia. Baby. I'm sorry."

He opened the passenger door for her, and she hopped off the car and got in. He whistled for Tequila and the dog loped across the beach towards them. She threw herself into the footwell with sandy paws and licked Julia's knees.

Daniel was quiet as he drove the short distance up the hill to her house. He pulled up in his usual spot but didn't quit the engine. He leaned across the console to kiss her goodbye and reached down to hold Tequila's collar so she didn't jump out when Julia opened the door. Then she found herself standing in her drive, still a little stoned, watching his red taillights recede.

And she realized then that there were two Daniel Castaños. There was the Daniel that watched her dance and made her feel perfect even when she wasn't. The Daniel that held her in the sand while she cried and offered to take her into the city in the middle of the night to get pancakes. The Daniel whose sweatshirt still hung in her wardrobe, like a protective talisman against her own dark thoughts.

Then there was the Daniel with bloodied knuckles and with the word ALONE down the side of his face. The Daniel who had gripped a man's throat until he'd gone blue and pointed a gun at another man's head like he'd done it a hundred times before.

The Daniel who had friends you didn't want to make enemies of.

It was that Daniel she didn't want to know. So, she shoved that version of him away. She forced it into that box in the back of her mind, where she kept all the other things she didn't want to face.

And she vowed never to examine its contents again.

———

"Goddammit."

Salsa splattered like horror movie gore all over Belinda's only good white shirt. She grabbed a handful of napkins from a holder on the table and tried to blot the stain but ended up making it twice as large.

A passing waiter saw her predicament and said in heavily accented English, "I'll get you a cloth, *señora*."

A damp dish cloth appeared, and she grabbed it, dabbing at the stain. Her attempts only turned the large red stain into a larger pink stain.

The waiter who had brought the cloth hadn't moved, as if watching Belinda dab at her left boob was fascinating.

Annoyed, she glanced up, only to find it wasn't a waiter at all. It was the proprietor, Mr. Tostá.

He looked fidgety and kept glancing around the restaurant floor. Beads of sweat had broken out on his forehead, as if talking to a customer had suddenly become an illicit business.

Belinda kept a lid on her impatience. Martín had called her last night, proclaiming to have information. Information he would only impart in person. She proposed a meeting at a downtown coffee shop to ensure neither of them would be recognized. But Martín clearly didn't trust Belinda any further than the tiny man could throw her, because he'd insisted on meeting her here, in familiar territory.

He dithered for a few more minutes, pretending to write something lengthy on his check pad. Finally, he stuck his hand into his apron pocket and pulled out his cellphone. He tapped at the screen, then placed it on the table by Belinda's right elbow. "Her name is Julia," he said in a low tone. "She's his girlfriend."

She dropped the cloth and picked up the phone. On the screen was a photo taken from within the restaurant. The photo, captured from the counter's vantage point, showed a young white woman seated at a table near the door. Belinda swiveled her head and saw the same table, currently occupied by an elderly couple.

The woman in the photo was blond. Early twenties. She was looking up at a man who had just come in the door. A man who was unmistakably Daniel Castaño.

Hello Blondie.

She swiped through, found three more photos of the same subject.

"You say she's his girlfriend?" she asked, looking up at Martín. "Are you sure?"

He nodded. "Sebastián introduced her that way. They left together."

She glanced over at the skinny Latino kid stacking dirty dishes onto a tray by the counter. They'd both agreed on the phone that Sebastián could never know about this little arrangement. Daniel was the only family the kid had left. There was no way he'd accept help from the government if he knew it had come with the price tag of putting his brother behind bars for a very long time.

Belinda looked back down at the photo. The two were looking at each other in a way that seemed intimate. But the images were grainy, the lighting poor. She could have just been imagining it. Three low resolution photos did not a relationship make.

She handed Martín back his phone. "Can you send these to me right now?"

He nodded, then walked back to the counter, tapping away at his phone.

Belinda's own phone rang. She took it out of her bag and glanced at the screen.

Oates.

"There's been an interesting development," he said. "Sasha Sokolov is no more."

That surprised her. The Sokolov brothers had been on the government's radar from the moment they set foot on US soil. A worse pair of entrepreneurial dirtbags she'd had yet to find. "No more, as in, gone to a better place?" she said hopefully.

"No more, as in, gone to a place where hopefully he won't need a good amount of his head."

"Shit." Belinda pushed her plate of half-eaten enchiladas away. "Has this been confirmed?"

"Let's just say, from a very well-placed source."

"Ah. The lovely Svetlana. Your favorite CI. How's she doing?"

Oates's tone was grim. "Not good."

Belinda sobered, too. Four months ago, stripper Svetlana Zeitseva had agreed to inform on the Sokolovs, putting her own life in extreme danger. It was the kind of bravery that was usually rewarded with a shallow grave and deserved more respect than Belinda often gave her. "Is she somewhere safe?"

"She's staying with a friend," Oates said. "I've been in contact with the OEO. I'm doing the paperwork now. Let's hope we can get her into witness protection before this mess gets even bigger."

"What happened?"

"*La Mano Negra* show up with the product, as agreed. Everyone seemed happy. For about five minutes, anyway."

Belinda ran a hand around the back of her neck, squeezing the muscles there. "Wait. Why would LMN want to blow up their deal with the Sokolovs? That relationship seemed like a match made in gangster heaven."

"Oh, no, that deal is still very much alive. The shot-caller wasn't Terry. It was Borya."

"Shit," she said again. "That's some Russian brotherly love for you right there."

"I'll say."

"And who was the trigger man?"

Oates didn't answer right away, and she instantly knew the answer.

"Castaño," she said.

"The one and only."

Belinda looked down at the photo of the young man on her phone. She was under pressure to wrap this operation up. And not just from the CPD who wanted their Body in the Dumpsters case solved. Oates himself believed they should just send in ICE to raid Castano's trailer. They'd almost certainly find evidence to link him to many of the crimes he'd committed. Then they'd make him an offer he couldn't refuse and wait until he flipped on his friends to save his own ass.

But Belinda knew better. Guys like Castaño didn't bend over

that easily. He'd take whatever they threw at him—deportation, even life in prison—and smile serenely back at them from his holding cell. No, she'd always known that to break him, she needed more leverage. She needed something, or someone, he cared about more than himself.

"Anyway," Oates said in her ear. "What you got?"

Her eyes went to the girl he was staring at in the picture.

"Not what," she said softly. "More like who."

THIRTEEN

"WHO THE FUCK uses cassette tapes anymore?"

Daniel nudged the toe of his boot against the wooden pallet in the back of the truck containing boxes and boxes of premium quality Maxell blank audio cassette tapes.

Milo looked from the pallet to Daniel, then back to the pallet. He said, "They ain't cassette tapes."

Daniel rolled his eyes. *Jesus, this guy.* "Yeah, I know they ain't fucking cassette tapes. I'm asking, why do they send this stuff up here disguised as shit that nobody even uses anymore? Last week it was ballpoint pens. And then waterbeds. Are they all still living in the eighties down there or what?"

Milo just shrugged, then grabbed the handle of the pallet jack. "Don't ask me, man. Ask Ferrera."

Daniel just shook his head. He wouldn't be asking José Ferrera for anything of the sort. Ferrera, better known as "El Merc", was the operations manager for Unidos Logistics, a distribution hub that operated out of an old dartboard factory on the outskirts of El Paso. More heroin moved through that factory in a year than some countries seized in a decade, and El Merc oversaw every gram.

Daniel had met him twice and would happily go the rest of his life without making it a third. The guy was deranged. He strutted around the factory floor, with two nickle-plated Desert Eagles holstered in a complicated shoulder rig and his entourage of mercenaries, each armed to the teeth. Daniel had heard stories about him that made Terry seem, by comparison, like a well-adjusted dude.

One of Ferrera's jobs was the hiring and firing of the drivers who worked for him. The hiring part was probably easy. El Merc paid triple what other transport companies paid their drivers. Something quadruple for a big load. Curiously, though, Daniel only ever saw those drivers at InterTruck two or three times and then never again. Apparently, the guy was as paranoid as fuck about undercover DEA agents infiltrating his operation. And the easiest way to prevent that happening was terminating your drivers every few weeks. Unfortunately for his drivers, being terminated by El Merc was literal.

Milo was struggling to shift the pallet jack. There were eighty 'keys on that pallet. Probably twice his body weight.

Daniel grabbed the handle off him and pulled hard. Once the wheels started turning, it was easier to maneuver toward the loading ramp at the back of the truck.

His phone buzzed in his pocket. He stopped, fishing it out of his pocket. A text from Julia.

Can you come over?

He texted back, **To ur house?**

Her reply was instant. **Yes.**

Right now?

When she replied with **If you can**, he stared down at his phone for a long moment, feeling his pulse speed up.

He knew Milo was watching him, so he stuffed his phone back into his pocket and finished unloading the pallet of phony cassette tapes. Then he crossed the warehouse floor and tapped on the large glass window of Paquito's office.

Paq looked up from his desk and nodded.

Daniel opened the door, then poked his head in. "I got a personal thing I gotta take care of. I'll be back later tonight to finish unloading this lot, alright?"

Paq regarded him for a moment, an unlit cigar clamped between his teeth. Daniel had never seen him light that thing; he just seemed to enjoy chewing on it. He nodded once, then returned his eyes to his paperwork. Paquito was a man of few words.

Milo intercepted him at the warehouse exit. "You going to see your little girlfriend?"

Daniel felt his jaw clench.

Milo's expression was slimy. "I hope you don't mind, but I did a little Googling of your girl. Saw some videos of her online doing that ballet shit. I bet she can fuck you in all kinds of positions, right?"

Daniel shoved the heel of his hand against Milo's shoulder. He hit the roller door, leaving a nice round dent in the metal.

Milo laughed, rubbing his shoulder where he'd hit the door. "Relax, man. Just making conversation."

Daniel didn't answer. He just held Milo's gaze for a beat too long, long enough for the smirk to falter. Then he turned and walked out.

The midday sun hit him like a slap, glaring off the windshields of parked trucks and making the pavement ripple with heat. He pulled out his phone again, rereading Julia's texts as he made his way across the lot.

Can you come over?

He opened the door, slid behind the wheel, and just sat there for a second, gripping the wheel. Then he exhaled, started the engine, and pulled out onto the highway, leaving the warehouse, and Milo's smug grin, behind him.

———

After leaving InterTruck, Daniel drove back to his trailer, showered, changed, fed and watered Tequila, then got back in his car and headed north on the interstate toward Lake Forest.

An hour later, he stood at her front door, hand raised to knock. But before he could, the door swung open.

Like she'd been waiting for him.

His eyes dragged over her. Black leggings. A tiny white T-shirt that barely reached her navel. Bare feet. Hair down.

She looked him over, too, in a slow, measured way, like she was taking inventory of his individual parts. It made him aware of himself in a way he never had been before. How he looked. How he stood. How he walked.

He'd never felt self-conscious before. Not until her.

"Hey," he said when he finally met her eyes.

She hesitated. Was she nervous? Of him? Or of having him here, inside her home?

He glanced past her at the grand entry hall. She noticed. "No one's here."

He leaned a shoulder against the doorframe. "Okay."

A long, heavy silence settled between them. Thick. Charged. The only sounds were their breathing and the quiet splash of the fountain behind him. Heat radiated off the white stone all around them.

She smiled, turned, and walked inside without a word.

He followed, stepping over the threshold, and stopped cold.

He let out a low whistle. "*Santa mierda.*"

The entry hall was massive, a circular expanse that could have fit four of his trailers, end to end. Twin marble staircases, their gold handrails curling like something out of a palace, rose along either side of the room, meeting in the center on the second floor. A chandelier the size of his entire damn living room hung overhead, its crystal facets glittering in the soft light. Floor-to-ceiling drapes. Patterned rugs. Alcoves with statues that probably cost more than his car.

Julia shut the door behind him and started up the staircase.

He was still staring when she looked over her shoulder. "Are you coming?"

His eyes dropped to her ass in those leggings, and he immediately forgot all about the chandelier.

Fuck, yes.

He followed her up. And it was a good thing she was leading, because he already knew he was fucking lost.

———

Julia ran a critical eye over her reflection in the mirror. The lingerie set she'd picked out on a shopping trip yesterday had seemed so pretty in the store. Lacy and pink and sheer. Little satin bows on the bra and satin ribbon ties on each side of the thong. It had seemed innocent and sweet. But now that she had it on, it seemed pornographic.

She swallowed hard, unable to decide whether what she was doing was a boss move, or the worst idea she'd ever had.

Smoothing her hair, she leaned forward and checked her makeup again. She realized she was just stalling.

She blew out a breath. "Showtime."

She'd left Daniel in her bedroom, telling him she'd only be a minute, which was quite a few minutes ago. She wondered if he'd figured out why she'd invited him to her house this afternoon, or if he was just sitting out there, confused. Then she remembered how he'd looked at her earlier, when she'd been climbing the stairs. Like she was something delicious, and he was starving.

She had to stop and balance a hand against the bathroom wall. If just the memory of his eyes on her could make her feel like a million volts had just shot through her, how was she going to cope with the feeling of him inside her?

She realized she was shaking. It wasn't just her hands or legs; the quiver seemed to emanate from her very core. It was like her heart wasn't beating so much as vibrating.

She didn't get this nervous before going on stage. Or even

before auditioning. Actually, she didn't think she'd ever been this nervous.

She took another deep breath, wishing she was wearing some actual fabric to wipe her sweaty palms on. She spied her silk robe hanging on the back of the door. The plan had been to saunter out in just the lingerie, like she regularly seduced men on idle Tuesdays. But at the last minute, she chickened out and grabbed the robe and pulled it on.

She felt better. And worse. So much for the boss move.

Before she could chicken out of the whole thing, she grabbed the door handle, pulled it open, and walked into her bedroom.

He was staring at her bedroom wall, his back to her. She realized he was looking at the rows of framed photos that hung there. One was of her dad. There were also some of her performing in various roles, on stages all around the world. He was studying one black and white wide shot of her performing a soaring grand jeté in the wedding scene of *Don Quixote*.

Heart hammering, she just stood there, wondering if she should make a sound or maybe clear her throat. Before she had to, he turned, first just his head, then his whole body.

His eyes roamed over her. Taking in her robe and her obvious lack of clothing underneath it. Her pulse skittered. Every single cell in her body felt like it had suddenly developed consciousness.

His throat worked in a thick swallow. "Can I see?" he said, in a voice barely above a whisper. "Can I see all of you?"

She didn't answer, because she couldn't seem to make her own throat work. With trembling fingers, she undid the belt of her robe and let it slip from her shoulders to fall in a puddle at her feet.

He said nothing, just took her in with his eyes. Lingering on certain parts more than others. The feel of his gaze on her was so intense, he may as well have struck a match to her skin.

"*Dios*," he breathed. "*Eres hermosa.*"

He crossed the distance between them and, gripping her ass in both hands, lifted her. She braced both hands on his shoulders, her legs coming up to wrap around his hips.

He carried to her bed and dropped her down onto it. Standing over her, he gently pushed her knees apart with his. Then he tilted her chin up with a crooked index finger and kissed her. His tongue glided across her lips, then slid into her mouth, and it was caressing and gentle, and then it was possessive and bold, and so deep in her mouth it felt like a foretaste of what was to come.

She didn't even notice he'd unclasped her bra until she felt him gliding the straps over her shoulders. Then it was off completely, landing in her lap.

He broke off the kiss to look down at her small breasts, his hands going to them as if they couldn't stop themselves. He cupped each one, taking advantage of her open-mouthed gasp to kiss her again.

Her hands went to tug at the hem of his t-shirt, communicating wordlessly that she wanted it off too.

He obliged, grabbing the back collar of his singlet and pulling it down over his head.

When he straightened, she got a little jolt, like she did every time she saw him shirtless. He had a beautiful body. Thick muscles covered his arms and shoulders, but his abdomen was long and lean, like a dancer's. It was his tattoos, however, that always gave her a slight shock. One in particular: the black hand on his left pec, right over his heart. She didn't mind any of his other tatts, though some of them were beautiful. Works of art. But that one she hated. Every time she saw it, she had an urge to cover it with her own hand, make it go away.

He dropped his t-shirt on the floor to join her bra. Then he came back to his spot between her legs and gripped her chin between thumb and finger. He lifted her head, making her look him in the eye. "Are you okay?"

She wanted to say yes, but her heart was making a filthy liar out of her. He must have been able to feel its beat pulsing in every vein under her skin.

He pressed his thumb against her lips. "You can tell me to stop. Anytime. I swear I will."

She looked up at him and said softly, but with certainty, "Daniel. I don't want you to stop."

She shifted higher on the bed. He bent over her and curled his fingers around the waistband of her panties. When she lifted her hips, he striped it off her with the practiced ease that made her think he'd done that move many times before.

She forced that thought away.

Some ingrained modesty made her try to close her legs, try to conceal herself from him, but he didn't let her. He gripped her knees, one in each palm, and then just looked at her. His gaze was so potent it was like he was touching her everywhere, all at once.

Her returning gaze was much less confident. His eyes went back to hers and she knew he'd heard the questions she hadn't asked. *"Eres perfecto."*

He leaned over her, his hands around her waist until she was lying flat against the bed. Then he began laying down a trail of kisses from her neck, over her breasts, down her ribs. Then lower…and lower… He pressed his tongue against her stomach.

"Quiero probarte," he said huskily.

She pushed herself up on her elbows. He was looking up at her, along the length of her body. There was a question in his eyes. She didn't need a translation to know what he was asking her. To know the destination of his relentless downward journey.

Her breath got stuck somewhere in her throat. She nodded, and it was all the permission he needed.

She fell back on the bed and covered her face with both hands like she could somehow contain the feeling of his mouth on her.

"Oh my God," she said, her voice muffled by her palms. She tried to wiggle away, but he gripped onto her thighs to hold her still. His tongue was hot and wet, smooth and rough. It was like some kind of torture dreamed up by angels.

She arched her back. Sensation exploded in her. She might have actually screamed, though she hoped that might have only been in her head. Daniel was grinning up at her like a devil, so she realized it must have been out loud.

He sank his teeth into the soft skin of her upper thigh. The sudden flip from pleasure to pain made her gasp.

She laughed shakily and said, "You're very good at that."

He grinned again, climbing back over her body like a lion over its prey. "Really? I couldn't tell."

He worked his way back up to her mouth, plunging his tongue now into her mouth. She could taste herself on him, salty and musky, and a little shocking that two separate people could be this intimate with each other.

"Damn," he murmured against her mouth. "You taste good everywhere."

He sat up, positioning himself between her legs, and undid his jeans. She pushed up onto her elbows and watched. The bulge of him in his tight boxers was obscene, and it made her mouth water. She had a sudden urge to reach out touch him, but fear stopped her.

He pulled a condom from his pocket. Using his teeth, he tore it open and rolled it on. He propped himself up with one arm, settling on top of her to avoid putting his weight on her. Taking her hand, he led it down between them to wrap around him. He was long and hot and hard.

She angled him until she could feel the blunt tip of him pressing against her.

He slid inside her, then stayed still for a moment, letting her body adjust to him. Leaning over her, he placed his forearms on either side of her head and kissed her, sucking her bottom lip and dragging it between his teeth. He made a low moan against her mouth, then he started to move. His lower body rolled sinuously against hers.

She bowed her back up to meet him, lifting her knees so they clamped around his ribs. He made a sound of almost misery and pressed his forehead against hers. "You like that, huh?" his words came on sharp pants between each thrust. "You like it when I'm all the way fucking inside you?" He grabbed both her hands and held them above her head and kissed her like he never had before.

Like it was the last thing he wanted to do before physically leaving this earth.

His movements formed a rhythm, both urgent and steady, and with each one came a growing sensation inside her. She felt like she was hurtling towards some precipice. When she finally reached it, she teetered on the edge for a moment, hanging suspended in a feeling of intense pleasure, then she shattered.

Above her, Daniel's body tensed, his legs shaking. His grip on her hands was so tight, it caused hurt. He stilled for a heartbeat, then thrust into her one more time. He broke off the kiss and groaned against her mouth. Whispered something unintelligible in Spanish or English, or maybe some made-up language of his own.

Rolling off her, he draped over his eyes. His torso glistened with sweat. "*Santa madre de Dios y dulce Jesucristo*," he panted, dropping his arm.

She just lay there, not even trying to move. She felt like she'd melted to the bed. He turned to look at her, propping his head up on his elbow.

She curled around to face him, too. She didn't want to say anything. She was content just to lie there and bathe in the way he was looking at her. He made her feel like she was truly beautiful, and not just in some superficial, physical way, but in some other nameless way that only he had the parameters for. It made her think that if she could spend the rest of her life being judged by him and only him, she might actually be happy.

He got up, kicked off his jeans and underwear, then went to dispose of the condom in the bathroom. She watched as he walked naked back to the bed.

He lay back down beside her, and she instinctively wiggled closer, their bodies drawn together like magnets.

"Can I ask you something?" she murmured.

He tensed. "What?"

"How many girlfriends have you had?"

His body relaxed. "None."

She blinked, caught off guard. For a moment she didn't quite believe him, then her eyes landed on the word ALONE inked along his skin by his jaw.

He held her gaze. "What do you really wanna know? How many girls I've fucked? Or how many I've been in love with?"

She hesitated, caught between two equally loaded questions. Then, finally: "The second one."

He propped an arm behind his head, a slow smile tugging at his lips. "One. Her name was Gabby. She was twenty-three. I was eight." A laugh rumbled low in his chest. "She was my babysitter. Guess I was punching above my weight even back then."

She smiled, in spite of herself. That seemed to soothe the nerves that had crept in, but only for a moment.

She hesitated, then asked—casually, or at least trying to sound that way—"So… ballpark, how many girls have you slept with?"

The second the words left her mouth, she regretted them. It sounded too insecure, too revealing. But she couldn't help it. Compared to her own history—short, sheltered, careful—his past felt like another universe.

He didn't answer right away. Just gave a slow shake of his head, eyes unreadable.

She waited, trying to read him. The quiet stretched, just long enough for her to wonder if she'd pushed too far.

"But there's no one else now, right?" she asked, more vulnerable than she meant to sound.

He reached out and ran his thumb along her cheekbone, gentle and sure.

"Baby, there's no one even close."

———

Daniel thought he could happily stay in that bed for hours. Between those thousand-thread-count sheets, in a room that smelled like her, with her warm body curled beside him—yeah, he could stay here for the rest of the afternoon. Maybe the rest of his life.

Lying on his side, head propped up on one elbow, he watched Julia sleep. Her hair fanned across the pillow like a halo, and with each slow breath, her bare shoulders rose and fell. His gaze trailed over her, memorizing the delicate curve of her spine, the way her lashes fluttered slightly in dreams.

Fuck, she was perfect.

One of her eyes cracked open. Then the other. She smiled, before her expression faltered into something almost shy. "Why are you staring at me?"

He grinned. "I'm just committing to memory how good you looked in that little lacy pink thing. Y'know, in case I get lonely later."

She rolled over to face him, smiling sleepily. He slid a hand behind her neck, drawing her closer. Their lips met, slow and unhurried, like they had all the time in the world. His thumb traced down the soft skin of her throat, settling in the hollow at the base of her neck.

She let him kiss her for a moment, then her fingers brushed his wrist, feeling the watch strapped there. Suddenly, she stiffened. "Wait, what time is it?"

Before he could answer, she grabbed his hand and twisted it so she could see the watch face.

"Shit." She sat up, swinging her legs over the side of the bed. "My mom's due home any minute."

Daniel didn't move. He just watched her, still lazy with sleep.

She glanced over her shoulder, exasperated. "You have to go."

"Now?"

"Yes, now."

He groaned and sat up, rubbing his face. "Isn't there, like, a window I can jump out of or something?"

"Not unless you don't mind a twelve-foot drop."

He moved behind her, draping an arm over her shoulder, his hand curving around her breast. His inked skin was stark against her pale complexion. He pressed a kiss to her shoulder, then along the slope of her collarbone. "I might not mind if it means I get to stay longer."

"Daniel," she murmured, tilting her head as if tempted.

But then her eyes flicked toward the driveway. His car was sitting out there, loud and unmistakable.

"You have to go *now*."

He caught her mouth again, kissing her deep, but she broke away too soon. So, he moved to the back of her neck instead, sweeping her hair aside with his fingers. "What do you think she'd do if she found me up here?" he murmured. "Call the cops?"

He meant it as a joke, but her expression instantly sobered.

"Shit, really?"

She pressed her lips together, looking both worried and a little irritated. "It's just better if she doesn't meet you this way."

He sighed but didn't argue. Instead, he rolled off the bed and started gathering his clothes.

Julia sat back against the pillows, watching him dress. "When can I see you again?"

He glanced at her hopefully. "Tonight? My place?"

The words hung between them. She hadn't been back to his trailer since that night. He wondered if she still saw the place in her nightmares.

She bit her bottom lip, hesitating. Then, so softly he almost didn't hear it, she whispered, "Okay."

Relief coursed through him. "Text me when you're ready. I'll come get you."

She smiled "You know, if we're gonna keep this thing on the down-low, you really need to get a better muffler for your car."

He tugged on his singlet and shook his head in mock frustration. "Baby, you don't put a muffler on a Hemi. It's like I've taught you nothing."

She stood, dragging the sheet with her. "Tonight, then."

He lifted her chin with his knuckles, his thumb tracing over her lower lip before he dipped his head and kissed her one last time. "*Esta noche*," he murmured. "*Te amo.*"

He turned to leave.

Behind him, Julia made a strangled noise. "Wait. Did you just say you love me?"

He paused in the doorway, a slow grin spreading across his face. "I thought you said you didn't speak Spanish?"

FOURTEEN

JULIA SLOWED as she approached the trailer, then stopped. It looked exactly like it had on that night.

There were the same steps leading to the door that she'd stumbled up in her stilettos. Inside would be the darkened interior where his hands had groped her, where breath had been hot and reeking of alcohol in her face.

She glanced at Daniel beside her. Squeezed his hand and he squeezed back.

Tethered in the long grass, Tequila wagged her tail and whined. Daniel went and let her off. She came bounding towards Julia, skidding to a halt just before she collided with her legs.

Julia squatted down and submitted to her daily drool session. While scratching the dog's ears, she remembered it was Tequila who had saved her that night. Her barking had alerted Daniel to what was happening in his trailer. She felt a hot lump rise in the back of her throat. She didn't know why that was making her emotional, but it was.

Daniel came over and looked down at Tequila resting her heavy chin on Julia's knees. *"No le gusta nadie. Solo a ti."*

"What?"

"She doesn't like anyone but you."

Julia stood up and followed him to the trailer steps. She climbed them slowly, stopping on the threshold.

As she stared around the room, an icy hand of fear gripped her by the throat. She'd seen this place so many times in her nightmares. There was the wall he'd held her against, which she now saw was a wardrobe door. The place where he'd held a hand over her mouth, stopping her from breathing. Where she believed she was going to die.

Daniel was standing near the bed, watching her with an expression that seemed caught between sadness and tenderness and something else. Something much darker. He exhaled and said, "I can take you back home."

She looked at him. He opened his arms, and she walked right into them. Instantly, the grip of fear receded.

"No," she said into his chest. "I want to stay here. With you."

With utmost care, he removed her clothing one piece at a time, treating her as gently as a delicate porcelain doll. He discarded his own clothes and pulled her into bed next to him. With his heavy arms, he embraced her and simply held her. She dozed, and when she dreamed, it wasn't about being paralyzed and in fear. It was of Daniel, wrapping her in his warmth, his scent, his firm hands.

When she woke, it was to find him wide awake and watching her. Their heads sharing a pillow, foreheads touching.

"You okay?" he whispered.

She nodded. They kissed. She let him in, his tongue feeling more at home in her mouth than her own.

The kiss grew hotter and more urgent. He sat up and took a condom from the beer crate and put it on. Then he sat up against the wall and pulled her onto his lap. She braced her hands on the wall on either side of his head and slid down, taking him fully inside with a soft moan. He gripped her hips and rocked her flush against him. His mouth was on her neck, his tongue branding her skin with its heat. Their bodies intertwined so seamlessly, it was hard to believe they served any other purpose than to be joined like this.

When she came, it was like coming apart and the only thing holding her together was him.

———

Sunlight pierced through the thin curtains, draping across her face. Julia stirred but didn't move, letting herself sink into the moment. She thought about the last time she had woken up in Daniel's trailer—how it had felt like clawing her way out of a nightmare, only to realize she was still trapped inside it.

This time, she felt like she had to pinch herself to make sure she wasn't still dreaming.

She turned her head toward him.

Daniel slept on his stomach, sprawled across the bed, taking up just as much space unconscious as he did awake. One arm was flung over the sheets, the other tucked beneath the pillow. The broad, muscular expanse of his back was half-covered by the crumpled sheet, his tanned skin smooth except for the faint scars and tattoos she was beginning to recognize as intimately as she knew her own reflection.

He was beautiful. Almost unbearably so.

She reached out and traced the scar on his temple, running her thumb lightly over the jagged line that disappeared into his dark hair. Then she smoothed her finger over the tiny cross tattooed on his cheekbone.

His lips curled into a lazy smile before he even opened his eyes. He made a low, sleepy sound and rolled onto his back, stretching, then lacing his hands behind his head. His dark eyes met hers, warm with amusement.

"Morning, *bonita*."

She smiled back, propping herself up on her elbow. The trailer was dim, the air thick with the lingering scent of sleep, sex, and him.

Daniel made a satisfied sound and rolled toward her, reaching out.

She scooted back. "I gotta brush my teeth before you even think about kissing me."

Before he could catch her, she slipped out of bed, scooping up her camisole and panties from the floor. She pulled them on as she grabbed her makeup bag and disappeared into the tiny bathroom.

She rinsed her face, then brushed her teeth with the spare toothbrush she had stashed in her bag. When she came out, he brushed past her, taking his turn.

While he was in the bathroom, she wandered into the little kitchenette. Opening the cupboard, she found the sum total of his dishware: one mug, a couple of glasses, one bowl, one plate. His pantry was even more depressing—a jar of instant coffee, an unopened box of Rice Krispies. She checked the fridge. A carton of juice. A six-pack of *Sol Cerveza*.

Clearly, he ate most of his meals at Martín's.

What he lacked in human food, though, he made up for in dog food. A full twenty-five pound sack of chow sat in the corner, like Tequila was the only one around here getting three square meals a day.

Daniel came up behind her, sliding an arm around her waist and tugging her back against him. His other hand pushed her hair aside, his lips brushing the sensitive spot just below her ear.

"I gotta go to work soon," he murmured, voice still thick with sleep. "But I was kinda hoping we could go back to bed for a bit."

She smiled over her shoulder. "And how am I getting home?"

His mouth skimmed lower, pressing warm, open-mouthed kisses down her neck. "I'll take you home. Unless…" He grazed her skin with his teeth, then soothed the spot with his tongue.

She sucked in a sharp breath. "Unless…?"

His lips found the shell of her ear. "Unless you wanna stay here. Forever."

She laughed softly. "Stay here? Forever? With you and your one bowl and your one box of Rice Krispies?" She reached out, pulled open a drawer, and laughed again. "And your one spoon."

His hands flattened against her stomach, smoothing over her skin. "We can share."

She chuckled, and he squeezed her tighter. The heat of his bare chest seeped into her back.

"I can't tell if you're joking or serious," she murmured.

She angled her head, trying to catch his expression—just like she had the day before, when he told her he loved her.

He smiled against her skin. Then his hand slid down the front of her panties.

She gasped, gripping the counter.

His voice was rough in her ear. "Can I please fuck you now?"

Later, as they lay tangled together, skin damp, hearts still racing, he propped himself up on his elbow.

He brushed his palm against her cheek, his fingers tracing the line of her jaw. His dark eyes searched hers, something unreadable in them. Then, in a voice barely above a whisper, he said—

"I wasn't joking."

———

Daniel legs swung over the edge of the lumpy mattress and sat up, pushing the tangled blankets away. Julia came up behind him and ran her hand over the tattoo on his biceps, the Death-like figure in a black robe and a red crown. "So, what's with the skeleton?"

"It's not a skeleton," he said. *"Es la Santa Muerte."*

"What's that?"

He glanced over his shoulder at her. "Not what. Who. *La Huesuda.* The Bony Lady."

She looked more closely at it. "The Bony Lady?"

"Sí. My mom had a shrine to her in our garden. Lit the candle every night. White for thanks. Gold for money. Red for love. Black for protection."

If he closed his eyes, he could see the painted stone statue of *La Huesuda* in the far corner of the courtyard of their house in Torreón. Her head was bowed, her bony hands strung with rosary beads and clasped in supplication. Like a skeletal Virgin Mary.

He said, "We had a statue of her. Sebastián used to be terrified of it. He thought she was like Death, you know. Like how the Grim Reaper is to Americans. He thought she was coming to take his soul in the night. But my mom told him, no, she's not like that for us. *Para nosotros, ella es la Niña Bonita, la señora que nos mantendrá a salvo.*" He looked at her, at the puzzled expression on her beautiful face. "For us she is the Pretty Girl, the lady who will keep us safe."

He could hear the hollowness in his voice as he spoke. He never talked about his mom. Not even to Sebastián, who was too young to remember much of their life in Coahuila.

But when he closed his eyes, he could see all of it. He could see his old house, blue with white shutters. His *mamá* under the jacaranda tree, sweeping up the violet flowers in the spring. He could see old Señor Gómez shuffled out of the house next door, yelling at him for using his wall for football practice on Sunday mornings. He could see the outdoor bathroom in the tin shed, which got so hot in the summer that the water in the toilet bowl steamed.

She reached out and trailed fingers over the image of an old, bearded man on his shoulder blade. "Who's this guy, then?"

"St Jude." He smiled back at her. "Patron saint of lost causes."

"So, you're Catholic then?" She rested her cheek against his back. "You don't seem very Catholic."

"Don't I?" He grinned. "And here's me thinking I was going straight to heaven."

She laughed, snaking both her arms around his torso. He could feel her breasts pressing into his back and he felt damn close to heaven right then.

She pressed her palm against the hand print tattoo that lay

over his heart. As if she could feel it on his skin without even seeing it. Her touch posed a question, despite her silence.

His answer was to place his hand over hers and gently pry it away. He curled his hand around hers, hoping she understood that one didn't have a simple explanation.

She propped her chin on his shoulder. 'Do you ever want to go back there?' she said.

He realized she was looking at *la Bandera de México* that hung above the door. "*No puedo volver,*" he said softly. "I can't go back."

"Why not?"

"Because if I did, I wouldn't be able to get back here again."

There was a long pause. She lifted her head from his shoulder, and he could practically hear her mind working.

"It scares me a little."

He frowned. "What does?"

"That you keep things from me. About your life. Your past."

He squeezed her hand. "Before I met you, I was someone else. Someone worse."

She studied him, like she could pull the truth straight from his skin. "Worse how?"

There was a loud banging on his trailer door. Terry's voice came from right outside. "Daniel! You in there?"

He leaped up, head snapped from the door to Julia sitting naked on his bed and back to the door again. "Jesus. Fuck."

Terry pounded again.

He didn't have time to come up with a plan. So, he just ripped the sheet off the bed, bundled Julia up in it, then unlocked his wardrobe and pushed her into it.

"Daniel, what—"

He silenced her by stamping a kiss on her lips. "Just stay in here a minute, okay? While I get rid of him."

She nodded mutely.

Terry had gotten fed up with waiting and pushed open the trailer door.

Daniel slammed the wardrobe door shut and whirled around.

He grabbed his jeans off the floor and pulled them on. "Ever heard of a little privacy, *güey*?"

Terry shrugged. "I tried knocking, man."

Daniel finished buttoning his jeans. "Yeah, you nearly took the fucking door off."

He grabbed his singlet off the floor and his phone from the table and, with a last look behind him at the wardrobe, headed for the door.

Terry climbed down the steps ahead of him. When he stepped onto the grass, the trailer visibly groaned in relief. Daniel always needed to reset the wheel chocks after Terry came calling.

He crossed his arms and peered up at Daniel through his sunglasses. "Paq said you never showed back up last night to finish that last drop."

Daniel scratched the back of his head. "Yeah, I, uh, had —"

"Personal stuff," Terry cut in. He turned his mirrored gaze to the trailer, as if he could see through its walls, its doors, right into his wardrobe.

Daniel didn't know what would anger Terry more: knowing that Daniel had broken his cardinal rule about getting involved with a woman or knowing that the woman in question was the same one who could go to the cops anytime she wanted and report what had happened in his trailer that night. Daniel had trusted Julia when she'd said she wouldn't do that. But Terry trusted no one.

Daniel lifted one shoulder but said nothing. He could feel his heart beating a steady drip of adrenaline into his veins. He ran through all the scenarios in his mind, imagining what lengths he'd go to protect Julia.

Any length, he realized.

Any fucking one.

He tried to keep his expression neutral. A confrontation wasn't something he could deal with right now. He had to stay calm and hope like hell the big man was bluffing.

Terry looked back at him. Took his cigarette from behind his ear and stuck it in his mouth. Then he turned his head toward the 'Cuda. Tequila, relaxed but alert, was tied up beside the car.

"Fuck, that thing's ugly," Terry said.

Daniel didn't know if he was talking about his car or his dog, but he let the insult slide.

For a long moment, neither of them said anything.

"Your old man was a mechanic, right?"

Daniel nodded.

Terry stuck the cigarette in his mouth and fumbled in his pockets for a lighter. "Pushed some stuff for the cartel too back in the day, no?"

Daniel shoved his hands in his pocket and didn't reply. Since they both knew the answer to that question, there seemed little point.

Terry gave another grunt that might have been a laugh. "Until he didn't no more."

He waited to see if Daniel had any kind of response to that. Daniel didn't. He knew this game. The smiles and easy laughs that always punctuated Terry's conversations were part of the act, too. In the same way that he was slow until he was fast, the big man was always friendly until he really, really wasn't. He was your best friend until he was distributing your body parts in so many dumpsters. For all the years Daniel had known him, he'd managed to stay in the gap between his two extremes.

Terry smiled, making the cigarette stick out the side of his mouth at a jaunty angle. "I don't give a fuck who you fuck, Daniel."

Daniel's blood seemed to have stalled in his veins. And he knew now, without a doubt, that Terry knew about Julia. Whether because Milo had told him, or by some other means.

The guy was still patting and poking at his pockets, looking for the lighter that he could never find. He stopped and looked at Daniel, as if expecting him to supply him with his lighter, as he usually did. Daniel kept his hands in his pockets.

He plucked the cigarette out of his mouth and stuck it back

behind his ear. "What I do give a fuck about is if you don't show when you say you're gonna show up. It's just basic manners. You know what I'm saying?"

Abruptly, he turned and started ambling toward his car parked on the street.

Daniel glanced behind him again at the trailer, but he had no choice: he had to follow. Maybe it was the reminder of his dad's choices, and where they had gotten them all. Or maybe it was something he had always known deep down. But it occurred to him now with the clarity it hadn't before: there was no running away from this life. It always found you.

And it was always really fucking angry when it did.

———

Julia heard the 'Cuda's engine rumble to life, gravel crunching beneath its tires as it reversed down the drive. She waited, listening, until the sound faded completely. Only then did she push open the cupboard door, the blanket wrapped tightly around her shoulders.

As she stepped out, her foot caught on something, dragging it out with her. A gym bag.

Her phone chirped from the beer crate. She snatched it up, her fingers cold despite the midday heat.

Sorry baby. B back soon to take u home xx.

She sank onto the edge of the bed, her mind circling back to the other man she'd glimpsed before Daniel had slammed the door shut. The one with the spiderweb tattoo stretched over most of his scalp. He was big. Rough-looking. Dangerous.

Sebastián's voice echoed in her head: *Daniel has friends. The sort of friends that, if they ever become enemies, well, your life expectancy goes down a lot.*

Was that man one of them?

She exhaled slowly, pressing her fingers against her temples. Her mind reeled back to their earlier conversation—Daniel's face hardening when she'd asked if he ever wanted to go back to Mexico. *I can't,* he'd said. *If I leave, I can't come back.*

He hadn't spelled it out, but she'd understood anyway.

He was undocumented. Sebastián, too.

A tight, aching feeling bloomed in her chest.

God.

She thought of all the things they must go without, the doors that were slammed shut before they could even knock. The risks they carried just by existing in a country that didn't want them. The ordinary, everyday indignities they had to endure.

And yet, Daniel never talked about it. Never let her see that weight on his shoulders.

Did he think she wouldn't understand? That she couldn't understand?

Maybe it was worse than that. Maybe, deep down, he didn't trust her.

The thought stung more than she wanted to admit.

She wiped her face with the edge of the blanket and stood up, pulling her panties and camisole back on.

Her gaze drifted over the inside of the trailer. Bare walls. No pictures. No trinkets or souvenirs. Just the Mexican flag tacked over the door. It was like he'd made no effort to carve out a space that was his own.

Did he even have photos of his family? Did he ever let himself have anything that felt like home?

She thought about all the things she'd told him about her own life—her childhood, her family, the things that shaped her. And how little he had shared in return.

This relationship—it wasn't equal. Not even close.

Her eyes flicked down to the gym bag she'd kicked earlier, still slumped on the floor.

She bent to pick it up, intending to shove it back into the wardrobe where it belonged. But when she lifted it, she noticed something off.

It was heavy. Too heavy for gym clothes. And oddly bulky.

A strange prickle crawled up her spine.

Slowly, she set it back down and unzipped it.

Her breath caught. The air inside the trailer seemed to shrink.

It wasn't gym clothes.

Sebastián's voice surfaced in her mind again, low and serious. *How well do you know my brother?*

Apparently, not well at all.

———

Daniel froze in the doorway of his trailer, pulse spiking as the sight registered.

Julia was curled up on his bed, barely dressed, with his life savings scattered in a messy pile by her knees. His loaded Beretta lay on the pillow beside her, a stark contrast against the soft, crumpled sheets.

Heat flared in his chest, anger, panic, betrayal all tangled up. She'd discovered the bag. The cash. Pieces of him he never meant for her to see.

He slammed the door so hard the walls rattled. The bang made her jolt awake.

She gasped, blinking against the midday light. Scrambling upright, she took in his face, his posture. "Daniel, I—"

He strode to the bed and started shoving the cash back into the bag. "If you were planning on robbing me, baby, I wouldn't recommend falling asleep on the job."

She gaped at him. "I wasn't robbing you. I was waiting for you to come home and explain why you've got a bag full of cash and a gun in your closet."

He gave her a flat look. "You knew I had a gun."

She sat up, crossing her legs. "Yeah, but I didn't know you had, like, ten grand in cash just lying around."

"Twenty, actually." He kept stuffing the bills away. "Unless you really did rob me."

Her jaw clenched. "Where's it from?"

He zipped the bag and slung it off the bed. "From working, baby. You know what that is?"

She swallowed, color rising in her cheeks. "Working. Right. And what exactly do you do for a job, Daniel? Builder, was it? Or mechanic?" She paused, her voice cooling. "Or something else entirely?"

"I make a living," he said. "You realize nothing's free in this world, right? Not in mine." He picked up the gun and checked the chamber, then shoved it into the back waistband of his jeans. "Everything seems to be free in yours."

"Don't do that."

"Do what?"

"Make this about something else."

He shook his head, already exhausted. "So, what is it about then?"

Her voice wavered, but her eyes stayed locked on his. "What do you do, Daniel? What do you really do?" She hesitated, then forced out, "Is it drugs? It's drugs, isn't it?"

He didn't answer. He just kept his hands busy.

Julia pushed off the bed. "That tattoo on your hand. The letters. And that black hand print on your chest." She grabbed her phone, her fingers tightening around it. "I Googled it. It says LMN stands for—"

"*La Mano Negra.*"

The words slipped from his mouth before he could stop them. Or maybe he didn't want to. Maybe he was tired of holding it in.

He jerked his chin at her phone. "What else does it say?"

Her breath hitched. She hesitated, then looked back at the screen.

"Read it," he said, voice low, firm. "Out loud."

She inhaled, slow and shaky, before speaking. The words came out in a rush, as if she hoped she could fast-forward to the end and find out none of it was true. "It says they're a street gang. Started in California in the nineties as a feeder for *La Eme*, the Mexican Mafia." She scrolled. "They use the black hand print and the number thirteen as symbols of allegiance, because M is the thirteenth letter of the alphabet. And…" She swallowed. "And it says they grew from a small gang to one of the largest criminal syndicates in the U.S. Responsible for hundreds of violent crimes, including execution-style murders, tortures, and beheadings—"

In one swift motion, he stepped forward, plucked the phone from her hand, and tossed it onto the bed. With his other hand, he pulled her in, backing her against the wardrobe.

Her breath caught, her wide blue eyes flickering between fear and defiance. He could feel her heart racing against him. "It's true though, right?" she whispered. "You're in that gang?"

"Yeah." His voice was even. "But I haven't beheaded anyone in ages."

Her lips pressed into a tight line. "Daniel. It's not funny."

She hesitated, then asked the one question he knew was coming. "Have you ever killed someone?"

He exhaled and dropped his head.

Her hands pressed against his stomach, a light push. "Daniel…"

He brushed his lips against her jaw, his breath hot against her skin. "So what? You scared of me now?" His voice dropped lower. "You weren't scared last night." He ran his tongue along the column of her throat, pausing where her pulse ticked beneath his lips. "Or this morning."

Her breath hitched. "Daniel, stop."

His hands curled under the waistband of her panties.

She pushed against his chest, firmer this time. "I said stop."

The adrenaline was still there, but it soured in his blood. His hands dropped from her hips. He straightened, stepping back, fists clenching and unclenching.

She wouldn't even look at him.

He let out a slow breath. "So, that's it? We're done? Just like that?"

She angled her face away, a hand swiping at the tears threatening to spill. "That night… those pills he gave me." Her voice was barely a whisper. "You knew what they were." A tear broke free, tracing a path down her cheek. "Did you sell them to him?"

His stomach twisted. "Is that what you think I do?" His voice was sharp, incredulous. "You think I sell rape pills to pieces of shit like that?"

She said nothing. Wouldn't look at him. That was worse than words.

"I just…" Her voice cracked. "I don't understand. Why would you get mixed up in something like this?"

Something bitter and sharp burned in his throat. "No. You don't understand shit, Julia." His voice was quiet but laced with something raw. "You skip through life like a fucking Bambi in the woods. You don't see the bad in the world. It just doesn't exist for you."

He stepped toward her. "But it exists for me. It's existed since I was fourteen. Since I was alone in a foreign country with a four-year-old to take care of. You have no idea the things I've had to do to survive." He let out a humorless laugh. "And I didn't want any of it, baby."

Her tear-streaked face lifted, something breaking open in her expression.

And then he saw it.

The thing he'd been dreading.

Fear.

But then something even worse. In her eyes, he saw himself. Every sin. Every regret. Everything he hated about who he was. Reflected back at him.

This thing between them was a minefield, and it was going to blow them both up.

He tore his gaze away, jaw tight. "I love you, Julia. But we are not the same. And I don't think you fucking get that."

Her lips parted, her face a battlefield of emotions—grief, anger, something fierce and unrelenting. But also, something that looked like surrender.

She grabbed her clothes from the floor, pulling them on with shaky hands.

He watched from the door as she walked down the dirt path, the midday heat blurring the edges of her figure. His chest rose and fell like he'd just faced down an opponent ten times her size. An army of his own emotions was doing battle.

The winner was loss, a feeling of crushing bereavement. Of something priceless shattering right in front of him.

FIFTEEN

DANIEL RATTLED the wrought-iron bars of the security gate, then stumbled backward into the gravel parking lot. It was past midnight. Martín's restaurant was shuttered, dark, and silent.

He tipped his head back, eyes searching the second-floor windows. "¡Sebastián! *¡Órale!*"

A minute later, a shadow moved behind the glass. Then the sound of locks clicking open—first one, then two chains sliding free. The door creaked, and Sebastián appeared in the dim hallway, arms crossed. He eyed Daniel from head to toe. *"Estás pedo, güey."*

Daniel was drunk. He lifted the bottle of bourbon by its neck and shrugged. "Getting there."

Sebastián didn't move. Another figure appeared behind him—taller, older than Sebastián, younger than Daniel. He was pulling on a t-shirt as he stepped into the light.

Daniel watched as Sebastián turned toward him, and they shared a brief kiss before the guy headed out the door and jogged down the steps. He passed Daniel with an unreadable glance before disappearing across the lot.

Daniel turned back, raising an eyebrow. "That Caleb?"

Sebastián nodded.

Daniel snorted and gave his brother a playful shove. "He come to get his book back?"

Sebastián just looked him up and down. "I take it you and Julia are over."

Daniel rubbed a hand over the scruff on his jaw. "*Mierda.*"

Three days had passed since that morning in his trailer, and each one had been progressively worse.

He let the door bang shut behind him and climbed the stairs, trailing after his brother. When they reached the room, he uncapped the bottle and took another swig before slumping to the floor beneath the window. The bourbon burned warm and cheap down his throat. He held the bottle out, and Sebastián took it, hesitating only a second before drinking.

Daniel fished a joint from his pocket, rolling it between his fingers. He planned on getting so drunk and so high that he wouldn't have to feel anything, not until tomorrow at least.

Before he could light it, Sebastián muttered, "You know Martín freaks when you smoke in here."

Daniel exhaled sharply and shoved the joint back into his pocket. He leaned his head against the windowsill. "I always knew I was gonna fuck this up."

Sebastián didn't say anything. Just took another sip of bourbon, grimacing like he regretted it.

The silence stretched between them. A streetlamp outside cast slanted gold light through the threadbare curtains, illuminating one side of Sebastián's face.

Daniel stared at the bottle in his hands. "You remember when we finally got to LA? After that fucking bus ride from Tucson?" He took another drink. "I had to give the driver Dad's Rolex and two of Mom's gold necklaces just to get us on board. Fare was probably forty bucks, but he saw two unaccompanied Mexican kids and figured he could take us for a fucking ride."

Sebastián stayed quiet.

Daniel let out a soft, humorless chuckle. "And when we finally got here, we had nowhere to sleep, so I stole that car from the bus terminal."

Sebastián's voice was quiet. "I don't remember any of that."

"You were, what, four? Still crying for Mom and Dad every night." Daniel turned the bottle in his hands. "So, I told you this was how people in America lived. That everyone slept in their cars so they could wake up someplace new every day."

He glanced at his brother, a half-smile tugging at his lips. "But you called bullshit on me right away. Told me people here don't live in their cars. They live in houses, same as people in México. And that's when I knew—shit, this kid is gonna be way smarter than me one day."

Sebastián's face was unreadable, but his voice was thinner than before when he said, "I remember you singing 'Macochi Pitentzin' to me when I couldn't sleep."

Daniel smiled. "You remember that?"

Sebastián nodded.

"You remember Mamá singing it to you?"

A pause. Then, quietly, "Maybe."

Daniel exhaled. Took another drink. Passed the bottle back. This time, Sebastián didn't wince as he swallowed.

"Then we ran out of gas," Daniel continued. "So, I dumped the car and was in the middle of lifting us another one when this huge guy comes running out of a tattoo shop across the street. He had an aluminum bat, and was shouting like a crazy motherfucker. I froze. Thought, this is it. This is how I die."

Sebastián listened, silent.

"But he didn't hit me," Daniel said, shaking his head. "Just grabbed me by the scruff and told me that if I was gonna steal cars, I needed to learn how to do a better fucking job of it." He reached across, taking the bottle back. "And that's how we met Terry."

Neither of them spoke for a long time after that. They just drank together in silence.

After a while, Daniel stretched his legs out and said, "You

know how I told you that once the 'Cuda was finished, and I had enough saved up, we'd be outta here?"

Sebastián stared at him. "We're leaving?"

Daniel nodded.

"All of it?"

By which he meant the gang. The drugs. Terry.

"All of it," Daniel said. "For good this time."

Sebastián was quiet. Then: "When?"

"Not tomorrow." Daniel looked down at the empty bottle. "But soon. Real soon."

Sebastián didn't respond right away. Then he turned and met Daniel's eyes. "What about Julia?"

Daniel squeezed his fingers against his temples. The thought of never seeing Julia again hit him in the chest like a physical blow.

He forced himself to his feet. It was harder than expected, and he had to grip the windowsill for balance. "I told you," he slurred. "It's over."

He was halfway to the door when Sebastián called after him.

"*¿Y a dónde vamos a ir, Dani?*"

"Where?" Daniel turned back, his voice quiet but certain. "*Nos vamos a casa, hermanito.*"

We're gonna go find someplace we can finally call home.

———

Everything was perfect. The bride looked beautiful in bespoke Dior, her six-foot train of handmade French lace trailing behind her down the rose petal-strewn aisle of the huge marque. The groomsmen all looked handsome in their tailored suits, the groom wiping away a tear as his bride approached. Proudly watching from the front row, the mother-of-the-bride wore a custom Versace gown, while the stepfather-of-the-bride looked regal in his kilt. Five hundred impeccably dressed guests filled the remaining marquee space. A string-quartet played Elvis's "Can't Help Falling In Love".

Julia stood stiffly on the dais, clutching her bouquet of pink roses to her chest and trying very hard not to cry. It was only when Natalie was gazing lovingly into Carter's eyes and saying "I do" that she couldn't hold back the dam any longer.

She dabbed at her eyes with the corner of a tissue, hoping everyone would just assume they were tears of joy. The main thing was to not ruin her makeup. It had taken two hours to apply and if she wasn't careful, it would be dripping off her chin before the ceremony was even over. Her mother was already eying her from her seat in a way that seemed to say, *pull yourself together*. The wedding had cost a small fortune—actually, quite a big one— and no one wanted it ruined by one bawling bridesmaid.

Finally, they signed the papers, and the ceremony ended. The reception was being held in the house, with a live band performing in the newly renovated gazebo. Julia made a beeline for the champagne table. She hardly ever drank alcohol. After that boozy night out in the city that had ended so disastrously, she'd quit the stuff altogether.

She was now reevaluating that decision. Double-fisting flutes of Dom Perignon, she looked around for a quiet spot where she could get drunk in peace.

Her studio seemed like the perfect place. She could curl up on the couch and cry properly, without worrying about her makeup. That was all she had been doing these past three days, anyway. Sleeping in his sweatshirt and crying in her studio. Stirring only when she heard a loud car engine. Then, when realizing that it wasn't the 'Cuda, sinking back down into her depression.

She wished now that she'd never found out what she had about him. That she'd never gone prying into his things. Gone opening boxes in her mind that she'd vowed to keep sealed shut. Her ignorance had been bliss. And now she could never get it back.

Gripping her glasses, she started making her way out to the

pool area. But it was like being stuck in one of those video games where obstacles kept popping up to block your path. Distant family members kept accosting her, telling her how beautiful she and her sister looked. Complete strangers came up to her, feeling it was their sudden duty to inform her that one day she, too, would get to walk down the aisle in a big white dress. A photographer stopped her to take her photo, which she wished she'd refused. She didn't want Natalie's wedding album to contain a snap of her standing there with smeared mascara and holding two empty champagne flutes like a lush.

A groomsman intercepted her and tried to start a conversation. He might have been flirting with her, but she wasn't paying enough attention to be sure.

By that point, both her glasses now being empty, she realized she need the bathroom. Glad for the excuse to get away from the groomsman, she diverted her course to one of the downstairs guest bathrooms.

She bent over the sink, washing her hands, when a wave of crippling pain hit her again. She missed Daniel more than she thought she could miss anyone. And it hurt, physically. It ached in her bones. Even her skin hurt; it was like all those pheromones had soured into neurotoxins and were now poisoning her from the inside out.

She wondered if he had been thinking about her as much as she'd been thinking about him. Or if he'd moved on already. He'd told her he loved her. But then, she knew nothing about love. Except that she sucked at it.

She turned off the tap and stood there, head bowed over the sink, tears dripping off the end of her nose.

The bathroom door opened, and someone came in.

"Oh, excuse me," said a woman's voice.

Julia straightened, hiding her tear-stained face. "I'm all done here now."

She didn't want to go back out there looking like this, but now she'd have to. She grabbed her clutch bag and tried to leave, but the woman was blocking her way. In her hand was a pack of tissues.

"Weddings always get me going," she said.

Julia forced a smile and took the offered tissue.

The woman put the pack back into her leather satchel bag. "Although, I feel like those ain't happy tears."

Julia swallowed but said nothing. With the tissue, she dabbed her face and studied the woman more closely. She was Black, fifty-ish, with short graying hair. Her attire was not exactly wedding appropriate. She had on a crumpled jacket, a white shirt with a faint pink stain on the right side and black pants. The leather satchel on her hip. She looked like she was on her way to a very boring business meeting.

"Boyfriend trouble?" she said.

Julia continued to say nothing. A feeling of uneasiness crept over her. There was something not quite right about this woman.

She seemed to sense Julia's disquiet and smiled. "My name's Belinda," she said, pulling something out of her satchel. "I'm a Special Agent with the U.S. Drug Enforcement Administration." She held open a leather wallet containing an ID that confirmed that fact. "And if you don't mind, Julia, I'd like to have a little chat with you."

"With me?" Julia shook her head. "Why?"

That small smile again. "It's about your boyfriend."

SIXTEEN

"DANIEL?"

Julia reached up and tapped on the door of his trailer. She called his name softly again. No response.

His car was here, but the trailer's lights were off, and the curtains were closed. She had a sudden, terrible feeling that he was here, but he wasn't alone.

The thought of that felt like a hot poker being jammed into her gut. And then twisted. The pain brought a fresh wave of tears to her eyes.

Coming here in the middle of the night wasn't just stupid, it was potentially heartbreaking. As if her heart needed any more of that.

But she'd had to. After she'd escaped from the DEA woman in the bathroom, she'd come straight here, not even taking the time to get changed. She'd just hugged her sister goodbye and fled the party before anyone could stop her.

She just knew she needed to see him. To tell him he was in serious trouble.

Except now, it seemed like it had been a wasted trip.

She descended the steps to the grass. The full moon illuminated the area better than streetlights. Tequila whined and wagged her tail from her bed on the grass nearby. Julia went over and gave her a pat. On cue, the dog started drooling on custom Valentino.

"You have good taste, girl," Julia whispered.

Behind her, the trailer door opened, and a wedge of light fell out onto the grass.

"Julia?" Daniel's voice was soft. "What are you doing here? It's the middle of the night."

She whirled around. Opened her mouth to speak, but all she could do was stare at him. He was standing in the doorway, one arm propped against the jamb. Barefoot and shirtless, just wearing low-slung loose jeans over white briefs, the glint of silver from the chain at his neck.

"Daniel, I…" She trailed off, just letting her eyes drink their fill of him. It had only been three days since she'd last seen him, but God, that had been too long. One second felt like too long. Blinking felt like too long.

His eyes tracked over her too, taking in her dress, her shoes dangling from one hand. His gaze shifted from the street, then back to her. "Where's your car?"

"I didn't drive."

"Why not?"

"I… I had two glasses of champagne."

He looked away quickly, like he was trying to hide a smile. "How'd you get here then?"

"A taxi. Two, actually. The Lake Forest guy wouldn't take me west of Chinatown. Not at this time of night."

He straightened from the doorjamb. "Baby. You should have called me. I'd have come pick you up."

Maybe it was hearing him call her 'baby' again or maybe it was the low concern in his voice, but she felt like crying all over again. "You would have?" she said in a small voice.

A tremor of emotion moved across his face. "You know I would have."

She practically ran up the steps. He moved back, letting her in. Kicked the door shut with his heel behind her.

They stood and stared at each other under the yellow light of the single overhead bulb. They were both breathing heavily, even though neither of them had said anything yet.

Julia tried to remember what she'd come here to tell him, but when she opened her mouth, those words weren't the ones that came tumbling out.

"Daniel, I'm sorry. About everything I said. If you thought I was judging you, because I wasn't. I mean, maybe I was, but..." She shook her head, frustrated that none of the words were coming out right. She couldn't afford to mess this up again by saying the wrong thing.

She exhaled. 'I know I'll never know what it's like to be you. I know my life is impossibly privileged and that I have about as much right to judge you as...as... Well, I have no right to judge anyone."

He said nothing for a long moment, and she thought she might have offended him even more with her little speech. Then he said bluntly, "Are you done?"

She opened her mouth, closed it, then said, "Yes."

"Good."

He crossed the space between them, gripped the back of her head with one hand, and kissed her. Hard. She could feel his stubble grazing her cheek, the edge of his teeth against her lips.

He broke it off but continued to grip the back of her head, his hand wrist deep in her hair. He said in a low, urgent tone, right against her mouth, "Fuck, I missed you."

Both his hands cradled the sides of her head as he turned her face up to his and kissed her again. Softer this time, but no less intense, his tongue caressing hers until she moaned against his mouth.

His hands slid down her hair to run down her shoulders and across her back. His fingers found the zip at the back of her gown and gripped it. He pulled away from the kiss to look at her, a question in his eyes.

She nodded.

He unzipped her dress. Pushed it down, and it slid off her in a sigh of silk and tulle.

There was a long pause as his eyes took her in. He looked adorably dismayed. Like a kid on Christmas morning who'd just unwrapped his present, only to find it wasn't what he wanted. He looked back up at her and gave his head a little shake as if to say, what the fuck?

"It's called shapewear," she said, unable to keep the amusement out of her voice.

He stepped back and stared at it in horror. "How do I get it off you?"

She laughed at the urgency in his tone. "Daniel, it's not a bomb vest."

"Fucking looks like one," he grumbled.

"It's not that difficult. Look, you just unhook it here…and then tug this bit here off…and then yank this part down…"

He shook his head, looked very grumpy. "Fuck this. I'm gonna go get some scissors."

She got it off without him having to resort to any drastic action. He watched her, arms crossed. "How do you go to the bathroom in all this?"

"Not easily."

"Baby, what do you need shapewear for, anyway? Your shape is perfect."

She kicked the last of it away. "Not according to my mother."

She was now naked, and his expression was one of pure male lust. He was reaching for her even before he'd closed the gap between them.

In a sudden movement, he cupped her butt with both hands and lifted her, then carried her backwards until she was pressed against his wardrobe door. He kept her pinned there with just his hips, his forearms bracing against the wood on either side of her head. The only other thing pinning her in place was his mouth. He groaned, and she felt it in the back of her throat.

She clung to him, arms and legs, like a koala to a tree. No way was she coming down. He straightened, dropping one arm to rather expertly unbutton his jeans with one hand. Just as she felt him pressing against her, he broke off the kiss. Maintaining eye contact with her, he guided himself inside her. Her body resisted him at first, then relented with a sharp thrill.

They both drew in quick breaths, exhaling into each other's mouths. He held her gaze the whole time, and it was so intimate. She couldn't imagine being closer to another human being.

"Please don't ever leave me again," he whispered.

She pressed her lips to his. "Please don't ever let me."

———

She trailed her fingers over the words that ran around his collarbone. THE WILL TO LIVE IS THE WILL TO DIE.

"What does it mean?"

Daniel had his arm flung over his eyes. He made a sound halfway between a groan and a sigh, lifted his arm and eyed her. 'It means the things that people want to stay alive for are the same things that they'd be prepared to die for. Money. Power. Family. It's, uh, what do you call it? *Una paradoja.*"

"A paradox?"

He nodded.

She looked down at the black hand print on his chest. Stop, it seemed to say. Do not approach. She pressed her hand over it. Dug her fingers in, her nails indenting his skin. Then she ran her nails over his chest, over the dark dusting of hair that grew thicker below his navel and ran down beneath the waistband of his jeans.

She said, "You should get a tattoo of my name."

He shrugged one shoulder. "Just tell me where you want it."

She regarded his upper body, which was pretty well covered.

"My ass cheek is free," he said helpfully.

She laughed. "Alright. Then everyone will know that your ass belongs to me."

He'd gotten hard again between her thighs. "Apparently, my dick already does. You might as well have the set."

She smiled, then lowered herself down onto him, resting her chin on his chest. "Do you want me to get a tattoo of your name?"

"No." He ran his hands up the backs of her thighs. "Because I already know that every single part of you belongs to me."

————

Moonlight slipped through a crack in the curtains, tracing silver strands in Julia's hair, making them glow. Her head rested on Daniel's shoulder, the rest of her curled against his side, their legs tangled together.

For a while, they just lay there, the quiet wrapping around them. Only their breathing and the distant hum of the city filled the space between them.

Something shifted in her expression, her eyes turning distant, as if suddenly lost in thought. A tiny crease formed between her brows.

A prickle of unease tightened in his stomach. "Baby, what is it?"

She looked up at him. "Daniel," she whispered. "There's something I still haven't told you."

————

Daniel's eyes were tracking over her face like he'd never seen it before. "And this Belinda woman said she works for the DEA?"

Julia hugged the sheet to her chest. "She cornered me in the bathroom at the wedding. She knew all about you. And me. And us being together." She chewed the inside of her cheek and added,

"She said that if I refused to talk to them, I could get in big trouble. That they could make me talk to them."

Daniel was still watching her intently. She sat forward again and placed her hand on his back. "I got out of there straight away and called a taxi and came here. I didn't tell her anything. I didn't even know most of the stuff she was asking me, and even if I did, I wouldn't have told her."

He twisted around and silenced her with a kiss on the mouth. "Baby, it's okay. I know you wouldn't rat on me." He placed a hand on her cheek. "I trust you."

She smiled, feeling herself relax.

He exhaled and turned back around, resting his elbows on his knees. "What I wanna know is how the fuck the DEA found out about us." He turned and swung his legs out of the bed. "It's not like we advertised it. The only places we've been together are your house, my trailer, Martín's restaurant, and that one time at the mercado. And the only person who sprung us down there was Milo, and that little shit doesn't have the balls to cross Terry and go snitching to the feds."

She didn't know who Milo was, so she said nothing.

Daniel went on, "Obviously Sebastián knew, but he'd never tell anyone."

She interrupted him. "Martín knows. When Sebastián and I were at the restaurant together, Sebastián introduced me to him as your girlfriend. He spoke in Spanish, but I'm pretty sure that's what he said."

"*Mierda.*" He kneaded his forehead. "You know what they're gonna do, right?" He looked back at Julia. "They're gonna try to turn you against me. Then they're gonna use you to get to me."

She'd already worked that out over the course of her two taxi rides. The shock of that realization had worn off, but it was still weird to think that government agents were looking at her like some kind of gangster's moll.

She crawled out of bed and closer to him. Placed a hand on the back of his head and turned it to face her. "They can try all they want. They'll never turn me against you."

His face softened. He leaned over and kissed her cheek, then tucked some hair behind her ear. "I know they won't. But I don't want them to even try. I don't want any of this shit coming anywhere near you."

She smiled, but it was tight-lipped and faded fast. Some of her anxiety had subsided, but there was still something that was gnawing at her. It had been gnawing at her for weeks, and she knew she had to confront it at last.

"Daniel. You need to tell me what this is all about. What you're involved in that's so bad."

He shook his head. "Julia, I can't."

Her voice was soft but firm. "Like it or not, we're in this together now."

He pressed his fingers into his eye sockets and said nothing for a long moment. Then he dragged his hand down his face, cupping his hand over his mouth. Finally, he turned to her, dropped his hand, and began to speak. She reached for his arm, bracing herself to hold on no matter what he said.

———

Daniel told her about the heroin, about its journey from the poppy fields of the Sierra Madre Occidental as raw opium paste, arriving at the border at Ciudad Juárez as pure China White. How it got carefully weighed and wrapped in glassine on long tables in an old dartboard factory, under the watchful eye of José "El Merc" Ferrera and his army of cartel soldiers. How the product then got loaded onto pallets in the guise of various unassuming items. Crap no one would look twice at. Like cassette tapes and ballpoint pens and waterbeds.

How smugglers then moved it north in the back of freight haulers, and how those vehicles arrived at InterTruck for routine servicing. How the product then made its way to buyers like the

Sokolovs. The Russians cut the keys down further, then further again, until it wound up on the street in the hands of the lowest level dealers of all.

And he told her about how he was just a cog in that wheel, a middleman. A guy who got shit done for Terry, who got shit done for *los jefes* back in L.A. Who in turn got shit done for the bosses even higher up the food chain than them.

Until about a year ago, that was Daniel's life, and he had accepted it. Death, prison, or deportation were the only endings to his story. Every year beyond fourteen had been a roll of the dice. If he made it to twenty-seven, he'd consider himself practically elderly.

But then Terry started sniffing around Sebastián. Making comments about bringing him into the gang. Soon, he'd be expecting his brother to start pulling shifts at InterTruck. Terry knew how smart his little brother was and was angling to put his brains to good use on the ledgers.

And it was then that he knew he had to get out. To get them both out.

So, for the past year, after every deal, he'd started skimming a little off the top. A couple of bills here and there, stuffed into the gym bag that she'd found in his wardrobe. He always adjusted the ledgers when he got back to base. He never took a lot. Never enough for Terry or Paq to notice.

I hope, he thought.

Julia listened to all of it. He kept his eyes glued to the ceiling. He didn't want to see her expression. He didn't want to watch as whatever good impressions she'd had of him were buried forever. Buried where they belonged.

After he'd finished talking, she was quiet for a long moment, digesting it all.

He closed his eyes, so he didn't have to see her eyes peering into his soul. He still felt them, though. And he felt her cool hand on his cheek, turning his face so he couldn't hide from her anymore.

"I'm getting out, Julia," he said, his voice flat. "That's what the money in the bag is for. Severance pay. I'm done with this life, and I'm taking Seb with me."

She frowned. "What changed?"

He sat up in bed, elbows resting on his knees, staring at the floor. "My brother is gay."

Julia sat up too, watching him. "And that's a problem?"

He shook his head. "Not to me. But in my world, baby, it's a death sentence." His fingers dragged over his face. "I saw a guy get killed right in front of me just because there was a rumor he was gay." His voice trailed off. His fingertips pressed hard into his eye sockets, as if he could erase the memory by force.

He knew what would happen if Terry got his claws into Seb. If the truth got out. It would end in blood.

His throat tightened as he looked at Julia. "Seb doesn't belong in this life. He's got too much ahead of him to be stuck slinging drugs. Or scrubbing dishes just to get by."

She moved closer, resting a tentative hand on his back. "So do you."

He said nothing. He didn't know what he had to offer the world. No one had ever given him the chance to figure that out. His life had been a fight for survival since the day he set foot on American soil.

Julia hesitated, then said, "There's that thing all the politicians have been talking about. DACA. It's for people who came here as kids. It lets them stay, work legally, get real jobs."

He turned his head slightly. "I know what it is. Sebastián's already an expert on it, trust me."

He'd thought about it, more than he wanted to admit. But his own record meant the door was closed to him. For Sebastián, though, it was different. For the first time in years, something like hope had started creeping in. The idea that maybe, just maybe, there was a way out. A way forward. If not for him, then at least for his little brother.

"But first," he said, "we gotta get the fuck out of here. Far away. Somewhere Terry can't find us. Somewhere the gang doesn't have a toehold. Somewhere we can start over. For real this time."

Julia's voice was soft. "When?"

Daniel sighed. "Soon. Real soon. I got a bad feeling that Terry already suspects something's going on with me. He keeps making these cryptic little comments."

He thought about what Borya Sokolov had said to him. Right after he'd told Daniel that his brother Sasha had deserved a bullet in his head because he'd been stealing from the business.

Terry said you got the message.

He looked at Julia. "If he ever found out I've been taking money from him. It would be the end." He didn't want to scare her with the truth. *If he ever found out, they'll never find all the pieces of me.* What he'd then do to Sebastián didn't even bear thinking about.

She wrapped her arms tightly around him, the heat of her bare skin setting a fire in his lower body. "So, we go. Like you planned. Together, and now."

He looked at her, his face just a few inches from hers. "I can't ask you to do that."

She smiled. Placed her hand on his cheek. "Daniel, I barely survived three days without you. So don't you dare think of leaving me behind again."

———

Something flashed through his eyes. Something that looked almost like pain. And she knew his last three days must have been pretty rough, too.

He dropped his head, shook it. "You have a whole life here. Your family's here."

"My life is with you." They felt like the truest words she'd ever spoken.

His face creased. "But your ballet."

"I can join another company. Or…" she let the word hang there, carrying with it possibilities she'd never had the courage to consider before. "I can do something else."

He still looked unconvinced, so she tried another tack. "If that DEA woman found out about me, then it means this Terry guy could, too. And if you just up and leave me here, he'll find me. He'll use me to get to you."

He turned to look at her, and his expression was grim. "I think he already knows about you."

A literal chill ran up her spine.

"I'm sorry," he whispered. "I told you I'd protect you from all this stuff and I haven't."

She put her hand on the back of his head, caressing the soft bristles of his cropped hair. "You are protecting me. You're getting out. We're getting out."

He was watching her seriously. "Are you sure about this? Because when we go, we won't be coming back."

She hesitated. Just for a moment. Long enough to picture her mom and sister's faces when they realized she was gone. The spartan studio where she'd spent half her life. The dream she'd clung to, chipped and imperfect as it was.

But then she looked at him—really looked at him—and all that noise quieted. "I've never been surer of anything in my life."

And, God help her, she meant it.

He nodded. "Okay. So we go."

"Where?"

"Texas. Corpus Christi. I have a cousin who lives there. He's legit. He'll help us out."

"When?"

He glanced at the curtains, where the first tinge of dawn was showing between the cracks. "Today."

She took a deep breath. So deep it hurt her chest. "Okay."

"We'll need your car and the 'Cuda. Both only have two seats, and we have four passengers."

"Four?"

"I'm not leaving Tequila behind."

She nodded. He got up and started pacing the small space. She could feel the nervous energy radiating off him. It was radiating off her, too.

"Go back home, pack everything you need. But not too much. We don't got a lot of trunk space."

She pushed the sheets away. "We'll need more money. We're going to have to start again, right? All of us, from scratch." She looked up at him. "I have my credit cards, money in my accounts."

He shook his head. "You won't be able to use any of that when we get to where we're going. They'll be the first things the feds will try to trace."

The feds. The word struck her like cold water. Of course she'd known, somewhere in the back of her mind, that what they were doing was illegal. Dangerous. But hearing it out loud made it real. This wasn't just sneaking off into the night. It was going on the run. From the government.

Her breath caught for a second. But then she looked at Daniel pacing like a caged animal, carrying too much weigh on his shoulders for someone so young, and she realized that he'd been living with this fear for most of his life.

At least now, he wouldn't have to do it alone.

"What are you going to tell your family?" he asked.

She swallowed a dry lump. "Nothing."

He closed his mouth, then ran a hand over his head. "You're not gonna tell them you're leaving?"

She pressed her hand to her forehead and looked up at him. "It'll be safer if I don't. For everyone."

He didn't seem happy with her answer, even though she could tell he knew it was probably the truth. She added softly, "Maybe I'll send them a postcard from Texas. When we're settled and everyone's calmed down."

Daniel shook his head immediately. "No postcards. Too easy to trace."

Her throat tightened, but she nodded. Even that small comfort was too dangerous.

He heaved a sigh. "From here on out, baby, it's us against the world. No credit cards. No contacting anyone. I'll swap out the 'Cuda's plates on the way. When we get closer to Texas, I'll offload it somewhere out of state. Too hot to sell nearby."

Her head snapped up. "What? No."

"She's worth at least forty grand. We might need that in case I can't find work right away."

"But she's your ride or die."

He looked down at her, his moss-colored eyes bright even in the semi-darkness. "Baby, you're my ride or die."

A tremor of emotion moved through her. It was love, a great quake of it, enough to shake her to her bones. She'd go with him anywhere, live however they had to, so long as she was with him.

She said, "I have some jewelry we could sell. Some diamond earrings, a Cartier watch. And a Piaget ring. Eighteen karat gold and diamond. Must be worth a bit."

"I'll replace it," he blurted.

She made a face, annoyed that he even had to think about that. "No, Daniel. God, I don't even wear it."

But he'd already turned around and opened his wardrobe. He began searching the upper shelf, shoving things aside and swearing in Spanish.

When he found what he was looking for, he turned back around and sat next to her on the bed.

"You'll wear this though, right? If I asked you to?"

She looked down at what he was holding. It was a gold ring. In the center was a blood red ruby, surrounded by tiny chips of diamonds. Not a Piaget, but easily as beautiful.

"Daniel," she breathed, suddenly feeling lightheaded. "What exactly are you asking me?"

He got off the bed and knelt on the floor of the trailer at her feet. Said in a soft voice, "I'm asking you to marry me, baby."

"Yes," she said instantly.

He looked down at the ring in his palm. "It was my *abuela's*, then my *mamá's*." He reached out, taking her hand and placing it on her finger. "And now it is yours."

She looked up at him, tears forming in the backs of her eyes. "I love you."

He placed a hand on the back of her head and kissed her so deeply, she felt the thrill down to her toes. Then, when it was over, he rested his forehead against hers and whispered, "I love you, too."

She placed a hand on his cheek. "That night. That I met you. Here, in this trailer. I thought it was the worst night of my life." The tears spilled over and ran down her cheeks. "Turns out it was the best."

SEVENTEEN

EVENTUALLY, they had to leave the safety of their cocoon and make a proper plan for the day. A plan that would involve Daniel driving them both to La Villita, where she would catch a taxi back to her house. She would pack a suitcase, then drive to the Joffrey Tower downtown and clean out her locker and her dressing room. She'd email her resignation to the ballet company when they got to Texas.

Daniel, meanwhile, would go to the restaurant and tell Sebastián their plan, before returning to the trailer and packing up his own stuff. They agreed to meet again at twilight at the secluded beach in Lake Forest, where they'd had their first kiss.

He gave her one now, in the middle of bustling West 26th, between street carts selling *elotes* and *aguas frescas*. She was wearing last night's dress. Its hem was bunched up in one hand, her bare feet showing.

"*Hoy vamos a comenzar una nueva vida, cariño,*" he murmured, pressing his forehead to hers. "Today we start a new life."

She smiled, the kind of smile she couldn't hold back if she tried. As she turned and jogged toward a waiting taxi, she had a feeling of floating. She was going to live in Texas with Daniel and Sebastián. They were going to get married and be a family. A family that had never existed before, one that they had made up only out of the separate parts of each other.

———

The taxi pulled up across from the house, and Julia hesitated before stepping out, her heels dangling from her fingers. The morning sun cut long shadows over the manicured lawn.

She held her breath as she opened the front door. The house was awake and busy, with cleaning staff moving through rooms, and workers on ladders taking down the floral arrangements. From the kitchen came the clinking of what must have been a hundred champagne glasses being washed.

Her mother was nowhere in sight.

In her bedroom, she stripped off the ruined dress and stepped into the shower, washing the lingering scent of Daniel from her skin. Dressed and made up, she dragged out her suitcase, throwing in what she'd need for Texas. No to knitwear, coats, and scarves. Yes to sundresses, tank tops, and jeans. She upended her jewelry box, tossed in a couple of designer clutch bags, and grabbed shoes she could sell online.

She shoved it all into the suitcase and turned for the door.

And stopped.

"Mom."

She stood in the doorway, arms crossed, flawless as ever at eight in the morning.

Julia's stomach clenched.

"Well," her mother said coolly. "That was quite the stunt you pulled. Walking out on your sister's wedding."

Julia swallowed, her pulse hammering. "I—"

"You could have at least waited until the cake was cut."

Julia forced a breath. "Why? It's not like I could have eaten any of it."

For the briefest moment, something flickered across her mother's face, but it was gone before Julia could name it. Her gaze dropped to the suitcase. "Where are you going?"

Julia's fingers tightened around the handle. "I'm moving out."

Her mom's tone was incredulous. "Today?"

"I'm twenty-two, Mom. I think it's time."

Her mother's head tilted slightly, assessing. "With only one suitcase?"

Julia stepped forward, determined to push past her if she had to.

"You're going with that boy, aren't you?"

Julia stopped mid-step.

Her mother scoffed softly. "You think I haven't noticed? Sneaking out at night. Skipping practice in the morning. The bruises on your neck. The smell of marijuana on your clothes."

Julia's jaw clenched. "You don't notice anything about me, Mom. Not since I was twelve. Not since Natalie started showing more promise than me."

Her mother exhaled, long and slow. "That isn't true."

Julia met her mother's eyes and held the gaze. "Isn't it?"

For the first time, her mother looked at her—really looked at her. And the anger in her face shifted. It was still sharp, still cutting, but now edged with something Julia hadn't expected.

Worry.

For a second, it threw her.

She wasn't used to her mother caring what she did, only how she appeared while doing it. The worry looked out of place on her face, like it didn't quite belong there. And yet, it was there. Real. Raw. Julia blinked, and for just a breath of a moment, she felt something soften in her chest.

Was I wrong about her?

Has she always cared, just never shown it the way I needed her to?

But then the steel came back into her mother's posture, the lines of judgment reforming like armor, and the flicker of connection vanished as quickly as it had come.

Her mother straightened. "So you're just leaving? Throwing everything away? Your ballet, too?"

Her hands trembled, her whole body wired with adrenaline, but beneath the fear was something else—a lightness, a strange, intoxicating sense of relief.

She met her mother's gaze, her voice steadier than she thought possible. "Ballet was always your dream, Mom. I think we both know it was never mine."

She descended the stairs, shoulders squared, forcing herself to believe she was making the right choice. The weight of her mother's disappointment pressed against her back, but ahead was something else.

Freedom.

Sliding into her BMW, she pulled out of the drive and onto the narrow lanes of Lake Forest. Her heart was still hammering from the confrontation, but already she felt lighter.

The trees lining the road cast long morning shadows, their leaves rustling in the warm breeze. She rolled the window down, letting the fresh air hit her face as she turned onto the highway. Every mile she put between herself and that house felt like peeling off another layer of suffocating expectations.

Then, in the rearview mirror, she spotted it.

A black SUV.

Her stomach clenched. It was probably nothing. Just another car on the road. But something about it, its dark-tinted windows, the way it hugged the lane behind her, made her uneasy.

She switched lanes. So did the SUV.

Her pulse quickened.

She eased her foot onto the gas, putting some distance between them. After a few bends, it disappeared from view. She exhaled, rolling her shoulders. Just paranoia.

But when she glanced in the mirror again—

The SUV was back.

Still behind her.

Her fingers tightened around the wheel. Could be a coincidence. Could be nothing.

She slowed slightly, hoping it would pass. It didn't.

Her heartbeat slammed against her ribs.

Trying to keep her breathing steady, she took the next exit, weaving onto a quieter stretch of road. She checked the mirror.

The SUV followed.

A trickle of sweat ran down her back.

She signaled right. The SUV signaled right.

Okay. Not paranoia. Not a coincidence.

She could hear her own breathing now, sharp and fast. Her mind raced through possibilities. Carjackers? No, too polished, too precise. A private investigator hired by her mother? Maybe.

Then she saw the plates.

Government.

Her breath hitched.

Red and blue strobes flared along the windshield and grille.

Shit.

Her foot hovered over the accelerator. Run? Try to lose them on the way into the city?

No. That was stupid. She'd wrap her car around a tree and end up in jail for fleeing a federal agent.

Adrenaline made her movements jerky, but she forced her foot onto the brake. Indicated. Pulled over. Prayed they would pass.

They didn't.

The SUV stopped behind her. A woman stepped out.

She was Black. Cropped, graying hair. A crinkled shirt with a pink stain on the front.

Julia closed her eyes. Whatever this was, it wasn't good. Not for her. Not for Daniel.

The woman reached the window, glancing between Julia and the suitcase on the passenger seat.

"Gee," she said, dryly. "I hope you weren't planning on going somewhere."

EIGHTEEN

Julia stared up at the camera that sat on the ceiling like a giant fly, red light blinking fiendishly. Fluorescent lights buzzed overhead. It must have been over an hour since they'd left her in this room, so narrow she could almost touch both walls with outstretched arms, with only a cup of water for company. Two plastic chairs faced her over a wonky trestle table, scarred over with gang graffiti.

The center of the table was claimed by tags from the usual suspects: the Vice Lords, *La Mano Negra*, the Gangster Disciples, the Latin Kings. There were, however, a few scribblings from unaffiliated outsiders. One was a little etching of a police officer being shot in the neck, complete with arterial spray and wafting gun smoke. She ran her hand over it, feeling the grooves etched deeply into the Formica surface. She could tell the victim was a cop because the artist had taken the time to chisel the word PIG above the dying stick figure's head and a triumphant ME over the smiling assassin. Probably not admissible in court, but still not smart to be decorating a table with in an CPD interrogation facility in Holman Square.

She wasn't under arrest. No one had specified any charges or read her rights. But then, she wasn't sure if DEA agents even did those things. What they had done was take her bag and phone off her, which meant she didn't know the time and no way of contacting anyone, even if she was under arrest. Each passing second stretched into an eternity.

Somewhere down a hall, she heard a toilet flushing, a door banging shut. Footsteps approached, voices sprang up outside the door. Then the door opened with a whoosh, sucking the stale air out of the room.

In came Special Agent Belinda Weck, buried behind an armload of binders. She shuffled into the room and unloaded the stack onto the table, dropping a leather satchel on top for good measure. Plastic cards and keys jingled from a lanyard around her neck.

Entering the room behind her was a man. He was Black, too, and wearing a suit that was so sharp it could have drawn blood. Compared to the parade of crumpled, stubbled and sweat-stained people she'd seen in the hallways of this place, this guy looked like he had just stepped out of the pages of GQ.

Weck jerked her head at the man. "This is my colleague, AUSA Malcolm Oates."

"Are you going to explain any of this to me?" Julia said. "Or is the suspense supposed to kill me?"

Weck didn't answer; she was too busy rummaging in her bag, occasionally coming up with items of interest. A yellow legal pad, a cellphone, a pair of blue-rimmed reading glasses.

Julia eyed the largest binder on the table. It was stamped with some kind of government crest and encircled by a long string of letters. She read them upside down: OCDETF.

Weck noticed her interest. "Organized Crime Drug Enforcement Task Force," she translated, taking her seat.

Catchy, Julia thought.

"We are part of a Chicago Strike Force of combined law enforcement agencies, whose job is to target CPOTs." She had put on the glasses; they magnified the clumps of mascara that had settled into the creases beneath her eyes. "Those are what call Consolidated Priority Targets. Or what others like to call drug lords."

She took a breath, tried to pull herself together. "Well, I'm a ballet dancer. And I'm afraid I don't know any drug lords."

Weck was tapping her pen on the pad. Her gaze went to the ring on Julia's finger. "That's not strictly true though, is it?"

Julia covered the ring up with her other hand and said nothing.

Oates said, "Just how much do you know about your new fiancé, Miss Mikkelsen?"

Julia reached out a shaking hand for the cup and took a sip of water. It was warm and tasted like plastic.

Weck said, "I take it you know about his involvement with *La Mano Negra*?"

The special agent seemed to take Julia's continued silence as a yes. "So, I expect you also know that said involvement places him smack bang in the middle of a transnational criminal enterprise that imports billions of dollars' worth of heroin, cocaine, and fentanyl into Chicago and other U.S. cities."

The only sound in the room was the tap of Weck's pen.

Julia wished she'd hadn't drunk the water because she now felt like she was going to throw it up.

Weck sat back in her chair and opened the binder. "How about I give you a brief bio on your boyfriend and you let me know which bits he left out?"

She began flipping pages. Julia dropped her head and closed her eyes, wishing she could so easily close off her mind to all of this.

"Danilo Amador Castaño, born in Torreón in the state of Coahuila. Father, Hector, was a mechanic who owned his own auto shop. Mom, María, was a schoolteacher. One younger brother, Sebastián. By all accounts, it was a stable upbringing and a happy childhood for both the Castaño boys. Until one day, when Daniel was thirteen, the family packed up in a hurry and vanished overnight. Paid coyotes a considerable sum of money to take them over the border near El Paso."

Weck turned a page, went on, "Turns out Hector had been both laundering money through his business and smuggling drugs for the *Sinaloa* cartel. His business had been failing, and they approached him and offered to help. But he soon learned that help from the cartel comes with quite the price tag. And when he decided he didn't want to pay that price anymore, there was only one way out. To run. As fast and as far away as he could.

"They tracked them down, of course. Maybe they had spies watching his house, or maybe they owned one of the coyotes. Who knows? What we do know is that they intercepted the van with him and his whole extended family in it, eight people in all, crossing the Chihuahuan Desert on the U.S. side. And, well, ended that little dream."

Weck removed several photos from the binder and slid them across the table to Julia. It took her a second to realize what she was seeing and, by then, it was too late to unsee them.

A white Sprinter van riddled with hundreds of bullet holes. They had shattered the windows, blown out the windshield, and warped the metal sides. The rear doors were open, revealing the damage the bullets had inflicted on the slumped bodies inside.

Weck had the decency to look away as she turned the page. "No one knows how the boys survived. The bodies of their mother and grandmother likely shielded them from the bullets. Daniel, however, received a shrapnel wound to the side of his face."

Julia swallowed a sharp lump in her throat. His scar. The one that sat just above the cross inked onto his left cheekbone. He'd gotten it from surviving an attack that had killed his whole family.

Weck said, "They hid under that pile of bodies, Daniel keeping his four-year-old brother quiet for hours. We know this because by the time a border patrol showed up, the turkey vultures already numbered in the dozens." She paused, then added, "They still had to pry him away from his mother's body, though."

Julia kept her head down, hot tears blurring the view of her hands clasped in her lap.

She didn't want to be hearing about Daniel's family like this. From her. She wanted him to have been the one to tell her. When he was ready to.

Weck took the photos back, apparently satisfied they had traumatized Julia enough. "Both boys wound up in ICE custody. But they escaped from the El Paso hospital where they'd been taken. From there, they vanished. It wasn't until Daniel reached sixteen that he came to the attention of the LAPD. Now sporting some interesting ink."

She presented Julia with another photo. This one was a mugshot of a teenaged Daniel, a baby-faced little troublemaker, with the smirk and the dimple but no stubble. No face tattoo either, although when Weck showed two more photos showing closeups of his torso, she saw he was on his way to becoming the canvas he was now. *La Huesuda* was there, along with the black hand print, and THE WILL TO LIVE IS THE WILL TO DIE.

"By now, obviously, he's well and truly affiliated with *La Mano Negra*," Oates said. 'LAPD arrested him in connection with a drive-by shooting in Inglewood. They would have sent him back to the border, but he escaped police custody and disappeared. Again." His irritation with the apparent incompetence of the local cops was clear in his voice.

Weck's pen had started tapping again, an ominous little drumbeat. "Of course, we know where he wound up next. In our backyard. Except, while he's been here, he's escalated from drive-bys to full execution-style murders."

She placed another photo on top of the pile. Julia squeezed her eyes shut, but not fast enough. She observed a man wearing mirrored sunglasses, his head tilted back like he was staring at something fascinating on the ceiling. There was a gaping, blood-rimmed gunshot wound in the center of his forehead. Gore was splattered behind him like the innards of a dropped watermelon. Even with her eyes closed, she saw the image so clearly in her mind it felt painted onto the back of her eyelids.

Oates finally spoke. "Meet Sasha Sokolov. Deceased, obviously."

Julia kept her eyes shut. Her heart was beating irregularly; it felt a small animal was trying to kick its way out of her chest. "Daniel didn't do that," she whispered.

"Oh, he did," Weck said. "We have eyewitness testimony of him as the shooter." She paused, then added. "Well, we did have eyewitness testimony. Sadly, our CI, a stripper by the name of Svetlana, is also deceased. She got shot leaving her apartment in Philly before U.S. marshals could get her into protective custody." She tapped the photo. "But she managed to take this photo before they disposed of Sasha's body, and she gave us a detailed account of how it all went down."

Julia tried to ignore the brief stab of jealousy in her gut that came from hearing that Daniel had been spending time in the company of strippers. Jealousy that was both pointless and insensitive, given that the stripper in question was dead. She rested her forehead in her hands and said, "And I suppose you're gonna try to make me believe he killed her, too?" she snapped.

"Nope," Oates said calmly, sitting back in his chair. "That was almost certainly the Russians."

Weck inhaled and folded her hands on top of the folder. Silence stretched to fill the room.

Julia kept her head in her hands. Her skin felt feverish. She simply couldn't reconcile the picture of Daniel they were painting with the man she knew. The man who adored his brother and loved her deeply. It just didn't compute.

Before I met you, I was someone else. Someone worse.

She wanted to fling the photos off the table and into Weck's face. "I know what you're trying to do." Her voice had taken on a wobble. "You're trying to make him out as some kind of monster.

But he's not. So you can show me all the pictures you want." She swallowed and looked Weck right in the eye. "But you won't ever turn me against him."

———

Belinda sighed and surveyed Julia over the top of her reading glasses. The girl was still crying. Actually, it had progressed to sniveling. But she was showing an admirable amount of steel in defense of her man.

Okay. So the vinegar hadn't worked. Time to try some honey.

Belinda turned to Oates and nodded at him. He got the message and stood, smoothing his tie. Then he left without a word, the door slipping shut behind him.

Belinda looked back at Julia and smiled. Just us girls, she communicated silently. Then she scooped up the photos and shoved them back in the binder, with enough irritation to imply that the only reason they were on the table was at Oates's's insistence.

She returned her hands to the table, adopting a passive expression. Bad cop wasn't her strong suit, but what she excelled at was good cop. She'd once had a high-ranking Vice Lord sobbing on her shoulder about how much it still hurt that his momma had abandoned him as a boy. Right before she slapped handcuffs on him for murdering someone else's momma.

"Look, I get it," she said. "The attraction. Guys like Castaño, they're magnetic. Charismatic. They can be charming and sweet and make you feel like nothing else in the world matters to them but you. They're like a drug, and when you're with them, it's the best high in the world." She adjusted her glasses. "But they're also volatile. Possessive. And very dangerous."

Julia wiped her nose with the back of her hand. "None of that sounds like Daniel. None of it."

Belinda rifled through her bag and pulled out a pocket pack of tissues and pushed them across the table at her. She ignored the gesture.

"Being wifey to one of these guys is no fairytale, Julia. I'm just trying to save you the heartache of finding that out for yourself."

"You don't know him," she insisted. She nodded at the binder. "You think you do from all your bits of paper. But you don't. And you sure as hell know nothing about me."

Belinda gave her a sad smile. "Honey, I've seen every kind of version of you. I've seen the ones who are young and in love and think they're the only ones in history who've ever felt like that. I've seen the ones who try to settle down with these guys and marry them, have kids with them, only to find out too late they ain't exactly the settling down type. I've seen the ones who find themselves out on the street because their boos have gotten their asses shot or thrown in jail. I've seen the ones who end up in the ER because their one true love got high on amphetamines and rearranged their faces. And I've also seen the ones who wind up under a white sheet in the morgue." She sat back from the table and shook her head. "Now I'm just sitting here wondering which one you are."

Julia shook her head. "I know he would never hurt me."

Belinda sighed. "Julia, a woman can never know a thing like that. That's the problem."

Julia raked her hair back from her face and stared at the table.

"Do you feel safe in the relationship?"

She glanced up, her expression defiant. "I've never felt safer with anyone in my life."

"He's a big guy. Tall. Clearly works out."

She shrugged moodily. "Yeah. So?"

"Ever felt physically threatened by him?"

"No."

"Has he ever hit you?"

She looked horrified at the mere suggestion. "No!"

"Is the sex always consensual?" she asked.

She glanced up, eyes furious. "Yes."

Belinda let the silence settle, then changed tack. "What about his personality?"

"What about it?" she snapped.

"Does he ever have mood swings? Fly off the handle over small things?"

"No," she said stubbornly. "He's a perfectly chill guy."

Belinda pictured Sasha Sokolov's head. "Hmm."

Julia seemed to have had enough with this line of questioning. Her face had gone very red, tears still rolling down her cheeks. She opened her mouth, closed it, then opened it again. 'You asked me how I could know that he wouldn't hurt me?' she finally blurted.

Belinda hadn't asked her that, but she waited, sensing she was on the brink of a breakthrough here.

"On the night we met, some guy tried to…to…" She swallowed hard. "He put pills in my drink, and he tried to assault me." She closed her eyes and gave a quick shake of her head. "Daniel saved me that night. He dressed me. He took care of me. That's the kind of guy he is, not the psycho you're trying to make him out to be."

Belinda kept her face impassive, masking her feeling of triumph. She reopened the binder.

Time to bring out the trump card.

"Ah, yes," she said, tapping her pen on her notepad. "Your little meet-cute. At a house party in Chicago Lawn, right?"

Julia blinked at her. Belinda could practically hear the cogs whirring in her brain, trying to work out how she could know that.

"And the other guy you mentioned?" She flipped pages, found another photo. "Floyd Monaghan, correct? Twenty-seven. A DJ from Utah."

She watched as Julia flinched away from the photo of the smiling young man that she'd printed off one of his social media accounts. All of which had turned into shrines for him now that his body had finally been identified and his death confirmed.

"It took them a while to, uh, piece it all together," she said. She produced her last photographs, placing each in front of her like a tarot reader, laying out her future in the cards. "Literally."

If she'd recoiled from the photo of Floyd Monaghan in one piece, the sight of him in five bloody lumps made her jerk back from the table, her chair hitting the wall behind her. "Oh my God."

Belinda sat forward on her forearms. "In the end, they had to use DNA because his hands and teeth were missing. The detectives investigating Monaghan's disappearance traced his last known whereabouts to a trap house on the West Side. The same trap house behind which Daniel Castaño's trailer is parked. It took CPD weeks of canvassing the neighborhood, but they finally got someone who'd attended the party to admit they saw Monaghan there. And not alone, either. With a pretty blond girl. Heavily intoxicated. Both were last seen heading for Castaño's trailer. People heard multiple gunshots shortly after. It's not drawing a long bow to conclude that Castaño didn't take kindly to trespassers in his trailer." She adjusted her glasses again. "But you were there, of course. You already know all of this."

As she was speaking, Julia had stood up and wheeled around to face the wall. She bent double and vomited onto the carpet.

Belinda waited patiently until she was done. Until she'd turned back around, scraping her hair back from her tear-soaked face. She indicated the chunks of bone, blood, and sinewy that had once been Floyd Monaghan. "There's no way he did that. He couldn't have."

"Oh, he did," Belinda said, putting as much conviction into the words as she could. "Like I said. He's volatile. Possessive. And very, very dangerous."

Julia gave a couple more sobs that sounded more like dry heaves, then said in a small, miserable voice, "I don't know what you want from me."

Belinda softened her expression. "All I want is to help you, Julia. Out of this great big mess that you've found yourself in."

She came back to the table, eyes averted from the horrors of her boyfriend's handiwork. Finally, she reached forward for the pack of tissues.

Belinda allowed herself a small smile of triumph. Then smoothed her features into a solemn expression. "But first, you have to help us."

NINETEEN

THE MOMENT DANIEL strode into Martín's restaurant, the man flinched, and the blood drained from his face. The reaction must have stemmed from the look on Daniel's face. Or maybe it was because he'd caught sight of the fists balled at his sides.

For a split second the old urge rose up in him—to make Martín pay for selling him out, to remind him what betrayal earned. His fists tightened, itching for it.

But Julia's face flickered in his mind, steadying him. He drew a slow breath, letting the anger settle in his chest. Then he walked past Martín into the kitchen.

Sebastián stood at the sink rinsing a stack of dishes. He glanced up, nodded once, then shut off the water. He yanked the apron over his head and tossed it onto the counter.

Daniel went up the stairs ahead of him; once inside his brother's room, he closed the door.

"We're leaving?" Sebastián said.

Daniel nodded.

Sebastián grabbed his backpack off the floor, started shoving in clothes. Neither of them owned a lot of stuff; their lives had revolved around what they could carry with them since they were kids. "When?"

"Tonight. We're meeting Julia by the lake."

He straightened. "She's coming with us?"

Daniel leaned against the door frame. "I should hope so. Seeing as how she's gonna be my wife and all."

The kid dropped the socks he was trying to roll up. "You're getting married?"

"I gave her Mom's ring. She said yes."

Sebastián said nothing for a long moment, and Daniel knew he was thinking about that ring, which was the only thing they had left of their *mamá*. Or of their family. It was only theirs due to a stroke of luck. Before they'd gotten in that van, their mother had stashed all their valuables on her children, believing that two little boys would be less likely to be robbed than her or their dad. Since then, Daniel had sold everything else to survive. But not that ring.

Sebastián said quietly, "You really love her."

He met his brother's eyes. "Yeah," he said softly. "I really fucking do."

He meant it, but he also couldn't quite believe he meant it. He couldn't believe that in a few short months he'd known her, he'd gone from a guy who'd sat in her driveway with a pistol in his hand, with every intention of hurting her with it, to a guy who was counting down the hours before he could get her before an altar and God and making her his forever.

He didn't even know what it was about her that had so thoroughly turned his head. If someone put that same gun to his head and demanded to know why he loved her, what would he say? Because she was beautiful, obviously; every time he looked at her, things started knocking in his chest. Watching her dance was an almost religious experience. It was like she was part-human, part-butterfly. It blew his mind that with just her body she could make him feel things that there weren't words for in any language. The only time his mind was similarly blown was when her body was beneath his.

But if that gun really was to his head, though, if he had to list one reason for loving her, it would be a purely selfish thing. It would be because she made him want things, too. Real things, things he'd never had the chance to want until now.

He wanted to make babies with her and watch them grow. He wanted a place with her he could finally call home. He wanted to live, and not just survive.

Sebastián went to the chest of drawers, the room's only furniture other than the bed, and started emptying it. He slung his backpack over his shoulder, then wrapped one arm around Daniel. "*Te quiero, hermano.*"

Daniel swallowed down something that felt suspiciously like a lump in his throat. "I love you too, *hermanito.*" Then he pushed his brother away and said, "So you wanna go say goodbye to what's-his-face?"

Sebastián shook his head. "We've already said our goodbyes."

Daniel steered him out the door in front of him. "Let's get the fuck outta here, then."

Sebastián turned and said to him over his shoulder, "So, wait. We're all going to be living together under one roof? You, me and Julia?"

"Uh huh."

"And you two are going to be having sex, like, all the time, right?"

Daniel nodded seriously. "Pretty much constantly."

'Right. So I'm gonna need not just my own room but an entire half of the house to myself. And the walls will need to be completely soundproofed—"

Daniel shoved his brother out the door and slammed it behind him. "Jesus Christ, do I look like a fucking realtor today or what?"

They finally let her out of that room in the dingy warehouse in Holman Square over two hours later. While being escorted out, she asked to use the bathroom, and Weck guided her to one at the end of a hallway. It was small, just two cubicles and one metal sink. Fluorescent lights buzzing eerily overhead. She turned on the tap, pooling water in her hands and dashing it against her face.

At some point, she realized she was crying. The hot tears mingled with the cold water, so at first, she couldn't feel them. She turned the tap off and allowed herself half a minute for self- pity, her head bent over the sink, her knuckles clenched into fists against the metal bench top, weathering each sob like a passing storm. Then she straightened, dried her face with a paper towel and inhaled shakily through her teeth. Her reflection floated in front of her like a mirage. Her skin looked waxy and taut, and her eyes were set in dark sockets. She balled up the paper towel and chucked it in the bin.

When she reached her car in the parking lot, she saw that dusk was settling in.

He'd be waiting for her. She pushed the speed limit all the way back to Lake Forest, her hands gripping the steering wheel so tightly her nails dug into her palms. Images kept flicking through her mind. Daniel's head resting on the pillow beside hers, wearing his soft smile. Sasha Sokolov's head, with its neat, blackened hole and watermelon innards. The bloody lump of Floyd Monaghan's head in the bottom of the black trash bag. And she had to grit her teeth against another wave of nausea.

At the end of the lane up ahead, she saw him. Leaning against the hood of the parked 'Cuda, between the shafts of light coming from the headlights. Legs crossed in front of him. White singlet, tattered jeans. The glow of the lit end of a joint illuminating his perfect face.

Sight for sore eyes didn't even begin to cover it. All the other images faded into darkness, leaving just him. The man she loved.

She abandoned her car in the middle of the lane, engine still running, and sprinted towards him.

He stood up, tossing the joint. She launched herself at him and he caught her as if she weighed nothing at all.

She wrapped her arms around his neck, burying her face against his shoulder.

When she looked up, she saw Sebastián sitting in the 'Cuda's passenger seat. The door was open, his legs hanging out. Tequila sat panting at his feet.

He smiled and gave Julia a wave.

Her heart crumbled some more. "I'm so, so sorry," she sobbed.

"Why?" He kissed the side of her neck. "'Cause you're a little late? Who gives a fuck?"

She could feel the vibration of his voice in his chest. She tried to permanently record this moment, absorbing each detail. The scent of his skin. His stubble against her cheek. The pressure of his firm hands wrapped around her body.

"I love you," she whispered. "Please don't hate me."

He cupped her head, tilting it back to see her face. He smiled. "I could never hate you, baby."

You will, she thought, and with a certainty that felt like a knife wound to the gut.

She kissed him, hard, like it was the last time she ever would. He kissed her back, just as urgently, but then he seemed to sense something was wrong and pulled away.

Behind him, she noticed shadowy figures drawing near. From the beach, from the woods on either side of the lane. In the gloom, all she could make out were the bright white letters on their dark jackets. CPD. DEA. DOJ. FBI. A mob of three letter acronyms converging on them. She remembered their acronym for Daniel.

CPOT. Consolidated Priority Target.

He dropped her like she was hot. Then backed away from her until his legs hit the fender of the 'Cuda.

The acronyms were all yelling things at them: "Hands where we can see them!"

"Get on the ground!"

"Slowly!"

Julia lifted her hands, but Daniel did no such thing. He

reached behind him, and she had a sudden fear he was going for the gun he sometimes carried in his waistband.

"Daniel, no!" she screamed.

But it was too late. A dozen law enforcement officers converged on him like a pack of wolves. They dragged him to the ground, knelt on his back and legs, and shoved his face into the road grit.

She saw a blur of movement from the car. Sebastián had darted out of the passenger door and was rounding the front of the car.

The gunshot sounded like cannon fire. It was the loudest thing Julia had ever heard. It seemed to shred through the night, leaving tatters in its wake.

Deafened, everything seemed to play out before her like a silent movie. Sebastián's body, caught in the car's headlights, falling backwards, hitting the ground. Tequila barking, tail between her legs, running to and from in agitated circles. Daniel's mouth open in an unheard roar. Behind her, red and blue police lights started strobing in unison, turning the forested lane into a sudden club scene.

Five agents restrained Daniel; one of their knees pressed his cheek. Yet, amid the chaos, he found her gaze.

And the look in them was one of pure hatred.

TWENTY

THIS ROOM, this nightmarish room again. The red blinking light. The cup of water. The scarred table. The smiling assassin carved onto the table. The word "ME" scratched above it.

Someone had cleaned up her sick from earlier, but she could still smell it. Her eyes felt swollen; she dipped her fingers into her cup and pressed them to her eyelids.

When she squeezed her eyes shut, she could see it all play out in her mind's eye. Sebastián's body hitting the ground. A moment of suspended animation when no one seemed able to move. But she had. Maybe it was her quick-twitch dancer's muscles or maybe it was just her desperation, but she'd made it to his body before anyone else did. Saw the gaping, sucking hole in his chest, the blood, the blood. It had already soaked through his t-shirt and was gleaming on the gravel.

She'd been useless, of course, unable to do much but hover her palms pointlessly over the wound, like some kind of faith healer. Too scared to touch him in case that would make the damage worse. As if she hadn't done enough of that already.

He just stared up at the stars, gulping air in breaths that grew shorter and shorter.

Someone had hauled her off him and applied actual first aid.

She'd heard Weck's voice, and the dreadful woman had dragged her away and bundled her into a car.

She opened her eyes and ran her hands over her face. Looked around the tiny room. Now she wanted to be anywhere but here.

The door opened and Weck entered, clutching a brown paper bag and her best friend, the binder.

Julia kept her eyes on the table, tracing the stick figure with the gun. "Is he dead?" she asked dully.

Weck came to stand by the table but didn't sit down. "He's in surgery. The bullet punctured a lung and there are some fragments near his spine." She paused, then added, "The doctor said he was very lucky to be alive."

Julia snorted. "You mean, he's lucky you people didn't kill him."

Weck said nothing. She didn't even have the decency to look guilty about what had happened. In her mind, she probably thought she wasn't.

The special agent placed the paper bag on the table and pushed it towards her. It had the name of a fast-food joint on it and smelled greasy. "You should eat."

"I'm not hungry." She sat back in her chair. "I did what you wanted. I gave you your probable cause to arrest him. Your Consolidated Priority Target, or whatever the hell you want to call him to dehumanize him some more—"

"Castaño isn't the CPOT," Weck interrupted. "Terry Bidois is. He's a high-ranking underboss in *La Eme*. Shot-caller for the whole Chicago operation, from importation to distribution. Answers directly to Mexico. We've been wiretapping his phone for months but haven't been about to make any headway on how he's getting the heroin into Chicago."

She placed the binder on the table, but Julia interrupted her before she could open it and show her any more of the horrors held within.

"I've seen him. He came to Daniel's trailer once when I was there." She swallowed, remembering her glimpse of him over

Daniel's shoulder as he was stashing her in his wardrobe. "Big white guy. Scary looking. A spider web tattoo on the back of his head." She sighed, massaged her temples. "Daniel told me about him."

"Perfect." Weck pulled out a chair. "Now *you* can tell me about him."

Julia looked down at her hands. The ring that Daniel had placed on her finger only that morning caught the light, glinting crimson. She thought about Sebastián's blood shining on the stones where he lay. And the look Daniel had given her, like she'd just ripped the heart right out of his chest.

Weck noticed her looking at the ring. "And then," she said, "we're gonna go pay a little visit to your fiancé."

———

Eight plastic chairs sat in empty booths facing thick plate glass. The telephones hung from their cradles like dead weights, beneath stern signs warning that all conversations were being monitored. From beyond the concrete walls came the muffled echoes of barking orders, angry shouts, and the occasional clatter of something heavy hitting the floor.

The no-contact visiting area of the Metropolitan Correctional Center in downtown Chicago was every bit as bleak as Julia had imagined.

She sat stiffly in one of the chairs, her pulse quickening with every second that passed. Her eyes locked onto the reinforced door in the concrete cubicle beyond the glass. The air here was thick with disinfectant and desperation.

When the buzzer sounded, she nearly jolted out of her skin.

Daniel shuffled through the doorway, a guard close behind him.

Her breath caught in her throat.

He wore the standard-issue orange jumpsuit, but it wasn't the uniform that made her stomach twist, it was the way he moved.

Slow. Tense. Like an animal on a short chain, his hands balled into fists at his sides. Then she saw his face.

His left eye was bloodshot, the surrounding skin already darkening into an ugly bruise. A fresh cut split through his eyebrow, the same one that had already been scarred before. His bottom lip was cracked, a smear of dried blood catching in the scruff along his jaw.

Even battered, he was still the most beautiful thing she had ever seen.

But he wasn't looking at her. His gaze stayed pinned to the floor as the guard gave him a sharp shove toward the chair.

"Daniel," she whispered, forgetting for a moment that the glass swallowed her words.

She pressed her hands against the cold barrier between them, as if she could somehow make it vanish, as if she could reach through and touch him. For all her longing, though, a sliver of hesitation coiled deep in her gut.

I know he would never hurt me.

Weck's voice came slithering back. *Honey, a woman can never know a thing like that. That's the problem.*

She forced herself to move, unhooking the phone from its cradle. She kept one hand against the glass. For a long moment, he simply stared at her palm.

Then, finally, he reached for the receiver on his side. His movements were sluggish, as if even this simple action drained him.

When he lifted it to his ear, she didn't waste time.

"Sebastián got out of surgery a few hours ago. They say he's going to be okay."

The lie tasted bitter on her tongue, but it was all she had to give. They hadn't said he'd be okay, only that he'd survived.

Daniel said nothing.

Her gaze drifted over his bruises again, then lower, to the cuts on his hands. Some were still raw, blood smudged against the ink on his knuckles. L-M-N-1-3.

How long before this place broke him? Or worse? Would his

own people turn on him? Would he survive long enough to even stand trial?

He followed her line of sight and gave a wry, humorless smile. He lifted a hand, fingering his split lip. "Apparently, I don't got a lot of friends in here."

Her stomach twisted.

She leaned in, slow, cautious, as if he might bolt. Now was the time to make her pitch. Or rather, Weck's pitch.

"The DEA doesn't want you, Daniel. They want Terry. If you testify against him, they'll cut you a deal. Protection. A fresh start somewhere new. Just like we always talked about—"

"No."

Desperation prickled beneath her skin. "If you don't cooperate, they'll throw everything at you. You're looking at a life sentence."

Still, he said nothing. He wouldn't even look at her.

Julia clenched the phone tighter. She knew she should stick to the script, but the need to explain herself clawed at her. "They told me... They showed me what you did to Floyd. That you shot him. And then..."

The words dried up in her throat. Her vision blurred.

At last, his gaze snapped to hers, copper-green, sharp as broken glass. A fierceness she'd never seen before burned behind them.

"If you want me to say I'm sorry for that," he bit out, "I ain't."

Her breath hitched.

"I'd do the exact same thing again to any other man who laid a hand on you."

Instinctively, she flinched.

Weck's voice whispered in her mind. *Volatile. Possessive. Dangerous.*

No, she shot back. *Not possessive. Protective.*

Please, let there be a difference.

Her throat tightened. She forced herself to ask the question she had been dreading. "Why did you come to my house that first time?"

The anger in his eyes wavered, replaced by something raw, something unguarded.

He exhaled sharply. Looked away. Shook his head.

"The first time," he admitted, voice hoarse, "I went there to scare you. To make sure you didn't go to the cops."

Julia shut her eyes. Nodded. She had already known the truth, but hearing it still stung.

"Why didn't you?" she asked.

His voice was quieter now, almost a whisper. "Because as soon as I saw you again, I knew I could never hurt you."

For the first time since she'd sat down, warmth flickered in her chest. A sliver of hope.

But then, just as quickly, the light dimmed. His jaw worked, and that same fire flared behind his eyes. "I just wish that went in reverse."

The words struck like a blade between her ribs.

She inhaled sharply. "Daniel, please. Take the deal. If not for yourself, then for Sebastián. They said they'd help him, too."

His voice turned to a snarl. "Jesus fucking Christ, you don't get it, do you? They ain't gonna help him. They fucking shot him."

He ran a hand down his face, exhaling harshly. When he resurfaced, his expression had hardened. The cold glint in his eyes sent a shiver down her spine.

"You told them everything, didn't you?" he asked. "Everything I told you. About the heroin. The pipeline. InterTruck."

She swallowed something sharp. Nodded.

His lips curled into a humorless smile. "Well, I ain't no snitch. If they kill me, they kill me. But at least I'll die knowing that."

Her grip on the phone tightened. She could feel something unraveling, something slipping through her fingers.

Hope.

Tears burned in her eyes. She thought of the way he had

looked at her when she'd said yes to his proposal. Like she had just lit a fire in a world that had been nothing but dark.

That was the man she loved.

Or had, anyway.

When she met his gaze again, his expression was desolate.

And in that instant, she saw him—really saw him. The eight-year-old who had declared his love to his babysitter. The eleven-year-old learning to drive his dad's old Chevy. The teenager who had been forced to survive in a world that never gave him a chance.

His voice was hoarse when he finally spoke. "You listen to me. Whatever protection they're offering you, you take it."

A chill crawled up her spine. "What do you mean?"

His knuckles whitened around the receiver.

"I mean, you've crossed the wrong people." His voice dropped to a whisper. "*La Mano Negra.* The *Cártel de Sinaloa.* Borya Sokolov."

Her blood turned to ice.

"They will come for you, Julia." He leaned in, his face inches from the glass. "And when they find you…"

He pushed to his feet so suddenly that the guard behind him tensed. His eyes locked onto hers, burning with something wild.

"You better run, baby."

TWENTY-ONE

THEY WERE the last words Daniel ever spoke to her.

Three days later, they cornered him in a prison shower stall. There was nowhere to run. Nowhere to hide. The blade punched into the side of his neck, swift and deliberate, severing his carotid.

His blood spilled out in thick ribbons, swirling into the drain with the dirty water. The last of him, washed away like nothing. His killer had a black handprint tattooed on his chest.

Sebastián never woke up from surgery. He lingered for three weeks in a sterile hospital room, tethered to a bank of beeping machines, before they finally shut him down like a faulty piece of equipment. No legal status. No insurance. No family.

No reason to keep him alive.

When he died, the only person in the room was the nurse who flicked the switch.

Julia was taken to a safe house somewhere in the city's southwest. A converted warehouse near an industrial park, faceless and gray, indistinguishable from the empty lots and shuttered buildings around it. Inside, the only things that stood out were a single bed with a wafer-thin mattress, a strip of green and orange carpet worn down to its threads, and a water stain blooming across the ceiling like an old bruise.

She spent most of her time lying on that mattress, staring at that stain. At first, she cycled through memories of Daniel, playing them over and over until they lost their shape—his voice turning unfamiliar, his touch fading into something half-remembered, like echoes from a dream she couldn't quite hold on to. Then, even those memories slipped away, replaced by nothing. She lay there, hollow, her will to live drifting like a tide pulling further and further from shore.

The will to live is the will to die. Una paradoja.

Searing light cut into her eyelids. She opened them and blinked, squinting against the sudden brightness in the room. Weck was standing by the curtains, silhouetted by the daylight now streaming in the window.

She went to Julia's bedside and looked down. "The good news is, your intel was solid. We took it to a grand jury, got indictments on eight members of LMN-13. Yesterday, we raided InterTruck and arrested Terry Bidois, Milo Bidois, Paquito Vasquez and Che Cardenas. They're being held at MCC. There are warrants out for four others."

Julia stared up at the ceiling and said nothing.

Weck went on, "U.S. federal agents and their Mexican counterparts raided that old dartboard factory in Juárez that Castaño told you about. They arrested José Ferrera. Cut off an entire arm of Sinaloa's heroin operation. Not the head, but still." She paused, then added, "We wouldn't have had any of that without you."

Julia did not know why this woman was telling her this. Like she cared. Like it fucking *mattered*.

"I just got off the phone AUSA Oates," she continued. "He said the Attorney General is ready to sign off on your application for the federal witness security program."

Another long pause.

"You just have to say the word."

Julia said nothing.

Weck sighed. "This story only has two endings, Julia. One

where you take what's being offered here. Or one where you leave here and in a few weeks' time, I have to watch as they dig your body parts out of a dumpster in Canaryville."

Her words bounced harmlessly off Julia's brain.

Weck leaned closer to the bed. "Listen, I know you wanted a different ending here. One where you got to live happily ever after with Castaño."

She swallowed, feeling a couple of hot tears leak out the side of her eyes. She closed her eyes, and she could see him as clearly as if it were right in front of her. His bright hazel eyes, his dimples, the way his expression could shift from guarded to open on the turn of a dime. She could still feel the heat of his skin, what it had felt like to rest her chin on his chest. The smell of him, the taste of him. She remembered the way he laughed. Few people made laughter sound sad, but he'd had that rare ability.

Weck sighed. "But when it came down to it, he didn't choose you, did he, Julia? He didn't choose his brother either. He chose the gang. A gang that stabbed him in the back of the neck in a shower stall."

She inhaled as pain, sharp and real, sliced through her. When Weck had told her about Daniel's death several days ago, after having first told her of Sebastián's, she had felt nothing. She'd been numb from head to toe. Now she could only wish for such numbness.

"A gang," Weck continued, "that's put out an order to kill you on sight."

As much as her mind tried to rebel against what Weck was saying, her words still sent a shiver down Julia's spine. She heard Daniel's voice again, and this time it frightened her.

You better run, baby.

"And I know this is hard for you to get your head around. Especially because you probably still think of Castaño as having been your protector. Your knight in shining armor. The one who came to your rescue in that trailer when no one else did."

Julia finally found some words to say. "He's dead," she croaked. "So what difference does it make to you what I think of him?" She turned her head to Weck. "Unless you want to destroy my memory of him, too."

"No," Weck said. "I want you to question your memory of him. Of everything that happened. Julia, you survived a traumatic experience that night with Monaghan. And trauma can manifest in all kinds of ways. One of those ways is forming strong bonds and attachments to people who we view as having saved us. I think that's what happened to you."

Julia just shook her head. This woman was trying to make out that her entire relationship with Daniel had just been some kind of prolonged PTSD episode.

And it hadn't been. It had been real.

Right?

"What I do know is that you need to talk to someone about what happened to you. Someone who can help you process it. There are people who can do that, people who specialize in this kind of thing."

Julia swallowed. Recalling that night in the trailer always filled her with panic. But there was a part of her now that also felt like it might be a relief. Painful, but necessary. Like the closing of a wound.

The special agent looked down at her. "You need to be the one to save yourself this time, Julia. You got a shot here. For a new life. A fresh start. That's what you wanted, isn't it?"

Hoy vamos a comenzar una nueva vida, cariño.

Today we start a new life.

She looked up at Weck, tears falling freely now. She took a shuddering breath. And even though the movement took an excruciating amount of effort, she nodded.

Weck smiled, and it seemed genuine. "Good girl." She stood up. "It might not feel like it now, but someday you'll look back and realize this was the best decision you ever made." She took her phone out of her bag. "I'll get someone from OEO down here for a preliminary interview, then hand you over to the marshals."

She paused tapping in numbers into her phone to look down at Julia. "They know what they're doing. They'll keep you safe."

TWENTY-TWO

JESSICA MEEKS STOOD in a square of light spilling from the windows of the diner behind her and took a hit off her vape. It was four in the morning, in a truck stop west of Mobile, and the air felt like hot soup.

She surveyed the gas station forecourt, but the marshal's car was no longer parked at the pumps where she'd last seen it.

In its place was an old silver sedan. Its headlights were on, engine idling.

She blew out a stream of smoke and stared at the car. She fantasized about running across the forecourt and jumping into its passenger seat. Then going wherever it was going. North, east or west.

As she stared, a plan took shape in her mind. She'd hitch a ride to the nearest city, then change her identity the old-fashioned way, by dumping her wallet in a bin and picking out a new name at random. She'd find work at another strip club easily enough. Those places were filled with girls running away from something.

There'd be no Baton Rouge safe house. No isolation rooms, no psychologists. No marshals following her around for the rest of her life. The thought was so tempting she felt her legs twitch in anticipation of a sprint across the forecourt.

The sedan hadn't moved. It sat gleaming under the LED canopy lights. Its driver was a silhouette behind the wheel. As if he were waiting for her.

A heavy hand gripped her shoulder. "Ma'am," said a voice in a thick Southern accent.

She spun around, heart pounding.

Inglis was standing right behind her. He looked in the silver sedan's direction, then back at her. His expression indicated he knew exactly what she'd been on the brink of doing.

She exhaled a thick cloud of vape that drifted around his face. He grimaced, waving it away with one hand.

"Sorry," she said. Then, to make sure he didn't think she was apologizing for the aborted escape attempt, she held up her vape pen and clicked it off.

A distant rumble of thunder came from the south, like a far-off battle beginning. She looked up and saw the stars had vanished.

As if taking its cue from the sound of the coming storm, the sedan suddenly reversed away from the pumps. She watched it speed out of the truck stop, taking with it any last-minute bid for freedom.

"We should get back on the road." Inglis turned and started towards his car, which she saw was now parked around the side of the diner.

She trotted after him. "They're saying on the news this storm is gonna be real bad."

Inglis didn't look back. "They say that about all of them."

"They say they're closing all the Waffle Houses."

He paused by the driver's door, one foot in the car. "Well," he said. "I guess it's time to panic."

———

The silver sedan sat in a shadowy layby, its sole occupant gripping a SIG pistol in his palm like he was holding hands with a loved one.

In his side mirror, he saw a car's headlights cut through the night and swing in a wide arc towards him. It was the marshal's Charger, pulling out of the truck stop and heading back toward the interstate.

He let them pass, then sat there for a full minute longer in the syrupy darkness. His heart was still beating a steady stream of adrenaline through his veins.

She'd been so close. She'd looked right at him and for a hot second he'd thought she was going to actually run across the gas station forecourt and get into his car.

What were the chances of that? He hadn't even known what he would have done. Killed her right there and then?

That wasn't the plan, and he knew it. The plan came from people way higher up the food chain than him. From people whose plans you simply didn't fuck around with.

He picked up a phone from the passenger seat. The metal was cool in his hand. Thirteen hours earlier, he'd taken it from a little bungalow in The Pines neighborhood of Panama City Beach. A souvenir, right before he'd left a souvenir of his own, in red spray-paint.

Then he'd sat across the street from her house, watching the chaos that had ensued. Watching as she realized just how weak the walls were that she'd built around her world.

Just the sight of her had made every muscle in his body tighten. She looked good. Real good. And that pissed him off more than anything. He'd gotten seven years in a federal prison. She'd gotten eleven years in the Florida sunshine.

Would she even recognize him anymore? These days, he barely recognized himself. Prison had stripped him of everything. His possessions, his dreams, even his own name. Nowadays, everyone just called him Roach. When he thought of his old name —his old identity—it felt like it belonged to a ghost.

Far to the south, lightning licked the horizon with its forked tongue. Roach placed the pistol on the front seat beside the phone and started the engine.

As he turned west onto the interstate, he saw banks of thick clouds, darker than the night sky and steadily rolling north.

214

TWENTY-THREE

AS JESSICA and the marshal drove west, the traffic started building in the eastbound lanes of the interstate. The sun was rising, smoldering through the thick bands of rain clouds. Its light glinted off a line of cars that stretched as far as the eye could see. A crawling metallic millipede, extending west, probably all the way to New Orleans. Some had pulled their vehicles to the side of the road to stretch their kids' or dogs' legs, or to stare despondently under the hoods of overheated engines.

The westbound lanes were deserted. Large variable message signs bordering the highway were flashing alerts: HURRICANE WARNING IN EFFECT and USE HURRICANE EVACUATION ROUTES and DRIVE TO THE CONDITIONS. Two Mississippi National Guard trucks passed them, also barreling west.

The pressure was already dropping. She shivered and hugged her arms.

The marshal glanced at her in the rearview mirror. Heat began blasting from the air vents. He gave her another quick glance, then returned his eyes to the road.

The guy sure wasn't big on small talk. Or maybe he just didn't want to make it with her.

She studied his profile, cut from the light seeping in the windshield. It was the first time she'd really noted his features. He was good-looking, in a wholesome, corn-fed kind of way. Early thirties, wavy blond hair swept back from his forehead. A strong jaw, shaded with a day's worth of stubble. Blue eyes, never still. Always moving, as if afraid to alight on anything for too long. One hand loosely grasped the steering wheel, low, almost in his lap. The other was resting on his knee.

Lightning tore across the western sky, its forks like the branches of a huge phosphorescent tree. Fat raindrops started falling onto the roof of the car, slow enough that she could count the seconds between each one. When the thunder arrived, the sound was so intense she could feel it in the floorboards.

She nervously twirled the ruby ring she wore on a chain around her neck, watching the trail of cars blur past the window. This hurricane was forecast weeks ago, yet people had predictably delayed evacuation until the last minute. Hoping, probably, that it would magically dissipate over the Gulf or alter its course to rain its destruction on some other poor souls. But it hadn't, so here they all were.

Hope could be a real bitch like that.

———

The air felt heavy with the coming storm. Ryan could feel it pressing against the windows of the car, an electric charge settling deep in his bones. The temperature had dropped like a stone. Voltage crackled in the air, lifting the hairs on his arms.

He gripped the steering wheel with both hands. His jaw was clenched, and he had to make a conscious effort to relax it.

Something didn't feel right. Not just the storm. Not just the road ahead. It was a familiar feeling, the kind that had once saved his life—and someone else's. But not always. Not every time.

He had learned the hard way that second chances weren't always given.

His eyes flicked to Meeks in the rearview mirror. She was

staring out the window, her hair falling over her shoulders in soft waves of pastel pink. Her t-shirt clung to her in the dim light, denim cutoffs leaving her legs bare and bronzed.

He dragged his gaze away.

It was an often-overlooked fact that there were almost no innocent witnesses in the WITSEC program. Anyone who thought differently had been watching too many movies. Most of its members were ex-bangers and dealers who turned snitch for a better deal in court, or aging crime bosses with gammy knees and arthritic trigger fingers who wanted out of the life for good. WITSEC was their endgame, their retirement plan. A new identity and a clean slate, all on the government's dime. It felt like a cosmic joke that the USMS was responsible for both hunting down the most dangerous felons in the country and, once they had them in custody, for shifting heaven and earth to keep them safe.

Meeks didn't fit the description of a dangerous felon, but she was clearly no angel. As if to underline that fact, his mind produced an image of her on stage at that strip club back in Florida. Wearing not much more than fresh air and a fake smile. The picture was impressively detailed.

He forced the image away. Gave himself a mental cold shower. Then returned his attention to the road. Her past had nothing to do with him. Nothing about her had anything to do with him. His job was to get her to Baton Rouge, that was it. Then she became someone else's problem.

Rain began to hammer the roof of the car, as suddenly as if a fire hose was being aimed at them from the heavens. The sky had gotten so dark it was like it had gone back to night. He turned the windshield wipers on full and set the headlights to bright.

Up ahead in the road was the unmistakable flash of red and blue police lights. Cursing under his breath, he slowed as he approached. A Ford Police Interceptor was parked across the lanes, bearing the badge of the Mississippi Highway Patrol. A State Trooper in a heavy-duty parka was waving a light stick to stop their progress. An LED sign on the side of the interstate read ROAD CLOSED AHEAD.

Shit. He slowed the car to a halt. But he kept his eyes trained on his rain-splatted wing mirror. Something was still bothering him. And it wasn't the storm that lay up ahead.

It was what lay behind.

———

Roach eased his foot onto the brake. Rain was lashing his windshield, the urgent beat of his wiper blades barely keeping up. His view came in second-long bursts between swipes, mirroring the pulses of red and blue from the lightbar on top of the state trooper's SUV.

The marshal's Charger had stopped in the road ahead. Roach brought his own car to a halt and watched as the marshal buzzed down his window. He saw the trooper bend down to the window and say something with a shake of his head. Then he saw the marshal hold something out the window. Probably his ID. The trooper pointed down the road, as if giving directions. Then he stepped back, and the marshal accelerated away, angling around the trooper's vehicle.

Lightning turned the world into a photo negative. He blinked the bright flare out of his eyes and saw the trooper was signaling to him with his light stick.

He pulled up next to the trooper and lowered his own window. The trooper leaned in, rain running in rivulets down the hood and over his face. "You need to head back the way you came," he shouted over the roar of the rain. "This whole area's under mandatory evac. Road's closed up ahead."

He nodded in the direction of the marshal's receding head-lights. He yelled back, "You let him through."

The trooper shook his head, flinging water left and right. His expression was firm. "You gotta turn back," he said, straightening up. "Go back the way you came."

Go back. Ha. Go back where? To Miami? To where he'd been living in a cockroach infested trap house with a bunch of dead-eyed junkies? Where he had no money, no family, and no prospects?

Or was he meant to go back further, to Chicago, to the life he'd once had? To the plans he'd been making, the dreams he'd been pursuing?

Yeah, he'd like to go back there, and he would, one day. But not before he'd taken out the little bitch who'd burned it all to the ground.

Roach took his gun from the passenger seat. "Yeah, I ain't going back."

As soon as the trooper saw the weapon, his face went slack with fear. He reached down for his own weapon, his hand getting obstructed by the heavy plastic of his wet parka.

Too slow.

The sky lit up like it was caught in the flash of a giant camera. In the boom of thunder that followed, no one heard the crack of the gunshot, not even the man who fired it.

The trooper fell back, hit square in the chest.

Roach hit the accelerator, water spraying out from under his tires.

The only way back was forward.

TWENTY-FOUR

RAIN POPPED LOUDLY against the roof of the car. The wind had picked up, too. Ryan could feel it buffeting the car. He had to drive at a crawl, his eyes glued to the white line, just to avoid driving off the side of the road. Visibility must have been ten feet at most. Beyond that was guesswork.

He calculated in his head how much further it was to their destination. The Louisiana line couldn't be far off. He guessed it was sixty-odd miles to New Orleans. Given that they were averaging twenty miles an hour right now, that was still hours of driving ahead. And they were heading straight into the storm.

They would never make it. He should've reversed course twenty miles back, when the trooper had flagged them down.

He could feel Meek's eyes on him as he drove. He realized he was still gripping the steering wheel tightly, that his back and shoulders were stiff. Forcing himself to relax, he glanced at her in the rearview.

The rain got even heavier, filling the car with a roar so loud it made it impossible to think straight.

Suddenly, he felt the car lift as they hit a patch of surface flooding. He de-accelerated to avoid hydroplaning, but the car had already lost traction. It slid across the pavement with a wet hiss. He corrected the spin and let the car come to a complete stop.

Meeks was shouting something from the backseat. He kept his eyes straight ahead, his focus on the short stretch of road he could still make out.

There was a movement over his right shoulder. She was climbing between the seats. "Ma'am, you really can't—"

Too late. She had angled herself over the center console and neatly into the passenger seat. "I said," she yelled, "should we be driving in this?"

Unless you'd prefer swimming, he thought. He knew they shouldn't be driving in this. Less than two feet of water could float a vehicle. Only one foot if it was flowing fast. And if even a tablespoon got into the electrics, this car was going nowhere fast. With them in it.

She said, "Shouldn't we find somewhere to shelter in place?" Her voice was raised against the sounds of the storm. "There was a turnoff a few miles back."

He looked around. They were on a stretch of interstate in the middle of nowhere. The view ahead and behind was an opaque curtain of rain. The slash pines that lined the road shook, like they possessed no more rigidity than blades of grass.

"We're not turning around, ma'am," he shouted back.

"Why not?"

"Because," he yelled, "we're being followed."

———

Jessica stared at him. "Are you sure?"

The marshal nodded. "Definitely since the truck stop. Possibly since Panama City."

"And you're only just telling me this now?"

He didn't respond, just restarted the car and put it back into gear.

She turned in the seat, craning to get a look out the back

window. There was nothing out there but water. There was nothing anywhere but water.

"I'm sure," he said, taking his foot off the brake and edging forward. "It's a nineties silver sedan."

She faced him again, recalling the silver sedan at the truck stop. "A Cadillac."

His eyes connected with hers for the first time since they'd met. The glance was brief, and he broke it off almost immediately. But in it, she saw the same knowledge that must have been showing on her face.

It was the silver sedan she'd been about to hitch a ride from. That she'd literally been about to climb into.

She reached into the backseat and grabbed her shoulder bag. She settled it in her lap and put her seatbelt on over the top of it.

Inglis glanced at her lap, then looked back out the windshield. "I take it you know how to use that thing?"

When she didn't answer, he glanced at her again. "The weapon in your bag, ma'am."

The only sound in the car was the drill of the rain, the thump of the wiper blades. "How did you know I had one?" she said finally.

"You've been hanging onto that bag like your life depended on it. So, I figured you probably thought it did."

She opened her mouth to say something, but nothing came out, so she closed it again.

He said, "It's not legal, I'm assuming. Is it loaded?"

She looked down at her bag. He was correct that it hadn't been acquired legally. An ex- boyfriend had hooked her up with it. The guy had been something of a gun aficionado. He'd also been a meth aficionado and a not-working or paying-taxes aficionado.

"Yes," she said. "It's loaded."

He looked at her again, right in the eyes, and this time didn't look away. "And do you know how to use it?"

She paused, then said, "I've fired it a few times at a range."

He said nothing, but she could tell from his face that he wasn't happy with her answer.

As he drove slowly forward, she could hear the water sloshing under the wheel wells. She imagined it wouldn't be long before this whole stretch of road was submerged. "But surely, we can't keep going in this? The storm is to the southwest, right? We can't keep just driving straight into it."

He kept his eyes on the road ahead. It was easier talking to him now that she was sitting right next to him, but he still left a lot to be desired in the conversation department. She'd met a few U.S. marshals in her life, and they all struck her as varying degrees of standoffish. Unapproachable. Arrogant, even. She sometimes wondered if they taught courses in it at Glynco. If so, this guy would have been top of his class.

"Hello?" she prompted.

He flicked her an irritated look, and she got the feeling he was wishing she'd decamp to the back seat.

"There's a turnoff up ahead," he said, nodding at the map app on the screen in the dash. It was one of many devices fitted into the car, including a laptop on a swivel mount, a head-up display on the windshield and a police radio built into the center console. "We'll find somewhere to stop and wait out the worst of it."

Outside, the rain kept smashing down around them. Inglis was forced to drive at a snail's pace, the wipers blades sluicing water as fast as it was falling. Up ahead, the interstate veered off onto a ramp with a forty mile per hour speed limit. They weren't doing anything near that. He took the turn onto another dead-straight road that ran due north.

From what she could make out of the view, the landscape ahead was flat, the trees scrubbed away to almost nothing from storms past. The sky was as dark as dusk, illuminated from time to time by brief flares of lightning on the horizon.

They drove several miles on the state road until a narrow track opened to the right. A mailbox sat off to the side, rocking from side to side with each wind gust. Inglis navigated the turn, inching along a lane already awash with water.

To the left, bordered by a shelterbelt of scraggly pines, was a house. It was an old clapboard bungalow, standing up on concrete piles. She peered at it through the fogged windshield. The place already looked like the after photo of storm damage: broken windows boarded up with plywood, rusted roofing with iron missing in sections. Near the house stood a corrugated iron shed. Parked at one end was an old Massey Ferguson tractor, but there was space for another vehicle. The marshal pulled the car in and quit the engine.

They sat there for a long moment, neither of them speaking. Just enjoying not being under aerial assault anymore. But it was far from quiet. The sound of the rain on the iron roof was like a hail of stones.

She glanced at him, to find him staring straight ahead. At the feel of her eyes on him, he gave her a quick glance and undid his seatbelt. "Stay here," he shouted, opening his door.

He got out and went around to the trunk. She swiveled in her seat to watch out the rear windows as he pulled out a heavy parka, with U.S. MARSHAL emblazoned on the back in yellow. He pulled the hood up, then disappeared into the volley of rain.

As soon as he was gone, she got out of the car and looked around. A workbench ran along one side of the shed. It was crammed with boxes and plastic crates. She peered into a couple. They were each carefully packed with dozens of the same item. Rolls of toilet paper. Bottles of hand sanitizer. Blister packs of AA batteries. Boxes of N95 masks. There were several crates of canned food, too, but their lids were rusty, and the labels gone.

Clearly, whoever lived here was either a prepper or a hoarder.

Everything else in the shed was junk. Broken appliances. Old paint cans. Rusted tools. Sacks of rotting potatoes. An ancient outboard motor. Suspended from the ceiling from hooks was a tiny aluminum-hulled boat.

She went to the door and looked out. The rain was coming in

at a steep angle from the east. Nearly a foot had flooded the drive and parts of the front yard already. Rising out of the puddles were strange objects: upturned shopping trolleys, orange buoys tangled in fishing net, misshapen lawn furniture.

The shed's raised concrete foundation kept it safe from the water. But not the wind. It sailed in, flinging stinging needles of rain into her face.

Lightning licked the sky with its sharp tongue. She could smell salt and ozone.

Right on cue, thunder boomed overhead, so loud she involuntarily dropped to a crouch, hands over her ears. The air moved around her, and the ground tremored under her feet.

She straightened, her pulse pounding in her ears. From here, the house was just a vague shape through the curtain of rain.

She wished the marshal would come back. Maybe he'd drowned before he made it to the porch. Or maybe he'd knocked on the door of a family of serial killers, who were at this very moment tying him in the basement next to the body of the last guy who'd been stupid enough to knock on their front door.

She dithered for another few minutes, then took a deep breath and held her bag over her head like a makeshift umbrella.

And then she ran through the storm to the creepy old house built up on stilts, trying not to think about how this was like the start of nearly every horror movie ever made.

TWENTY-FIVE

A DIRT PATH, already a muddy stream, led from the shed to the house. Jessica took it at a run but got drenched within seconds. Rain ran in rivulets down her arms, cascading down her chest and filling her sneakers to overflowing. She'd become a human water feature.

She splashed up the wooden steps. A tiny arched awning over the front door served as the house's porch. Cowering under it, she reached down for the doorknob, but just as her hand closed around it, it was yanked out of her grasp. The door sprung open, revealing Inglis standing there in his dripping wet parka. One hand was resting on the grip of his holstered handgun.

He blinked at her, then removed his hand from the gun and stepped aside to let her in. She entered a small entrance hall, squeezing water from her hair as she went. "Anyone home?"

He shook his head. "Nope."

"No serial killers?"

He gave her an odd look, then said, "The place is pretty cleaned out. Hard to know if whoever lived here left yesterday or last year."

"Was the door locked?"

"Key was under the mat."

She looked around the entrance hall, noting its threadbare carpet and mold-spotted wallpaper. "What happens if the owners come back?"

A gust of wind barreled into the house, making it shiver on its stilts.

Inglis shook his head. "No one's going about in this."

She caught his eye, and she knew what he was thinking. That whoever had been following them was probably still stuck out there in the storm. And hopefully not seeking shelter anywhere near them.

He turned and led her down the hall to the kitchen. The air hung heavy with the smell of stale smoke and mold, making the room feel dingy and oppressive. The linoleum was ancient, the wallpaper peeling. Inglis was right about the place having been cleaned out: there was just an old stove with a coil range, a refrigerator that might have been new in the sixties, and a chest freezer in the corner.

She wandered around the rest of the house. It had been reduced to its bare bones. A single, sagging couch sat in the otherwise empty living room; the only other piece of furniture was a double bed in the bedroom, beneath a boarded-up window.

Jessica stood in the doorway, taking in the depressing digs. A ceiling fan had a milky center light entombing dozens of dead bugs.

It suddenly flared to life. She turned to see the marshal standing behind her, hand on the switch.

"Power's still on." As soon as the words had left his mouth, a gust slammed into the house. The bulb dimmed, then grew bright again. "Though maybe not for long," he added ominously.

She looked at the bed, which was just a mattress covered with an old sheet.

Inglis glanced at it, too, his face expressionless. Then he turned and left without another word.

If the guy were any less animated, he'd be dead, she thought.

Next door was a bathroom, which was as sparse as the rest of the place. Toilet, pedestal basin, old enamel bathtub with a shower head above. Metal shower curtain rail, sans curtain.

She sighed. *Home sweet home for the night.*

She went back into the kitchen to find Inglis standing there. They were both soaked through and dripping trails of water everywhere they went.

"What have we got for food?" she said. Not waiting for an answer, she went to the cupboards over the sink, opened them, found nothing but a few stacked plates and mugs. The refrigerator was unplugged and filled only with a musty odor. A pantry by the oven yielded more promising results: a couple of cans of chicken soup, another of beef stew and one can right at the back with no label.

She pulled out the mystery can and gave it an experimental jiggle. "What'd you suppose this is?"

He came closer and took it from her. Turned it over to exam the bottom of the can. "Whatever it is, it expired three years ago."

She spied something amber glinting at her from the back of the cupboard. A bottle of whiskey. *That might come in handy later.*

The chest freezer was plugged in and switched on, so she went to it and cracked it open.

She immediately dropped the lid and skipped back from it.

"Oh my God," she yelped. "It's a body. And it's been…" she swiveled to look at the marshal, her face aghast, *"chopped into pieces."*

———

Ryan closed the distance in two quick strides, instincts kicking in before thought. The air in the kitchen was cool, but he felt the warmth radiating from Jessica as he stepped beside her. A faint scent clung to her—something floral, a contrast to the sharp, damp chill of their surroundings.

Ryan forced himself to focus, pushing aside the distraction. He lifted the door, the cold air rushing out in a cloud of frost. He leaned in and pulled out a plastic bag containing a frozen slab of meat.

Jessica came close enough to peer over his shoulder. "Is it a… person?"

He dropped the bag with a clunk onto the rest of the dismembered carcass. "Venison's my guess." He shut the freezer door. "I hope you're not a vegan."

Jessica exhaled sharply. "Oh good. Just a hacked-up woodland creature." She gave him a look. "Next time, maybe lead with 'don't worry, it's not a corpse.' Just for me."

Another enormous gust of wind shook the house from floor to ceiling. Heavy rain hammered the iron roof. He left the kitchen and walked through to the derelict living room that overlooked the front drive.

Two of the three windows were already boarded up, probably the causalities of previous hurricanes. He went to the one that wasn't and looked down at the yard. Everywhere there used to be grass was now water. The wind was making a constant assault on the house. It wasn't strong enough to turn the items on the lawn into missiles, but it was getting there.

He tried to guess how far away they were from the coast. Five miles, maybe six? Far enough away to escape a storm surge? He knew they should have kept driving, kept pushing as far from the sea as possible. But he also knew that being swept away in a car while trying to outrun a hurricane was one of the leading ways people actually died in hurricanes.

Jessica joined him at the window. He kept his gaze locked on the glass, though his peripheral vision was doing a damn good job of reminding him she was right there.

He hadn't meant to stare when she came bursting through the door, but the wet t-shirt had made it physically impossible not to. The rain had plastered the sheer fabric to her skin like a second layer, leaving absolutely nothing to the imagination. And clearly, bras weren't part of her emergency weather protocol.

He cleared his throat and tried to focus on the storm outside. If she noticed the flush creeping up his neck or the way he'd suddenly forgotten how to breathe properly, she didn't let on. Calm as ever, she followed his gaze out the window.

"How long do you think we're going to be stuck here?" she asked, as if she wasn't standing there dressed like a goddamn temptation in a disaster movie.

He forked dripping hair off his forehead with his fingers. "At least tonight."

Lightning, thin and mean, sliced across the sky.

Her eyes moved apprehensively to the ceiling. "This place is gonna hold up, right?"

As if to underline the dubiousness of that prospect, thunder boomed overhead. It was so loud it seemed to shift the air in the room.

They glanced at each other, and he succeeded at holding her gaze. "God willing," he said grimly. "And the creek don't rise."

TWENTY-SIX

JESSICA HAD DREAMED of being cold for weeks, but now she couldn't remember what it felt like to be warm.

Inglis had made two mad dashes back to the shed to retrieve their things from the car. He'd left her soaked suitcase in the hall, beside his equally sodden duffel.

She dug through it and pulled out a sweatshirt—an old Nirvana hoodie she'd swiped from a guy she'd lived with back in Florida. Fifty-seven days, her longest relationship to date. He was a musician, the kind who gigged all night, smoked all day, and left the fridge empty. She'd liked his tattoos, and the sex had been decent, but it had ended the way they always did—with him calling her a slut and a bitch, and her leaving with his drugs and his sweatshirt.

She yanked it over her head, mostly for warmth, but also to end the marshal's misery. He was going to give himself whiplash with his effort to keep his eyes off her chest.

She didn't know why he was so bothered. It wasn't like he hadn't seen tits before. Hell, half of Bay County had seen hers. Once upon a time, she might've found his politeness endearing. Chivalrous, even. But she'd long since stopped believing men were capable of either.

When she came back into the kitchen, Inglis's gaze flicked to the hoodie. She expected relief, but his face betrayed nothing. She wondered if he played poker because boy, he'd be good.

"You hungry?" he asked.

She nodded. She hadn't eaten since last night, but given their limited menu, she regretted not grabbing something at that diner back in Alabama.

"We should eat now," he said. "While we got light. And power."

He held up two cans. "Beef stew or chicken noodle?" Then he picked up the mystery can. "Or are you feeling lucky?"

She pulled out a chair at the Formica table. "Not particularly."

"Chicken noodle it is, then."

She watched as he rattled through drawers for a can opener, rinsed out a pot in the sink, and dumped the soup into it. His shirt was still damp, clinging to his arms, the fabric stretching tight across lean muscle.

To break the silence, she asked, "Where are you from?"

"East Tennessee, ma'am."

There was a pause.

"How long have you been a marshal?"

"Twelve years."

"Bet you've seen a lot."

He didn't answer. The conversation died.

She tried again. "You live in Tennessee?"

He nodded. "Memphis. When I'm there."

"So, you travel often?"

He glanced at her, wary now. "It's kinda in the job description."

"Right. Hunting down bad guys. And occasionally babysitting nosy witnesses, too, huh?" She flashed a smile, but he didn't return it.

Jeez. Tough crowd.

She gave up on conversation, figuring it for a lost cause.

Inglis poured the soup into two bowls and turned to bring

them to the table—but he froze when he spotted the revolver in her right hand.

His eyes went from the gun to her face. Then back to the gun.

"Well," he said, setting the bowls down slowly. "That escalated quickly."

"I lied," she admitted. "About knowing how to use it. I've never even fired it."

His hands slid to his hips, his gaze locked on the gun.

"And I was thinking you could show me."

His voice stayed even. "You said that thing's loaded, right?"

She nodded.

"First lesson—never point a gun at someone you don't fully intend to shoot."

She followed his gaze and realized she was aiming at his groin.

His eyes lifted, pinning her with a dry, knowing look. "Unless, of course, that is what you intend."

She swallowed.

Only then did she notice his right hand resting, casual but firm, on the grip of his own weapon.

Heat crept up her neck. She quickly placed the revolver on the table and shook her head.

He exhaled and something told her she'd thrown him off more than he liked.

He pulled out the chair and sat. "Why'd you get a weapon you don't know how to use?"

She tilted her head. "Because I didn't feel safe, okay?" She gestured vaguely to their surroundings. "And, clearly, for good reason."

Inglis said nothing, just studied her, his sharp blue eyes scanning her face like he was reading something written between the lines.

She leaned forward on her elbows. "Look, someone broke into my house and trashed it. Spray-painted that shit on my wall. Someone who you say might've followed us across two state lines. No offense to you or the Marshals Service, but if push comes to shove, I need to be able to defend myself."

She held his gaze, willing him to understand.

Finally, he leaned back, arms folding across his chest.

"Alright," he said. "After we're done eating, we'll find something for you to shoot at." He paused, then added, deadpan, "Preferably something that ain't me."

———

With a final heave, they managed to drag the big roller door closed, the metal groaning against its tracks as they sealed the shed against the fierce wind.

Jessica could hear things pinging off the corrugated iron: branches, gravel, and other small projectiles. As the day went on and the storm hit its straps, she knew those missiles would only get bigger.

A back door opened onto the yard beyond. Wind and rain whirled in, rattled the tools and chains that hung from the walls.

Inglis shook the water from his hands, then held out one for her gun. Jessica took it out of her pocket and handed it to him.

He turned her pistol over on his palm. It was burnished silver with a pale pink grip. In his big hands, it looked ridiculous.

He pressed the thumb catch and swung the cylinder open. Then he pushed a pin and dumped all five rounds into his hand. He reloaded it one by one. "Who gave it to you?"

"Just some guy I used to know. Said it was ideal for a woman. Easy to use."

He closed the barrel with a neat little flick of his hand. "He was patronizing you. If he really cared about your personal safety, he'd have got you a can of Mace and a jackknife instead."

"What's wrong with it?"

He held it up. "This is a .38 Special snub-nose revolver. They're marketed to women because they look like they're easy to fire. In fact, the opposite is true. They're hammerless, see?" He showed her a blank space at the back of the gun. "That means the trigger pull is heavy. And the recoil is a hell of a thing. If you're not ready for it, it'll snap your hand right back. Plus," he added, as if he hadn't dressed down her little gun enough, "they can't shoot worth a damn."

"You seemed pretty twitchy a minute ago, when I had it pointed at your junk."

He pressed his lips together but didn't deign to reply. Then he slid his own weapon from its holster with his other hand. It was matte black with a heavy stippled grip. Long, rectangular barrel. It looked well-handled and, in the dull light, coldly lethal. It made hers look like a Mattel accessory.

"This is a Glock 22," he said. "See how much longer the barrel is?"

She shrugged. "So, yours is bigger than mine. Big deal."

"The longer the barrel, the higher the velocity of the shot. And the faster the shot, the more accurate it is." He gestured with her gun. "This thing? You'd have a better chance of hitting someone with it if you threw it at him."

She raised her eyebrows. "Now who's being patronizing?"

He didn't reply, just handed it back to her.

She looked down at it, tiny and pink, and realized the asshole who'd sold it to her had been low key trolling her.

He swiveled her until she was facing out into the backyard. Through the haze of rain, she could just make out the dark shapes of objects: rubbish bins, a ride-on mower half covered by a tarp, and a couple of forty-four-gallon drums.

Pointing at one of them, he said, "Aim for that drum. See it? Imagine it's your target. Don't try and be fancy and think you're gonna put one between his eyes. Go for the center mass. Shoulders, torso, stomach, back."

She looked up at him. "What about aiming for the leg or something? Seems more…humane."

"Way harder than it looks." He met her gaze directly. "You

shoot him where you have to, ma'am. And you keep on shooting until he goes down. Got it?"

She held it in her right hand, palm around the grip and her index finger under the trigger guard. He got behind her, lifting her elbow until her arm was out in front of her. Then he angled her until she was pointing it at the drum.

She said quietly, "Have you ever shot anyone?"

His voice was next to her ear. "No one I wanted to."

She looked back at the drum, squinted one eye to bring it into focus. When she thought she had it lined up with her hand, she squeezed the trigger. There was more resistance against her finger than she was expecting, which made her think it was stuck or something, but then it went off with an almighty bang.

The recoil shot up her arm and pushed her whole body back against him. He steadied her with both hands on her upper arms. The sound reverberated and died away. 'Did I hit it?'

"You pulled it to the right. Try again."

She did, trying to focus on the drum and not on the feel of Inglis's hands on her shoulders or his body heat radiating through the damp fabric of his shirt. Three more times she tried, and on the last, saw a bright yellow spark and heard the faint metallic ping of the bullet hitting the target.

"Woo hoo," she said, lowering the gun and glancing up at him. "What'd I win?"

He was still standing right behind her. His gaze fell upon her, the corners of his mouth quirking up in the closest approximation of a smile she'd seen on him.

Registering their proximity, he promptly released her and retreated a step. "Okay. That's enough practice."

Neither of them spoke for a long moment. They just stood there listening to the drum of rain on the roof and the thump of each wind gust against the roller door, like they were the most fascinating sounds on Earth.

Finally, she broke the silence. "He's still out there, isn't he?"

Inglis met her eyes again, his expression tense. He nodded.

Jessica cast her gaze upwards. Their shelter was dubious at best. The fragile structure felt like a metaphor for her own precarious situation, each gust a painful reminder.

She looked down at the little gun in her hand. Sure, it was better than nothing. But would it be enough to protect her from the men who were hunting her?

TWENTY-SEVEN

THE RAIN WAS RELENTLESS; it crashed like a waterfall over Roach's windshield. Visibility in the dead state trooper's SUV was better than it would have been in his abandoned Catera. But even with the wipers going full tack, he still couldn't see shit.

He'd turned off the interstate some miles back, but he had no idea where he was. Didn't even know what direction he was driving in.

He gripped the steering wheel in both hands, face inches from the windshield. His breath fogged the glass, making it even harder to see. He smeared his balled-up fist against the cold surface, using the split-second gap between the dash of the wiper and the bloom of rain against the windshield to get a blink-and-you'll-miss-it glimpse of his surroundings.

A squat gray building with a wide overhang to his left. He didn't even think, just jerked the steering wheel around and slammed his foot on the accelerator. It was only when he was under the shelter of the overhang that he realized it was a gas station. The place was dark inside, and it was hard to tell if it had been shut for the storm or closed for good.

Only one way to find out. He directed the front grille of the Ford straight at the automatic doors and hit the gas. The vehicle rammed right through the middle of them, glass raining down on the hood in glinting shards. The sound of the crash was almost completely drowned out by the roar of the storm.

He shoved the door open, jumped down. Pulling his SIG out from his waistband, he squeezed around the front of the SUV.

Glass crunched under his boots as he surveyed the darkened store. Food lined the shelves, and along the far wall, a beverage refrigerator glowed blue. Overhead, an alarm wailed, the noise barely audible over the drum of rain on the roof. It'd turn off eventually, and he knew it wouldn't send anyone running in his direction anytime soon. Not unless they had a boat.

He grabbed a bag of Cheetos off the shelf and squatted down against the counter.

Now it was just a waiting game.

Inglis dropped her suitcase onto the linoleum with a dull thud. "We should get some rest while we still can."

Jessica watched as he stepped back into the hall to retrieve his bag. But instead of bringing it into the kitchen with hers, he carried it into the lounge and set it carefully on the sagging sofa in the corner.

She frowned. The thing was ancient—water-stained fabric, fraying seams, the base so worn it nearly touched the floor.

"You're not sleeping on that," she said. "We can share the mattress."

He hesitated, jaw working slightly. "Are you sure?"

She exhaled sharply, resisting the urge to roll her eyes. It wasn't like she was propositioning him for a night of wild sex. "Yes, I'm sure." She bent down to drag her suitcase into the bedroom. "But if you snore, you're back on the couch."

Inside the bedroom, they stripped the dusty sheet off the mattress. She tried not to notice the patchwork of old stains, all roughly at groin level. The pillows were worse—mildew-spotted, damp to the touch. She tossed them into the corner.

Without hesitation, Inglis took the worse side of the bed. She stretched out on the other, facing the wall.

Sleep felt impossibly far away. The longer she lay there, the further it drifted.

She glanced over her shoulder. Inglis had his back to her, lying as close to the mattress edge as he could without falling off. He wasn't sleeping either.

Outside, the storm raged; it crashed against the sides of the house like waves upon a cliff. But in here, in this dark, airless room, it was as if they were in a box at the bottom of the ocean, weighed down by unimaginable pressure.

She stayed perfectly still, fighting the urge to toss and turn. Sleepless nights were never good for her. That was when her past came creeping in, flickering like a cruel film reel behind her eyelids, each scene a reminder of what she'd lost.

Not the house. Not the money. Not even her mother or sister, though she sometimes let herself imagine a fresh start with them.

No.

Mostly, it was two faces.

Sebastián.

Daniel.

Their names were carved into her ribs, pressed deep into the hollow spaces of her chest.

She wiped a hand across her wet cheeks, thinking she'd been silent. But then the mattress dipped.

Inglis sat up carefully.

He didn't say anything. Didn't ask if she was okay or offer some useless reassurance. He just rose from the bed, walked to the door, and slipped out, closing it gently behind him.

Jessica let out a breath she hadn't realized she was holding.

She turned onto her back, stared at the ceiling, and went back to counting her losses.

TWENTY-EIGHT

ROACH LINED up the beer can with the sight on his handgun and pulled the trigger. It exploded like a geyser, spraying beer in a wide arc, then landed on its side and spun until its contents joined the growing puddle on the floor. Fourteen other cans and several ruptured tubes of Pringles made up the snack graveyard.

He picked up the half-empty bottle of Dewars and took a long pull. He'd found it in a drawer in the back office after he'd finished prying the safe from the wall.

Placing his gun on the ground, he slipped the gold phone out of his pocket.

It had only taken him a few minutes back in Florida to bypass Julia's passcode with some firmware he'd downloaded onto his old laptop. The one that was probably now bobbing in the Catera's backseat.

Now he accessed her device tracking app and saw where her synced Garmin smartwatch was. Less than nine miles away. Which, presuming it was still attached to her pretty little wrist, meant she hadn't gone far.

He looked out the shattered front door, beyond the state trooper's SUV, to where the rain was near horizontal. The road had become a river, and the gas station forecourt was half a foot submerged. Water was everywhere; it dripped from between cracks in the ceiling tiles; it trickled down the walls; it crept in from under the SUVs tires like a slow tide.

He took another hit from the bottle, thinking about what was awaiting Julia in her immediate future. Wondering if she had any inkling of it. He wondered if she could sense the fear that would soon be emanating from every pore in her body, the way that cats could detect a coming earthquake.

Fear.

In his opinion, it ruled the world. It dictated nearly every decision a person made. Fear of missing out. Fear of failure, fear of success. Fear of getting old. Fear of death. Fear of pain. The latter being the most powerful fear of all. He knew of places you could put a razor blade in a person that would make death feel like a kindness.

Roach had learned that himself the hardest way possible.

But he was getting ahead of himself. He had to play this right, and that meant taking it one step at a time.

After all, good things came to those who wait. He smiled around the mouth of the bottle.

Bad things, too.

———

Jessica jolted awake, sitting bolt upright in bed.

The house shuddered as a gust of wind slammed into it with the force of a wrecking ball. Her pulse pounded in her ears. She wasn't sure if it was the storm or the nightmare that had wrenched her from sleep.

In the dream, she'd been lying on an old mattress—one disturbingly similar to this one—in a dark, damp room. Metal chains shackled her wrists to the wall, a cruel detail where, thankfully, dream and reality diverged.

Then Daniel had appeared, stepping out of the darkness.

That familiar jolt hit her—pain and happiness tangled into

something unbearable. She'd strained against the chains, desperate to reach him. She'd tried to speak, to tell him again how sorry she was, but the words had choked into ragged sobs.

He'd knelt beside her, fingers tracing the metal cuffs. Then he'd smiled—that same sad, beautiful smile that haunted her—and said, *"You better run, baby."*

Then Inglis had walked in, holding out her gun. His voice was calm, steady. *"Shoot him where you have to, ma'am."*

And then, mercifully, she'd woken up.

Jessica let out a shaky breath and rubbed her arms, the cold seeping deeper than skin. The fear still clung to her, that creeping terror that lingers at the edges of sleep, threatening to spill into the waking world. The memory left a hollow ache in its wake, a yawning emptiness she couldn't shake.

On the other side of the bed, the sheets were rumpled. Inglis must have come back after she finally passed out.

She checked her watch. The screen lit up in the gloom. Nearly seven in the evening. She'd slept longer than she thought. But her mind ached, as if it had been running at full speed while her body lay still.

She slid out of bed and padded to the bathroom, then wandered through the darkened living room. Outside, fingers of rain tapped against the bare windowpane. The wind howled through the trees, bending them violently. It rattled the roller door on the shed like something was trying to claw its way in.

The house felt eerie. Empty. Like she was the last person left alive.

Light glowed from the kitchen.

She went in, finding Inglis sitting at the table, nursing a glass of whiskey. His shirt was unbuttoned at the collar, his sleeves rolled up, forearms flexing as he swirled the liquid.

Jessica grabbed a second glass. "You drinking alone?"

He glanced up, studying her face like he could still see the remnants of her nightmare. "Didn't think you'd be up."

"Couldn't sleep."

The silence stretched. Outside, the storm howled, rattling the walls.

She poured herself a drink, sliding into the chair across from him. "I dreamed about you."

Inglis stilled, his grip tightening on the glass. "That so?"

She tilted her head, watching him. "You were telling me to pull the trigger."

His jaw clenched, something flickering behind his eyes. "Did you?"

She took a slow sip of whiskey, letting the burn settle in her chest. "Guess I woke up too soon."

His gaze dropped to her mouth, just for a second, before he looked away. "Lucky for me."

Jessica smiled. "Lucky for both of us."

The air between them felt thick, humming with a tension neither of them acknowledged.

Inglis took another sip of whiskey, then made a face like he wished he hadn't.

Jessica swiveled the bottle to face her. "Says here it's Tennessee's finest."

Inglis eyed the off-brand logo. Raised an eyebrow.

She poured another glass. "You know what they say about people from Tennessee, right?"

"I'm sure I do," he drawled.

"They make other Southerners look like they're in a hurry."

That half-smile again. "See, now, I heard the exact same thing about people from Arkansas."

She nodded at the bottles of water lined neatly on the counter, alongside matches, candles and their remaining tins of food. "Why do I get the feeling you were a Boy Scout?"

This time, he actually smiled, if only for a second. Some of the tension unwound from his frame.

Jessica studied him. She still couldn't get a read on him. Unavailable? Uninterested? Just plain shy? Probably not the first, and not just because he wasn't wearing a ring. She'd worked in a strip club for years. She could spot the taken ones from ten feet. And she hated them most of all— hated knowing she was scratching some itch for a guy, giving him something he wasn't getting at home, but which he didn't have the goddamn balls to do anything about. Except ogle her and drool.

Inglis pulled his hand from his pocket, set his phone on the table.

She glanced at it. "I'm guessing no service, right?"

"Satellite calls only."

Another violent gust slammed into the house. The roller door groaned under the strain.

A second later, the kitchen lights flickered, plunging them into semi-darkness before surging back to life.

"Whew." Jessica exhaled. "That was close." She unscrewed the whiskey bottle and topped off both their glasses. Then she leaned back in her chair, tilting her head at him.

"So, Ryan. What's your story, then?"

———

Ryan had a problem. Well, he had a lot of problems, but the main one facing him right now was, in fact, facing right now.

He shouldn't be sitting here drinking with her. He wasn't exactly sure how many ethics codes he was violating, but it had to be a few.

And there were other reasons, too.

This house could come down around them at any moment. If that were to happen, at least one of them should be sober. Plus, tomorrow they'd both be better off without hangovers.

So, yeah, that was a bunch of reasons. And yet, he couldn't make himself get up and leave this damn table.

The more he looked at her, the more his impression of her seemed to shift in front of his eyes. He was finding it increasingly difficult to maintain his earlier conviction about there being no innocent witnesses in the program. About her deserving this transient, fear-filled life.

And he was becoming more and more convinced that he was a judgmental prick for ever having thought that.

She was still waiting for an answer to her question, so he cleared his throat and said, "My story?"

She shrugged. "Tell me about yourself."

He swallowed and stared down at his glass, mystified how to go about doing such a thing. Small talk wasn't his strong suit. "Uh, what do you want to know?"

She shrugged, "Tell me about your job. You work for the... Violent Fugitive...something, right?"

"Two Rivers Violent Fugitive Task Force."

She snapped her fingers like that had been on the tip of her tongue. Then took another sip of her drink. "Hunting down violent fugitives. That sounds terrifying."

He tilted his head. "Sometimes." He took a sip of his own. "Most of the time, though, it's as boring as any other job."

She smiled and raised her eyebrows like she didn't believe that. But he wasn't just trying to sound modest. His job really was about ten percent beating down doors and ninety percent reading tedious case files and chasing down dead-end leads. Some fugitives he'd hunted had been on the run for over twenty years. They were living quiet lives in small towns, thinking the law had forgotten about them. But the USMS never forgot. It was a long game for them, not an all guns blazing kinda thing.

And that was the secret of their success: keeping their successes a secret. It was a company motto. If they did their jobs right, no one would even know they'd been there.

Overhead, the light flickered again, and they both cast their eyes ceiling-ward as if in prayer to the electricity gods.

"What's the worst case you ever had?"

Ryan chewed his bottom lip for a moment, not looking at her. Then he exhaled and said, "Well, the first runner-up would have to be the angel-dusted Neo Nazi with enough homemade explosives strapped to him to blow us both to Jesus." He shook his head at the memory. "Guy had more swastikas on him than brain cells, that was for damn sure.

"But the actual worst one was this house we raided in Jackson. This guy was up on a bunch of sex crime charges across multiple states. We finally tracked him down to this old shack on the outskirts of town. It was maybe five o'clock in the morning. We knocked his door down. Dragged the guy out of bed. He was pretty much as loathsome as you'd expect a guy like that to be. But it was what we found in the other bedroom that was worse. A girl, filthy and starving, tied to a mattress. She'd been locked in there for God knows how long."

Jessica held her glass to her lips but didn't take a sip.

"I say girl," he went on, "but she was in her twenties. Although so malnourished, she looked about twelve. Turns out, he'd murdered her mother when she was a baby and then kidnapped her. He'd been living with her all those years. First as her father. Then as her husband." He shook his head. "To say that was disturbing is an understatement."

She said nothing for a long moment. Then she said quietly, "When I see those kinds of stories on the news, I never know whether those are good days or bad days for you guys."

Inglis eyed her over his glass. "Yeah," he said softly. "Me either."

Then the lights went out without even a flicker of warning and the room plunged into darkness.

TWENTY-NINE

JESSICA BOLTED UPRIGHT, her chair toppling over behind her with a thud. The darkness was so complete it felt like she was blindfolded. Instinctively, she thrust out her arms, unable to recall a single thing about her surroundings. Another thud: a glass or the whiskey bottle falling over onto the table.

She felt panic crowd in around her, hot hands and breath, and the sensation that she couldn't control any part of her body.

Bright white light burned into the backs of her eyeballs, and she shut them tight. When she opened them again, she saw Ryan holding out his phone.

He lowered the light. "Hey," he said softy. "It's okay. It's alright."

She was still breathing fast, her pulse beating in her jugular. It wasn't just the dark that had frightened her. The similarities between the marshal's story and her dream had also troubled her. She tried to shake the eerie feeling away, but it seemed to have settled in her bones.

He came around the table and gently pulled her into him in an awkward one-armed hug. She relaxed into it, into the solidness of his chest, the comforting bulk of his biceps. She could smell cologne on his shirt. Something fresh and marine.

"I'm sorry," she said, panic giving way to a feeling of foolishness. "You must think I'm such a wimp. It's just something happened to me in the dark a long time ago."

Inglis was looking down at her, concern bracketing his mouth. He opened it to say something, then seemed to think the better of it and closed it. Stepping back, he let her go, and the feeling of security he'd wrapped her in melted into the darkness.

He turned to the kitchen counter, and she heard the click of a lighter. When he faced her again, he was holding a candle propped in a mug.

She gave a shaky laugh. "Definitely a Boy Scout."

He placed the mug on the table and sat back down, letting his phone light die.

She forced herself to say something irreverent to lighten the mood. "Well," she said, looking around their little candlelit table. "This is romantic."

He raised an eyebrow. "We're drinking terrible whiskey, with a candle that smells like an old crayon, in a house that may not make it through the night. You have a low bar for romance."

She laughed, still feeling a little giddy from her fright. "Oh, honey, my bar is, like, underground." She unscrewed the cap, poured them both some more of the terrible whiskey. "Most of the men I've dated think opening a can of beer for a woman constitutes a grand gesture. The fact that you're wearing cologne and haven't tried to cop a feel yet puts you in the top one percentile, easy."

He tilted his head slightly, eyes glinting with something unreadable. "Yet?"

That one word sent a spark through her. She didn't know whether it was her calling him honey, the talk of copping feels, or maybe the detail that she knew what he smelled like because of their hug, but suddenly, he wasn't looking at his drink anymore. He was looking at her.

She regarded him for a long moment and realized she was making him nervous. But not in a bad way.

So. Not uninterested, then. Just restrained.

She knew that type, too. They were the ones who got dragged into the club by boorish friends. They actually dressed up or at least put on a shirt with buttons. And when they got peer-pressured into going into the Champagne Room with her (which, in all her time working at Femme Fatale, had never once featured champagne), they wanted to know her name, where she was from, how her day had been, instead of just attempting to dry hump her. Choir boys, the other girls called them. She thought of them as men whose mamas raised them right. And of all the men she'd had to wade through in a night working at that awful place, they had been the ones she'd disliked the least.

She took another sip of her drink, aware that on her empty stomach it was going straight to her head. "So. You married?"

He said nothing for a long time, and she thought he wouldn't answer. Then he cleared his throat and said, "I was. Long time ago."

Hmm. There's definitely a story there, she thought. "Got anyone back home in Memphis?"

"No."

"See, that surprises me," she said, tilting her glass at him. "I figured someone like you would be beating women off with a stick."

He shifted in his seat, looking for all the world like someone who'd rather not be having this conversation. But she knew he was a little intrigued because he said, 'Someone like me?'

"Oh, yeah," she said, warming to her topic. "You've got this whole inscrutable thing going on. Taciturn and mysterious. Alpha, but not assholey with it."

"Right," he said, getting three syllables out of the word. His accent was getting thicker with every sip he took.

"Women love that shit." She surveyed him some more over the rim of her glass. She was flirting with a federal marshal. Flirting hard. Was that even legal? "Plus, there's your face. And what I can assume is a fair amount going on underneath your shirt." She propped an elbow on the table. "I mean, I wouldn't kick you out of bed. Unless you were better on the floor."

He choked on his drink.

She hid a smile. Teasing this guy could keep her entertained for hours.

When he recovered, looking a lot pinker than he had before, she held one hand in surrender. "I'm sorry. I will keep it in my pants, I promise."

He cleared his throat but didn't reply. Neither of them spoke for a long moment. All her shameless flirting had thickened the air between them. She'd only been joking, but now it felt... real.

And the way he was looking at her? Like maybe he wasn't planning to run either.

It was her turn to clear her throat a little nervously. And it was then she realized that the room was silent. There was no constant drill of rain on the roof. No incessant howling of the wind. She didn't know how long it had been quiet, but now that she was aware of it, the silence was deafening.

Her ears popped, and the low pressure made her feel breathless. The air smelt like salt.

Inglis cast his eyes upward, noticing it, too. "Means the back half of the storm's still coming our way," he said.

She got up, went through to the living room. Stood in front of the one clear window, surveyed the new, calm world. There were stars overhead. They glinted off the water that now lapped gently against the side of the house.

Wait. *Water that lapped against the side of the house?*

She stared out, wondering if she was seeing things or if there'd been something in the whiskey.

The eerie calm continued.

Ryan joined her at the window, and she said, "How long do you think it will it last?"

He shook his head. "Depends on where we are in the eye. Could be half an hour. Could only be a few minutes."

They both stood there for a long time, not speaking. Soaking in the silence. Then she heard it: a distant roar like an enormous wave approaching from the west.

She turned her head and squinted, certain that she could actually see the wind as it came towards them. But that was impossible, right? And yet there it was, a physical ripple that seemed to shimmer in the darkness. It smacked down trees as it went, their branches and leaves vanishing before the blast like a special effect. She could only stare in horror as the ripple approached the house—

Ryan threw himself on top of her as the window exploded. The building shifted beneath them. The sound was like nothing she'd ever heard: a great, deep vibration that she felt in bones as much as perceived with her ears.

The wind was inside the house now, like an invisible wild animal, ripping and tearing at her hair and clothes. Inglis bundled her up and half-dragged, half-carried her out of the room, broken glass and debris crunching underfoot.

The candle had snuffed out, but he grabbed it and the lighter, and by the illumination from his phone, they made their way to the rear of the house.

He slammed the bedroom door shut behind them and twisted the lock while she slid down the wall and hugged her knees. "So, I guess that was the back end," she managed.

Ryan relit the candle in the mug and set it down on the floor at her feet. "Are you hurt?"

She raised her hands and looked at them, then at her bare arms. "A few scratches, nothing major." She realized her arms were shaking, so she lowered them. "What about you?"

He came to sit beside her against the wall. "I'm fine."

Silence set up camp between them. Outside the room, the sounds of the storm had returned with gusto. The unholy howl of the wind, the sudden volleys of rain against what was left of the roof.

She rested her head back against the wall and sighed. "Shit. The whiskey."

Inglis made a sound of resignation. "Probably better watered down, anyway."

She snorted, which prompted him to chuckle, and then they were both laughing like idiots while the house groaned and the roller door in the garage sounded like it was being ripped from its hinges.

When they finally calmed down enough to speak, he said, "So. What's your story, then? Since we're sharing."

She turned to him, smile fading. "Oh, you don't wanna hear mine."

"Why not?" He rolled his head on the wall to face her. "We got nothing but time to kill."

———

Jessica looked away from his penetrating blue stare. She realized she'd been doing the thing she always did to people, especially men: pressing them into talking about their lives, so she didn't have to talk about her own.

Because she couldn't talk about her own. Not to anyone. Not ever.

She'd learned a long time ago that men liked it when she made the conversation all about them. They liked to believe that she really was fascinated by every banal detail about their job or their sports team or their truck. By every opinion that came out of their mouths, no matter how stupid or offensive. And they never once realized that her interest in them was as fake as her smile.

Because, to them, she didn't actually exist. She wasn't a real person; she was just a figment of their fantasies. She was Fuck Me Barbie. Which was fine, because deep down, she didn't believe she existed either. Deep down, she knew that Jessica Meeks was a lie, and that her whole life was, too.

She wondered what he knew about her past. At least some of it. Maybe all of it.

He wasn't asking for her life story because he wanted to know about it. He was asking because he wanted her to tell him.

And no one had ever wanted that from her before. At least, not for a very long time.

She swallowed, not knowing where to start. She wished she did have the whiskey bottle in hand. It felt like a necessary aid if she was going to go digging up things in her past.

Dead and buried things in her past.

She looked down at her hands and said, "I used to be a ballet dancer." She could feel his eyes on her, but she kept her head down. "I trained my whole life for it. Turned out it was more my mom's dream than mine.' She lifted her knees, draping her wrists over them. "But I still miss it, you know. I miss having a dream, a purpose, even if it wasn't mine."

He said nothing for a while, just stared at her like she was the most fascinating thing he'd ever seen. Then he looked away and said, "You know, you didn't have to work in that place." He snatched a quick glance at her. "I mean, not that I'm judging you or anyone who does that kinda thing for a living. I'm just saying..." he trailed off awkwardly, then cleared his throat and tried again. "There's federal assistance available. The USMS can arrange for you to attend to college, if that's something you wanted to do one day."

She said nothing for a long moment. Just listened to the wind and chewed her inner cheek. Obviously, working at Femme Fatale was never her life's ambition. At first, she told herself that stripping was some kind of feminist power move, that she was making men pay for what they would otherwise just take for free. But deep down, she knew it was less about feminism and more about capitalism. It paid better than waiting tables or cleaning motel rooms, plain and simple.

"I'm sorry," he said, shaking his head like he felt stupid for bringing it up. "It's none of my business."

His embarrassment made her want to say something concessionary. Made her want to acknowledge his attempt to give her life advice, even though he had precious little right offering it.

"Dance therapy," she blurted.

He looked at her, a question in his eyes.

"I was thinking of becoming qualified in it one day." *When I have my shit together*, she added mentally.

"Dance therapy?" he repeated.

She nodded. "After a traumatic event, the brain tries to suppress it, while the body holds on to it. It remains reactive. For years afterwards. And the theory is that physical movement, like yoga or dance, can help. It sort of rewires the brain. There's all this research that's proves how effective it is." She gave him a dry look. "But you probably think that's a load of woke nonsense, right?"

"No," he said softly. "I do not."

She examined his face, but it showed no signs of skepticism. In fact, he seemed genuinely interested. "I mean, I'd need a Master's degree, and to go through a clinical internship and all that. It'll be a lot of work."

He took her hand. The gesture didn't seem romantic, so much as comforting. "How about I make you a deal?" he said. "If we make it out of this mess, if I get you to Baton Rouge—come hell or high water—promise me you'll consider it, okay?"

She was amazed that he was invested enough in her life to bother making such a deal. But she nodded and said, "Okay." Then she smiled and added, "I mean, obviously, I can't keep stripping forever. I'm over thirty. Getting a little long in the tooth to be prancing around the stage in nothing but a thong, don't you think?"

The question was meant to be rhetorical, but he seemed to think it needed answering. He turned his head on the wall to look at her and said softly, "Oh, I thought you looked real pretty." His hand was still closed around hers, his thumb brushing her knuckles. "Matter of fact, I couldn't take my eyes off of you."

He didn't sound like a lawman anymore. He sounded like a

Southern boy in a bar trying to pick her up. And she remembered exactly how he'd been looking at her, standing under the Exit sign while she'd been up on stage. Like he'd strayed into a dream instead of a dingy dive bar.

She had a sudden desire to lean over and kiss him, just to see if his mouth tasted as good as the syrupy drawl that came from it. And she knew now that he'd kiss her back. He'd do whatever she let him do.

She'd read somewhere that when people found themselves in life-threatening situations, the desire to procreate became front of mind. Basically, when everything was fucked, people just wanted to fuck. There was probably something Freudian in it, something about how sex was a coping mechanism, a way of warding off the fear of death. Or maybe it was for the same reason those people left evacuating to the last minute. Maybe it was simply about hope.

She dragged her gaze away, her fingers going to the ring around her neck. Daniel's memory flared in her mind, and any desire to kiss the marshal flickered out and died.

Crossing her arms over her knees, she said, "What happened with your wife? Since we're, you know, sharing."

His jaw clenched, then released. He glanced down at his hand, as if expecting to still see a ring there.

"Sorry," she said. "I mean, if she died of some awful disease or something."

"No, it's just, you know, complicated." He gave his head a quick shake. "We were together for seven years. We've been separated for longer than that now."

She stared at him, trying to do the math. "Wait, how old are you?"

"Thirty-four."

"So, you got married when you were...?"

"Seventeen."

"Whoa. I mean, I know they do things differently in the mountains, but seventeen?"

He shot her a droll look. Then he sighed and said, "I'd gotten her pregnant."

Okay. Choir boy, maybe not. "So your parents made you get married?"

He shook his head. "Not mine. My daddy gave me three hundred dollars, the keys to his truck, and directions to a clinic in Knoxville." He glanced at her quickly. "Only if she'd wanted too, of course."

"But she didn't?"

A deep wail, precursor to another massive gust, interrupted him before he could answer. It sounded like an incoming freight train, and it hit the house with about as much force. She grabbed Inglis's arm as the room buckled sideways. Outside, she heard things falling and hitting the ground. Crockery, the tins of food, the kitchen chairs. The door to their room rattled like the hurricane herself was trying to get in.

They both stared at the door and then at each other. She swallowed, letting go of his arm. Then she nodded at him, wanted him to go on with his story, wanting to think of anything else but the storm outside.

He inhaled deeply. "Her folks wouldn't let her get a termination. Her daddy was a pastor. Of the fire and brimstone variety. Threatened to disown her if she went through with it. Threatened to come after me with a twelve bore if I didn't do right by her."

"Seriously?"

He nodded. "I had to go hide out in my daddy's hunting cabin in the mountains till he calmed down." He said it with a smile that quickly faded. "We didn't seem to think getting married was the worst idea at the time. We were young. And dumb. And in love."

"Yeah," she said softly. "I know how that goes."

He didn't respond, and they were both quiet for a spell. "So…" she drew the word out, "you have a kid?"

The ball of his jaw tightened again. He forked his fingertips through his hair, then gave his head a quick shake. "No. She lost the baby. She was nearly full term, eight and a half months. But there was no heartbeat. So, she had to go through labor, the whole birth and everything. But the baby was…" He swallowed hard and didn't continue.

"I'm sorry," she whispered.

He dropped his head, pressed his fingertips to his eyelids. "It was awful. For everyone. But mostly for her. Her daddy told her it was God punishing us for having been so ungrateful of His gift in the first place."

Her eyebrows flew up, and he gave her a wry look. "Oh, yeah. Randy Hyssop was a mean son of a bitch on a good day." He sighed, looking down at his lap. "I'd just turned eighteen. I had no idea how to deal with any of it. All I could think was that I wished we'd taken the three hundred bucks and the trip to Knoxville."

He glanced at her, right in the eyes, like he expected to see some judgment reflected in them. She took his hand again and squeezed it, like he'd done to hers earlier.

"We tried to make it work," he said. "Moved west, to Memphis. I went to college; she went to nursing school. But she wasn't coping. She had a lot of guilt, I think. Over the baby. She seemed to think it was her fault somehow. Like she actually believed what her daddy said about the miscarriage. She'd started taking these antidepressants, and then she started taking pain pills. Then she started stealing scrips and meds from the hospital where she worked." He looked down at his lap. "She just spiraled. I found out she had a dealer. Then I found out she was screwing her dealer." He inhaled, then shook his head. "So, yeah. That ended that."

He stared down at their joined hands, like he expected them to enter the conversation. "We never actually got divorced. We just kind of stopped being married. She took off up north some-where." He shrugged. "I think she has a kid now. A boy."

They were both quiet again. Listening to the heavy beat of the rain and the soft hiss of the candle. The building continued to sway with the wind, like a ship at sea. She'd gotten so used to it now that she expected when the storm was finally over, she'd have trouble walking on steady ground.

"You don't still keep in touch?"

"Oh, she still calls and texts me occasionally." His jaw tightened. "When she wants something. Money, usually." He shook his head and sighed. "But whatever else we had is over. Which is for the best." He paused, then added, "Relationships are like glass. Sometimes it's better to leave them broken than to hurt yourself trying to put them back together."

She smiled at him. "That was deep."

He returned the smile. "It's something my mama said to me once. I never forgot it."

"She sounds like a wise lady."

He nodded, his smile turning sad. "She was."

She looked up and, without thinking, reached out a hand to smooth the back of his hair, at the place he was constantly fidgeting with. "But your wife knew, right? That you loved her?"

He shook his head, although she knew he wasn't saying no. "Yeah. Kylie knows." The way he said it, in the present tense, made her think he did still love her. And that maybe she loved him, too. He turned to look at her. "But it's not enough, you know. Love."

No, she thought. *Sometimes it's not.*

THIRTY

IN A SUDDEN DRAFT from under the door, the candle guttered and nearly went out. Ryan sat up and adjusted it in its mug, making it flicker and casting eerie shadows onto the walls.

Everything felt strange. That they were stuck in this one small room in a house in the middle of nowhere. In the middle of a hurricane. That she was sharing deeply personal stories with this man, who was basically a stranger.

Except he wasn't a stranger. She realized she knew him now better than she knew anybody else in her life. Which was probably the strangest thing of all.

When he settled himself against the wall again, she said, "So there's been no one else? Since she left?"

He rested his head back, so he was looking at the ceiling. "Nope. And I figure that if I could have found somebody else, I would of by now."

She drew her feet under her until she was sitting cross-legged. "I haven't been able to make any kind of relationship work, either," she said, her fingers finding their way to the ring again. "Not since Daniel."

Ryan's tone was skeptical. "This is the guy who got you into this whole mess?"

Her gaze fell upon the ring, triggering the familiar ache she always felt when she saw it.

"He wasn't a bad guy," she whispered. "He was just playing the hand he'd been dealt."

She looked at the marshal, but he didn't look like he believed her.

She said, "The drugs, the gang, he hated all of it. It was just a means to an end. A way to survive." She squeezed the ring between her thumb and fingers, feeling something hot backing up behind her eyes.

It wasn't lost on her that of all the dangerous things he'd survived in his life, she'd been the one thing he couldn't.

The tears spilled over, rolling down her cheeks.

"You still love him."

She swallowed and wiped the tears away with the back of her hand. Then she looked at him and nodded.

"And I'm guessing you ain't found anyone else either."

"No. When Daniel went, it was like he turned out the light behind him." She swiped away another tear and made a face. "Actually, it's like he burned down the whole fucking house."

It wasn't like she hadn't tried to find that kind of spark again with someone else. In the first few years after she'd arrived in Florida, she had gone through a phase of bringing warm bodies home every night, hoping to catch one of those mythical other fish that apparently populate the sea. Mostly she just caught STIs. Nowadays, she was more discerning in her choice of bedfellows, and definitely more particular about her sexual health. But she'd all but given up on finding anyone who could make her feel like he had. Even the mere memory of his hands on her was more thrilling than any other man's.

She sighed and leaned her head back against the wall. "I dunno why I've never been able to get my shit together. Get a proper job. Form mature relationships. Resume normal transmission." She gave him a wry smile. "Honestly, I think half my problem is that I have terrible taste in men. It's my fatal flaw. I'm like an asshole-seeking missile."

He smiled and shook his head, like what she said both amused and annoyed him.

"It's like I have this flashing neon sign above my head that reads 'Fuck me, then forget me'." She turned her head toward Ryan. "You're a guy. Can you see it?"

He wasn't looking above her head. His eyes were roving all over her face. They were so blue, like the color of a gas flame.

Finally, they settled on her lips. "No," he said in a low burr.

The room trembled from the impact of another gust of wind, and she heard a metallic grinding that could only be the sound of the tin sheets parting company with the roof. Their attention snapped from each other back to the precarious situation they were in.

Ryan got to his feet, dragging her up with him.

"We need to get out of this room."

"And go where?"

"The bathroom."

He half-led, half-dragged her into the adjoining room, wrenching the door shut behind them. The sounds of the storm were muted in here, but the whole house still shuddered with every wind gust.

Ryan pointed at the tub. "Get in."

She climbed in at one end. He squatted in the other. They both gripped the sides and stared at each other in the dark.

Jessica exhaled shakily. *Well. That was a mood killer.*

Her lips tingled, like they still remembered what almost happened.

Ryan cleared his throat, shifting his grip on the tub edge. His hand brushed against hers.

Jessica squeezed her fingers into a fist. "If we die in here, how long do you think it'll take them to find our bodies?"

Ryan's hand found hers again. This time, he squeezed it tight. "We're not gonna die in here."

Jessica tried to smile.
She failed.

———

Ryan tried to make himself comfortable in the bathtub, but it was too short by several feet. His legs were bent to the side and the rolled-up towel he was using as a pillow was damp and hard. Curled up at the other end, Jessica was dosing, her cheek pressed against her forearm.

He stared at the ceiling, listening to the never-ending drone of the wind and rain outside, and the steady trickle closer at hand, where water was running down the side of the wall and pooling on the floor.

He shifted onto his other hip bone. At least the discomfort gave him the impetus to think.

He pulled his phone out of his pocket. The battery was half-gone; he shouldn't be using it. Yet, when it came to Kylie, he'd given up counting the things that he shouldn't have done for her.

He brought up the last text she'd sent him. From an unknown number, of course. Nearly every time she contacted him, it was from a different cellphone. Sometimes the gap between those times was weeks. Sometimes it was months. Once, about five years back, she'd gone a whole year without contacting him and he'd thought, finally, it was over. She'd gotten clean, she'd gotten her shit together. And he'd begun entertaining ideas of getting his own together. Finalizing their divorce. Maybe dating again. Carlita Owens, a sheriff's deputy he worked with in Memphis, had been chomping at the bit to put his profile up on Tinder.

And then, an unknown number on his cell. She was back in trouble. Except she now had a kid with her.

He looked down at the screen. This last text was from two days ago.

Ryan, I'm so sorry. For everything. I know I've put you through hell.

He stopped reading. He'd read it all before and not just in this text. That she was sorry. That she was getting help. That she was going to rehab.

And yet, she continued to compromise him in every way possible. She'd destroyed their marriage. Trashed his dignity. Jeopardized his job.

This shit had to stop. He needed to pull the ripcord on their pathetic excuse of a relationship and salvage what was left of his youth. But what weakened his resolve was the knowledge that none of it was her fault. Addiction was an illness. He saw the damage narcotics wrought in people's lives nearly every day of his own. He observed the futility of this country's ill-fated war on drugs everywhere he looked.

His wife was sick. She needed help. And he wasn't providing that. Every time he sent her money or showed up to strong-arm some asshole who'd tried to get more than money from her, he wasn't helping her. He was just enabling her to continue living that life. He was, in fact, making her sicker.

Underlying everything was his own bone-deep feeling of guilt. If he hadn't gotten her knocked up, if they hadn't gotten married so young, what would the trajectory of their lives have been?

It was an unanswerable question. All he knew was that he couldn't let guilt destroy what remained of his life.

He hit *delete*, and the text vanished.

As soon as he got back home, he'd get a new number. And the first call he'd make with it was to a divorce lawyer.

"I really hope this rehab is real this time, Kylie," he muttered. Then he turned his phone off and slipped it back in his pocket.

Carefully, so as not to wake Jessica, he climbed out of the tub and stretched his stiff limbs. Then he sloshed across the inch of water that now covered the bathroom floor.

The hallway was pitch black, like the rest of the house. Too dark to see any of the damage the storm had done, but he could tell from the wind tunneling down the narrow passage that some parts of the living room and kitchen had been left exposed to the elements. Leaks had sprung up all along the passage, and the carpet was sopping. Every step was like walking on a wet sponge.

He returned to the bathroom, closing the door before the wind could follow him in.

The candle was burning low in the mug on the floor. Jessica stirred and sat up. "What's wrong?"

"You hear that?"

"What?"

"The storm. I think it's moving away."

THIRTY-ONE

JESSICA WOKE to find light seeping through the busted bathroom window. Bright light. It took her a moment to realize that there was no wind, no rain. Birds were singing.

She climbed from the bathtub, her stiff, sore limbs protesting with each movement. Her body ached with fatigue, but there was also a sense of relief that she'd survived the night unscathed.

She doubted the building had, though. Opening the bathroom door, she half expected a wave of water to flood the room, but the only thing that came in was a damp breeze.

Venturing out, she took a survey of the house. The living room had fared the worst, with the window and a good amount of the front wall ripped away. She could see patches of blue sky through holes in the roof. The kitchen was a mess too; the cupboards had all been blown open, their scant contents lying shattered in deep puddles on the floor. Broken foliage and bare branches covered every surface and crunched underfoot. The air smelt of pine needles and brine.

She saw Ryan standing on the little porch just outside the door. "You do realize," she called as she approached him, "if we stay here for much longer without power, that thing in the freezer is going to start coming back to life—"

She stopped abruptly beside him. Water covered what had once been land. It filled the front yard and lapped at the top of the porch. It stretched all the way to the road and beyond, as far as the eye could see. Things were floating in it: downed pine trees, junk from the yard, dead fish and birds.

She said, "I hope you know I'm not very good at swimming."

"You should never swim in floodwaters," he said, looking out over the newly formed lake. "It's full of all kinds of crap. Not to mention leaches. Water snakes. Gators."

She glanced back at the house. From out here, the damage looked worse than it did inside. A huge pine tree had embedded itself in the front wall. The flood had taken the roller door and completely submerged the garage. The Charger was up to its windows in saltwater.

She couldn't get over how quiet it was. She could hear the lap of the water, the light breeze in the trees. It was almost idyllic.

Ryan unclipped his Glock from its holster and held it out to her. "You see anything moving in the water, you go right ahead and shoot if for me, okay?"

She took the gun from him, managing not to drop it. "Wait, what?"

He walked down the porch steps and start wading through the water. It was up to his shins, then his knee, then his hips.

She looked down at the gun. It was heavier than it looked; the rubber was warm in her grip. "Does it have a safety or something?" she called after him.

"Nope. Just pull the trigger."

"What if I miss and hit you?"

He turned and gave her a wry smile over his shoulder. "Oh, I happen to know you're a crack shot."

As he waded deeper, she yelled, "What did you just say about not swimming in floodwaters?"

"I said you shouldn't," he called back. "Not me."

She watched him make it to the safety of the shed without

being eaten by anything. He was gone about ten minutes, then she heard a motor starting. It wasn't the Charger's.

When he reappeared, it was at the helm of the tiny aluminum boat she'd seen in the shed yesterday.

"Seriously?" she yelled.

"I said I'd get you to Baton Rouge, didn't I?" he shouted over the sound of the outboard motor. "Come hell or high water."

———

Ryan got dressed in dry clothing for what he hoped would be the last time for a while. Then he went and finished carting all their things onto the porch.

Jessica joined him a little while later, wearing a fresh t-shirt and a denim skirt, her hair piled on top of her head. He couldn't seem to stop staring at her. Because soon, he knew he would never get to lay eyes on her again. The thought was like a sharp stab right above his kidney.

Together, they packed their things into the Jon boat, in the small space between the bench seats.

She picked up the rifle case, containing a Remington 870 shotgun and an AR-15 patrol rifle. Most field offices kept them in their vehicles, and every marshal was trained to use them.

Next, she passed him the last two bottles of their water. Their lack of food was also a concern. The few tins they'd had left were underwater in the kitchen somewhere. He was starving and suspected Jessica was, too. But he figured they would survive until they got to a town or managed to flag down help.

When everything was loaded, he helped her in. The little boat had a flat hull and rocked dangerously with them both standing in it. He had a moment of fear that he was going to wind up in wet clothes again, but she had excellent balance and quickly sat down on the bench seat to steady it.

He started the motor and used the tiller steer to guide the boat toward the road.

From her perch at the bow, she turned around to look at the house. Her eyes caught his, and she smiled.

He tried to smile back, but it got stuck somewhere behind his mouth. And it dawned on him how strange this situation was. Less than two days ago, he hadn't known her from a can of paint. And now he was experiencing actual chest pains at the thought of losing her.

"You're doing that thing again."

He looked up to find her watching him. And he realized he was indeed raking at the hair on the back of his head. He stopped, resting his hand on his knee.

She gestured at the floodwaters surrounding them in every direction. "You ever see anything like this?"

He looked around. The water was the color of milky coffee and was so deep in parts that he could only see the tops of road signs and power poles. Trees sprouted from the water, stripped of all their leaves, like the masts of some lost armada.

He said, "My sister was living in Galveston during Harvey. I went to stay with her to help with the cleanup." He shook his head at the memory. "It was a hell of a mess. Water so high you could fish off the porch."

She gave him a long look. "I bet you can't wait to get back home."

He thought of his tidy brick and tile house, with its empty rooms and kitchen that never got used and plastic lawns that never needed mowing. Nestled in a homogenous subdivision on Memphis' eastern edge, the house was so indistinguishable from its neighbors that he frequently drove right past it and parked at the wrong address.

It now seemed like the last place in the world he wanted to go back to. In fact, he'd rather stay in that falling-down house with the dead thing in the freezer because at least it would be with…

Her.

He squeezed his eyes shut for a second, trying to figure out what the hell was going on inside his head. He wanted to…what?

Run off into the sunset with her? A protected witness who he'd known for a grand total of thirty-six hours, and who had at least one psychopath on her tail?

Yeah, he'd made some fairly poor decisions in the past when it came to women, but doing a thing like that would take the cake.

He remembered the psychopath was still out there somewhere. Waiting out the tempest, planning his next move.

He knew guys like that. Better than most. He knew they didn't stop until someone made them.

And he knew if the storm hadn't killed him, Ryan would have to.

———

Roach woke up with a splutter as water trickled into his mouth from above and made him cough. It took him a full ten seconds to figure out where he was and why he was sopping wet.

He was lying flat on his back on the gas station countertop, staring at the ceiling, which had sprung dozens of leaks, including the one that had erupted right above his head. When he rolled over to escape it, he knocked the empty bottle of Dewars off the edge. But it didn't shatter on the floor; it made a splash instead.

He scrambled into a sitting position. "Jesus fucking Christ."

The bottle was bobbing in about three feet of water, which spread out and filled the entire store. Small islands had formed of chip bags and confectionery packets and plastic sunglasses and everything else that had fallen from the shelves and was light enough to float.

The trooper's SUV was sitting in water up to the top of its wheels. Beyond it and the shattered store window, the forecourt and the street were both flooded.

He scrubbed his hand down his face. Despite his wet wake-up call, his mouth felt dry and tacky, and his head ached. He really shouldn't have polished off that bottle last night.

He grabbed Julia's phone out of his jacket pocket and turned it on. Opened the tracking app. Saw the little arrow that showed where her smartwatch was now.

Julia Mikkelsen was on the move.

THIRTY-TWO

JESSICA MASSAGED HER TEMPLES, fighting a headache. She knew she should feel happy that this whole ordeal was nearly over—and she did—but she also felt other things. Complicated things she didn't have the energy to unpack right now.

The boat zipped north, following the approximate path of a road. A damp breeze ruffled her hair, carrying with it the smell of rotting vegetation and the sour whiff of sea brine.

The further north they went, the shallower the flood waters became, until road markers appeared, then letter boxes, and soon raised patches of dry land. She could feel things start to bump and scrape against the bottom of the hull. When there came a loud, long crunch against the aluminum, Ryan quit the motor, and they came to a halt.

He swung one leg out, then the other. There was still at least half a foot of muddy water on the ground. She stood up too and was about to step down into it when Ryan turned back and scooped her up in his arms.

He carried her to where the asphalt of the road emerged on a slow rise out of the water and set her down on her feet. Then he looked away, raking his hand through his hair. For a second, he seemed like he was going to say something. But without a word, he went back to the boat and started unloading their stuff.

And she knew he had complicated things going on in his head, too.

Before setting off on foot, they drank some water, then distributed their belongings between them. He had his duffel, the rifles and the water bottles; she had her shoulder bag and her battered suitcase. She wheeled it behind her as they picked their way along the road, skirting deep pools of water and tree branches. There was nothing to see on either side of the road except a sodden brown shoulder and the skeletons of pine trees.

They walked in silence. Neither of them was in the mood to make conversation. The sun beat down, making the puddles steam. The road ahead appeared wavy in the heat haze. Her camisole was stuck to her back and Ryan had sweated through his shirt.

They'd been walking about a mile when they saw a vehicle up ahead. It was an old white minivan, parked half on the shoulder and half on the asphalt. It looked abandoned. As they neared it, she saw why. A branch had landed on it, denting the roof and cracking the windshield.

After dropping her suitcase on the road, she jogged up to it, cupping her hands against the driver's window. There was no one inside, but some smears of blood on the steering wheel and the seat. Apparently, the driver had hit the brakes in a hurry and their face had taken the impact. There wasn't enough blood, though, to indicate any life-threating injuries.

She peered into the back windows while Ryan tried the driver's door. It wasn't locked, but there were no keys in the ignition.

He dropped his duffel off his shoulder and rested the rifle case on the ground next to it. "Check in the back," he said. "See if there's a toolkit or something."

She lifted the rear hatch. The seats had been folded into the floor and a four by eight sheet of plywood took up the entire cargo area. It was probably a last-minute hurricane preparation for someone's house. Too last minute, in this case.

On top of it was a large dog bed, and some bags filled with groceries. She kept looking around and found a compartment built in the sidewall. She unlatched it and it dropped open. Inside was a tire iron and first aid kit and canvas pouch tied closed with a piece of string. She opened it and found it contained a variety of tools.

She brought it around to the front of the car, where Ryan was busy extricating the branch from the windshield and clearing the hood of broken glass.

He brushed off his hands, opened the bag and rattled around inside until he found a screwdriver. Then he kneeled on the ground and bent down into the driver's side footwell. Started unscrewing the steering column.

She'd seen someone hot-wire a car before—the gun aficionado had also been a grand theft auto aficionado—but didn't think that the skill was in Ryan's wheelhouse.

She leaned against the door, watching him strip the wires and reattach them. The radio turned on, then the windshield wipers started thumping. Then the engine spluttered to life. "They teach you how to do that at Glynco?" she asked.

He looked up at her and gave a quick smile. "Boy Scouts."

———

The Grand Caravan's engine roaring to life was the sweetest sound Ryan had heard in days. The gas tank was half-full—hopefully enough to get them to civilization.

Jessica had loaded their belongings into the cargo area and climbed into the passenger seat, a bag of salvaged groceries in her lap. As the van idled, she rummaged through it.

"They must've been on their way back from getting storm supplies when they crashed," she said, pulling out batteries, toilet paper, and thank God—a twelve-pack of bottled water. She tore off the plastic and handed him one.

Ryan cracked the seal and drank in greedy gulps, draining it in seconds.

Next, she unpacked a bottle of wine, a bag of apples, a loaf of bread, peanut butter, and a container of yogurt—spoiled. She grimaced and tossed it onto the floor.

She ripped open the bread bag and grabbed a few slices, passing the rest to him.

They ate in silence, tearing hunks of bread and dipping them into peanut butter. The simple act grounded him, settling something raw inside. His mood lifted with each bite. He sank his teeth into an apple, the crisp snap breaking the quiet, while out of the corner of his eye, he watched Jessica prop her feet up on the dash, leaning back in her seat like she belonged there.

Ryan fit the apple between his teeth and slipped the van into gear, easing them off the muddy shoulder. With the windshield shattered, he had to crane his head out the window to see where they were going.

At a four-way intersection, the traffic lights were dead, the road signs long gone. The asphalt was littered with broken branches, twisted metal, and the pieces of debris that hinted at lives upended.

He chose to head north. The destruction lessened in that direction.

Jessica leaned forward and flicked the radio on. A pop song blasted from the speakers.

She grinned, bouncing in her seat, singing along.

When most people danced in their seat, they looked like they needed a bathroom. Somehow, she made it look effortless. Graceful. Sexy. Hell, even the way she ate peanut butter straight from the jar was mesmerizing.

She glanced over and saw him watching.

"Come on," she said. "You love this song."

Ryan chucked his apple core out the window. "I hate this song."

She sighed and twisted the dial. Static hissed before "Islands in the Stream" crackled through the speakers. She turned to him expectantly.

He shook his head. "Nope."

Her mouth dropped open like he'd just confessed to drowning kittens for sport. "Seriously? You're from freaking Tennessee. How can you not love Dolly?"

He shrugged, and she rolled her eyes, twisting the dial again. "You're a hard man to please."

His gaze flicked to her bare legs, stretched out on the dash. *Not true.*

"You remember our deal, right?" he said. "That when you're safe, settled someplace new, you'll look into getting qualified for that dance therapy thing?"

Jessica swallowed and nodded. But something flickered in her eyes—hesitation, uncertainty. If he didn't know any better, he'd think she felt the same stomach-drop at the idea of her leaving. Of putting distance between them.

She gave up on the radio and tilted her seat back, arms resting behind her head. Her hair was down again, spilling around her in a soft pink veil. His gaze traced her, lingering on the delicate undersides of her arms, the curve of her breasts, the long line of her legs.

The way she stretched out, completely at ease, was so effortlessly sensual it hit him like a gut punch. He pictured her lying on his bed like that. Naked. Waiting for him.

His mouth went dry.

"You should keep your eyes on the road, Marshal," she murmured.

Their eyes met. Her expression told him she knew exactly what he was thinking. Exactly how much he wanted her.

Did that mean she wanted him too?

Then her gaze flicked past him, widening.

"Ryan, *the road!*"

His stomach plunged. He tore his gaze away, just in time to see—

"Shit."

He slammed on the brakes.

———

The water was up to Roach's knees, soaking the bottoms of his jeans and his shoes. He waded across the shop floor toward the Ford Interceptor. Under his feet, he could feel things crunching. Glass, broken plastic from the vehicle's headlights, sunken items from the shelves.

Outside, the sky was alarmingly blue. And it was so quiet. He'd gotten so used to the constant drum of rain on the roof that he'd almost forgotten there was such a thing as silence.

But it wasn't completely silent. Far off, he heard a chopper. People would come by soon to survey the damage and look for anyone who'd been stranded by the floodwaters.

He yanked open the door of the SUV and climbed in, trying to shake the water out of his shoes as he did. He turned the key in the ignition and the engine roared to life.

Twisting in his seat, he pulled his SIG out of his waistband and checked it was still dry. He placed it on his lap. Then he took out the woman's phone and smiled at the little arrow. And threw the vehicle into reverse.

THIRTY-THREE

"CHRIST ON A BIKE," Ryan muttered as he climbed out of the van. "If it's not one damn thing, it's another."

Several huge pine branches lay across the road, blocking their path. The grass shoulders and medians had turned to swamps, making it impossible to drive around it without sinking two feet deep.

He could feel the heat radiating up from the ground like warmth from a body. He went to the nearest branch and wrapped his hands around the thickest part. It was so heavy he could drag it only a few yards before having to stop.

Suddenly, it grew lighter, and he saw Jessica had grabbed hold of the thinner section and was hauling it up.

"I got it," he said. "I don't want you to do yourself an injury."

"I'm stronger than I look," she said. "Core muscles."

He didn't want to think about her core muscles right now, so he focused on lifting the branch. Together, they got it out of the path. He returned to do the same with the second one, only to find that she was no longer helping him. She was just standing in the road. Staring at that last branch like was the only thing between her and a fate worse than death.

He straightened. "What is it?"

She shook her head and swallowed hard. "I don't want to go to Baton Rouge."

He put both hands on his hips. "What?"

She looked at him and her face was stricken. "I don't want to go to the safe house. I don't want to keep running anymore." She looked back the way they had come, then crossed her arms across her chest. "I'm tired of being a burden. Of being someone's job. *Your* job. To get me from A to B, until I become someone else's problem."

"You're not anyone's burden," he said, even though he'd been thinking something very similar only two days ago.

"I'm tired of it," she said again. "I just want it all to be over."

He shook his head. "Jessica, there's a reason witness protection is for life. You crossed some very dangerous people back in Chicago. And these guys, they don't quit. They'll happily spend the rest of their lives hunting you down. It's like a blood sport to them."

She took a step towards him. "You could keep me safe."

'What?' he said again, but this time it was a whisper.

She scraped her hair back with both hands and gave a shaky laugh. "I know, it's crazy. I can't even believe I'm saying this. I've only known you for like," she glanced down at her watch, "forty-three hours or something."

The action of her looking at her watch triggered a memory, but he ignored the feeling. He was too busy trying to process what she was suggesting. What he *thought* she was suggesting.

"But," she went on, shaking her head, "even though it's only been that long, I already feel like I know you. Better than anyone else in my life." She gave him an almost apologetic smile. "Which, admittedly, is a pretty sad reflection of my life."

He tore his eyes away from hers. "You don't really know me." He didn't want to say those words. He didn't want to make her think he was pushing her away, but it was the truth.

Her smile faded. "But what I do know about you," she said with a soft sincerity, "I really like."

His heart felt like it had stopped beating.

"You're a good guy, Ryan," she said. "And I know that because my life has been a parade of really shitty ones. But you're decent. And you're kind. And smart. And for some reason, I find all your over-thinking weirdly soothing. Then there's the way you look at me, like…" She swallowed, and he was amazed to see her cheeks had gone pink.

Like I'd charge hell with a glass of ice water for you? he finished for her in his mind. *Because I would. With bare feet.*

"Like you might have feelings for me," she mumbled.

He wanted to tell her he did have feelings for her. A whole damn lot of them. And that while she was wrong about the good man thing, he wanted nothing more than to be one for her.

But when he opened his mouth, he didn't end up saying anything like that. Because the thing that had been trying to get his attention, the thing waving at him from the back of his mind, finally broke through into his consciousness.

So, the words that came out were, "Jessica, your watch."

She blinked at him in surprise. Probably wondering why, when she was standing there baring her soul, he was more interested in what she was wearing on her wrist.

He strode forward and lifted her arm, looking at the watch. She'd had it on this whole time, but he'd never paid it any attention. Maybe because he'd been too busy paying all his attention to various other parts of her.

He said, "That is a smartwatch."

"Yeah," she said, baffled.

"It syncs your location to your phone, right?"

She nodded.

"Your phone that went missing from your house back in Florida?"

"Yeah," she said again, an uneasy note creeping into her tone.

"So, you've basically been walking around with a tracking device on your wrist this whole damn time. A tracking device that is currently beaming your location to a phone that we don't know who has."

She swallowed hard. "But everything is offline because of the storm. There's no cell signal or mobile data. So surely it can't be sending out any kind of signal—"

"It can through its GPS receiver," he interrupted. "Satellites. Nothing to do with cell or internet coverage."

"But my phone is locked!"

"Is it an older phone?"

She paused. "It's a couple of years old."

He shook his head. "Then there are ways into it."

She visibly paled, then stared down at her wrist in horror. "The silver Cadillac," she whispered, her eyes darting back up to his. "The one that was following us."

He nodded grimly.

With shaking fingers, she took the watch off and held it out to him like it was a bomb that was about to go off. He grabbed it, then turned and pitched it as hard as he could into the swamp beyond the road. He stared after it for a long moment, then he looked back at her and said, "This is why you have to stay in WITSEC."

"No. This is why I have to stay with you."

He sighed. "If I'd been doing my job properly, Jessica, you wouldn't be in this mess."

"What do you mean?"

He eyed her tiredly and scrubbed his hand through his hair. "I mean, I shouldn't have let you leave Florida with that thing on your wrist." He started walking back towards the pile of branches in the road. "You remember I told you to leave all your devices behind?"

She followed him. "Then it's my fault, not yours."

He stopped walking, just stood there in the road.

"I'm not going to Louisiana," she said to his back. "And you can't make me."

No, he couldn't. She wasn't in his custody. She was free to leave him and the program anytime she wanted.

"Where will you go?" he said dully.

When she didn't answer, he turned to face her. She rolled her eyes and raised her hands into the air. "Memphis," she said, as if it should have been obvious. "With you."

He stared at her like she'd just told him she was planning on moving to Mars. And while one part of him was ecstatic that she wanted to stay with him, a far more practical part of him knew it could never work.

He swallowed and shook his head. "I…it's…it wouldn't be allowed."

"So we don't tell anyone."

He threw up a hand. "Jessica, I gotta answer to a bunch of people. People who are gonna wanna know what the hell happened here. Why you up and vanished mid-route and washed up back in Tennessee with me. And I don't think we'll be able to blame it on the hurricane."

She took a step closer to him. Blew out a breath. "Okay. So you tell them that while you were filling up at a gas station outside Mobile, I got out of your car and, before you could stop me, climbed into an old silver Cadillac. And that was the last you saw of me. You don't even know if I survived the storm."

He opened his mouth, but no words came out. Was he actually considering this?

"I'll change my name when we get to Memphis," she said. "I have to start again from scratch, anyway." She paused, then added, "No one has to know about us."

All he could do was stare at her for a long time. When he could finally engage his vocal cords, the only word that came out was, "Us?"

"There doesn't have to be an 'us'," she said quickly. "I mean, I could stay at an Airbnb or something for a while, then—"

"Do you want there to be an us?" he interrupted.

She chanced a glance at him. When she spoke, her voice was barely above a whisper. "Do you?"

He appeared to have lost the ability to do anything but stare at her. Like an idiot. Then he felt something in him break. The part of him that always tried to do the right thing. The decent thing. The thing that would assuage that permanent feeling of guilt he carried around with him. It just snapped, like a ligament off a bone. He almost heard it go.

He took two steps towards her, took her face in his hands and kissed her. She gave a little gasp against his mouth, and he pulled back, only to have her press her lips more firmly against his. Her mouth opened for him with a soft moan. When he finally broke it off, he kept her face cupped between his palms and rested his forehead against hers. "Good God, I want there to be an us."

She wrapped her hands around his back and clamped herself to him. Their mouths locked together again, and he didn't realize they had been walking backward until she bumped into the van.

He placed his hands on the hot metal roof, on either side of her head. Her hands were everywhere, running over his chest, tugging at his belt.

He encircled hers, stopping them. Wishing he didn't have to be the pragmatic one. "Jessica, we gotta get off this road. We'll keep heading north. Find a town. Find a motel room. Figure out what the hell we're gonna do next."

Actually, he knew exactly what they were gonna do next. Motel rooms had beds. With sheets. Clean ones. Where he could lay her down. Take his time with her. Taste her. Make love to her real slow. And then do it all over again.

He tilted up her chin and kissed her mouth again. Then he took his phone out of his pocket, turned it on and unlocked it, then handed it to her. "See if you can find a couple of bars of signal. Figure out where the hell we are. I'll finish clearing the road."

THIRTY-FOUR

JESSICA LEANED back against the van door, the metal warm against her skin. She watched as Ryan dragged the last of the branches off the road, muscles flexing with each movement. Her body still hummed with the lingering imprint of his—of the way he had pressed against her moments ago, heat and strength wrapped in the scent of rain and earth.

For the first time since leaving Florida, hope didn't feel like some distant, unattainable thing. It swelled inside her, displacing the weight that had been crushing her chest for days. A lightness spread through her, as if a storm had passed, not just the hurricane, but the one inside her.

She looked down at his phone, suddenly remembering what she was supposed to be doing. Finding a signal. Figuring out where they were. Searching for a place to sleep tonight.

Although, she had the distinct feeling there wouldn't be much sleeping involved.

That thought sent a rush of warmth through her veins, the lingering tingle in her blood turning into something effervescent.

She focused on the screen. The phone had finally latched onto a network, and notifications began rolling in, one after another.

Missed calls. Texts. Updates. A string of alerts scrolled past, but her eyes caught on one name—*Dad*. Ryan's father had tried to reach him. More than once.

News alerts pinged in rapid succession. Headlines about Hurricane Petra flashed across the screen, each one painting a picture of devastation. The storm had carved a path of destruction from Galveston to Pensacola, ripping off roofs, washing out roads, and setting off landslides. It had now tracked northeast, unloading months' worth of rain onto North Carolina.

But as she scrolled, one alert stood out—something that had nothing to do with the hurricane.

And the moment she read it, that lightness inside her turned to lead.

U.S. Marshals hunt for one of their own after a woman is abducted from Panama City Beach, FL.

Her thumb jabbed at the screen, leaving a sweaty mark behind. The story took forever to load because the signal kept losing bars. She swallowed, her throat suddenly dry, and glanced up at Ryan.

"Anything?" he called.

She shook her head quickly, trying not to notice that her hands gripping the phone were shaking. Finally, the article finished loading.

TALLAHASSEE, FL. U.S. Marshals are today hunting for one of their own after a Florida woman, 31, was abducted from her home in Panama City Beach on Friday night by Deputy U.S. Marshal Ryan Inglis, 34. The woman is believed to be a member of the ultra-secret Witness Security Program, and the alleged abduction was carried out by Inglis under the guise of relocating her to a safe site in Louisiana. The motive remains unknown, as does the location of the two individuals.

Inglis, who serves as a Deputy U.S. Marshal with the U.S. Marshals Service in the Western District of Tennessee, is a veteran fugitive hunter with a sterling record. He is the second-in-command of the Two Rivers Violent Fugitive Task Force, based out of Memphis. It is understood that he used his position within this multi-agency Task Force to access highly confidential information about the missing woman, including details about where she was living and working. He then used this information to gain her trust and convince her to leave with him.

The U.S. Marshal for the Western District of Tennessee, Kirk Leacham, made this statement today: 'I am deeply disappointed to learn that one of our own has betrayed his oath of service and integrity, and has tarnished the reputation of the WITSEC program, which remains a sacred responsibility for all sworn U.S. marshals.

'We are in the process of tracing the deputy marshal's vehicle and phone, as well as any devices the woman may have on her, but our attempts have been hampered by Hurricane Petra. Cell towers are damaged in many areas and some of the roads are in bad shape. There really couldn't be worse timing for an operation like this.'

The U.S. Marshals Office of Public Affairs released this statement: 'The federal Witness Security Program, colloquially known as WITSEC, has been in place since the 1970s. In that time, we have only a handful of breaches and no participant who followed security guidelines has been harmed while under the active protection of U.S. marshals. The United States Marshals Service is committed to ensuring the woman is located, the offender is brought to justice, and that this incident remains an isolated one.'

She looked up, her eyes going to Ryan, wide with horror. Even as she stared at him, her brain was desperately trying to process what she'd just read.

Because it didn't make any sense. She hadn't been kidnapped. She'd gone with the marshal willingly, because her house had been broken into and her cover blown.

Ryan hadn't been responsible for any of that. He hadn't ransacked her place and painted that thing on the wall. There was no way he had.

Right?

She looked back down at the phone, an absurd hope blooming that this was all some kind of elaborate joke. One part of the article jumped out at her: *he used his position within this multi-agency Task Force to access highly confidential information about the*

missing woman, including details about where she was living and work-
ing. He then used this information to gain her trust and convince her to
leave with him.

It suddenly dawned on her that this was no joke. And while she didn't understand the how or the why of it, she understood one thing.

She had to get the fuck out of here.

Right now.

The moment that realization hit her, adrenaline kicked in. She dropped the phone, and it landed with a splash in a pothole at her feet. She yanked open the van door and hauled herself into the driver's seat. Her hand automatically went to turn the key in the ignition, but of course there wasn't one. The engine was already running.

She rammed the shifter into reverse and when she looked up, she saw Ryan through the side window. He was still standing there in the road, looking profoundly confused. She had a moment again of thinking that this couldn't possibly be real, that it was Ryan, the sweet, shy, uptight man who'd held her hand last night when she'd been scared. Who cared about her dance therapy dream. Who'd called her pretty. And who'd just told her he wanted there to be an *us*.

Then she saw his eyes flick to his dropped phone—and then to hers. In an instant, the confusion vanished from his face, replaced by dawning horror.

And just like that, she had her answer.

It was all true.

He jogged towards her. "Jessica, wait, please let me explain."

She buried the accelerator.

The car shot backwards, bouncing over the potholed pavement. She shifted into drive and yanked the steering wheel around. The van turned in a wide arc, narrowly avoiding running off the blacktop and into the muddy verge.

She kept her foot on the accelerator, lurching over the rutted asphalt. She couldn't see where she was going because the windshield was cobwebbed with cracks. The tears filling her eyes weren't helping, either. She dashed them aside with the back of her hand. She was driving blind, but it didn't matter. The only thing that mattered was getting as far away from Ryan Inglis as possible.

THIRTY-FIVE

RYAN SANK onto the thick branch he'd just dragged off the road, his body heavy with exhaustion that had nothing to do with physical labor. He dragged a hand through his damp hair, then stared down at his phone, its mud-splattered screen balanced on his knee.

Then he lifted his head, straightening as his gaze followed the road ahead, the same road Jessica had disappeared down, leaving behind nothing but a set of muddy tire tracks.

Everything—*everything*—had turned to shit.

And now, looking back, he saw the truth with brutal clarity: his plan had never stood a chance. He might've told himself otherwise, clung to hope like a drowning man to driftwood, but deep down, he must have known. It was always going to end this way.

His name was a news alert now. A flashing, blaring warning to the world. He was a wanted man.

They were hunting him. *His own people.*

Except they weren't his people. Not anymore.

He was the one running now. *He* was the fugitive.

A sharp, aching pressure built behind his eyes, and he squeezed his fingers against his sockets as if he could physically push back the flood of memories. The last three days had unraveled his entire life, ripped it apart at the seams. It all traced back to one moment—the phone call that had started this.

Three days ago.

A lifetime ago.

———

The sound of his phone buzzing on his nightstand had woken him up.

Unknown number.

Kylie.

He'd sighed and sat up in bed. The glowing red digits of his clock floated in midair through the darkness. 2.07 AM.

Dragging a hand down his face, he'd wondered what fresh hell she was going to rain down upon him this time.

Then he'd cleared his throat and taken the call. "Deputy U.S. Marshal Ryan Inglis speaking."

Nothing from the other end of the line. It was an ominous silence, muffled and thick with foreboding.

Ryan had frowned, then added, "Kylie, is that you?"

"Well, shit." The voice was male, and it sounded coarse and laced with menace. "The bitch was telling the truth. You are some fancy federal cop."

Ryan had swung his legs out of bed. The man on the other end seemed to be waiting for him to respond. So, he'd said nothing.

"Don't you wanna know how your wife's doing? I got her right here with me." Still, he'd said nothing. Just gripped the phone with damp fingers.

The man had laughed. Like he'd been deriving some sick glee from Ryan's attempt to stonewall him.

There'd been a muffled sound, then a woman's gasp. Kylie's voice, in a desperate tone, had come on the line. "Ryan, please, he's—"

He'd heard another indistinct sound, then the man's chuckle

again. "She's fine, she's fine. I found her shooting up on my front step. I invited her in, like you do, and we got to talking."

The nasty way he'd said it had made Ryan think there was no way Kylie had gone into this guy's house of her own volition.

"She said her name's Addison, so I guess that was a lie."

Ryan's jaw clenched. Kylie used aliases when she wasn't sober, when she didn't want to be found by the people in her life that cared about her.

"She told me you was a U.S. marshal. And I thought, shit, I know about you guys. You're stone-cold sons of bitches. Man hunters."

Ryan had stared at the wall straight ahead of him. Light from the street outside was filtering through the blinds and casting strange shadows. "What do you want?"

The man had inhaled deeply, like he'd needed to think about it. Like he'd just been offered three wishes and didn't want to waste a single one of them. Then he'd said, "Eleven years ago, your people made a girl disappear. A girl that fucked my life up, big time. I want you to find her for me."

Ryan swallowed hard but said nothing. The silence drew out long and taut. Finally, Ryan cleared his throat and said, "I can't do that."

"Oh, really?" the voice said. "Because I can make people disappear too, Mr. Marshal. I'm a motherfucking magician at it. I can make it so the only thing they find of your wife are her pretty green eyes. I'll dig 'em both out and leave 'em for you as a little memento."

Ryan's pulse sounded like a drumbeat in his ears. "I just said, I can't do it. It doesn't work like that. WITSEC is a closed loop. I can't access that kind of information, even if I wanted to."

Another pause, filled only with the man's raspy breathing and the dull thud of Ryan's heartbeat in his ears. Then the man had spoken again, and he'd lost some of his joviality. "Don't bullshit me, man. I used to be in the army. Special Ops. I know how the fucking system works, alright. I know that you can find out anything if you really want to. If there's a will, there's a way, right? And I'd have thought keeping your wife's head attached to her body would have been a pretty fucking compelling reason to find a way." There was a pause, then Ryan had heard the unmistakable sound of a power tool. A buzz saw. "But maybe I'm wrong."

Ryan's blood seemed to have stalled in his veins. He wasn't sure he could feel his heart beating anymore. All he'd been able to feel was the phone pressing against his ear and the pain in his jaw from gritting his teeth. "Alright. I'll do it. Whoever you're trying to find, I'll find her."

The buzz saw had gone quiet. Then the voice came back on the line and told him the name of the woman he wanted located. "Text this number everything you find out," he'd said. "Involve anyone else, and she's dead. You have until midday tomorrow."

It had taken a great deal of effort, but Ryan had kept his voice low and calm. "If you hurt Kylie, I can promise you there's one person I will find. You."

He'd waited for a response. But all he got was that soft chuckle. Then the line had gone dead.

———

Ryan had sat there in the dark for a full half hour, his mind cycling through every possible option. Weighing the risks. Calculating the fallout.

The most logical course of action—the one he'd been trained to take—was to call the FBI immediately. Then his boss, Marshal Leacham.

But logic didn't mean shit when someone had a buzz saw to your wife's head.

The man's voice echoed in his skull, low and calm, like he was discussing the weather. *Involve anyone else and she's dead.*

His gut reaction had been to trace the call, pinpoint a location, and go there himself. Hunt the bastard down and put him in the ground.

But he only had until midday tomorrow.

And Kylie could be anywhere.

He pressed his fists against his eyes, forcing his mind to focus. The voice on the phone had given him almost nothing—just scraps of information that weren't nearly enough. Ex-military. Special Ops. A Northeastern accent. White. Older, maybe fifties or sixties.

That narrowed it down to about a hundred thousand people.

Useless.

He exhaled hard through his nose, and for a moment, he saw Kylie at sixteen again. Long red hair. Sweet smile. Sitting in the bleachers, pretending not to watch him play football. She was too cool for cheerleading; she ran with the kids who smoked under the bleachers and skipped school to hang out at Cashmore's Clearing. He never understood why she turned those beautiful green eyes his way, but when she did, he'd felt like the goddamn king of the world.

They started skipping school together after that. Then whole weekends at his dad's hunting cabin in the mountains. She'd gotten his name tattooed high on her thigh, where her parents couldn't see it.

That tattoo was still there.

It would probably be what they used to ID her body.

Ryan shot to his feet, yanked on his jeans, and was out the door before he'd fully decided where he was going.

By the time he made it downtown, his pulse was pounding in his throat.

In his office, he ran the name through every database he had access to. *Julia Mikkelsen.* Eleven years and one month ago, she'd vanished into thin air. The last trace of her was buried in a sprawling federal indictment against over a dozen Chicago members of *La Mano Negra.*

One of those members? Her fiancé, Daniel Castaño.

Then, just like that, her name disappeared. Became a number. Became nothing.

He hadn't been bullshitting the man on the phone. Only four government officials and God knew what had happened to Mikkelsen after that.

And if there was one thing the USMS was better at than tracking people, it was hiding them.

But he'd found something. A thread to pull.

One of those four officials. A WITSEC inspector by the name of *Inez Sharrow.*

His only lead. Which meant she was his only option.

He spent nearly an hour picking apart every angle of the story he'd use, searching for weak spots. But there were too many. He could never plug them all.

In the end, he realized what he should have known from the start—he was going to have to white-knuckle this thing.

He braced his elbow on his desk, exhaled, and tapped out Sharrow's number.

No more stalling.

As the phone rang, adrenaline burned through his veins like an electric current. This call would either cost Kylie her life. Or cost him everything in his.

Maybe both.

When Sharrow had picked up, he'd introduced himself, polite but brusque, one marshal to another. It had been six in the morning, and she'd sounded a little dazed, although she'd quickly composed herself when she'd heard who he was. He'd made something of a name for himself in the Southeast after a couple of high-profile arrests that had made the national news. It wasn't a reputation he'd had any desire or cause to lean upon. Until now.

He'd gone straight to the point: "We've developed some information that concerns one of your witnesses."

There'd been a pause on the other end, and Ryan had sensed Sharrow sitting up a little straighter.

"We raided a *La Mano Negra* compound in Collierville

yesterday morning and found a laptop that contained some disturbing contents. Not least of which were recent surveillance stills of a woman. When the FBI guy ran facial rec, it turned her up as one of yours. Witness number 11672."

The lie had rolled off his tongue with surprising ease. But that hadn't meant she'd bought it. The long pause that had followed felt like the longest in Ryan's life.

Finally, Sharrow had responded. "Shit."

Okay, so she was buying it. So far. "The footage was of her at what looked at her house," he said. "It was time-stamped two days ago."

An exhalation, and then Sharrow's voice had come out in a wince. "Shit."

"Yeah," he'd lied. "Someone's found her, somehow."

There'd been another long pause. "But how?" she'd said, eventually. "It's impossible. You know the precautions—"

"What I know," he'd interrupted, "is that we gotta get her the hell outta there. Right now."

The use of *we* had been deliberate. It made them sound like they were in this together, that they had each other's backs. That they were a team. He knew it had worked because he could hear the relief in the woman's voice. "Yeah. Right. Of course."

So far, so good. He'd swallowed some of his own relief. "Where are you?"

"In Denver. At my parent's house. I'm on maternity leave."

He'd closed his eyes and pressed his palm against his forehead. Finally, something had gone his way. "And where's the witness?"

Another long pause. Ryan hadn't even dared to breathe. If Sharrow told him this piece of information that she meant she was all in. It meant she'd bought his entire story. It meant that soon this whole mess would be over.

"Southwest Florida," she'd said.

If Ryan hadn't already been sitting, he would have had to find a chair to keep from buckling from relief. But he'd managed to keep his tone cool and collected. "Well, that means I'm a hell of a lot closer to her than you are."

He'd paused before making his request. It was a request that went against every oath of service and integrity and justice he'd taken when he became a marshal. It was wrong, and he knew the consequences of it would haunt him for the rest of his life.

But it was the only way to save Kylie's life.

In the end, he'd just blurted it out, knowing there was no way around it. "But I'm gonna need you to send me all her details."

During the long pause that had followed his question, Ryan had bitten down on his tongue so hard he'd thought he might bite through.

"All her details?"

"Everything you got on her. I can get to her place and get her into protective custody right away. But I gotta know where I'm going and who I'm dealing with here."

She said nothing for a long moment and Ryan had gripped the phone, thinking that for sure that the jig was up. Then she'd said, a little breathlessly, "Okay. I'll send you her file."

He'd heard the anxiety in her voice and realized what had been motivating her long pauses. Fear. She'd been terrified of being the first U.S. marshal to wind up with a dead witness on her hands. The one-hundred-per-cent survival rate of WITSEC participants had been bandied about so often it had become folkloric. It had entered popular culture, had captured the public's imagination. And it was the feather in the cap of the USMS. Unlike every other law enforcement agency in this country, U.S. marshals got to hold their heads up high and say, *we don't screw things up. We don't get people killed under our watch.*

Ever.

And it was probably the only reason anyone agreed to join the damn program in the first place.

He'd felt a deep twist of guilt that it would be him at fault if the woman got killed because what he was about to do.

Not Sharrow. And certainly not the Service.

He'd swallowed down his apprehension and said with as much confidence as he could muster, "Inez. I'll handle this. She's going to be fine."

But even as he'd said them, he'd realized they'd sounded like someone's famous last words.

After he'd ended the call, he'd booked the first flight to Tallahassee. It had departed at thirty-four minutes past noon.

At ten minutes to twelve, he'd been waiting in the departure lounge at Memphis International Airport. Sharrow had emailed him the witness's file, and he'd read it as he paced. The woman's name was now Jessica Meeks. She lived in some tourist town by the sea and worked as a stripper in some dive bar near the beach.

In her hurry, Sharrow had attached not just Meeks' file, but a whole sheaf of information about Daniel Castaño, too.

Or maybe it hadn't been a mistake. Maybe she had thought it was relevant. He didn't know, and at that point, he didn't care.

At one minute to midday, his phone had buzzed in his hand. Unknown number. Speak of the devil.

He'd put the phone to his ear but had said nothing.

"Time's up, Mr. Marshal," the voice had said, in that dry rasp. Then there'd been a muffled sound, like the phone had been handed to someone else. Then a woman's scream. Kylie's. Then the unmistakable sound of a power tool.

A buzz saw.

The call had ended.

Ryan's hands had been shaking so much he'd barely been able to tap the buttons on his screen. They'd just skidded uselessly over the surface. A cold dread, like icy fingers, gripped his stomach.

He'd forced his fingers to work.

To attach the woman's file.

To hit *Send*.

And then he'd sunk down into a plastic seat in the middle of the bustling airport. Knowing that eight hundred miles to the south, in a small town called Panama City Beach, Jessica Meeks had just become a dead woman walking.

If there was such a place as purgatory, Ryan thought it might resemble the departure lounge of Hartsfield-Jackson Atlanta International Airport, as he waited to find out which of the two women was dead because of him.

As Ryan had paced back and forth, waiting for his connecting flight to Florida, he'd got a text from the unknown number. He'd had to suck in a breath and steel himself before opening it.

It had been from Kylie.

Ryan, I'm so sorry. For everything. I know I've put you through hell. But it's over now. Everything's going to be better. You'll see.

He'd known he should feel relief, and he did. But undercutting it had been a sharp stab of anger. Anger at his wife and her inability to get her shit together. To go get help. To go get therapy. To quit being such a goddamn liability.

The anger had promptly spawned guilt, and the sharp switch had made his head ache. His phone had rung again.

Sharrow.

"I'm on a flight to Florida," she'd said. "I should be there around six tonight."

"But you said you're on maternity leave."

"As long as I don't give birth on the plane, I'll consider it a win."

Rubbing a hand over his face, he felt even more guilty for making a heavily pregnant woman fly across the country.

She'd said, "A neutral site in Baton Rouge can take her."

He'd nodded, even though Sharrow hadn't been able to see him. "Okay. Good. I can get her there."

"But there's a hurricane coming in. Big one, they say."

He'd heard. The news had been full of it. Right then, though, he'd had bigger problems to worry about. "I'll get her there."

"Are you sure? There are warnings out for the whole Gulf coast."

They'd been calling his flight, so he'd stood up. "I'll be fine. They always say they're gonna be worse than they are."

When he'd landed in Tallahassee, he'd contacted Mark Lyman, a deputy marshal he'd worked with on a case in the Caribbean a year ago. He'd given him the same story he'd given Sharrow, about the phony Collierville raid and the laptop and the subsequent need to get Jessica Meeks into immediate protective custody.

Only this time, the need was genuine. But not because of some fictitious surveillance stills.

Because of him.

He'd borrowed the deputy's vehicle and driven like hell to Panama City Beach. The view out the window had been monotonous: stands of slash pine and the yellowing grass verge of the interstate, pocked with divots of sand as white as snow.

A little over two hours later, he'd arrived at Meek's house. Flashing blue lights painted the ransacked building in an eerie glow, and the officers' grim faces spoke of a horrifying scene.

He'd been too late.

When he'd discovered that the woman hadn't been home during the invasion, that she'd been at work, he'd nearly dropped to his knees in relief. He'd raced to Femme Fatale in time to find her safe and sound. Albeit scantily clad.

And he'd known the moment he'd laid eyes on her, he couldn't let anything happen to her. He was going to get her to that neutral site in Baton Rouge if it killed him.

It nearly had. And yet he'd still failed.

Now she was lost and alone and terrified. And it was all his fault.

It occurred to him now, sitting on that log in the middle of nowhere, that it was always going to end this way. That at some point, someone was going to investigate his story. Someone was going to put the pieces together and realize the whole thing was a lie.

Jessica would have figured it all out eventually, too. In his heart of hearts, he'd known that all along, too. Which made all his hopes for some kind of a…*thing* working out between them seem even more futile.

What on earth had he been thinking? That he'd get to live happily ever after with the woman he'd sold out to the men who were trying to kill her?

He stared down that muddy road in the direction she'd had gone. And was reminded with a sickening jolt that those same men were still out there.

THIRTY-SIX

JESSICA GRIPPED the steering wheel with both hands, her eyes glued to the yellow line in the middle of the road. It was her only guide. Tears blurred her vision, and she swiped them away irritably.

She'd trusted him completely.

Why? Because he was a lawman?

At least partially, yes. Trust was the invisible scaffolding that supported every law enforcement agency on the planet. Without it, they simply wouldn't exist. Sometime in history, humans had collectively agreed that a person with a rank and a badge and a gun was to be held in higher esteem than anyone else. That, based solely on the presence of those items, they were to be listened to. They were to be believed. They were to be trusted.

But she hadn't just trusted him as a cop. She'd trusted him as a man. She'd let him in, mentally and emotionally. She'd told him things she'd told no one else. She'd *felt* things.

She gave a brittle laugh, remembering one thing she'd told him.

I'm like an asshole-seeking missile.

And she'd just struck another doozy of a target.

She wondered now what his plan had actually been. Where

had he really been taking her? Or, more likely, to whom had he been taking her? And what had been his motive? Money? Was he expecting payment on delivery of her, like she was boxed goods?

She closed her eyes briefly, remembering their last conversation. How he'd said he was taking her back to Tennessee with him. Right after he'd kissed her so passionately, it had made her knees buckle.

So maybe he had developed feelings for her. And maybe because of that, he'd decided to not go through with whatever terrible scheme he'd set in motion.

Or maybe she was just plain delusional when it came to men.

You don't really know me, he'd said. He'd been right about that. Perhaps he'd even been trying to warn her.

She glanced in the rearview mirror, saw nothing but an empty road. Surely, she had to come upon someone soon.

Glancing down at her bare wrist, she cursed. He'd thrown away her smartwatch. Its battery was nearly dead, but she could have used to contact emergency services. Not to mention, the real marshals who were trying to find her might have been attempting to track it at this very moment. Unfortunately, where they'd find it was in the middle of a swampy forest.

She swiped more tears away, squinting through the cracked windshield. Up ahead was the four-way intersection they'd passed earlier. She braked hard and yanked the steering wheel to the right. The minivan careened through the turn, rocking from one side to the other. When it regained its balance, she sped up again, keeping to the middle of the road and its strips of yellow. This road was narrow and clumped in places with thick silty mats of pines needles and debris. Her tires bounced over them, jerking her about in her seat.

To her right, she saw a wooden split-rail fence. Most of it was missing, but it was a sign of civilization. Soon, another sign appeared: a road sign, or what was left of it. There were just two wooden poles, and the bottom panel remaining. In white lettering, it read 3 MILES.

So, she was close to something. Hopefully, a town. She gripped the steering wheel tighter and kept her foot on the gas.

Up ahead, between the latticework of cracks in the windshield, she noticed a vehicle coming towards her. An SUV. Dark grey, a light bar on the top. She veered into the left lane and, as it passed, she saw the blue stripe and yellow badge of the Mississippi Highway Patrol on its side door.

"Oh, thank God."

She slammed on the brakes. Tires squealed and skidded, and the minivan rocked to a halt. In her rearview mirror, she glimpsed the trooper had come to a stop too.

She wrenched open the minivan's door and practically fell out of it. She heard the SUV's door open and clunk close, heard the trooper's footsteps crunch over the strewn pine needles.

"Boy, am I glad to see you," she called, leaning back into the van to grab her shoulder bag off the front passenger seat. As she straightened, she felt a hard cylinder of metal pressing against the back of her skull.

"Snap," the trooper said.

Except he wasn't a trooper. She knew that with the same certainty she knew it was a gun aimed at her head. She could almost feel the pressure that sat waiting in the barrel, ready to explode a bullet into her brain.

Her body was dumping adrenaline into her bloodstream by the bucket load. Somehow, though, she kept her voice steady. "Who are you?"

"You don't know who I am?" He rubbed the barrel of the gun into her hair. The sharp metal bit into her scalp. "I'm hurt," he said right in her ear. "Seeing as how you and your boyfriend burned my whole fucking life to the ground."

She darted a glance at him out of the corner of her eye. He was scrawny and no taller than her. Wearing jeans and an oversized singlet that showed off ropy arms. A patchy buzz-cut revealed a lumpy skull and a pale scalp. It was laced over with pink scars. He was white, with a narrow face, with a bony nose and high cheekbones. Fading tattoos covered his forehead and jawline, the most legible being the letters LMN over his left eyebrow and the number 13 over his right.

He said, "My name's Milo, little bitch. And that's a name you're gonna remember. 'Cause it's a name you're gonna be screaming real soon."

She heard a loud crack, and a second later, felt a searing pain. Her vision tunneled, then dimmed, and then died out altogether.

———

Jessica opened her eyes, but the realization that she was still alive didn't bring the relief she thought it would. Instead, it just brought a dull pain in the back of her head and the deep sense that her ordeal was far from over.

She was on the floor in the rear of the van, and it was driving. Fast. She could feel it rocking from side to side as it sped over bumps in the road.

What she didn't know was what direction they were going, or for how long they'd been going in it. Nor did she know where their intended destination was, or how long it would take to get there.

It occurred to her that this guy was smart enough to have kidnapped her in the minivan and not the Highway Patrol vehicle, which would have been easier for the authorities to locate.

She doubted anyone would be combing the land for an abandoned Dodge Grand Caravan. Not in the aftermath of a hurricane. The owner might not report it missing for days or weeks. Or even at all.

Which meant she was completely on her own.

Rap music was blaring from the radio, and the scrawny guy was bobbing his head and attempting to rap along. He was terrible. Watching him would have almost been funny in any other situation than this.

This situation, though, was anything but humorous. She was

lying on her front, arms pinned beneath her, her cheek pressed against the rough surface of the plywood that filled the cargo area. When she tried to move her limbs, they wouldn't cooperate. Something bound her wrists and ankles. She guessed they were plastic zip-ties by the way they were cutting into her skin.

Her squirming attracted the attention of the scrawny guy. Milo. He turned to her and smiled, revealing stained teeth, the front one chipped almost in half.

"Comfy?"

She swallowed down a thick lump in her throat and said, "What do you want?"

He reached down with his right hand and lifted his gun off his lap. It was matte black, like Ryan's, with a chunky rubber grip and some kind of complicated sight attached to the top. "What I want," he said, "is to put this bullet in your head, little bitch. But there's a bit of line to do that. And sadly, I ain't at the front."

He turned more fully and grinned at her again. She noticed his other arm, the one gripping the steering wheel. It had needle marks running up the skin of his inner forearm, like the bites of some bloodthirsty insect.

"Where are you taking me?"

He didn't answer, just cranked the radio louder and resumed his off-beat rapping.

She engaged all her stomach muscles and flipped herself onto her back. The plywood cracked underneath her. She swiveled her head from side to side, looking for anything that could help her. A tool. A weapon. But other than the dog bed, there was nothing.

Ryan's rifles. She thought back to where she'd seen him stash them. Behind the driver's seat. There was no way she could get to them. And even if she could, she wouldn't be able to get them out of their case with her hands bound.

Milo turned his head half to her and brandished his gun again. "You keep moving around back there and I might just have to jump that line, bitch."

She tried to remember what had become of her own gun. It

was still in her shoulder bag. She cast her eyes about for it, but she couldn't see it anywhere.

It was probably lying on that sodden and potholed Mississippi state road. Many miles behind them.

———

As the miles passed, a feeling of dread settled heavier on her. Milo had given up on trying to be a rap god and turned the radio off, so they drove in silence.

The back of her head throbbed, and she used the pain to keep herself awake and alert. She had a vague sense they were heading north, based on the feel of the road beneath her. There were fewer potholes and storm debris. The asphalt was smoother, and it whirred beneath the tires.

She heard no other traffic sounds, not the rumble of a truck or the purr of another vehicle passing them. So, they likely weren't on an interstate. Still in the middle of nowhere, then.

From her position on the floor of the minivan, her view out the window was only of the sky. It was cloudless, and so blue it seemed to belong to an alien world.

Every so often, she rocked herself from side to side, fighting a cramp in her legs and pins and needles in her arms. She knew when the minivan finally stopped, she had to be ready. For whatever that was waiting for her at their final destination.

Eventually, the minivan slowed, its tires crunching over gravel, then came to a stop. She heard her captor open the driver's door, slam it shut. More crunching, this time his boots on the loose rocks.

She peered up through the window, but there was still nothing to see, except that the sky had burned off its blue. It had to be late in the afternoon. Which meant it would be dark in a matter of hours. And the night brought with it a whole host of new fears.

Voices now, Milo's and another man's. Too low to make out the content of the conversation. Other than it sounded ominous.

The back hatch of the minivan opened. Bright white light filled the cargo area. Jessica squeezed her eyes shut, then blinked quickly.

The dark shapes of two men stood there, surveying her. One was the diminutive form of Milo. The other shape was taller, although equally skinny. His hands seemed overly large for his thin arms.

As her eyes adjusted to the light, they became more than just silhouettes.

The new guy was young, maybe only in his early twenties. He was pale, with stringy blond hair tied at the nape of his neck. Wire-rimmed glasses and a scruffy goatee. He smiled at her.

She struggled against her bindings again, out of reflex. Her earlier attempts to free herself had rubbed the skin around her wrists and ankles raw.

Both men climbed into the cargo area, making the whole minivan dip with their weight.

Using her feet, she pushed herself as far away from them as she could, until she hit the back of the driver's seat. "Don't you touch me."

Ponytail, still grinning, ducked down to grab her legs. She kicked them out of his reach.

Milo went to shove the dog bed away, then stopped. He bent down. Picked up her cheap, faux-leather shoulder bag with the gold clasp.

Her *shoulder bag*.

He twisted the clasp and opened it. She squirmed again, her heart dropped through her ribcage. He'd find the gun. He'd find it and take it for himself or toss it away, and with it, her only viable means of defending herself.

Ponytail was staring down at her skirt. "You think she's wearing any underwear?"

Milo's head jerked up, the bag in his hands instantly forgotten. His smile turned slimy. "Only one way to find out."

She thrashed about, an automatic fear response. Milo bent

down and grabbed hold of her knees, dragging her out of her corner and towards the open door. She flailed at them with her bound hands, attempting to push them away.

The little creep was stronger than he looked. She also noticed that he seemed twitchier than he had earlier. His eyes were blood-shot and opened wide, like he was trying to see in the dark. There was a greasy sheen of sweat on his forehead. Her gaze went to the needle marks on his arms. She suspected his last hit had been a while ago.

He crawled his hands up her legs to the hem of her skirt, still wearing that evil grin.

She went motionless. She'd been on the receiving end of shit like this from men more times than she could count. When she'd worked at Femme Fatale, it had been daily. She remembered something Jade had told her on her first night at that place: "Not all men are dogs, honey. But some are real mongrels."

The only good thing about having suffered through years of this kind of crap was that it didn't terrify her like it might have once. She didn't panic or struggle. She waited, biding her time, collecting her strength. Until the moment his attention became fully focused on what he was hoping to find under her skirt.

Engaging all her muscles, she reared up, angling the point of her elbow into the center of his forehead. There was an audible thud. The impact hurt her arm, but from the way Milo lurched back, she knew it hurt his head more.

"Fuck's sake." He pressed his palm to his forehead, his face contorted with rage. "Little bitch."

He looked down at his hand as if he expected to find blood there. There wasn't any, but she could already see a white and red raised lump forming.

Milo looked back down at her, his smile now a snarl. She had a sudden fear that he'd come at her twice as forcefully, but he seemed to realize the moment had passed. He gestured at Pony-tail. "Get her legs."

He grabbed her hair, yanking it so hard it brought tears to her eyes.

Together, they hauled her out of the back of the minivan like she was a roll of old carpet. Milo slammed her shoulder against the side and raked her back on the tow bar as he swung her down. Tears prickled in her eyes, but she blinked them away.

Outside, she tried to snatch a glance at her surroundings. But from the way they were carrying her, all she saw was the sky, a grass verge, and a glimpse of a road. An empty road. Then she saw a pale gold sedan, parked only a few feet from the rear of the minivan. With its trunk open.

"No," she said. "Please—"

They dumped her into the trunk. The last thing she saw before he slammed the lid was Milo's furious face, with a bright red welt in the middle of his forehead.

But seconds before the trunk came down, he tossed her bag in after her. It bounced off her hip bone with a dull clunk.

She knew what that clunk was.

With trembling fingers, she undid the clasp. Every movement made the plastic zip ties around her wrists bite into her raw skin. She got her hands inside and felt about until her fingers grasped the cold metal barrel of the gun.

Her little gun, the one that couldn't shoot worth a damn. She knew her odds of successfully using it against these guys were low.

But low was better than zero.

And as she lay there in the pitch blackness, hugging her bag against her lap, she felt for the first time like she might just survive this.

———

Darkness, she realized, was like pain. Once she got over the initial shock and panic it induced, once you yielded to it and quit trying to fight it, it became bearable. Almost soothing. It blocked everything else out and whittled her world down to one very basic fact.

She was still alive. Even if she wished she wasn't.

The space in the trunk was so cramped she couldn't move her legs or arms. She tensed them from time to time, to keep her circulation moving, but she knew they'd be useless to fight or to run with if she got the chance. And because she was in the very rear of the vehicle, she was thrown around every turn like a rag doll. She'd long ago lost any sense of direction.

She could smell gasoline, rubber, and hot metal. For a while, she'd worried about carbon monoxide poisoning. She'd heard of teenagers dying of that while joyriding in the trunks of cars.

But after the fourth hour in there and no relief in sight, she started to think that a painless death in her sleep might be quite nice.

She was so thirsty her stomach burned for want of water. Her bladder was uncomfortably full. Every turn the car took was agony.

Just when she thought she was going to be forced to wet herself, she felt the vehicle slow and veer to the right. Then it stopped altogether.

Doors opened and slammed shut. Feet crunched over gravel. The trunk lid was raised.

She closed her eyes instinctively, but no light burned into her eyeballs. It was dark outside. Ponytail was leaning over her.

"She's still alive," he called.

Milo's response came from too far away to hear.

"I need water," she rasped.

He ignored her. Just yanked her upright by her forearms. He produced a switchblade and, before she could flinch, sliced through the zip ties around her ankles.

She scissored her legs out of the trunk. He was keeping a painfully firm grip on her upper arm to keep her from running. She knew she wouldn't be able to, even if he wasn't keeping hold of her. Her legs felt like jelly.

He jerked her to a standing position. It was too dark to detect anything about her surroundings beyond the fact that they were parked in some kind of rest area. Traffic zipped by a hundred yards away. She saw headlights winking at her between a line of trees.

So close, yet so far.

Milo was approaching them, zipping up the fly of his jeans. She tried to pull away, but Ponytail yanked her forward.

He marched her to a grassy bank that dropped down toward a boggy paddock. He let go of her arm and said, "Do whatever you gotta do."

She turned her head around, gaging her options. She could run, but there was nowhere to escape to. Except down a steep drop to a darkened swamp. She still had bound hands, and her legs were shaking under her own weight.

"There's no one watching," he said, watching her with a nasty smirk.

He went to grab at her skirt, but she stepped away. She'd shoved the gun down her waistband, and she couldn't let him see it. Not yet. Not until she had free hands and a clear shot, and then she planned on letting both these fuckers see it.

So, she squatted in the grass and went. And forced herself not to be embarrassed. If he got off on watching kidnapped women urinate, then he was the only one who should be ashamed.

When she was done, he hauled her back to the car. Milo was waiting by the trunk. She felt a swoop of fear at having to return to the tiny, dark space. But any attempt to break free of her captors would be impossible. She was dehydrated, starving, and her whole body ached.

Milo was holding a water bottle in one hand. He uncapped it and held it above her mouth. She drank greedily, not stopping until the bottle was empty.

Then they shoved her back in the trunk.

She lay there in the darkness again, curled in the fetal position.

Maybe she was only halfway to wherever to they were taking her. Maybe only a quarter.

Maybe when she got there, she'd wish she was back in here.

Her eyelids felt heavy. Soon, they were so heavy she couldn't keep them open. An overwhelming desire to sleep came over her. And it occurred to her then that there must have been something in the water.

It was her last coherent thought. That there'd been...something...in...the...

THIRTY-SEVEN

JESSICA WOKE up with a full body jerk. It drove her feet and head into hard metal. It hurt, and the crashing sound of her collision made her heart beat wildly.

She lay there, breathing fast, trying to figure out where she was.

It was dark. But she wasn't in the trunk anymore. She was lying on her side, legs bent, on a cold floor. It was concrete. Gritty and damp and hard.

Something solid was pressing against the soles of her shoes and the top of her head. She tried to straighten her legs but couldn't. When she tried to pull apart her hands, she found they were still bound with the zip ties.

Her eyes roamed around, feeling dilated, trying to make sense of her surroundings in the darkness.

A cage. She was in a fucking *cage*.

Panicking, she pushed herself into a sitting position, only to hit her head again on the top of the cage. It made a sound like cymbals crashing every time she struck it.

She tried to calm down and think for a moment, but her body was going haywire on her. Her heart was galloping in her chest, and she couldn't seem to get enough oxygen into her lungs. She wasn't claustrophobic, but the feeling of being trapped in the dark by unknown assailants was a primal fear. Her body's only response was pure panic.

She closed her eyes and rode the wave of terror until it slowly ebbed. When she opened them again, she realized the room wasn't as dark as she'd thought. Light was filtering in from a rain splattered window to her left. It was an artificial orange, which meant it came from a streetlight. Which suggested she was in a town or a city.

She peered around the room. It looked like a kitchen. She could make out a sink and a counter that ran the length of the wall beneath the window. More shapes to the right took the form of a table and chairs. A darker gap beyond indicated a doorway.

The small lump pressing into her hip bone told her the gun was still there. She didn't know how she'd get to it with her wrists tied—if she could at all—but just knowing it was there kept the panic from swallowing her whole.

She went to the bars of the cage and ran her hands over them. The metal strips were thin but closely spaced. It was, she realized, a large dog crate. She closed her fingers around the railings and pulled as hard as she could, but they didn't even bend.

A good quality dog crate.

She followed the bars around until she found the opening. Shaking it, she discovered it was fastened with a length of galvanized chain and a chunky combination lock. She twirled the numbers a few times, knowing it was hopeless. Without some incredibly good luck, there was no way out via that door.

It was then that she realized her crate wasn't the only one in the room. Butted up against hers was another.

And inside it was a person.

Pulse thudding in her ears, she gripped the bars and pressed her face against them. "Hello?" Her throat was so dry, the word came out as a croak. "Can you hear me?"

The person didn't move. Maybe they were asleep. Or maybe they'd been drugged, like she'd been.

They were leaning against the side of their cage, their arm pressing against the bars, their head twisted in the opposite direction. Jessica stared hard into the darkness, trying to make out more details about the other prisoner. It was a woman. And she still wasn't moving.

She pressed her palms together and wedged her hands through a gap in the bars. She reached through into the other cage and shook the woman's shoulder.

She let go instantly and yanked her fingers back through the bars. The woman's arm was bare. And cold. And stiff.

At the sudden jostling, the woman slumped further against the cage. Her head lolled to the other side, so she was now staring directly at Jessica.

With blank, dead eyes.

Sucking in a scream, Jessica scrambled to the far side of her cage. Her back hit it, making the thing clang loudly.

The dead woman's eyes had followed her. The light from the window glinted off them, so that even through the darkness, Jessica could still see them staring right at her.

Run, they seemed to say. *Run while you can.*

But she couldn't. There was no more running. It was over. She reached the end of the line.

Instead of fear, a part of her felt relief. *I don't want to run anymore,* she'd told Ryan. So, in one way, she'd gotten what she wished for.

She pressed herself into the corner of her cage and lifted her knees to her chest, drawing some strength from the hard lump of her revolver.

Sitting in the darkness, her mind took strange turns down dark paths. She saw Daniel again, lying beside her in bed. Smiling at her. Then he became Ryan. Then the dead girl with the staring eyes. Then she was gazing at her own dead body.

She jerked out of the half-dream, making the cage rattle.

Through the window above the sink, she saw that the sky had lightened to a soft gray, and the streetlights had turned off. Rain still streaked the glass. It was probably the remnants of the hurricane she'd survived many miles to the south.

Thinking about the storm made her think about Ryan. Where he was now. If the authorities had caught up with him and, if so, what was going to happen to him. And then she found herself wondering why she cared.

And yet she did. For reasons she didn't have the strength or the desire to examine any further.

As the sky grew lighter, she could make out more details of her surroundings. The kitchen was in terrible shape. There were no appliances left, just gaps in the counter where once an oven and a fridge might have been. Most of the countertop itself was gone, the chipboard eaten away as if a giant rat had gnawed it, exposing the wooden framework beneath. Every cupboard door had been ripped from its hinges and the linoleum floor had been torn up in large strips. The whole place stunk like mildew, unwashed clothing, and urine.

She glanced at the dead woman in the cage next to hers.

And death, too.

With the increasing light, the sounds of the traffic outside grew, too. Cars, trucks, the distant rattle of a city rail. The rain kept up a steady patter. Then, those noises were joined by a much nearer one. A sound coming from within the house. A sound getting closer.

Footsteps.

Jessica took slow, controlled breaths, determined not to succumb to panic again. She held her hands close to her waistband, resisting the urge to tug the gun out.

A dark figure appeared in the doorway. Bald head, shoulders so wide they brushed each side of the frame. Made even wider by the bulky military jacket he was wearing. She would have recognized him from his shape alone, but as soon as he came further into the kitchen, there was no doubt who he was. A spiderweb tattooed, now faded, covered his pale scalp.

The infamous Terry.

At his feet was a humongous black dog. It was a German Shepard, with enormous paws that clipped as it walked. It stopped when Terry stopped. Stared when Terry stared.

The man squatted down in front of her cage. Smiled at her. "Well, hi there, darling."

She stayed in the far corner, feeling lightheaded. She tried to keep still, but her whole body was shaking.

He smiled again. Like she'd confirmed something for him. "Yeah, Daniel always had a weakness for the pretty girls." He pushed himself to his feet with a groan. "I told him it would be his downfall one day. But he wouldn't listen." He chuckled. "Stubborn son of a bitch, wasn't he?"

He turned to the table. She noticed it was littered with bulky objects. There were several power tools, their cords draped over the edge and plugged into a powerstrip. One was a circular saw; the other, an angle grinder. Like they were doing renovations on the kitchen.

There were several guns, too. Very big ones.

He picked one up. It was a military rifle. He held it in both hands and gave a low whistle. "An AR-15. Nice" He looked at the other weapon on the table. Some kind of pump-action shotgun. "And a Remington 870. Your marshal had some very fine firearms."

So, he'd found Ryan's rifle bag. She swallowed the hard lump in her throat and said hoarsely, "If you're going to kill me, you might as well get it over with."

He chuckled like she'd said something funny. Then pulled out the chair and turned it so it was facing her. "I ain't gonna kill you, darling." He sat down, bracing the rifle across his knees. "Though it's not like I ain't got a whole bunch of reasons to. Ten of 'em, actually. One for every year I spent in that fucking place."

He was talking about prison. Jessica hadn't followed the trial of the twelve *La Mano Negra* gang members after she'd helped to indict them. She'd had no interest in what became of Daniel's so-called friends. Not after what they'd done to him. But she learned from a vague source, possibly Inez or maybe just from idle online scrolling, that all of them had been convicted. Their sentences had varied from a couple of years to fifteen, and she'd heard Terry had received a lengthier one.

He leaned forward and said, "But you see, I now got a better reason to keep you alive. Borya Sokolov has agreed to pay me a lot of money for you."

Sokolov. That name conjured the image Jessica still carried around in the back of her mind of Sasha Sokolov's brain matter splattered behind him.

Daniel's handiwork.

She'd heard about his brother Borya, too. He was a Russian businessman who owned multiple brothels and strip clubs in New York City and Philly. A few of the women working at Femme Fatale were former employees of his establishments. And the stories they'd told of the way those places were run—stories of girls being beaten and gang raped by the patrons—had made her sick to her stomach. Apparently, he produced porn too, the kind you could only find on the filthiest corners of the dark web. The kind that involved animals and knives and hooks and chains and other things she didn't even want to think about.

And she still remembered the story Special Agent Weck had told her about poor Svetlana, who'd been about to testify against him, but had been murdered before marshals could get her into protective custody.

Terry smiled when he saw Jessica had recognized the name. "Yeah, he hasn't forgotten you either. See, you and your boyfriend pissed off a lot of people when you went blabbing to the feds. Sokolov had to go underground for years until they stopped sniffing around him. So, when I called him up just now and told him I'd found you, he offered me fifty grand *not* to kill you."

He sat back in the chair, the gun still in his lap. "But I've seen the place you're going. The girls don't last very long in those rooms. And he told me I could watch, so I guess everybody wins."

He laughed again, like he'd made a great joke. But she knew he wasn't joking.

And she knew she'd rather take a bullet from that sniper rifle than to go to Sokolov. Or, if it came down to it, a bullet from her own gun.

If it came down to it, she'd do it. But it hadn't, yet.

So, she stayed silent. Stayed in the back of her cage. And waited.

———

If anything, daylight only made the room drearier. It seemed to ooze through the dirty window and illuminate just how filthy and dilapidated the place was.

It illuminated other things, too.

The dried blood that was smeared on the concrete and floor. On the table, too. And on the power tools. The blades of the circular saw. And the angle grinder. She realized they hadn't been using them for kitchen renovations.

Terry had left, thank God, but he'd ordered the dog to stay. It sat in the middle of the floor, a yard away from the bars, and stared at her. Like it was trying to work out why she was in the cage, and he was out of it.

He looked like he was quite enjoying the switch in the dynamic.

She finally mustered the courage to face the dead woman again. It seemed necessary. Facing her felt like facing her future. She had to not be frightened. She had to at least try to be as brave as that woman must have been, right until the end.

Crawling on her knees, she crossed the cage until she was staring right at her. And the woman stared right back.

She looked to be a few years older than Jessica. Very pretty, although it appeared she'd had a hard life even before her terrible death. Her red hair was frizzy and dry, and her face, now ashen and waxy, was lined prematurely around her mouth and eyes. Jessica couldn't help but notice the purple needle marks on the inside of her forearm.

She noticed another mark, this one collaring her neck. It was almost black against the woman's white skin and had the unmistakable imprint of thick fingers.

There was no way to tell in this dim light if that had been her cause of death. But she kind of hoped it was. There were no good ways of dying at the hands of these men, but when she thought of the power tools on the table, she knew that there were worse ones.

They had stripped her down to her underwear, which made Jessica want to find something to cover her. But there was nothing nearby, and no way she could reach far enough through the bars of the cages, anyway.

One of the woman's legs was pressed against the railings, as if she too had tried a futile escape from the inescapable. Jessica noticed she had a small tattoo on her upper thigh, right below her hip joint. It was a love heart with a name in the middle. The kind of tattoo you got when you were young. And dumb. And in love.

It read *Ryan.*

Jessica exhaled, resting her forehead against the metal.

So this was Kylie. Ryan's Kylie.

Suddenly, it all made sense to her. Why he'd done what he'd had. Why he'd betrayed his oath and risked everything. Why he'd betrayed her.

It wasn't for money.

It was for love.

She wrapped her fingers around the bars and squeezed, feeling hot liquid burn the backs of her eyes. He didn't know she was dead. He couldn't have known. He probably still didn't know.

She rested her head right next to the woman's stiff one. She couldn't cover her with anything. All she could do was reach through the bars with shaking hands and close Kylie's eyes for her one last time.

———

Jessica kneeled on the concrete floor and rasped, "I need water."

Milo leaned back in his chair, clamping the tourniquet between his teeth and pulling his head back. The rubber bit into the skin of his upper arm. He spat out the tourniquet and said, "Bitch, you got water."

She looked at the dirty dog bowl they'd provided for her. It sat two feet outside of the cage. Wedging both her hands through a gap in the bars, she could just about reach it at full stretch.

But the dog sat another foot away, watching her intently. And every time she so much as placed her fingers through the gap, it lunged for them.

She didn't know if Terry had trained it to do that, or if it was just a sadist like everyone else in this place. And she realized now that some of the blemishes she'd seen on Kylie's wrists were bite marks.

So, the thing had a taste for humans. She kept her hands inside the cage and went thirsty.

Milo and Ponytail were sitting around the table, shooting up from a dose they'd cooked up on a metal spoon and drawn into a syringe that they then shared. Terry had disappeared. Which was a good thing. Of the three of them, these two were the weaker links, especially if they were high as fuck.

Which they were right now.

Milo dropped the syringe, his head lolling back against his shoulders. She had a brief flare of hope that maybe he'd ODed and that would be one down. But no, he was still breathing, just in la la land.

That only left Ponytail.

For a second, she thought about yanking the gun out of her

skirt and shooting them both while they were out of it. It was as good a time as any.

But Ponytail was still lucid. His eyes were a little glazed, but he was watching her. And right beside him on the table were multiple weapons.

And even if she was successful in killing them, she'd remain stuck in this cage. With no water. And a psychopathic German Shepard continuing to observe her every move.

So, she scratched that plan. And quickly came up with a new one.

Crawling forward on her knees, she gripped the bars with her fingers. "I need to go to the bathroom."

Ponytail smirked. "So go."

She shook her head. "I can't."

"Sure you can."

She gave the cage a little shake, aware that the dog's focus on her increased. "Just let me use the bathroom. Please."

Ponytail sat and stared and smirked.

She swallowed hard. The back of her throat felt like sandpaper. "You can watch."

His smile grew wider. "I can watch now."

"But then you'll have to clean it up. They'll make you."

She watched his reaction, hoping she'd got the dynamic right between the three of them. She'd gaged that Ponytail was the lackey, the guy that the others would indeed make clean up any messes. Not that she saw much evidence of cleaning going on around here.

She must have been right, though, because he scraped his chair back across the torn-up linoleum and got to his feet. Muttering curses, he went to the opening in the cage's side and twisted the lock. She didn't bother trying to see what the combination was. She had no intention of going back into that crate.

The lock sprung open, and he pulled open the door.

She squeezed herself out before he could change his mind. But as soon as she was on her feet, he took a firm grip of her upper arm and yanked her toward the doorway.

He led her down a dark hallway, stopping in front of a small toilet cubicle. Something brown and foul-smelling stained the rim and pedestal. But she was less concerned with the state of hygiene in there and more interested in the small window above the tank.

The small open window.

Ponytail shoved her shoulder, forcing her into the stinking room.

She turned back to him. "Can you untie my hands?"

He shook his head and pushed her again. "Hurry it up. I don't got all day."

She held out her bound wrists to him in supplication. "Please. I'd be so grateful. And if I had my hands free, there're all kinds of ways I could show you how grateful."

He paused, and she could see his mind working. She knew he was having doubts. But she also knew that he wasn't the brightest crayon in the box. And that he had very poor self-control.

He rummaged around in the pocket of his cargo pants until he came up with a small folding knife. Flipping it open, he sawed through the plastic zip tie on her wrist. Then he returned the knife to his pants and immediately began unbuttoning them.

Before she could even let her disgust register, she reacted. She jammed her elbow into his gut, then got her foot around the door and shoved it shut on him. She pressed all her weight against it, then fumbled for the lock under the handle. By the time she had twisted it into place, he had recovered from the gut punch and was now thudding his fists against the door.

She thought for a second about trying to shoot him through the wood. But then she considered the dangers of firing a weapon in such a confined space.

Then all those thoughts were eclipsed by one: run.

Heart hammering in her ears, she turned from the door and slammed the toilet seat down. She climbed on top and, with both hands, shoved the window open as far as it would go. It was a couple of feet: not much, but enough to push her head and shoulders out. And if she could get those out, she could get the rest of her body out.

She had both knees on the cistern and was preparing to test her theory, hoping there was something soft below to break her fall, when the door behind her crashed open. It slammed against the wall with so much force it shook the entire house.

"Get her back inside," Terry said.

———

"Hold her legs down. This bitch ain't ever running away again."

Terry had her pinned down on the kitchen table, his fat fingers around her neck like a vise. Sweat covered her body like cold grease. Something warm and wet running down the side of her face, and she could taste blood in the back of her mouth. When they'd pulled her in through the window, she hit the sill with her cheek. Pain had burst inside her skull like fireworks.

Ponytail did as he was told, grabbing her ankles and gripping them. She tried to kick out but was met with impossible resistance.

Twisting her head to the side, she saw the butt of the rifle a few inches above her left ear. She lifted her arm to reach for it, but Ponytail noticed what she was trying to do and slammed her wrist down.

Milo was pacing back and forth across the kitchen, scraping his hands through his hair and muttering to himself. He seemed to be trapped in his own private nightmare, unaware of what was going on just a few feet away from him.

Jessica's nightmare was about to get even worse. Right beside her ear came the shrill whine of a circular saw.

Ponytail yelled over it, "She'll be no use to Sokolov if she's got bits missing."

"I don't give a fuck about Sokolov," Terry shouted back, lifting the saw so she could see it. "This bitch is done."

Fear ran through her veins like ice water. The desire to escape was so intense, she felt an overwhelming urge to leave her own body. To just abandon it there on that dirty table and float off up to the ceiling.

Then she saw Terry direct the whirring blade toward her leg, right above the knee. And her mind decided it didn't want to abandon her body just yet.

Cortisol and adrenaline were pumping into her bloodstream, making everything move slower. She shoved her free hand into the waistband of her skirt, closed her damp fingers around her gun. Pulled it out, worked her finger under the trigger guard. Her fingers were shaking so much it was a miracle she didn't drop it.

The hot draft from the spinning saw blade brushed the skin of her leg. She felt the first snick of searing pain as it bit into her flesh just as she leveled the gun at Ponytail's chest.

She heard Ryan's voice in her head saying, *Shoot him where you have to.*

She pulled the trigger. The little gun spat its bullet, jerking her hand back. The sound stopped everything. Ponytail lurched backward, like someone had grabbed hold of the collar of his shirt and tugged him backward. He stared at her gun in confusion, as if it had just asked him a complicated question. One that he didn't have an answer for. Then he stared down at the rapidly growing bloodstain on the front of his chest.

And don't stop until he goes down.

She pulled the trigger once more, and Ponytail lurched back again, then collapsed onto the floor.

The whole thing had only taken seconds, but Terry had processed the situation much quicker than Ponytail. He'd dropped the saw, still whirring dangerously close to her leg, and had produced a handgun of his own from an unseen holster beneath his jacket. He brought it around to aim between her eyes. She swung her arm in his direction and pulled the trigger three times in quick succession.

The sound of each gunshot was like the crack of a whip. The force of the recoil meant her hand lurched all over the place.

She heard an almighty thud. Terry was no longer looming over her. Instead, he had crashed onto the kitchen floor, his body sprawled in a growing pool of crimson, the metallic scent of blood filling the air.

She didn't have time to inspect the accuracy of her shots. Milo had emerged from his trance and was looking even more wild-eyed. He sprang forward, suddenly agile, and grabbed for the rifle on the table.

Jessica didn't think; she just acted. She had one bullet left in the revolver. She couldn't miss.

It hit him in the neck. He stopped in his tracks and lifted both hands to stem the flow of blood jetting from his jugular like a geyser.

"You…little…*bitch*…" he hissed, blood and spit spraying from his mouth.

She tossed the gun aside and rolled off the table. She dived for the door, then sprinted down the hallway.

She made it to the front door and yanked it open, the daylight stunning her for a second. Blinking her eyes clear, she threw herself down a short flight of concrete steps.

She turned right, towards a busy road. And she ran.

THIRTY-EIGHT

THREE WEEKS LATER

JESSICA FOLDED the last of her clothes and tucked them into the suitcase. It was brand new—bought especially for the move. Her old one had vanished somewhere on that lonely Mississippi highway, lost for good. She didn't miss it. If anything, it felt like a fitting metaphor: leaving the past behind, untethering herself from the weight of everything she'd been carrying.

And she was leaving behind more than just a battered old suitcase.

She glanced around her bedroom, taking in the empty spaces where her life had once been. When she'd finally been discharged from the hospital and cleared by the alphabet soup of agencies that had pried into every corner of her existence, she'd booked the first flight back to the sun-drenched familiarity of Florida. But the moment she arrived in Panama City Beach, reality hit hard.

Her house, still wrapped in crime scene tape, stood like a monument to everything she had endured. Inside, the wreckage remained untouched—clothes scattered, furniture overturned, food all over the floor. The air still felt thick with the ghost of that night.

For three days, she had sifted through the mess, tossing what was unsalvageable into a skip bin, boxing up the rest for long-term storage. Now, all that remained was a single suitcase, over-stuffed with the last remnants of her life.

She had gotten good at this—packing up, starting over.

Practice makes perfect.

She zipped it up and grabbed the handle, ready to drag it off the bed. Then she froze. There was someone standing in her bedroom doorway.

Heart pounding, she turned to face the intruder. When she saw who it was, she exhaled, her pulse slowing but not quite returning to normal.

He looked very different from the last time she'd seen him in that doorway. When he'd worn a chromium star on his belt and a Glock on his hip. Now he lacked both, though she doubted he was unarmed.

Because he wasn't a deputy U.S. marshal any longer. Now he was Ryan Inglis, a wanted fugitive.

He was wearing jeans and sneakers and a dark blue hoodie. The casual clothes seemed out of character. Whenever she thought about him—and she was embarrassed to admit that she had thought about him—it was always in a crisp white shirt, with his hair neatly combed.

Then she reminded herself that she didn't really know him at all. She never had.

He looked tired, and he hadn't shaved in about a week. Some-how, the dark circles and the golden scruff on his jaw made him look more attractive. Less boy-next-door and more ruggedly handsome. Life on the run apparently suited him.

He glanced at the wall over her bed, where she'd attempted to scrub the spray-paint off. It had taken two bottles of turpentine and cost her all her acrylic nails on one hand, but she'd faded it to a faint mark.

Neither of them spoke; they just stared at each other. Finally, she ended the standoff. "There are a lot of people out there looking for you."

He broke eye contact with her but said nothing.

"I heard every U.S. marshal in the country has joined the hunt. I heard they set up a special task force just for you."

His jaw worked, but still he remained silent.

"One of them could have been watching this house," she said.

Finally, he spoke. "There wasn't. I made sure."

She put her hands on her hips and looked down at her bare mattress. "I hope you're not here to apologize. Because that would be supremely inadequate."

He didn't answer. She looked up at him and raised her eyebrows.

He raked his hand through his hair, finally looking a bit more like the Ryan she remembered. "I came to see if you were okay."

She gave a dry laugh. "I'm alive. Okay would be pushing it."

He was looking at her, and she could feel his eyes taking in her still-bruised face. The swelling around her broken cheekbone was subsiding, but the dark purple and yellow hues of her two black eyes remained quite vivid.

"I heard what happened," he said softly. "That you killed them. All three."

She looked away, squeezing the handle of her suitcase.

"You did good."

She glanced at him, her stomach twisting. She knew what she had to say to him, but making the words leave her mouth took a tremendous effort. "Ryan, your wife. Kylie." She swallowed hard, then just forced them out. "She's dead."

The ball of his jaw tightened again, and he inhaled. When he looked at her, his expression was stoic. "I know. I found out on the news." He looked down at his feet. "The guy on the phone, he told me they'd let her go if I gave them what they wanted."

Me, she thought.

"And I got a text from her right after, saying she was sorry." He closed his eyes for a moment. "I guess she never really sent that text. I guess she was probably already dead at that point."

"I'm sorry."

He looked at her, and his face suddenly crumpled. The stoic

expression was replaced by a look so anguished, so despairing, that she desperately wanted to go to him and wrap her arms around him.

It took all her strength to stay where she was.

"I'm sorry, too," he said, in a voice barely above a whisper. "For everything."

She swallowed down a bubble of rising tears. Because she couldn't trust herself to speak, she just nodded.

When she finally felt like she was on top of her emotions, she cleared her throat and said, "The FBI agent who took my statement told me she had a son. A little boy called Noah. He said they'd contacted Kylie's mother, and that she was going to take him back to Tennessee to live with her."

Ryan nodded. "Diane's a good woman. She'll take care of him."

Jessica glanced down at her suitcase, then back at him. "The agent also told me you caught two flights and drove all day to get to me before they did. He said that there really is a safe house in Baton Rouge, and that you insisted on being the one to take me there, despite the hurricane warnings."

She stared at his face, but he gave no reaction. "But if you think that somehow doing any of that somehow makes us square—"

"I don't think that," he interrupted softly.

"Good. Because it doesn't. Not by a long shot."

He looked down, and she couldn't see his expression. Couldn't see if her words had hurt him or snuffed out some hope he'd been clinging to.

She didn't want to do either of those things. But she had to tell him the truth. No matter how much it pained her.

When he looked back up at her, his face was carefully neutral, and she was reminded how good he was at concealing himself behind that cool facade.

"Where will you go?" she asked.

He paused before answering, like he was still weighing his

options. Or maybe weighing how much he could trust her with his answer. Finally, he said, "South."

"Mexico?"

He didn't reply. Just nodded at her suitcase. "What about you?"

She lifted it off the bed. "I guess I've realized running away isn't the same as moving on. Sometimes you actually have to go back to move forward." She turned to look at him. "So that's what I'm doing."

"You're going back to Illinois?"

She shook her head. "San Francisco first. To see my sister. Then after that, I don't know. Maybe I'll enroll in that dance therapy course."

He nodded and gave her a brief smile, like that genuinely made him happy. Then he reached his hand into the pocket of his hoodie and took something out. "Well, there's one place you might want to consider going first."

He held it out to her. It was a small piece of folded paper.

She stayed where she was and just stared at it. Then, when it became clear he wouldn't come any further into the room, she crossed the space between them, reached out and took it from him.

When she unfolded it, she saw a handwritten name at the top and underneath, an address in Texas.

She looked up at him and gave a little shake of her head. "What is this?"

"His contact details," he said softly.

She stared at him, searching his eyes with hers.

He exhaled, and she was close enough to him to feel it wash over her face. "Daniel Castaño's."

Something brushed down her spine. Like fingertips, sending shivers all over her body. "But he's dead," she whispered.

Ryan shook his head. "He's not. Neither is his brother Sebastián."

She opened her mouth and tried to make it work. "What?"

"They both entered the witness security program roughly eleven years ago. Right after Daniel agreed to testify against members of *La Mano Negra.*"

She shook her head, not able to make any of this compute. "But he didn't testify. He refused to cooperate with the DEA. He'd told me he'd rather die than become a snitch."

"I guess something changed his mind. Because it was his testimony against Terry Bidois and the rest of his crew that brought the whole thing crashing down. He agreed to testify against Borya Sokolov, too, but that case was more complicated, and they couldn't get an indictment."

She continued to just stare at him, his words bouncing harmlessly off her brain. "But she told me he was dead. Belinda Weck, the DEA agent. She told me he got stabbed in prison. And Sebastián, she said he died after surgery."

Ryan shook his head again. "Sebastián survived his surgery. Straight afterwards, he was taken to a neutral site in Chicago, along with his brother. After the trial, they were both relocated to Texas and given new identities." He shrugged. "I guess they told you they were both dead for your own protection. And for theirs."

She was still reeling from the news, but it was finally sinking in. "How do you know all this?" she whispered.

"I got sent his whole file. It was all in there. The only stipulations he made before agreeing to the DOJ's terms was that his brother be kept safe." He paused, then added, "And he insisted that you be accepted into the program, too."

She realized she was shaking all over and had to take a step back and sink down on the mattress. She looked back down at the piece of paper he'd given her. Ran her thumb over the handwritten address. In Texas.

She swallowed down a sudden uprising of tears. Then she glanced back up at him, realizing that this was why he was here. That he'd come all the way back to Florida, at huge personal risk, just to give her another man's address.

It caused her heart to squeeze. "Ryan…" she whispered. She didn't know how to continue that sentence. Didn't know how to say both thank you and I'm sorry at the same time.

His eyes went to the ring on the chain around her neck. When his gaze met hers again, they were full of feeling. They contained sadness, pain, regret, and maybe even something like love.

They were two broken people who, for a heartbeat, had imagined that they could make each other whole again. And maybe they could have.

They'd never know now.

"Goodbye Jessica," he said softly. Then he turned and walked away, down the hall and out the open front door.

She followed him and watched from her porch as he jogged across her yard, his hoodie pulled up over his head.

"Ryan," she called after him.

He stopped and turned back to her.

"Jessica is not my real name."

He nodded once, then kept jogging toward the road.

She watched him as he turned left, then rounded the bend and was gone.

EPILOGUE

THE GPS in Jessica's rented Corolla announced she was nearing her destination.

"If you say so," she muttered back to it. She had no idea where she was. Thirty miles west of Corpus Christi, and somewhat south of Agua Dulce—a town comprising little more than a Dollar General, a grain silo, a gas station, and an auto shop.

When Jessica glanced in her rearview mirror, a trail of brown dirt stretched behind her as far back as the farm road. Ahead, dust and heat radiating off the baked earth obscured the view. The land was so flat it could have been ironed.

Then she saw it: a wooden fence. Then a tree. Then a house. They stood alone in a little cluster, the only vertical things for miles.

She slowed to a halt in front of the gate and turned off the ignition. As much as she wanted to get out and stretch her legs, she stayed seated inside. She closed her eyes. Burned into her eyeballs was the same view she'd been staring at through the windshield all day: shimmering blacktop, endless white lines and a wedge of hazy blue sky. And all around, the flat, empty nothingness of southern Texas.

She exhaled and opened her eyes. Took a sip of water from the bottle on the seat next to her. She knew she was just stalling. Knew she had to get out of this hot car and do what she'd come here to do.

She pushed open the car door, feeling more nervous than she had in a long time.

It had been over eleven years since she'd last seen Daniel. And their last conversation in that prison visitation room had been ugly. He'd said things that had hurt her, in retaliation for the things she'd done to hurt him. But, according to Ryan, he'd secretly bargained for her safety. That gave her hope that maybe he hadn't hated her at the end.

And that maybe, just maybe, he might not hate her now.

She'd Googled his new name, but the search had turned up almost nothing. No social media accounts, not even Facebook. The only mention of him she found was in an archived article from 2019 in a small Nueces County gazette. It identified him as the best man at his brother Santiago's wedding. According to the piece, both grooms were doctors at a hospital in Corpus Christi, which was where they'd met. Accompanying it was a photo, grainy and badly scanned. But she'd recognized them both, standing side-by-side in their suits, smiling at the camera. Sebastián and Daniel Castaño might both go by different names now, but there was no changing their striking good looks. Or, it seemed, the bond the two shared, visible even in that tiny, blurry photo on her phone screen.

She climbed out of the car. The heat of the earth was radiating up through the bottoms of her sandals. She smoothed the crumpled skirt of her sundress, then finger-combed her hair. It was back to its natural blond. She resisted the urge to check her reflection in the side mirror. She was trying not to be presumptuous, or to assume that this reunion would go a certain way.

Eleven years was a long time. He might be married or in a serious relationship. He might be happy on his own. He might not be attracted to her anymore. People change, after all.

And while all those scenarios felt like sucker punches to her heart, she'd steeled herself to handle it. She'd resolved to come here and accept whatever she found. If the best-case scenario was that they could part as friends, then so be it.

She approached the split-rail fence and stopped at the open gate. The house sat at the end of the dusty drive. It was a small white structure, with black batons and a gray iron roof. To the side of it stood a large jacaranda tree, the ground below carpeted in its violet flowers.

Near to the gate was an old red car, half-covered by a tarp and propped up on axle stands. The front fender had distinctive shark fin gills on it.

In the shade beneath the tarp lay an old Rottweiler, panting in the heat. The dog spotted Jessica and pricked up its ears. It turned its head on its side and regarded her thoughtfully. Like it was trying to remember her face. Then it gave a solitary woof that sounded more like a cough.

"¡Tequila!" came a man's voice from under the car, followed by several mumbled curse words in Spanish. His legs appeared first, then the rest of him. He clambered to his feet, shielding his face from the sun, to look at her.

He was late-thirties. Hispanic. Bright hazel eyes under dark eyebrows. A faded tattoo of a cross on his left cheekbone and the word ALONE barely visible under his stubble. His hair was longer now and curling over his ears and almost to his shoulders. He was wearing a white singlet that showed off thick arm muscles covered in an impressive array of tattoos, and a pair of low-slung jeans that looked like they were on borrowed time.

Neither of them spoke; they just stared at each other. His eyes drifted over her, his gaze like a caress. He took in the ruby ring she wore on a gold chain around her neck. When he met her eyes again, his were charged with such emotion that the air between them seemed to almost shimmer.

And she knew from that one look it was all still there between them. That fire, that hunger. That want and need. That longing. That love.

She rested her hands on the gate and tilted her head at the car. "Is that a 1970 Plymouth Hemi 'Cuda?"

He nodded, still not taking his eyes off her. "Yeah."

"I heard they're really rare."

"They are." He smiled, revealing a dimple in his left cheek. "Never thought I'd find two in one lifetime."

He picked up a rag from the hood of the car and started wiping his hands with it. Held one out to her. "I'm Dante, by the way."

She walked in the gate. Dried her own sweaty hands on her dress. As she placed her hand in his and felt his fingers wrap around hers, she realized it was true: that old saying about people, not places, being home.

"Jessica," she said with a smile.

ALSO BY S.K. MUSKAT

Love on the Run

Jessica, Not Her Real Name

South of Justice

You Can Run

ABOUT THE AUTHOR

S.K. Muskat is the pen name for Shannon Hart. She writes romantic thrillers where love is risky, secrets kill, and no one gets out unscathed. With a passion for storytelling that has taken her around the world, she now calls New Zealand home—along with an ever-growing collection of plants that, unlike her characters, thrive under her care.

www.ingramcontent.com/pod-product-compliance
Lightning Source LLC
Chambersburg PA
CBHW020237010826
48973CB00006B/1554